Homeland

Homeland

CORY DOCTOROW

A TOM DOHERTY ASSOCIATES BOOK

NEW YORK

HOMELAND

Copyright © 2013 by Cory Doctorow

Edited by Patrick Nielsen Hayden

A Tor Teen Book
Published by Tom Doherty Associates, LLC
175 Fifth Avenue
New York, NY 10010

www.tor-forge.com

Tor® is a registered trademark of Tom Doherty Associates, LLC.

ISBN 978-0-7653-3369-8 (hardcover)
ISBN 978-1-4668-0587-3 (e-book)

First Edition: February 2013

Printed in the United States of America

0 9 8 7 6 5 4 3 2 1

For Alice and Poesy, who make me whole

Homeland

Chapter 1

Attending Burning Man made me simultaneously one of the most photographed people on the planet and one of the least surveilled humans in the modern world.

I adjusted my burnoose, covering up my nose and mouth and tucking its edge into place under the lower rim of my big, scratched goggles. The sun was high, the temperature well over a hundred degrees, and breathing through the embroidered cotton scarf made it even more stifling. But the wind had just kicked up, and there was a lot of playa dust—fine gypsum sand, deceptively soft and powdery, but alkali enough to make your eyes burn and your skin crack—and after two days in the desert, I had learned that it was better to be hot than to choke.

Pretty much everyone was holding a camera of some kind—mostly phones, of course, but also big SLRs and even old-fashioned film cameras, including a genuine antique plate camera whose operator hid out from the dust under a huge black cloth that made me hot just to look at it. Everything was ruggedized for the fine, blowing dust, mostly through the simple expedient of sticking it in a ziplock bag, which is what I'd done with my phone. I turned around slowly to get a panorama and saw that the man walking past me was holding the string for a gigantic helium balloon a hundred yards overhead, from which dangled a digital video camera. Also, the man holding the balloon was naked.

Well, not entirely. He was wearing shoes. I understood that: playa dust is hard on your feet. They call it playa-foot, when the alkali dust dries out your skin so much that it starts to crack and peel. Everyone agrees that playa-foot sucks.

Burning Man is a festival held every Labor Day weekend in the middle of Nevada's Black Rock Desert. Fifty thousand people show up in this incredibly harsh, hot, dusty environment and build a huge city—Black Rock City—and *participate*. "Spectator" is a vicious insult in Black Rock City. Everyone's supposed to be *doing* stuff and, yeah, also admiring everyone else's stuff (hence all the cameras). At Burning Man, everyone is the show.

I wasn't naked, but the parts of me that were showing *were* decorated with elaborate mandalas laid on with colored zinc. A lady as old as my mother, wearing a tie-dyed wedding dress, had offered to paint me that morning, and she'd done a great job. That's another thing about Burning Man: it runs on a gift economy, which means that you generally go around offering nice things to strangers a lot, which makes for a surprisingly pleasant environment. The designs the painter had laid down made me look *amazing,* and there were plenty of cameras aiming my way as I ambled across the open desert toward Nine O'Clock.

Black Rock City is a pretty modern city: it has public sanitation (portable chem-toilets decorated with raunchy poems reminding you not to put anything but toilet paper in them), electricity and Internet service (at Six O'Clock, the main plaza in the middle of the ring-shaped city), something like a government (the nonprofit that runs Burning Man), several local newspapers (all of them doing better than the newspapers in the real world!), a dozen radio stations, an all-volunteer police force (the Black Rock Rangers, who patrolled wearing tutus or parts of chicken suits or glitter paint), and many other amenities associated with the modern world.

But BRC has no official surveillance. There are no CCTVs, no checkpoints—at least not after the main gate, where tickets are collected—no ID checks at all, no bag searches, no RFID sniffers, no mobile phone companies logging your movements. There was also no mobile phone service. No one drives—except for the weird art cars registered with the Department of Mutant Vehicles—so there were no license plate cameras and no sniffers for your E-ZPasses. The WiFi was open and unlogged. Attendees at Burning Man agreed not to use their photos commercially without permission, and it was generally considered polite to ask people before taking their portraits.

So there I was, having my picture taken through the blowing dust as I gulped down water from the water jug I kept clipped to my belt at all times, sucking at the stubby built-in straw under cover of the blue-and-silver burnoose, simultaneously observed and observer, simultaneously observed and unsurveilled, and it was *glorious*.

"Wahoo!" I shouted to the dust and the art cars and the naked people and the enormous wooden splay-armed effigy perched atop a pyramid straight ahead of me in the middle of the desert. This was The Man, and we'd burn him in three nights, and that's why it was called Burning Man. I couldn't wait.

"You're in a good mood," a jawa said from behind me. Even with the tone-shifter built into its dust mask, the cloaked sand-person had an awfully familiar voice.

"Ange?" I said. We'd been missing each other all that day, ever since I'd woken up an hour before her and snuck out of the tent to catch the sunrise (which was *awesome*), and we'd been leaving each other notes back at camp all day about where we were heading next. Ange had spent the summer spinning up the jawa robes, working with cooling towels that trapped sweat as

it evaporated, channeling it back over her skin for extra evapo-
rative cooling. She'd hand-dyed it a mottled brown, tailored it
into the characteristic monkish robe shape, and added crossed
bandoliers. These exaggerated her breasts, which made the whole
thing entirely and totally *warsome*. She hadn't worn it out in
public yet, and now, in the dust and the glare, she was undoubt-
edly the greatest sand-person I'd ever met. I hugged her and she
hugged me back so hard it knocked the wind out of me, one of
her trademarked wrestling-hold cuddles.

"I smudged your paint," she said through the voice-shifter
after we unclinched.

"I got zinc on your robes," I said.

She shrugged. "Like it matters! We both look fabulous.
Now, what have you seen and what have you done and where
have you been, young man?"

"Where to start?" I said. I'd been wandering up and down
the radial avenues that cut through the city, lined with big camps
sporting odd exhibits—one camp where a line of people were
efficiently making snow cones for anyone who wanted them,
working with huge blocks of ice and a vicious ice-shaver. Then
a camp where someone had set up a tall, linoleum-covered slide
that you could toboggan down on a plastic magic carpet, after
first dumping a gallon of waste water over the lino to make it
plenty slippery. It was a very clever way to get rid of gray water
(that's water that you've showered in, or used to wash your dishes
or hands—black water being water that's got poo or pee in it).
One of the other Burning Man rules was "leave no trace"—
when we left, we'd take every scrap of Black Rock City with
us, and that included all the gray water. But the slide made for
a great gray water evaporator, and every drop of liquid that the
sliders helped turn into vapor was a drop of liquid the camp
wouldn't have to pack all the way back to Reno.

There'd been pervy camps where they were teaching couples to tie each other up; a "junk food glory hole" that you put your mouth over in order to receive a mysterious and unhealthy treat (I'd gotten a mouthful of some kind of super-sugary breakfast cereal studded with coconut "marshmallows" shaped like astrological symbols); a camp where they were offering free service for playa bikes (beater bikes caked with playa dust and decorated with glitter and fun fur and weird fetishes and bells); a tea-house camp where I'd been given a very precisely made cup of some kind of Japanese tea I'd never heard of that was delicious and sharp; camps full of whimsy; camps full of physics; camps full of optical illusions; camps full of men and women; a kids' camp full of screaming kids running around playing some kind of semisupervised outdoor game—things I'd never suspected existed.

And I'd only seen a tiny slice of Black Rock City.

I told Ange about as much as I could remember and she nodded or said "ooh," or "aah," or demanded to know where I'd seen things. Then she told me about the stuff she'd seen—a camp where topless women were painting one another's breasts; a camp where an entire brass band was performing; a camp where they'd built a medieval trebuchet that fired ancient, broken-down pianos down a firing range, the audience holding its breath in total silence while they waited for the glorious crash each piano made when it exploded into flinders on the hardpack desert.

"Can you believe this place?" Ange said, jumping up and down on the spot in excitement, making her bandoliers jingle.

"I know—can you believe we almost didn't make it?"

I'd always sort of planned on going out to see The Man burn—after all, I grew up in San Francisco, the place with the largest concentration of burners in the world. But it took a lot of work to participate in Burning Man. First, there was the matter of packing for a camping trip in the middle of the desert where you had to pack in *everything*—including water—and then pack it all out again, everything you didn't leave behind in the porta-potties. And there were *very* strict rules about what could go in *those*. Then there was the gift economy: figuring out what I could bring to the desert that someone else might want. Plus the matter of costumes, cool art, and inventions to show off . . . every time I started to think about it, I just about had a nervous breakdown.

But this year, of all years, I'd made it. This was the year both my parents lost their jobs. The year I'd dropped out of college rather than take on any more student debt. The year I'd spent knocking on every door I could find, looking for paid work—*anything!*—without getting even a nibble.

"Never underestimate the determination of a kid who is cash-poor and time-rich," Ange said solemnly, pulling down her face mask with one hand and yanking me down to kiss me with the other.

"That's catchy," I said. "You should print T-shirts."

"Oh," she said. "That reminds me. I got a T-shirt!"

She threw open her robe to reveal a proud red tee that read MAKE BEAUTIFUL ART AND SET IT ON FIRE, laid out like those British KEEP CALM AND CARRY ON posters, with the Burning Man logo where the crown should be.

"Just in time, too," I said, holding my nose. I was only partly kidding. At the last minute, we'd both decided to ditch half the clothes we'd planned on bringing so that we could fit more parts for Secret Project X-1 into our backpacks. Between that and taking "bits and pits" baths by rubbing the worst of the dried sweat, body paint, sunscreen, and miscellaneous fluids off with baby wipes once a day, neither of us smelled very nice.

She shrugged. "The playa provides." It was one of the Burning Man mottoes we'd picked up on the first day, when we both realized that we thought the other one had brought the sunscreen, and just as we were about to get into an argument about it, we stumbled on Sunscreen Camp, where some nice people had slathered us all over with SPF 50 and given us some baggies to take with. "The playa provides!" they'd said, and wished us well.

I put my arm around her shoulders. She dramatically turned her nose up at my armpit, then made a big show of putting on her face mask.

"Come on," she said. "Let's go out to the temple."

The temple was a huge, two-story sprawling structure, dotted with high towers and flying buttresses. It was filled with robotic Tibetan gongs that played strange clanging tunes throughout the day. I'd seen it from a distance that morning while walking around the playa, watching the sun turn the dust rusty orange, but I hadn't been up close.

The outer wings of the temple were open to the sky, made of the same lumber as the rest of the whole elaborate curlicue structure. The walls were lined with benches and were inset with niches and nooks. And everywhere, every surface, was covered in writing and signs and posters and pictures.

And almost all of it was about dead people.

"Oh," Ange said to me, as we trailed along the walls, reading the memorials that had been inked or painted or stapled there. I was reading a handwritten thirty-page-long letter from an adult woman to her parents, about all the ways they'd hurt her and made her miserable and destroyed her life, about how she'd felt when they'd died, about how her marriages had been destroyed by the craziness she'd had instilled in her. It veered from wild accusation to tender exasperation to anger to sorrow, like some kind of emotional roller coaster. I felt like I was spying on something I wasn't supposed to see, except that everything in the temple was there to be seen.

Every surface in the temple was a memorial to something

or someone. There were baby shoes and pictures of grannies, a pair of crutches and a beat-up cowboy hat with a hatband woven from dead dried flowers. Burners—dressed and undressed like a circus from the end of the world—walked solemnly around these, reading them, more often than not with tears running down their faces. Pretty soon, I had tears running down my face. It moved me in a way that nothing had ever moved me before. Especially since it was all going to burn on Sunday night, before we tore down Black Rock City and went home.

Ange sat in the dust and began looking through a sketchbook whose pages were filled with dense, dark illustrations. I wandered into the main atrium of the temple, a tall, airy space whose walls were lined with gongs. Here, the floor was carpeted with people—sitting and lying down, eyes closed, soaking in the solemnity of the moment, some with small smiles, some weeping, some with expressions of utmost serenity.

I'd tried meditating once, during a drama class in high school. It hadn't worked very well. Some of the kids kept on giggling. There was some kind of shouting going on in the hallway outside the door. The clock on the wall ticked loudly, reminding me that at any moment, there'd be a loud buzzer and the roar and stamp of thousands of kids all trying to force their way through a throng to their next class. But I'd read a lot about meditation and how good it was supposed to be for you. In theory it was easy, too: just sit down and think of nothing.

So I did. I shifted my utility belt around so that I could sit down without it digging into my ass and waited until a patch of floor was vacated, then sat. There were streamers of sunlight piercing the high windows above, lancing down in gray-gold spikes that glittered with dancing dust. I looked into one of these, at the dancing motes, and then closed my eyes. I pictured a grid of four squares, featureless and white with thick black rims and sharp corners. In my mind's eye, I erased one square. Then another. Then another. Now there was just one square. I erased it.

There was nothing now. I was thinking of nothing, literally. Then I was thinking about the fact that I was thinking about nothing, mentally congratulating myself, and I realized that I was thinking of something again. I pictured my four squares and started over.

I don't know how long I sat there, but there were moments when the world seemed to both go away and be more present than it ever had been. I was living in that exact and very moment, not anticipating anything that might happen later, not thinking of anything that had just happened, just being *right there.* It only lasted for a fraction of a second each time, but each of those fragmentary moments were . . . well, they were something.

I opened my eyes. I was breathing in time with the gongs around me, a slow, steady cadence. There was something digging into my butt, a bit of my utility belt's strap or something. The girl in front of me had a complex equation branded into the skin of her shoulder blades, the burned skin curdled into deep, sharp-relief mathematical symbols and numbers. Someone smelled like weed. Someone was sobbing softly. Someone outside the temple called out to someone else. Someone laughed. Time was like molasses, flowing slowly and stickily around me. Nothing seemed important and everything seemed wonderful. That was what I'd been looking for, all my life, without ever knowing it. I smiled.

"Hello, M1k3y," a voice hissed in my ear, very soft and very close, lips brushing my lobe, breath tickling me. The voice tickled me, too, tickled my memory. I knew that voice, though I hadn't heard it in a very long time.

Slowly, as though I were a giraffe with a neck as tall as a tree, I turned my head to look around.

"Hello, Masha," I said, softly. "Fancy meeting you here."

Her hand was on my hand and I remembered the way she'd twisted my wrist around in some kind of martial arts hold the last time I'd seen her. I didn't think she'd be able to get away with bending my arm up behind my back and walking me out of the temple on my tiptoes. If I shouted for help, thousands of burners would . . . well, they wouldn't tear her limb from limb, but they'd do *something*. Kidnapping people on the playa was definitely against the rules. It was in the Ten Principles, I was nearly certain of it.

She tugged at my wrist. "Let's go," she said. "Come on."

I got to my feet and followed her, freely and of my own will, and even though I trembled with fear as I got up, there was a nugget of excitement in there, too. Of course this was happening now, at Burning Man. A couple years ago, I'd been in the midst of more excitement than anyone would or could want. I'd led a techno-guerrilla army against the Department of Homeland Security, met a girl and fell in love with her, been arrested and tortured, found celebrity, and sued the government. Since then, it had all gone downhill, in a weird way. Being waterboarded was terrible, awful, unimaginable—I still had nightmares—but it happened and then it *ended*. My parents' slow slide into bankruptcy, the hard, grinding reality of a city with no jobs for anyone, let alone a semiqualified college dropout like me, and the student debt that I *had* to pay every month. It was a pile of misery that I lived under every day, and it showed no sign of going away. It wasn't dramatic, dynamic trouble, the kind of thing you got war stories out of years after the fact. It was just, you know, reality.

And reality sucked.

So I went with Masha, because Masha had been living

underground with Zeb for the better part of two years, and whatever else she was, she was someone whose life was generating a lot of exciting stories. Her reality might suck too, but it sucked in huge, showy, neon letters—not in the quiet, crabbed handwriting of a desperate and broke teenager scribbling in his diary.

I went with Masha, and she led me out of the temple. The wind was blowing worse than it had been before, real whiteout conditions, and I pulled down my goggles and pulled up my scarf again. Even with them on, I could barely see, and each breath of air filled my mouth with the taste of dried saliva and powdery gypsum from my burnoose. Masha's hair wasn't bright pink anymore; it was a mousy blond-brown, turned gray with dust, cut into duckling fuzz all over, the kind of haircut you could maintain yourself with a clipper. I'd had that haircut, off and on, through much of my adolescence. Her skull bones were fine and fragile, her skin stretched like paper over her cheekbones. Her neck muscles corded and her jaw muscles jumped. She'd lost weight since I'd seen her last, and her skin had gone leathery brown, a color that was deeper than a mere summer tan.

We went all of ten steps out from the temple, but we might have been a mile from it—it was lost in the dust. There were people around, but I couldn't make out their words over the spooky moan of the wind blowing through the temple's windows. Bits of grit crept between my goggles and my sweaty cheeks and made my eyes and nose run.

"Far enough," she said, and let go of my wrist, holding her hands before her. I saw that the fingertips on her left hand were weirdly deformed and squashed and bent, and I had a vivid recollection of slamming the rolling door of a moving van down on her hand as she chased me. She'd been planning to semikidnap me at the time, and I was trying to get away with evidence that my best friend Darryl had been kidnapped by Homeland

Security, but I still heard the surprised and pained shout she'd let out when the door crunched on her hand. She saw where I was looking and took her hand away, tucking it into the sleeve of the loose cotton shirt she wore.

"How's tricks, M1k3y?" she said.

"It's Marcus these days," I said. "Tricks have been better. How about you? Can't say I expected to see you again. Ever. Especially not at Burning Man."

Her eyes crinkled behind her goggles and her veil shifted and I knew she was smiling. "Why, M1k3y—*Marcus*—it was the easiest way for me to get to see *you*."

It wasn't exactly a secret that I was planning to come to Burning Man that year. I'd been posting desperate "Will trade work for a ride to the playa" and "Want to borrow your old camping gear" messages to Craigslist and the hackerspace mailing lists for months, trying to prove that the proverbial time-rich kid could out-determination cash-poorness. Anyone who was trying to figure out where I was going to be over Labor Day weekend could have googled my semiprecise location in about three seconds.

"Um," I said. "Um. Look, Masha, you know, you're kind of freaking me out. Are you here to kill me or something? Where's Zeb?"

She closed her eyes and the pale dust sifted down between us. "Zeb's off enjoying the playa. Last time I saw him, he was volunteering in the café and waiting to go to a yoga class. He's actually a pretty good barista—better than he is at being a yogi, anyway. And no, I'm not going to kill you. I'm going to give you something, and leave it up to you to decide what to do with it."

"You're going to give me something?"

"Yeah. It's a gift economy around here. Haven't you heard?"

"What, exactly, are you going to give me, Masha?"

She shook her head. "Better you don't know until we make

the handoff. Technically, it would be better—for you, at least—if you *never* knew. But that's how it goes." She seemed to be talking to herself now. Being underground had changed her. She was, I don't know, *hinky*. Like something was wrong with her, like she was up to something, or like she could run at any second. She'd been so self-confident and decisive and unreadable. Now she seemed half crazy. Or maybe one-quarter crazy, and one-quarter terrified.

"Tonight," she said. "They're going to burn the Library of Alexandria at 8 P.M. After that burn, walk out to the trash fence, directly opposite Six O'Clock. Wait for me if I'm not there when you show up. I've got stuff to do first."

"Okay," I said. "I suppose I can do that. Will Zeb be there? I'd love to say hello to him again."

She rolled her eyes. "Zeb'll probably be there, but you might not see him. You come alone. And come out dark. No lights, got it?"

"No," I said. "Actually, no. I'm with Ange, as you must know, and I'm not going out there without her, assuming she wants to come. And no lights? You've got to be kidding me."

For a city of fifty thousand people involved with recreational substances, flaming art, and enormous, mutant machines, Black Rock has a remarkably low mortality rate. But in a city where they laughed at danger, walking after dark without lights—*lots* of lights, preferably—was considered borderline insane. One of the most dangerous things you could do at Burning Man was walk the playa at night without illumination: that made you a "darktard," and darktards were at risk of being run into by art bikes screaming over the dust in the inky night, they risked getting crushed by mammoth art cars, and they were certain to be tripped over and kicked and generally squashed. Burning Man's unofficial motto might have been "safety third," but no one liked a darktard.

She closed her eyes and stood statue-still. The wind was dying down a little, but I still felt like I'd just eaten a pound of talcum powder, and my eyes were stinging like I'd been pepper-sprayed.

"Bring your girly if you must. But no lights, not after you get out past the last art car. And if both of you end up in trouble because you wouldn't come out alone, you'll know whose fault it was."

She turned on her heel and walked off into the dust, and she was out of my sight in a minute. I hurried back to the temple to find Ange.

Chapter 2

They burn a *lot* of stuff at Burning Man. Of course, there's the burning of The Man himself on Saturday night. I'd seen that on video a hundred times from a hundred angles, with many different Men (he is different every year). It's raucous and primal, and the explosives hidden in his base made huge mushroom clouds when they went off. The temple burn, on Sunday night, was as quiet and solemn as The Man's burn was insane and frenetic. But before either of them get burned, there are lots of "little" burns.

The night before, there'd been the burning of the regional art. Burner affinity groups from across America, Canada, and the rest of the world had designed and built beautiful wooden structures ranging from something the size of a park bench up to three-story-tall fanciful towers. These ringed the circle of open playa in the middle of Black Rock City, and we'd gone and seen all of them the day we arrived, because we'd been told that they'd burn first. And they did, all at once, more than any one person could see, each one burning in its own way as burners crowded around them, held at a safe distance by Black Rock Rangers until the fires collapsed into stable configurations, masses of burning lumber on burn-platforms over the playa.

Anything that burned got burned on a platform, because "leave no trace" meant that you couldn't even leave behind *scorch marks*.

That had been pretty spectacular, but tonight they were going to burn the Library of Alexandria. Not the original, of course: Julius Caesar (or someone!) burned that one in 48 B.C., taking with it the largest collection of scrolls that had ever been assembled at that time. It wasn't the first library anyone had burned, and it wasn't the last, but it was the library that symbolized the wanton destruction of knowledge. The Burning Man Library of Alexandria was set on twenty-four great wheels on twelve great axles and it could be hauled across the playa by gangs of hundreds of volunteers who tugged at the ropes affixed to its front. Inside, the columned building was lined with nooks that were, in turn, stuffed with scrolls, each one hand-written, each a copy of some public domain book downloaded from Project Gutenberg and hand-transcribed onto long rolls of paper by volunteers who'd worked at the project all year. Fifty thousand books had been converted to scrolls in this fashion, and they would all burn. LIBRARIES BURN: it was the message stenciled at irregular intervals all over the Library of Alexandria and sported by the librarians who volunteered there, fetching you scrolls and helping you find the passages you were looking for. I'd gone in and read some Mark Twain, a funny story I remembered reading in school about when Twain had edited an agricultural newspaper. I'd been delighted to discover that someone had gone to the trouble of writing that one out, using rolled-up lined school notepaper and taping it together in a continuous scroll that went on for hundreds of yards.

As I helped the librarian roll up the scroll—she agreed that the Twain piece was really funny—and put it away, I'd said, unthinkingly, "It's such a shame that they're going to burn all these."

She'd smiled sadly and said, "Well, sure, but that's the point, isn't it? Ninety percent of the works in copyright are orphan works: no one knows who owns the rights to them, and no one can figure out how to put them back into print. Meanwhile, the copies of them that we do know about are disintegrating or getting lost. So there's a library out there, the biggest library ever, ninety percent of the stuff anyone's ever created, and it's burning, in slow motion. Libraries burn." She shrugged. "That's what they do. But maybe someday we'll figure out how to make so many copies of humanity's creative works that we'll save most of them from the fire."

And I read my Mark Twain and felt the library rock gently under me as the hundreds of rope-pullers out front dragged the Library of Alexandria from one side of the open playa to the other, inviting more patrons to get on board and have a ride and read a book before it all burned down. On the way out, the librarian gave me a thumbdrive: "It's a compressed copy of the Gutenberg archive. Fifty thousand books and counting. There's also a list of public domain books that we *don't* have, and a list of known libraries, by city, where they can be found. Feel free to get a copy and scan or retype it."

The little thumbdrive only weighed an ounce or two, but it felt as heavy as a mountain of books as I slipped it gravely into my pocket.

And now it was time to burn the Library of Alexandria. Again.

The Library had been hauled onto a burn-platform, and the hauling ropes were coiled neatly on its porch. Black Rock Rangers in their ranger hats and weird clothes surrounded it in a wide circle, sternly warning anyone who wandered too close to stay back. Ange and I stood on the front line, watching as a small swarm of Bureau of Land Management feds finished their inspection of the structure. I could see inside, see the incendiary charges that had been placed at careful intervals along the Library's length, see the rolled scrolls in their nooks. I felt weird tears in my eyes as I contemplated what was about to happen—tears of awe and sorrow and joy. Ange noticed and wiped the tears away, kissed my ear and whispered, "It's okay. Libraries burn."

Now three men stepped out of the crowd. One was dressed as Caesar in white Roman robes and crown, sneering magnificently. The next wore monkish robes and a pointed mitre with a large cross on it. He was meant to be Theophilus, Patriarch of Alexandria, another suspect in the burning of the Library. He looked beatifically on the crowd, then turned to Caesar. Finally, there was a man in a turban with a pointed beard—Caliph Omar, the final person usually accused of history's most notorious arson. The three shook hands, then each drew a torch out of his waistband and lit it from a firepot burning in the center of the Library's porch. They paced off from one another and stationed themselves in the middle of the back and side walls and, as the audience shouted and roared, thrust their torches lovingly in little holes set at the bottom of the walls.

There must have been some kind of flash powder or something in those nooks, because as each man scurried away, great arcs of flame shot out of them, up and out, scorching the Library walls. The walls burned merrily, and there was woodsmoke and gunpowder in the air now, the wind whipping it toward and past us, fanning the flames. The crowd noise increased, and I realized I was part of the chorus, making a kind of drawn-out, happy yelp.

Now the incendiary charges went, in near-perfect synch, a blossom of fire that forced its way out between the Library's columns, the fire's tongues lashing at sizzling embers—fragments of paper, fragments of books—that chased high into the night's sky. The heat of the blast made us all step back from one another, and embers rained out of the sky, winking out as they fell around us like ashen rain. The crowd moved like a slow-motion wave, edging its way out of the direction of the prevailing wind and the rain of fire. I smelled singed hair and fun fur, and a tall man in a loincloth behind me smacked me between the shoulders, shouting, "You were on fire, sorry!" I gave him a friendly wave—it was getting too loud to shout any kind of words—and continued to work my way to the edge.

Now there were fireworks, and not like the fireworks I'd seen on countless Fourth of July nights, fireworks that were artfully arranged to go off in orderly ranks, first one batch and then the next. These were fireworks with *tempo*, mortars screaming into the sky without pause, detonations so close together they were nearly one single explosion, a flaring, eye-watering series of booms that didn't let up, driven by the thundering, clashing music from the gigantic art cars behind the crowd, dubstep and funk and punk and some kind of up-tempo swing and even a gospel song all barely distinguishable. The crowd howled. I howled. The flames licked high and paper floated high on the thermals, burning bright in the desert night. The smoke was choking and there were bodies all around me, pressing in, dancing. I felt like I was part of some kind of mass organism with thousands of legs and eyes and throats and voices, and the flames went higher.

Soon the Library was just a skeleton of structural supports in stark black, surrounded by fiery orange and red. The building teetered, its roof shuddered, the columns rocked and shifted. Each time it seemed the building was about to collapse, the crowd gasped and held its breath, and each time it recovered its balance, we made a disappointed "Aww."

And then one of the columns gave way, snapping in two, taking the far corner of the roof with it, and the roof sheared downward and pulled free of the other columns, and they fell, too, and the whole thing collapsed in a crash and crackle, sending a fresh cloud of burning paper up in its wake. The Black

Rock Rangers pulled back and we rushed forward, surrounding the wreckage, crowding right up to the burning, crackling pile of lumber and paper and ash. The music got a lot louder—the art cars were pulling in tight now—and there was the occasional boom as a stray firework left in the pile sent up a glowing mortar. It was glorious. It was insane.

It was over, and it was time to get moving.

"Let's go," I said to Ange. She'd taken the news about Masha calmly, but she'd said, "There's no way I'm letting you go out there alone," when I told her that Masha had insisted on meeting me.

"That's what I told her," I said, and Ange stood on tiptoes, reached up, and patted me on the head.

"That's my boy," she said.

We threaded our way through the dancing, laughing crowd, getting faceful of woodsmoke, pot smoke, sweat, patchouli (Ange loved the smell, I hated it), ash, and playa dust. Soon we found ourselves through the crowd of people and in a crowd of art cars. It was an actual, no-fooling art car traffic jam: hundreds of mutant vehicles in a state of pure higgeldy-piggeldy, so that a three-story ghostly pirate ship (on wheels) found itself having to navigate through the gap between a tank with the body of a '59 El Camino on a crane arm that held it and its passengers ten feet off the ground and a rocking, rolling electric elephant with ten big-eyed weirdos riding on its howdah. Complicating things was the exodus of playa bikes, ridden with joyous recklessness by laughing, calling, goggled cyclists and streaming off into the night, becoming distant, erratic comets of bright LEDs, glowsticks, and electroluminescent wire.

EL wire was Burning Man's must-have fashion accessory. It was cheap and came in many colors, and glowed brightly for as long as the batteries in its pack held out. You could braid it into your hair, pin or glue it to your clothes, or just dangle it from anything handy. Ange's jawa bandoliers were woven through and through with different colors of pulsing EL wire, and she'd carefully worked a strand into the edge of her hood and another down the hem of her robe, so she glowed like a line drawing of herself from a distance. All my EL wire had been gotten for free, by harvesting other peoples' dead EL wire and painstakingly fixing it, tracking down the shorts and faults and taping them up. I'd done my army surplus boots with EL laces, and wound it in coils around my utility belt. Both of us were visible from a good distance, but that didn't stop a few cyclists from nearly running us down. They were very polite and apologetic about it, of course, but they were distracted. "Distracted" is a permanent state of being on the playa.

But as we ventured deeper into the desert, the population thinned out. Black Rock City's perimeter is defined by the "trash fence" that rings the desert, not too far in from the mountain ranges that surround it. These fences catch any MOOP ("matter out of place") that blows out of peoples' camps, where it can be harvested and packed out—leave no trace—and all that. Between the trash fence and the center of the city is two miles of open playa, nearly featureless, dotted here and there with people, art, and assorted surprises. If Six O'Clock Plaza is the sun, and The Man and temple and the camps are the inner solar system, the trash fence is something like the asteroid belt, or Pluto (allow me to pause for a moment here and say, PLUTO IS TOO A PLANET!).

Now we were walking in what felt like the middle of nowhere. So long as we didn't look over our shoulders at the carnival happening behind us, we could pretend that we were the only people on Earth.

Well, almost. We pretty much tripped over a couple who were naked and squirming on a blanket, way out in the big empty. It was a dangerous way to get your jollies, but nookie was a moderately good excuse for being a darktard. And they were pretty good-natured about it, all things considered. "Sorry," I called over my shoulder as we moved past them. "Time to go dark ourselves," I said.

"Guess so," Ange said, and fiddled with the battery switch on her bandolier. A moment later, she winked out of existence. I did the same. The sudden dark was so profound that the night looked the same with my eyes open and shut.

"Look up," Ange said. I did.

"My God, it's full of stars," I said, which is the joke I always tell when there's a lot of stars in the sky (it's a killer line from the book *2001,* though the idiots left it out of the movie). But I'd never seen a sky full of stars like this. The Milky Way—usually a slightly whitish streak, even on clear, moonless nights—was a glowing silvery river that sliced across the sky. I'd looked at Mars through binox once or twice and seen that it was, indeed, a little more red than the other stuff in the sky. But that night, in the middle of the desert, with the playa dust settled for a moment, it glowed like a coal in the lone eye of a cyclopean demon.

I stood there with my head flung back, staring wordlessly at the night, until I heard a funny sound, like the patter of water on stone, or—

"Ange, are you *peeing?*"

She shushed me. "Just having a sneaky playa-pee—the porta-sans are all the way back there. It'll evaporate by morning. Chill."

One of the occupational hazards of drinking water all the time was that you had to pee all the time, too. Some lucky burners had RVs at their camps with nice private toilets, but the rest of us went to "pee camp" when we needed to go. Luckily, the bathroom poetry—"poo-etry"—taped up inside the stalls made for pretty good reading. Technically, you weren't supposed to pee on the playa, but way out here the chances of getting caught were basically zero, and it really was a long way back to the toilets. Listening to Ange go made me want to go, too, so we enjoyed a playa-pee together in the inky, warm dark.

Walking in the dark, it was impossible to tell how close we were to the trash fence; there was just black ahead of us, with the slightly blacker black of the mountains rising to the lighter black of the starry sky. But gradually, we were able to pick out some tiny, flickering lights—candle lights, I thought—up ahead of us, in a long, quavering row.

As we got closer, I saw that they were candles, candle lanterns, actually, made of tin and glass, each with a drippy candle in it. They were placed at regular intervals along a gigantic, formal dinner table long enough to seat fifty people at least, with precise place settings and wineglasses and linen napkins folded into tents at each setting. "WTF?" I said softly.

Ange giggled. "Someone's art project," she said. "A dinner table at the trash fence. Woah."

"Hi there," a voice said from the dark, and a shadow detached itself from the table and then lit up with EL wire, revealing itself to be a young woman with bright purple hair and a leather jacket cut down into a vest. "Welcome." Suddenly there were more shadows turning into people—three more young women, one with green hair, one with blue hair, and . . .

"Hello, Masha," I said.

She gave me a little salute. "Meet my campmates," she said. "You've met before, actually. The day the bridge went."

Right, of course. These were the girls who'd been playing on Masha's Harajuku Fun Madness team when we'd run into them in the Tenderloin, moments before the Bay Bridge had been blown up by parties unknown. What had I called them? *The Popsicle Squad.* Yeah. "Nice to see you again," I said. "This is Ange."

Masha inclined her chin in a minute acknowledgment. "They've been good enough to let us use their dinner table for a little conversation, but I don't want to spend too much time out here. Plenty of people looking for me."

"Is Zeb here?"

"He went for a pee," she said. "He'll be back soon. But let's get started, okay?"

"Let's do it," Ange said. She'd stiffened up beside me the minute I'd said hi to Masha, and I had an idea that maybe she wasn't as cool about this meeting as she'd been playing it. Why should she be?

Masha brought us down to the farthest end of the table, away from her friends. We seated ourselves, and I saw that what I'd thought were bread baskets were in fact laden with long-lasting hippie junk food: whole-wheat pop-tarts from Trader Joe's, organic beef jerky, baggies of what turned out to be home-made granola. High-energy food that wouldn't melt in the sun. Masha noticed me inspecting the goods and she said, "Go ahead, that's what it's there for, help yourself." I tore into a pack of jerky (stashing the wrapper in my utility belt to throw away later at camp—turning gift-economy snacks into MOOP was really bad manners) and Ange got herself a pop-tart, just as Masha leaned across the table, opened the little glass door in the candle lantern, and blew the candle out. Now we were just black blobs in the black night, far from the nearest human, invisible.

I felt a hand—Masha's hand—grab my arm in the dark and feel its way down to my hand and then push something small and hard into my fingers, then let go.

"That's a USB stick, a little one. It's a crypto key that will unlock a four-gigabyte torrent file that you can get with a tor-rent magnet file on The Pirate Bay and about ten other torrent sites. It's called insurancefile.masha.torrent, and the checksum's on the USB stick, too. I'd appreciate it if you would download and seed the file, and ask anyone you trust to do the same."

"So," I said, speaking into the dark toward where Masha was sitting. "There's this big torrent blob filled with encrypted *something* floating around on the net, and if something happens, you want me to release the key so that it can be decrypted, right?"

"Yes, that's about the size of things," Masha said. I tried to imagine what might be in the insurance file. Blackmail photos? Corporate secrets? Pictures of aliens at Area 51? Proof of Bigfoot's existence?

"What's on it?" Ange said. Her voice was a little tight and tense, and though she was trying to hide it, I could tell she was stressing.

"Are you sure you want to know that?" Masha said. Her voice was absolutely emotionless.

"If you want us to do something other than throw this memory stick into a fire, you're goddamned right we do. I can't think of any reason to trust you, not one."

Masha didn't say anything. She heaved a sigh, and I heard her unscrew a bottle and take a drink of something. I smelled whiskey.

"Look," she said. "Back when I was, you know, *inside* at the DHS, I got to know a lot of things. Got to see a lot of things. Got to know a lot of people. Some of those people, they've *stayed* in touch with me. Not everyone at DHS wants to see America turned into a police state. Some people, they're just doing their jobs, maybe trying to catch actual bad guys or fight actual crime or prevent actual disasters, but they get to see things as they do these jobs, things that they're not happy about. Eventually, you come across something so terrible, you can't look yourself in the mirror anymore unless you do something about it.

"So maybe you copy some files, pile up some evidence. You

think to yourself, *Someday, someone will have the chance to speak out against this, and I'll quietly slip them these files, and my conscience will forgive me for being a part of an organization that's doing such rotten stuff.*

"So what happened is, someone you used to work with, someone who got a bad deal and has been underground and on the road, someone you trust, that person contacts you from deep underground and lets it be known that she'll hold on to all those docs for you, put them together with other peoples' docs, see if there are any interesting connections between them. That person will take them off your hands, launder them so no one will ever know where they came from, release them when the moment comes. This is quite a nice service to provide for tortured bureaucrats, you see, since it's the kind of thing that lets them sleep at night and still deposit their paychecks.

"Word gets around. Lots of people find it useful to outsource their conscience to a disgraced runaway outlaw, and, well, stuff does start to trickle in. Then pour in. Soon, you're sitting on gigabytes of that stuff."

"Four gigabytes, by any chance?" I said. I was feeling a little lightheaded. Masha was giving me the keys to decode all the ugliest secrets of the American government, all the stuff that had so horrified loyal DHS employees that they'd felt the need to smuggle it out. Masha herself would be so hot that she was practically radioactive: I could hardly believe that space-lasers weren't beaming out of the sky to kill her where she sat. And me? Well, once I had the key, no one could be sure I hadn't downloaded the insurance file and had a look, so that meant I was, fundamentally, a dead man.

"About that," she said.

"Gee, thanks."

"You have no right to do this," Ange said. "Whatever you're

up to, you're putting *us* in danger, without asking us, without us knowing anything about it. How *dare* you?"

Masha cut her off with a sharp *"Shh"* sound.

"Don't shush me—" Ange began, and I heard/felt/saw Masha grab her and squeeze.

"Shut *up*," she hissed.

Ange shut up. I held my breath. There was the distant *wub wub wub* of terrible dubstep playing from some faraway art car, the soughing of the wind blowing in the slats of the trash fence, and there—had I heard a footstep? Another footstep? Hesitant, stumbling, in the dark? A soft crunch, there it was again, *crunch, crunch,* closer now, and I felt Masha coil up, get ready to run, and I tasted the beef jerky again as it rose in my throat, buoyed up on a fountain of stomach acid. My ears hammered with my pulse and the sweat on the back of my neck dried to ice in an instant.

Crunch, crunch. The steps were practically upon us now, and there was a *bang* that made me jump as Masha leaped away from the table, knocked over her chair, and set off into the dark of the playa.

Then there was a blazing light, right in my face, blinding me, and a hand reaching out for me, and I scrambled away from it, grabbing for Ange, screaming something in wordless terror, Ange shouting, too, and then a voice said, "Hey, Marcus! Stop! It's me!"

I knew that voice, though I'd only heard it for an instant, long ago, on the street in front of Chavez High.

"Zeb?" I said.

"Dude!" he shouted, and I was grabbed up in a tight, somewhat smelly hug, my face pressed against his whiskered cheek. His blazing headlamp blinded me, but from what I could feel, he'd grown a beard of the same size and composition as a large animal, a big cat or possibly a beaver. The terror drained out of me, but left behind all its nervous energy, and I found myself laughing uproariously.

Suddenly, small strong hands separated us and Zeb was rolling on the playa, tackled by Masha, who must have circled back and recognized his voice. She was calling him all sorts of names as she wrestled him to the ground, straddling his chest and pinning his arms under her elbows.

"Sorry, sorry!" he said, and he was laughing, too, and so was Masha, and so was Ange, for that matter. "Sorry, okay! I just didn't want to disturb you. The girls told me you were down here. Thought a light would kill the atmosphere."

Masha let him up and gave him a kiss in a spot on his cheek where his beard was a little thinner.

"You are *such* an idiot," she said. He laughed again and tousled her hair. Masha was a totally different person with Zeb, playful and younger and not so totally lethal. I liked her better.

"Ange, this is Zeb. Zeb, this is Ange." He shook her hand.

"I've heard of you," she said.

"And I've heard of you, too," he said.

"Okay, sit down, you idiots, and turn off that damned light, Zeb." Masha was getting her down-to-business voice back, and we did what she said.

I still felt angry at her for what she'd done to us, but after being scared witless and then let down an instant later, it was hard to get back to that angry feeling. All my adrenaline had been dumped into my bloodstream already, and it would take a while to manufacture some more, I guess. Still, things were far from settled. "Masha," I said, "you know that what you've done here is really unfair, right?"

I couldn't see or hear her in the dark, and the silence stretched on so long I thought maybe she'd fallen asleep or tiptoed away. Then, suddenly, she said, "God, you're still a kid, aren't you?"

The way she said it made me feel like I was about eight years old, like I was some kind of hayseed with cow crap between my toes, and like she was some kind of world-traveling superspy underground fugitive ninja.

"Up yours," I said, trying to make it sound cynical and mean, and not like I was a widdle kid with hurt feewings. I don't think I was very successful.

She gave a mean laugh. "I mean it. 'Fair'? What's 'fair' got to do with anything? There is stuff going on in the world, bad stuff, the kind of stuff that ends up with dead people in shallow graves, and you're either part of the solution or you're part of the problem. Is it fair to all the people who risked everything to get me these docs for you to walk away from them, because you don't want to have your safe little life disrupted?

"Oh, M1k3y, you're *such a big hero*. After all you bravely, what, bravely told *other people's stories* to a *reporter*? Because you held a *press conference*? What a big, brave man." She spat loudly.

Yeah, it got me. Because you know what? She was right. Basically. Give or take. There'd been plenty of nights when I lay in bed and stared at the ceiling and thought *exactly* these thoughts. There'd been kids in the Xnet who did stuff that was way crazier than anything I'd done, kids whose jamming had put them right up against Homeland Security and the cops, kids who'd ended up in jail for a long time, without any newspaper coverage advertising their bravery. Some of them were probably still in there. The fact that I didn't know for sure—didn't even know all their names, or how many there were—was yet another reason that I didn't deserve anyone's admiration.

Every bit of clever, flashy wit ran and hid in the furthest corners of my mind. I heard Zeb shuffle his feet uncomfortably. No one knew what to say.

Except Ange. "Well, I suppose not everyone can be a sell-out," she said. "Not everyone can be a snitch who gets to sit in the hidden bunkers and spy on the ones who're getting beaten and jailed and tortured and disappeared. Not everyone can draw a fat salary for their trouble until the day comes that it's all too much for their poor little conscience and they just have to go and run away to a beach in Mexico somewhere, lying in the bed they made for themselves."

It made me smile, there in the dark. Go, Ange! Whatever my sins were, they were sins of omission: I could have done more. But Masha'd done the worst kind of evil: sins of commission. She'd done wrong. Really, really wrong. She'd tried to make up for it since. But *she* was in no position to shame *me*.

Another one of those long silences. I thought about dropping the USB stick in the dust and walking off in the dark. You know what stopped me?

Zeb.

Because Zeb *was* a hero. He'd broken out of Gitmo-by-the-Bay and instead of running, he'd come and found me at Chavez High so that he could pass on Darryl's note. He could have just hit the road, but he hadn't. And I'd told his secrets to the world, put him in harm's way. This wasn't just Masha's mission, this was Zeb's mission, too. They were a team. I owed him. We all did.

"Enough," I said, swallowing hard on all the stupid emotions, trying to find some of that Zen calm I'd attained at the temple. "Enough. Fine, it's not fair. Life's not fair. I've got this thing now. What do I do with it?"

"Keep it safe," Masha said, her voice back in that emotionless zone that I guessed she was good at finding when she needed it. "And if you ever hear that I've gone down, or Zeb's gone down, release it. Shout it from the mountaintops. If I ever ask you to release it, release it. And if you haven't heard from me by the Friday of the next Burning Man, one year from now, release it. Do you think you can do that?"

"Sounds like something I could manage," I said.

"I figure even you can't screw this up," she said, but I could tell she was just putting up her tough-chick front, and I didn't take it personally. "Okay, fine. I'm out of here. Don't screw up, all right?"

I heard her feet crunch away.

"See you at camp, babe!" Zeb called at her retreating back, and his headlamp came back on, dazzling me again. He grabbed a pop-tart from the basket and opened it, chewed at it enthusiastically. "I love that girl, honestly I do. But she is so *tightly wound!*"

It was so manifestly true that there was nothing for it but to laugh, and so we did, and it turned out that Zeb had some beer that he gift-economied to us, and I had some cold-brew coffee concentrate in a flask that we dipped into afterwards, just to get us back up from the beer's mellow down, and then we all needed pee camp, and we went back into the night and the playa and the dust.

Chapter 3

All day long, people had been telling me that the weather man said we were in for a dust storm, but I just assumed that "dust storm" meant that I'd have to tuck my scarf under the lower rim of my goggles, the way I had been doing every time it got windy on the playa.

But the dust storm that blew up after we left Zeb behind and returned to the nonstop circus was *insane*. The night turned white with flying dust, and our lights just bounced back in our faces, creating gloomy gray zones in front of us that seemed to go on forever. It reminded me of really bad fog, the kind of thing you get sometimes in San Francisco, usually in the middle of summer, reducing all the tourists in their shorts and T-shirts to hypothermia candidates. But fog made it hard to *see,* and the dust storm made it hard—nearly impossible—to breathe. Our eyes and noses streamed, our mouths were caked with dust, every breath triggered a coughing fit. We stumbled and staggered and clutched each other's hands because if we let go, we'd be swallowed by the storm.

Ange pulled my ear down to her mouth and shouted, "We have to get inside!"

"I know!" I said. "I'm just trying to figure out how to get back to camp; I think we're around Nine O'Clock and B." The ring roads that proceeded concentrically from center camp were lettered in alphabetical order. We were at Seven Fifteen and L, way out in the hinterlands. Without the dust, the walk would have taken fifteen minutes, and been altogether pleasant. With the dust . . . well, it felt like it might take *hours.*

"Screw that," Ange said. "We have to get inside somewhere *now.*" She started dragging me. I tripped over a piece of rebar hammered into the playa and topped with a punctured tennis ball—someone's tent stake. Ange's iron grip kept me from falling, and she hauled me along.

Then we were at a structure—a hexayurt, made from triangular slabs of flat styrofoam, duct-taped on its seams. The outside was covered with an insulating layer of silver-painted bubble wrap. We felt our way around to the "door" (a styro slab with a duct-tape hinge on one edge and a pull-loop). Ange was about to yank this open when I stopped her and knocked instead. Storm or no storm, it was weird and wrong to just walk into some stranger's home.

The wind howled. If someone was coming, I couldn't hear them over its terrible moaning whistle. I raised my hand to knock again, and the door swung open. A bearded face peered out at us and shouted, "Get in!"

We didn't need to be asked twice. We dove through the door and it shut behind us. I could still hardly see; my goggles were nearly opaque with caked-on dust, and the light in the hexayurt was dim, provided by LED lanterns draped with gauzy scarves.

"Look at what the storm blew in," said a gravelly, jovial voice from the yurt's shadows. "Better hose 'em off before you bring 'em over here, John, those two've got half the playa in their ears."

"Come on," said the bearded man. He was wearing tie-dyes and had beads braided into his long beard and what was left of his hair. He grinned at us from behind a pair of round John Lennon glasses. "Let's get you cleaned up. Shoes first, thanks."

Awkwardly, we bent down and unlaced our shoes. We *did* have half the playa in them. The other half was caught in the folds of our clothes and our hair and our ears.

"Can I get you two something to wear? We can beat the dust out of your clothes once the wind dies down."

My first instinct was to say no, because we hadn't even been introduced, plus it seemed like more hospitality than even the gift economy demanded. On the other hand, we weren't doing these people any kindness by crapping up their hexayurt. On the other other hand—

"That'd be so awesome," Ange said. "Thank you."

That's why she's my girlfriend. Left to my own devices, I'd be on-the-other-handing it until Labor Day. "Thanks," I said.

The man produced billowy bundles of bright silk. "They're salwar kameez," he said. "Indian clothes. Here, these are the pants, and you wrap the tops around like so." He demonstrated. "I get them on eBay from women's clothing collectives in India. Straight from the source. Very comfortable and practically one size fits all."

We stripped down to our underwear and wound the silk around us as best we could. We helped each other with the tricky bits, and our host helped, too. "That's better," he said, and gave us a package of baby wipes, which are the playa's answer to a shower. We went through a stack of them wiping the dust off each other's faces and out of each other's ears and cleaning our hands and bare feet—the dust had infiltrated our shoes and socks!

"And that's it," the man said, clasping his hands together and beaming. He had a soft, gentle way of talking, but you could tell by the twinkle of his eyes that he didn't miss anything and that something very interesting was churning away in his mind.

Either he was a Zen master or an axe murderer—no one else was that calm and mirthful. "I'm John, by the way."

Ange shook his hand. "Ange," she said.

"Marcus," I said.

Lots of people used "playa names," cute pseudonyms that let them assume new identities while they were at Burning Man. I'd had enough of living with my notorious alter ego, M1k3y, and didn't feel the need to give myself another handle. I hadn't talked it over with Ange, but she, too, didn't seem to want or need a temporary name.

"Come on and meet the rest."

"The rest" turned out to be three more guys, sitting on low cushions around a coffee table that was littered with paper, dice, and meticulously painted lead figurines. We'd interrupted an old-school gaming session, the kind you play with a dungeon master and lots of role-playing. I'm hardly in any position to turn up my nose at someone else's amusements—after all, I spent years doing live-action role-play—but this was seriously nerdy. The fact that they were playing in the middle of a dust storm on the playa just made it more surreal.

"Hi!" Ange said. "That looks like fun!"

"It certainly is," said a gravelly voice, and I got a look at its owner. He had a lined and seamed face, kind eyes, and a slightly wild beard, and he was wearing a scarf around his neck with a turquoise pin holding it in place. "Are you initiated in the mysteries of this particular pursuit?"

I slipped my hand into Ange's and did my best not to be shy or awkward. "I've never played, but I'm willing to learn."

"An admirable sentiment," said another man. He was also in his fifties or sixties, with a neat gray Vandyke beard and dark rimmed glasses. "I'm Mitch, this is Barlow, and this is Wil, our dungeon master."

The last man was a lot younger than the other three—maybe

a youthful forty—and clean-shaven, with apple cheeks and short hair. "Hey, folks," he said. "You're just in time. Are you going to sit in? I've got some pre-rolled characters you can play. We're just doing a minidungeon while we wait out the storm."

John brought us some cushions from the hexayurt's recesses and sat down with crossed legs and perfect, straight yoga posture. We settled down beside him. Wil gave us our character sheets—I was a half-elf mage, Ange was a human fighter with an enchanted sword—and dug around in a case until he found hand-painted figurines that matched the descriptions. "My son paints them," he said. "I used to help, but the kid's a machine—I can't keep up with him." I looked closely at the figs. They were, well, they were *beautiful*. They'd been painted in incredible detail, more than I could actually make out in the dim light of the yurt. My character's robes had been painted with mystical silver sigils, and Ange's character's chain mail had each ring picked out in tarnished silver, with tiny daubs of black paint in the center of each minute ring.

"These are amazing," I said. I'd always thought of tabletop RPGs as finicky and old-fashioned, but these figs had been painted by someone very talented who really loved the game, and if someone *that* talented thought this was worth his time, I'd give it a chance, too.

Wil was a great game master, spinning the story of our quest in a dramatic voice that sucked me right in. The other guys listened intently, though they interjected from time to time with funny quips that cracked one another up. I got the feeling they'd known one another for a long time, and when we took a break for fresh mint tea—these guys knew how to live!—I asked how they knew one another.

They all smiled kind of awkwardly at one another. "It's kind of a reunion," Mitch said. "We all worked together a long time ago."

"Did you do a start-up together?"

They laughed again. I could tell that I was missing something. Wil said, "You ever hear of the Electronic Frontier Foundation?" I sure had. I figured it out a second before he said it: "These guys founded it."

"Wait, wait," I said. "You're *John Perry Barlow*?" The guy in the kerchief nodded and grinned like a pirate. "And you're John Gilmore?" John shrugged and raised his eyebrows. "And *you're* Mitch Kapor?" The guy with the Vandyke gave a little wave. Ange was looking slightly left out. "Ange, *these guys founded EFF*. That one started the first ISP in San Francisco; that one commercialized spreadsheets; and that one wrote the Declaration of Independence of Cyberspace."

Barlow laughed like a cement mixer. "And turned teraliters of sewage into gigaliters of diesel fuel with tailored algae. I also wrote a song or two. Since we're on the subject."

"Oh yeah," I said. "Barlow also wrote songs for the Grateful Dead."

Ange shook her head. "You make them sound like the elder gods of the Internet."

"Enough with the 'elder' stuff," Mitch said, and sipped his tea. "You certainly seem to know your Internet trivia, young man."

I blushed. A couple of times on the playa, people had recognized me as M1k3y and come over to tell me how much they admired me and so on, and it had embarrassed me, but now I *wanted* these guys to know about that part of my life and I couldn't figure out how to get it out without sounding like I was boasting to three of the all-time heroes of the Internet. Again, Ange saved me. "Marcus and I worked with some EFF people a couple years ago. He started Xnet."

Wil laughed aloud at that. "That was *you*?" he said. He put on a hard-boiled detective voice: "Of all the yurts in all the playa, they had to walk into mine."

Mitch held out his hand. "It's an honor, sir," he said. I shook his hand, tongue-tied. The others followed suit. I was in a daze, and when John told me that he "really admired the work" I'd done, I thought I'd die from delight.

"Enough!" Ange said. "I won't be able to get his head out of the door if it gets any more swollen. Now, are we here to talk or to roll some goddamned dice?"

"I like your attitude," Wil said, and thumbed through his notebook and set down some terrain tiles on the graph paper in front of us. Ange turned out to be a master strategist—which didn't surprise me, but clearly impressed everyone else—and she arrayed our forces such that we sliced through the trash hordes, beat the minibosses, and made it to the final boss without suffering any major losses. She was a born tank, and loved bulling through our adversaries while directing our forces. Wil gave her tons of extra XP for doing it all in character—barbarian swordmistress came easily to her—and her example led us all, so by the time we got to the dragon empress in her cavern at the middle of the dungeon, we were all talking like a fantasy novel. Barlow was a master at this, improvising heroic poetry and delivering it in that whiskey voice of his. Meanwhile, Mitch and John kept catching little hints that Wil dropped in his narration, discovering traps and hidden treasures based on the most obscure clues. I can't remember when we'd had a better time.

Mitch and Barlow kept shifting on their cushions, and just as we broke through into the main cavern, they called for a stretch break, and got to their feet and rubbed vigorously at their lower backs, groaning. Wil stretched, too, and checked the yurt's door. "Storm's letting up," he called. It was coming on to midnight, and when Wil opened the door, a cool, refreshing breeze blew in, along with the sound of distant music.

Part of me wanted to rush back out into the night and find some music to dance to, and part of me wanted to stay in the yurt with my heroes, playing D&D. That was the thing about Burning Man—there was so *much* I wanted to do!

Wil came over and handed me another cup of mint tea, the leaves floating in the hot water. "Pretty awesome. Can't believe these guys let me DM their game. And I can't believe I ran into *you*." He shook his head. "This place is like nerdstock."

"Have you known them for long?"

"Not really. I met Barlow and Gilmore awhile back, when I did a fund-raiser for EFF. I ran into Gilmore at random today and I told him I'd brought my D&D stuff along and the next thing I knew, I was running a game for them."

"What kind of fund-raiser were you doing?" Wil looked familiar, but I couldn't quite place him.

"Oh," he said, and stuck his hands in his pockets. "They brought me in to pretend-fight a lawyer in a Barney the Purple Dinosaur costume. It was because the Barney people had been sending a lot of legal threats out to websites and EFF had been defending them, and, well, it was a lot of fun."

I knew him from *somewhere*. It was driving me crazy. "Look, do I know you? You look really familiar—"

"Ha!" he said. "I thought you knew. I made some movies when I was a kid, and I was on *Star Trek: The Next Generation*, and—"

My jaw dropped so low I felt like it was in danger of scraping my chest. "You're *Wil Wheaton*?"

He looked embarrassed. I've never been much of a Trek fan, but I'd seen a ton of the videos Wheaton had done with his comedy troupe, and of course, I knew about Wheaton's Law: *Don't be a dick.*

"That's me," he said.

"You were the first person I ever followed on Twitter!" I said. It was a weird thing to say, sure, but it was the first thing that came to mind. He was a *really* funny tweeter.

"Well, thank you!" he said. No wonder he was such a good narrator—he'd been acting since he was like seven years old. Being around all these people made me wish I had access to Wikipedia so I could look them all up.

We sat back down to play against the megaboss, the dragon empress. She had all kinds of fortifications, and a bunch of lethal attacks. I figured out how to use an illusion spell to trick her into moving into a side corridor that gave her less room to maneuver, and this made it possible for the fighters to attack her in waves while I used a digging spell to send chunks of the cave roof onto her head. This seemed like a good idea to me (and everyone else, I swear it!), right up to the time that I triggered a cave-in that killed us all.

But no one was too angry with me. We'd all cheered every time I rolled a fifteen or better and one of my spells brought some roof down on the dragon's head, and no one had bothered too much about all those dice rolls Wil was making behind his screen. Besides, it was nearly 1 A.M., and there was a party out there! We changed out of John's beautiful silk clothes and back into our stiff, dust-caked playa-wear and switched on all our EL wire and fit our goggles over our eyes and said a million thanks and shook everyone's hands and so on. Just as I was about to go, Mitch wrote an email address on my arm with a Sharpie (there was plenty of stuff there already—playa coordinates of parties and email addresses of people I planned on looking up).

"Ange tells me you're looking for a job. That's the campaign manager for Joseph Noss. I hear she's looking for a webmaster. Tell her I sent you."

I was speechless. After months of knocking on doors, sending in résumés, emailing and calling, an honest-to-goodness job—with a recommendation from an honest-to-goodness legend! I stammered out my thanks and as soon as we were outside, I kissed Ange and bounced up and down and dragged her off to the playa, nearly crashing into a guy on a dusty Segway tricked out with zebra-striped fun fur. He gave us a grin and a wave.

We didn't see Masha or Zeb again until the temple burn on Sunday night, the last night.

We'd burned The Man the night before, and it had been in-freaking-*sane*. Hundreds of fire-dancers executing precision maneuvers, tens of thousands of burners sitting in ranks on the playa, screaming our heads off as fireballs and mushroom clouds of flame rose out of The Man's pyramid, then the open-throated roar as it collapsed and the Rangers dropped their line and we all rushed forward to the fire, everyone helping everyone else along, like the world's most courteous stampede. I flashed on the crush of bodies in the BART station after the Bay Bridge blew, the horrible feeling of being forced by the mass of people to step on those who'd fallen, the sweat and the stink and the noise. Someone had *stabbed* Darryl in that crowd, given him the wound that started us on our awful adventure.

This crowd was nothing like that mob, but my internal organs didn't seem to know that, and they did slow flip-flops in my abdomen, and my legs turned to jelly, and I found myself slowly sliding to the playa. There were tears pouring down my face, and I felt like I was floating above my body as Ange grabbed me under my armpits, struggling to get me to my feet as she spoke urgent, soothing words into my ears. People stopped and helped, one tall woman steering traffic around us, a small older man grabbing me beneath my armpits with strong hands, pulling me upright.

I snapped back into my body, felt the jellylegged feeling recede, and blinked away the tears. "I'm sorry," I said. "Sorry." I was so embarrassed I felt like digging a hole and pulling the playa in over my head. But neither of the people who'd stopped to help seemed surprised. The woman told me where to find the nearest medical camp and the man gave me a hug and told me to take it easy.

Ange didn't say anything, just held me for a moment. She knew that I sometimes got a little wobbly in crowds, and she knew I didn't like to talk about it. We made our way to the fire and watched it for a moment, then went back out into the playa for the parties and the dancing and forgetting. I reminded myself that I was in love, at Burning Man, and that there might be a job waiting for me when I got back to San Francisco, and kicked myself in the ass every time I felt the bad feeling creeping up on me.

Temple burn was very different. We got there really early and sat down nearly at the front and watched the sun set and turn the temple's white walls orange, then red, then purple. Then the spotlights went up, and it turned blazing white again. The wind blew and I heard the rustle of all the paper remembrances fluttering in its nooks and on its walls.

We were sitting amid thousands of people, tens of thousands of people, but there was hardly a sound. When I closed my eyes, I could easily pretend that I was alone in the desert with the temple and all its memories and good-byes and sorrows. I felt the ghost of that feeling I'd had when I'd sat in the temple and tried to clear my mind, to be in the present and throw away all my distractions. The temple had an instantly calming effect on me, silenced all the chattering voices in the back of my head. I don't believe in spooks and ghosts and gods, and I don't think the temple had any *supernatural* effect, but it had an absolutely *natural* effect, made me sorrowful and hopeful and calm and, well, *soft-edged* all at once.

I wasn't the only one. We all sat and watched the temple, and people spoke in hushed tones, museum voices, church whispers. Time stretched. Sometimes I felt like I was dozing off.

Other times I felt like I could feel every pore and every hair on my body. Ange stroked my back, and I squeezed her leg softly. I looked at the faces around me. Some were calm, some softly cried, some smiled in profound contentment. The wind ruffled my scarf.

And then I spotted them. Three rows back from us, holding hands: Masha and Zeb. I nearly didn't recognize them at first, because Masha had her head on Zeb's shoulder and wore an expression of utter vulnerability and sadness, absolutely unlike her normal display of half-angry, half-cocky impatience. I looked away before I caught her eye, feeling like I'd intruded on her privacy.

I turned back to the temple just in time to see the first flames lick at its insides, the paper crackling and my breath catching in my chest. Then a tremendous column of fire sprouted out of the central atrium, *whoosh*ing in a pillar a hundred yards tall, the heat and light so intense I had to turn my face away. The crowd *sighed*, a huge, soft sound, and I sighed with it.

There was someone walking through the crowd now, a compact woman in goggles and gray clothes in a cut that somehow felt military, though they didn't have any markings or insignia. She was moving with odd intensity, holding a small video camera up to one eye and peering through it. People muttered objections as she stepped on them or blocked their view, then spoke louder, saying "Sit down!" and "Down in front," and "Spectator!" This last with a vicious spin on it that was particularly apt, given her preoccupation with that camera.

I looked away from her and tried to put her out of my mind. The temple was burning along its length now, and someone near me drew a breath and let out a deep, bassy "Ommmmmm" that made my ears buzz. Another voice joined in, and then another, and then *I* joined in, the sound like a living thing that traveled up and down my chest and through my skull, suffusing me with calm. It was exactly what I needed, that sound, and as my voice twined with all those others, with Ange's, I felt like a part of something so much larger than myself.

A sharp pain in my thigh made me open my eyes. It was the lady with the camera, facing away from me, scanning the fire and the crowd with it, and she'd caught some of the meat of my thigh as she stepped past me. I looked up in annoyance, ready to say something *really* nasty, and found myself literally frozen in terror.

You see, I knew that face. I could never have forgotten it.

Her name was Carrie Johnstone. I'd called her "Severe Haircut Woman" before I learned it. The last time I'd seen her in person, she'd had me strapped to a board and ordered a soldier hardly older than me to waterboard me—to simulate my execution. To torture me.

For years, that face had haunted my nightmares, swimming out of the dark of my dreams to taunt me; to savage me with sharp, animal teeth; to choke me out with a tight bag over my face; to ask me relentless questions I couldn't answer and hit me when I said so.

A closed-door military tribunal had found her not guilty of any crime, and she'd been "transferred" to help wind down the Forward Operating Base in Tikrit, Iraq. I had a news alert for her, but no news of her ever appeared. As far as I could tell, she'd vanished.

It was like being back in my nightmares, one of those paralysis dreams where your legs and arms won't work. I wanted to shout and scream and run, but all I could do was sit as my heart thundered so loud that my pulse blotted out all the other sounds, even that all-consuming *Ommmm*.

Johnstone didn't even notice. She radiated an arrogant disregard for people, her face smooth and emotionless as the people around her asked her (or shouted at her) to move. She took another step past me and I stared at her back—tense beneath her jacket, coiled for action—as she strode back through the crowd, disappearing over the horizon, hair beneath a stocking cap that was the same desert no-color as her clothes.

Ange squeezed my hand. "What's wrong?" she asked.

I shook my head and squeezed back. I wasn't going to tell her I'd just seen the bogeywoman on the playa. Even if that *was* Johnstone, so what? Everyone came to Burning Man, it seemed—software pioneers, fugitives, poets, and me. I hadn't seen any rules against war criminals attending.

"It's nothing," I choked out. I looked over the crowd. Johnstone had disappeared. I turned back to the burning temple, tried to find the peace I'd felt a moment before.

By the time the temple burned down, I'd nearly convinced myself that I'd imagined Johnstone. After all, it had been dark, the only light the erratic flicker of the temple. The woman had held a camera to her face, obscuring it. And I'd seen her from below. I'd been visiting all my ghosts that night, seeing the faces of friends lost and betrayed and saved in the temple's fire. I'd only seen the face for a moment. What were the odds that *Carrie Johnstone* would be at *Burning Man*? It was like finding Attila the Hun at a yoga class. Like finding Darth Vader playing ultimate frisbee in the park. Like finding Megatron volunteering at a children's hospital. Like finding Nightmare Moon having a birthday party at Chuck E. Cheese.

Thinking up these analogies—and even dumber ones that I won't inflict upon you—helped me calm down as Ange and I walked slowly away from temple burn with the rest of the crowd, a solemn and quiet procession.

"Going home tomorrow," I said.

"Exodus," Ange said. That's what it was called at Burning Man, and it was supposed to be epic—thousands of cars and

RVs stretching for miles, being released in "pulses" every hour so that the traffic didn't bunch up. We'd scored a ride back with Lemmy from Noisebridge, the hackerspace I hung around at in San Francisco. I didn't know him well, but we knew where he was camped and had arranged to meet him with our stuff at 7 A.M. to help him pack his car. Getting up that early would be tricky, but I had a secret weapon: my contribution to the Burning Man gift economy, aka cold-brew coffee.

You've had hot coffee before, and in the hands of a skilled maker, coffee can be *amazing*. But the fact is that coffee is one of the hardest things to get right in the world. Even with great beans and a great roast and great equipment, a little too much heat, the wrong grind, or letting things go on too long will produce a cup of bitterness. Coffee's full of different acids, and depending on the grind, temperature, roast, and method, you can "overextract" the acids from the beans, or overheat them and oxidize them, producing that awful taste you get at donut shops and Starbucks.

But there is Another Way. If you make coffee in *cold* water, you *only* extract the sweetest acids, the highly volatile flavors that hint at chocolate and caramel, the ones that boil away or turn to sourness under imperfect circumstances. Brewing coffee in cold water sounds weird, but in fact, it's just about the easiest way to make a cup (or a jar) of coffee.

Just grind coffee—keep it coarse, with grains about the size of sea salt—and combine it with twice as much water in an airtight jar. Give it a hard shake and stick it somewhere cool overnight (I used a cooler bag loaded with ice from ice camp and wrapped the whole thing in bubble wrap for insulation). In the morning, strain it through a colander and a paper coffee filter. What you've got now is coffee concentrate, which you can dilute with cold water to taste—I go about half and half. If you're feeling fancy, serve it over ice.

Here's the thing: cold-brew coffee tastes *amazing,* and it's practically impossible to screw it up. Unlike espresso, where all the grounds have to be about the same size so that the high-pressure water doesn't cause fracture lines in the "puck" of coffee that leave some of the coffee unextracted and the rest overextracted, cold-brew grounds can be just about any size. Seriously, you could grind it with a stone axe. Unlike drip coffee, which goes sour and bitter if you leave the grounds in contact with the water for too long, cold brew just gets yummier and yummier (and more and more caffeinated!) the longer the grounds sit in the water. Cold brewing in a jar is pretty much the easiest way to make coffee in the known universe—if you don't mind waiting overnight for the brew—and it produces the best-tasting, most potent coffee you've ever drunk. The only downside is that it's kind of a pain in the ass to clean up, but if you want to spend some more money, you can invest in various gadgets to make it easier to filter the grounds, from cheap little Toddy machines all the way up to hand-blown glass Kyoto drippers that look like something from a mad scientist's lab. But all you need to make a perfectly astounding cup of cold-brewed jet fuel is a mason jar, coffee, water, and something to strain it through. They've been making iced coffee this way in New Orleans for centuries, but for some unknown reason, it never seems to have caught on big-time.

All week, I'd been patrolling the playa armed with a big thermos bottle filled with cold-brew concentrate, pouring out cups to anyone who seemed nice or in need of a lift. Every single person I shared it with had been astounded at the flavor. It's funny watching someone take a sip of cold brew for the first time, because it looks and smells *strong,* and it is, and coffee drinkers have been trained to think that "strong" equals "bitter." The first mouthful washes over your tongue and the coffee flavor wafts up the back of your throat and fills up your sinus cavity

and your nose is all, "THIS IS INCREDIBLY STRONG!"
And the flavor *is* strong, but there isn't a *hint* of bitterness. It's
like someone took a cup of coffee and subtracted everything
that wasn't totally delicious, and what's left behind is a pure,
powerful coffee liquor made up of all these subtle flavors: citrus
and cocoa and a bit of maple syrup, all overlaid on the basic and
powerful coffee taste you know and love.

I know I converted at least a dozen people to the cult of cold
brew over the week, and the only challenge had been keeping
Ange from drinking it all before I could give it away. But we'd
have jet fuel in plenty for the morning's pack-up and Exodus.
I'd put up *all* the leftover coffee to brew before we went to the
temple burn, and if we drank even half of it, our ride would
have to let us out of the car during the Exodus pulses to run
laps around the playa and work off the excess energy.

Thinking about this, I took my thermos off my belt and
gave it a shake. "Want some magic bean juice?" I asked.

"Yum," Ange said, and took the flask from me and swigged
at it.

"Leave some for me," I said, and pried it out of her fingers
and drank the last few swallows. The deep, trancelike experience of temple burn had left me feeling like I wanted to find
someone's pillow camp and curl up on a mountain of cushions,
but it was my last night on the playa, and I was going to *dance*, so
I needed some rocket fuel.

Just as I lowered the flask, I spotted Masha and Zeb again,
walking stiffly beside each other, faces set like stone, expressionless. They were at least fifty yards away from me, in the dark
of night, and at first I thought they were just in some kind of
deeply relaxed state from the extraordinary events of the night.
But I soon saw that there was something definitely wrong.
Walking *very* close behind them were a pair of large men in
stocking caps just like the ones Carrie Johnstone—or her twin—

had been wearing, and they had tight gray-black scarves pulled over their faces, though it wasn't blowing dust just then. The crowd parted a little and I saw that they were dressed as Carrie Johnstone had been, the same semimilitary jackets and baggy pants and big black boots. There was something wrong with them, and I couldn't place it for a moment, but then it hit me: they were darktards—no EL wire, no lights. And for that matter, Zeb and Masha had gone dark.

I saw all this in a second and mostly reconstructed it after the fact, because I was already moving. "This way," I said to Ange, and grabbed her hand and started to push through the crowd. There was something *really* wrong with that little scene, and Masha might not be my favorite person in the world, but whatever was going down with her and Zeb and those two guys, I wanted to find out about it.

Even as we pushed through the crowd, part of my brain was already telling me a little story about how it would all be okay: *It's probably not even them. Those two guys probably have EL wire all over their clothes, but they're saving battery. Boy, is Ange going to think I'm a paranoia case when I tell her what I thought I saw—*

The four were heading out into the dark of the open playa now, and there was someone bringing up the rear, emerging from the crowd behind them. It was Carrie Johnstone, and I saw her profile clearly now, silhouetted by the orange light of a flamethrower flaring a fireball into the night as a mutant vehicle zoomed past. There was no doubt at all in my mind now, this was *her.* She was sweeping her head from side to side in a smooth, alert rhythm, like the Secret Service bodyguards that shadowed the president when you saw him on TV.

Ange was saying something, but I couldn't hear her, and she was pulling on my hand, so I let go of her, because I *knew* it was Carrie Johnstone, and I *knew* that Zeb and Masha were under her power. I had been under her power. So had Ange. I knew what that meant, and I wasn't going to let her snatch anyone else.

All five of them were vanishing into the night and I began to push and shove my way through the crowd, not caring anymore if I stepped on someone's toes or bumped into them. People swore at me, but I barely heard them. My vision had shrunk to a narrow tunnel with Carrie Johnstone at the end of it. I patted at my utility belt and found my thermos, which was made of hard metal alloy. It didn't weigh much, but if you hit someone from behind with it, as hard as you could, they'd know they'd been hit. That's what I was going to do to Carrie Johnstone.

I was making a wordless noise. It started off quietly, under my breath, but it was quickly turning into a roar. No, not a roar, a *battle cry*. For years, this woman had haunted and hunted me in my dreams. She'd humiliated me, broken me—and now she was doing it again to someone else. And I had her in my sights and in my power.

Someone on a playa bike nearly ran me down but swerved at the last moment and fell over right in front of me, clipping my shin. I didn't even slow down. In fact, I sped up, leapt over the bike, and took off at a run.

I'd never run like that in my life, a flat-out sprint with my feet barely touching the ground. I was just taking another step when the whole night turned hellish orange around me, and then there was a terrible *whoomph* sound, and a blast of heat and noise and wind lifted me off my feet and threw me face-first into the dust.

I was dazed for a moment—we all were—and then I rolled over and picked myself up. My nose was bleeding, and when I put my hand up to it, it brushed against my lip and it felt *weird*, numb and wet, and I thought, in a distant, abstract way, *I've really done a number on my face, I guess*. That same part of me quietly chided myself for violating first-aid protocol by moving around after an injury. Even if I didn't have a spinal injury or a concussion, I might have broken some small bone that hadn't had a chance to start sending pain signals to my brain yet, might be mashing that broken bone under all my weight as I climbed to my feet.

I told the voice to shut up. I remember that very clearly, actually thinking, *Shut up, you, I'm busy,* like you'd do to a yappy dog. Because whatever had turned the sky orange, whatever had sent that gust of heat and wind and sound through the night, *Carrie Johnstone had been responsible for it, and it had been part of her plan to take Zeb and Masha out.* I knew it. Not in the way I knew what my address was, but in the way that I knew that a ball thrown straight into the air would come straight back again. A logical certainty.

I set off back in the direction that Masha and Zeb and Johnstone and her goons had been heading, out into the darkness, limping a little now as my right knee started to complain, loudly. I told it to shut up, too.

They were gone. Of course they were. Unlit, moving fast, out there on the playa, they could have disappeared just by moving off a hundred yards in nearly any direction. They probably had night-scopes and all sorts of clever little asshole-ninja superspy gadgets that they could use to avoid me if they wanted to.

If she wanted to. Carrie Johnstone probably could have killed me without breaking a sweat, and I'm sure her goons could have done the same. They were some sort of soldiers, while I was a scrawny nineteen-year-old from San Francisco whose last fight had been settled in Mrs. Bapuji's day care with a firm admonishment to share the Elmo doll with little Manny Hernandez.

But I didn't care. I was on a mission. I wasn't a coward. I wasn't going to sit back and wait for other people to do all the work. So I lurched into the dark.

There was no sign of them. I called out their names, screaming myself hoarse, running this way and that, and I was still running when Ange caught up with me, grabbed my arm, and pulled me bodily back to the infirmary tent. There were a lot of us there, waiting to be seen by the paramedics, nurses, EMTs, and doctors who streamed from across the playa to help with the aftermath of the worst disaster in the history of Burning Man.

Octotank, the art car that exploded, had started out life as a ditch digger, and it retained the huge, powerful tank treads and chassis. A maker collective working out of a warehouse in San Bernardino had removed everything else and meticulously mounted an ancient Octopus carnival ride atop it. You've seen Octopus rides, though your local version might have been called "the Spider," "the Schwarzkopf Monster," or "the Polyp." They've got six or more articulated arms, each one ending in a ride seat, sometimes just a chair with a lap bar and sometimes a full cage.

Now, that would have been cool enough, but then the mutant vehicle designers had mounted a flamethrower to the roof of each of Octotank's cars and hooked them up to an Arduino controller that caused them to fire in breathtaking sequences. They all drew their fuel from the same massive reservoir mounted to one side of Octotank's body, but each one had a mechanism that injected the fuel with different metal salts, and these impurities all burned with different bright colors. When Octotank was in motion, all eight cars swinging around in the night as it trundled across the playa, shooting tall pillars of multicolored flame into the sky from the swirling mandalas of its cars, well, it was magnificent.

Right up to the moment it exploded, of course.

The fuel reservoir was already half empty, thankfully, otherwise it would have done more than knock me (and about a hundred other people) on my face—it would have incinerated us.

Miraculously, no one *was* incinerated, though a couple dozen were burned badly enough that they were airlifted to Reno. Octotank had been built by careful, thoughtful makers, and they'd put in triple fail-safes, the final measure being that the reservoir had been built with its thinnest wall on the outer, lower edge, so if it ever did blow, it would direct its force into the ground and not the driver or the riders. The force of the blast had knocked Octotank over, snapping off two of its arms, but the riders had been strapped down by their lap belts and had rolled with the vast, broken mechanisms, getting scrapes and a few broken bones.

As for me, my nose was broken, I had a pretty ugly cut to my forehead, and I'd bitten partway through my lip and needed three stitches. I had a sprained knee and a headache that could have been used to jackhammer concrete. But compared to a lot of the people who crowded in—and around—the infirmary camp that night, I'd gotten off light.

Ange and I sat with our backs against an RV in the infirmary camp. A woman in a pink furry cowboy hat and a glittering corset who'd identified herself as a nurse asked me to stick close so that they could watch for signs of concussion. I didn't want to sit still, but Ange made me and called me an idiot when I argued.

We didn't find out what had happened right away, couldn't have. We weren't looking at Octotank when it blew. Ange, being short, had been lost in a forest of taller bodies, trying to catch up to me (one of the reasons she didn't get hurt is that she was in among everyone else, and found herself in the middle of a pile of people—once she was sure that the people on the bottom were being seen to, she'd taken off again after me). I'd been running around in the dark, looking everywhere for Masha, Zeb, and the goon squad.

So we got the story secondhand and thirdhand from people in the infirmary. There were lots of wild theories, and everyone was buzzing about the Department of Mutant Vehicles, which certified all the art cars on the playa, and which was staffed with legendary mechanics and pyrotechnicians. Could they have missed some critical flaw in Octotank's build?

I didn't think so.

Chapter 4

I convinced Ange to let me go and get some water from the infirmary's big cooler—"My butt's getting numb"—and took the chance to survey the human wreckage. It was terrible, and I thought I knew what had caused it.

When I got back to Ange, I handed her my water bottle and watched her drink, then said, "Ange, if I told you something crazy, would you listen?"

She rolled her eyes. "Marcus Yallow, you've been telling me crazy things since the night I met you. Have I ever not listened?"

She had a point. "Sorry," I said. I leaned in close to her. "Back at the temple burn, do you remember a woman walking around with a camera, right in front?"

She shrugged. "Not really. Maybe?"

I swallowed. What I was about to say sounded crazy in my head, and it was going to sound crazier out in the air, and it was just for starters. "It was Carrie Johnstone," I said.

Ange looked puzzled for a moment, like she was trying to place the name.

"Wait, *Carrie Johnstone*? *The* Carrie Johnstone?"

I nodded. "I got a couple of good looks at her. I'm sure." I didn't sound sure. "I'm pretty sure."

"So she's a burner now? That's weird."

"I don't think she's a burner, Ange. I think she was here to kidnap Masha and Zeb."

"Uh-huh," Ange said. "Marcus—"

"Dammit," I said, "you *said you'd listen!*"

She shut her mouth, opened it, shut it. "I did. Sorry. Go on."

So I told her about what I'd seen, Zeb and Masha and the goons, and my stupid, half-baked attempt to catch them as they'd marched into the night.

"So what are you saying?"

"What do you *think* I'm saying, Ange?"

"It sounds like you think that Johnstone and her pals kidnapped Masha and Zeb."

I didn't say anything. Of *course* that's what I was thinking, but that was just for starters. I had another idea, one that was even more crazy-sounding. I wanted to know—*had* to know—whether it would occur to Ange, too, or whether I'd just had my brains rattled when I face-planted into the gypsum flats of Black Rock Desert.

"What?" she said. Then she opened her eyes a little wider. "You think that Johnstone blew up Octotank to . . . what, to cover her getaway?"

I closed my eyes. I couldn't bear to look at Ange, because she was staring at me like I was nuts.

"Look at it this way: they've been driving fire-breathing art cars around the desert for decades now, without a single major mishap. The first time one goes boom, it happens *just* as Carrie Johnstone, a war criminal with a history of ruthless disregard for human life, is in the middle of kidnapping a rogue agent who has been trafficking in giant troves of secret documents. The timing of the explosion is perfect, and a hundred percent of the attention on the playa is occupied for the next several hours. Meanwhile, they could get away in a million ways—hell, they

could just stroll over to the trash fence and hop over it and leg it
out over the mountains, or jump into a waiting car. The Black
Rock Rangers will all be scrambling to help the wounded, not
patrolling with night-scopes for people trying to sneak in without a ticket."

"Yeah," Ange said. "I suppose." She squeezed my hand
again. "Or: people have been driving homemade flamethrow-
ermobiles around the desert for decades, and it was only a matter
of time until one blew up. And you saw someone, in the dark,
do something that looked like a kidnapping, but at a distance,
and right before you had your head knocked around and broke
your nose, after a week's worth of sleep deprivation, recreational chemical use, and caffeine abuse." She said it calmly and
evenly, and kept hold of my hand as I struggled to go.

"Marcus," she said, grabbing my chin and forcing me to
look into her eyes. I winced as she put pressure on the sutures
in my lip, but she didn't loosen her grip. "*Marcus,* I know what
you've been through. I went through it, too; some of it, at least.
I know that improbable things happen sometimes. I was there
when Masha gave you her key. You have the right to believe
what you believe."

"But," I said. I could hear there was a *but* coming.

"Occam's Razor," she said.

Occam's Razor: the rule that says that when you're con-
fronted with a lot of explanations for a given phenomenon, the
least complicated one is the one that is most likely to be right.
Maybe your parents won't let you into the locked drawer in
their bedroom because they're secret spies and they don't want
you finding their cyanide capsules and blowdart rigs. Or maybe
that's just where they keep their (eww) sex toys. Given that you
know that your parents have had sex at least once, and given that
(in San Francisco, at least) odds are good they've bought the
odd dildo or two over the years, the superspy hypothesis has to

be shuffled to the bottom of the pile. Or, to put it another way, "Extraordinary claims require extraordinary evidence."

"I like Occam's Razor," I said. "It's a useful thinking tool. But it's not a *law*. Sometimes, the unlikely happens. It's happened to both of us. I saw what I saw, and I saw it just a few days after I saw Masha, who *is* mixed up in all kinds of espionage stuff, and who was acting paranoid as hell. Maybe she had a good reason for that."

"Yeah. And maybe all that stuff primed you to interpret anything that happened in the days that followed in dramatic and scary ways." She let go of me and looked away at the crowds of people. "Marcus, if you think you know what happened, you know what you should do. Masha *told* you what to do."

If you ever hear that I've gone down, or Zeb's gone down, release it. Shout it from the mountaintops.

You know what? I hadn't even thought of that. I'd been so fixated on rescuing Masha, or proving I wasn't losing my mind, I'd totally forgotten that I was her insurance policy, that she'd fully expected that she might "go down" and that she'd entrusted me with her personal countermeasure.

Now that I thought of it, I found that the idea terrified me.

"I don't know what's in her insurance file," I said, "but I've got an idea that if we were to make it public, it'd make some very powerful people *very* angry at us." I flashed on how I'd felt when Johnstone had been standing right over me, that paralyzing horror that started somewhere at the bottom of my spine and froze me to the spot. I believed that Johnstone had kidnapped Masha to keep the contents of that file a secret. What would she do to me if *I* released it?

Worse: what would she do if Masha told her *I* had the insurance file?

"Oh, crap," I said. "Oh, Ange, what'll we do?"

———

We both agreed that we didn't have to do *anything* that night. I was injured, we were in the middle of the playa without functional laptops, and, to be honest, we were both scared witless about the insurance file and what might happen if we were to go public with it. I still had the USB stick with me—I'd kept it in my utility belt, in its little secure zip-up money belt section. I kept compulsively checking it until Ange made me stop. After a few hours, we decided that I didn't have a concussion and snuck away before anyone could disagree with us. We caught a few precious hours' sleep in the tent, holding tight to each other, before the alarm on Ange's cheap, rugged plastic watch went off, *weep-weep-weep,* and we got up to break camp and start Exodus.

We'd slept in our clothes—it got cold at night in the desert, even with our sleeping bags zipped together for shared warmth—and when we got outside the tent and stood, I saw that my burnoose and the front of my T-shirt were crusted with dried blood from my broken nose and swollen lip. My nose and lip felt like they'd ballooned to elephantine proportions in the night, though when I brushed the dust off a nearby car's side mirror and checked my reflection, I saw that they were merely double their normal size. I looked like I'd been run over by a tank, one of my eyes blackened, my mouth distorted in a weird, pouty sneer, my taped-up nose misshapen and bulbous.

"Groagh," I said, and my lip split again and began to seep blood. My face *hurt.* They'd given me some Tylenol 3s at the infirmary and I took two of them, washing them down with cold brew, undiluted straight from the mason jar, then kept on swigging at the bean juice. I needed energy if I was going to help Ange break down our camp and lug our gear across Black Rock City to the camp where the guy who was giving us our ride had been staying.

Ange said, "You just sit down, Marcus, I got this."

I shook my head and said, "Nogh," a painful syllable that made my face bleed some more.

"Forget it, sit down."

I shook my head again.

"God, you're stubborn," she said. "Fine, kill yourself. Don't come running to me when you're dead."

I waved at her and handed her the cold-brew jar. She made a face. "There's blood in that one." I looked at the rim and saw it was smeared with red from my lip. I dug another jar out of the ice chest and passed it to her. She went to work on it. "Got to drink plenty of water, too," she said. "Remember, this stuff is a diuretic."

She was right. I alternated two swigs of water for every swig of cold brew at regular intervals over the next forty-five minutes as I crammed, jammed, piled, and mashed our stuff into our bags. The biggest item to pack, by far, was Secret Project X-1 and all its assorted bits and pieces.

When I joined Noisebridge, I hadn't really known what I wanted to do. All I knew was that these maker-types had set up a hackerspace in the Mission, filled it with lathes and laser cutters and workbenches and drill presses, and that anyone could join and use the gear to make, well, anything. I'd hung around for a month or two, dropping by after classes to just sit on the sofa and see what people were up to, bringing along my laptop and schoolbooks and studying in between watching as my fellow Noisebridgers invented every mad and amazing thing under the sun.

Noisebridge was a fantastic place. It had its own *space program*. Seriously. Almost every month, they launched homebrew weather balloons crammed with cameras and instrument packages to heights of seventy thousand feet and more and retrieved them. There were people hacking robots, cars, clocks, pet doors, toys, and rollerblades—not to mention video-game consoles, server hardware, autonomous flying drones, and so on and so on.

And they had *3D printers,* devices that could produce actual physical objects on demand, based on 3D files they made or downloaded from the net. Most of these had started off life as MakerBots, an amazing and popular open-source 3D printer kit that you assembled yourself. MakerBots printed in plastic, using spools of cheap plastic wire, and the results were pretty amazing, especially considering that the kits cost less than a thousand dollars, and you could make one for less if you scrounged around for the parts in surplus catalogs and the prodigious bins of spare electronics at Noisebridge.

Being open source, MakerBots were a hacker's paradise, and people all over the world had modified their printers to do extraordinary and amazing things. The big excitement when I joined Noisebridge was a successful conversion to laser-based powder printing, which involved using an apparatus to spread a thin layer of plastic powder on the printing surface, then melting it into specific forms with a laser, then adding another layer of powder and melting it again with the laser, over and over, until you'd built up the whole solid shape.

Powder-based printers cost a *lot* more than MakerBots—like $500,000 or more—and they were all locked up in a complicated set of patents that meant that only a few companies could make and sell them. But patents didn't stop *people* from modding their MakerBots to do powder, and once they started, it became the most popular form of MakerBot modding in the world. Naturally it was: the objects that came out of a powder printer were much smoother and more detailed than the stuff that came out of a plastic wire printer, and with a powerful enough laser, you could use metallic powders and produce precisely made objects in stainless steel, brass, silver—whatever you wanted.

But what interested me wasn't printing in steel: it was printing in *sand*. There were lots of people around the world who were experimenting with alternatives to plastic or metal powder as a printing medium, because, well, anything you could melt with a laser could be fed into a printer. You could print the most wonderful stuff with sugar or make brittle, tragically short-lived stuff out of the whey powder they sold in bulk for bodybuilding. But like I say, *sand* was the stuff that caught my imagination. When you melt sand, you get *glass,* and a beautiful, streaky kind of glass it was, and every day brought more amazing sculptures and jewelry and action figures and, well, *everything* made of melted sand. As a printing material, sand was as cheap as it got, cheaper even than whey powder.

But there wasn't any sand on the playa. What we had instead was *dust*. Gypsum dust, the stuff that they make drywall out of. In other words, stuff that you could (theoretically) make some wicked structures out of.

That was *my* plan, anyway. I made my own MakerBot, downloading the plans from their site, laser-cutting the balsa wood, building the Arduino-based controller, scrounging parts when I could, buying them when I absolutely couldn't find them, but only through surplus stores. In the end, it cost me less than $200, and took me about two months, and it worked *beautifully.* As soon as I got it working, I promptly broke it (of course) and tried to get it running as a powder printer. That was a *lot* more complicated, and the powerful laser it required cost as much as the rest of the printer. But I got it working, too.

And while I was gutting through that breakdown/upgrade/fix cycle, I hated every minute of it, felt like the world's biggest idiot for not being able to do something that everyone else (for some extremely specialized definition of "everyone else") seemed able to pull off. But you know what? I couldn't stop. Because whenever something went wrong, it always seemed like the solution was tantalizingly within reach, and if I just did *one more thing* I'd have it all working. One more thing and one more thing and one more thing again, and then, miraculously, *it worked!* I went from nearly comatose to elated beyond all reason in one millionth of a second, as the air above my workbench was filled with the sweet, toxic smell of melting sand and a bead of glass formed on the build platform. The bead took form, and my calibration testfile, a block with several holes in it that were sized to snugly fit a collection of standard bolts I kept in my pocket for testing, began to take shape.

I didn't need to use them. I could *see* that it was working. I'd taken that stupid printer apart and put it back together hundreds of times. I knew its movements like the movements of my own hands and its sounds like I knew the sound of my own heart. I laughed and danced on the spot, for real, and watched it go through its paces for a few minutes, before the excitement got to me and I raced out onto Mission Street, ready to grab the first person I could lay hands on and drag them back to Noisebridge to see *my machine working!* Of course, as soon as I got out the door, I realized it was three in the morning, and there was no one to be seen.

So that was my MakerBot, and the plan had been—what else—to mod it to print in playa dust, using melted sugar as a fuser. Sugar's *strong*—melt some caramels and brush them onto a 2×4 and clamp another 2×4 to the spot overnight while the "glue" sets and you'll get a joint that's so strong the wood will tear apart before the glue gives. But sugar is also water-soluble, so when I was done, my playa-dust prints could be dissolved in water. "Leave no trace," just like Burning Man principle eight says. I did some test runs, using powdered drywall that I ground up in an old hand-cranked coffee grinder, and I had it working pretty well when I disassembled the MakerBot and packed it up to take to the playa.

That was Secret Project X-1, and I *swear* it worked like a charm when I left San Francisco. I have no idea why it failed so miserably when we got to Black Rock City. The solar panels tested out good, and I borrowed a multimeter from another camp and checked every circuit and contact, and everything seemed to be in working order. But the stubborn, evil bastard refused to even turn on.

Even bloodied and bruised and traumatized and terrorized, I still felt a pang when I packed away X-1 again. I had this incredible plan to 3D print the most amazing shapes and objects out of playa dust—fanciful animals, busts of famous monsters, all the best junk from Thingiverse, the online library of free 3D forms. I was going to be the best, coolest, cleverest burner in the history of the playa. A legend. Instead, I was the guy who sweated and swore at his invention for twenty-four hours straight before his girlfriend went upside his head and told him to stop swearing at his printer and *get out there* and enjoy Burning Man. She was totally right, and everyone liked my cold brew, but man, it hurt to pack away X-1 without having printed a single widget.

"You'll get it working next year," Ange said. "Don't worry." She looked off at the cloud of dust rising from the playa as fifty thousand burners packed up and got ready to turn Black Rock City back into Black Rock Desert (though there'd be cleanup teams staying behind for a few months going over the whole desert, erasing the final signs of human occupation). "We have to go."

Chapter 5

We hardly spoke on the long drive home. Our ride, Lemmy—a guy in his forties who had been coming to Burning Man for twenty years—told us that Exodus was usually like a party, with people getting out of their vehicles between pulses and hanging out, dancing, chatting. But after the night's explosion and injuries, no one wanted to party down. The hourly pulse of cars released onto the winding road to Reno was like a funeral procession, and it was no better once we got to the little Indian reservation towns on the way to Reno and stopped for gas.

That matched my mood perfectly, to tell the truth. I was all beat up, and the painkillers made me groggy, while the jerking and jouncing of the car on the roads kept me from sleeping. Ange took over the driving in Reno, and I finally found my way into sleep, waking up briefly when we gassed up again in Sacramento, and then the next thing I knew, I was back home on Potrero Hill, at my parents' front door.

I kissed Ange good-bye and dragged my knapsack and duffel bag to the front door, fumbling my key into the lock. I had planned on calling my parents from Reno to let them know I was on the way, but sleep had taken precedence, and now I was heading home with a face that looked like it had been through a meat grinder and a pocket full of government secrets that were being hunted by a ruthless torturer. *Hey Mom, hey Dad! Funny thing, you'll never guess what happened to me while I was out in the middle of the desert.* Yay, this was going to be f-u-n.

The house was a mess. That was the new normal. It started when Dad lost his job and started spending a lot of time at home. Who knew he was such a slob? Mom refused to pick up after him (yay, Mom!), but she also turned out to have a high grodiness tolerance. By the time she lost *her* job, well, the place was already a pit. And it didn't get better after that.

I stepped over the scatter of shoes by the front door and dragged my junk through a pile of old newspapers, knocking them over and sending them slithering to the floor. "Hi, guys," I said. I wished that I'd be able to get my butt upstairs and into bed before I had to hold down a conversation, but I knew it wasn't very likely.

"Marcus!" Mom called from the living room. "We were so worried!" And one second later, there she was in the hallway, and gasping at my face. "Oh my word," she said, her British accent and funny little Britishisms ramping up the way they did when she was stressing.

"It's okay, Mom," I said. "There was an accident at Burning Man and—"

"We heard all about it," she said.

Duh. It hadn't even occurred to me that the stuff that happened at Burning Man would be news in the rest of the world. San Francisco was the birthplace of Burning Man, so of *course* they'd heard. And then they hadn't heard from me. Christ, I was a rotten son.

"I'm sorry," I said. "Really. It's better than it looks. I just had some painkillers before we left and fell asleep or I would have called—"

Now Dad was in the hallway, too. "God, Marcus, what happened?"

I closed my eyes, took a deep breath. "Can I make you a deal? How about if I tell you what happened really quickly, then I go have a shower and sleep, and then we can talk it over?"

This is what I love about my parents: they both looked at each other with their eyebrows up, like, *That sounds reasonable to me,* and nodded, and said, "Okay," and then gave me a crushing hug that felt *so* good, even if I was so tired I could barely stay vertical.

I unlaced my boots—bending over caused a fresh headache to blossom right behind my eyes—and kicked them off with two little puffs of playa dust. Dad cleared a pile of books off the sofa while Mom made tea for me and her and coffee for Dad (I'm embarrassed to say that despite all my efforts to educate him, Dad still drank—*ugh*—instant). I told them the story as quickly as I could, leaving out the part about Masha and Zeb and Carrie Johnstone. Here, back in San Francisco, it all seemed, I don't know, remote? Like something that happened to someone else, or something I'd read about in a book. Maybe it was the pain-killers, or Ange's (understandable) skepticism, but I found myself questioning my own memories.

"Oh," I said, as I was finishing up. "Someone offered me a job, too! Someone running for senator who needs a new webmaster or something. I'm going to drop them a line in the morning."

"That's fantastic, sweetie," Mom said, looking like she meant it. Dad said some nice things, too, but I could tell that he was thinking about the job he *didn't* have. After my trial and conviction—for stealing Masha's phone, of all things—he "mys- teriously" found that he couldn't get his security clearance renewed. So that meant that a lot of his consulting gigs dried up. We'd been worried, but not totally freaked, because at least he had his adjunct professorship at UC Berkeley. But then California went broke—really, really broke, not like all the other times it had gone broke as I was growing up—and the UC system got its budgets slashed to practically nothing. Adjuncts had been the first to go. And of course, when he lost his job, I lost my discount on tuition, and started piling up the student debt. That's right: my Xnet stuff cost my dad his job, and that cost me my college education. I think that's called "the law of unintended consequences," but I just like to think of it as FAIL.

"Okay, shower now," I said, having a sip of my tea. It was milky and sugary and strong, the way Mom liked it, and it was the taste of my childhood, the flavor of the sick days when Mom had taken care of me while I lay in bed with the flu or a stomach-ache. I decided to take it up with me, to finish after I showered. But I didn't make it into the shower. I didn't even undress. I flopped down on my bed amid the piles of clothes I'd pulled out of my bag while I was repacking the week before to make room for X-1, and I was snoring in seconds.

When I woke up the sky was dark and my tea was cold. I finally had that shower, staying under the hot water until it ran ice cold, scrubbing the dust out of my pores. Then I went into my room and started piling up laundry and separating out gear that needed to be hosed down outside in the driveway or wiped down on my workbench. Finally, I unpacked my utility belt and found myself holding on to a dusty USB stick.

Normally I'm pretty careful with my data. That means that I don't leave anything important on a USB stick. People lose those things all the time. The first thing to do with something important is to stick it in a computer—my latest frankenbook, a hand-built laptop called Lurching Abomination that was the distant descendant of Salmagundi, the first laptop I ever built for myself. Lurching Abomination had a whopper of a hard drive, two terabytes, and I used TrueCrypt to give myself a "plausible deniability" partition, so that if you just turned it on and entered a crypto key, you'd get what looked like a normal Paranoid-Linux installation with a browser and an email client that was hooked up to my public email addresses and Xnet accounts, where I got all the spam and friend requests from strangers and bots and stuff.

But if you—or if *I*—entered *another* password when starting up the machine, there was *another* ParanoidLinux instance hiding on that monster disk, and this one was only hooked up to my private accounts, my private bookmarks, my private calendars, my private social nets, and so on. With a little bit of monkeying, I could boot into the secure, secret version of my computer, fire up a virtual computer in a window, and put the plausible deniability version in that.

Next to Lurching Abomination was a stand-alone hard drive, and Lurch was smart enough to check every few minutes and see if the disk was connected, and if it was, to back itself up. That disk was also encrypted (duh—what would the point of doing all the crazy stuff with Lurch's disk be if I was going to make an unscrambled copy of all the data and leave it on my *desk*?). The disk's enclosure had enough smarts to try to periodically hook up to one of the big servers at Noisebridge and try to make a copy of itself there.

This all more or less worked, most of the time, and it meant that within a few minutes of copying any files onto my laptop, they would be encrypted, copied to my desktop drive, and copied again to Noisebridge's array. *That* server was synched up with a massive storage farm run by and for hackspaces, located in an old nuclear fallout shelter somewhere in England (seriously!). So yeah, do your worst, steal my laptop, burn down my house, nuke San Francisco, and I'll *still* have a backup.

Mwa–ha–ha. Yeah, it's crazy-paranoid, but: a) I'd been through some paranoid stuff, and b) it wasn't much harder than just using a commercial backup program, only my solution was safer and more robust and cheaper.

My hand hovered over the USB port. The USB stick was a no-name version, squarish and cheap looking, its case glued shut unevenly by some fifteen-year-old chained to a machine in China. You saw them lying smashed on the sidewalk, and people advertising banks or soda pop pressed them into your hands when you came out of the BART station. There was no way to tell if it was a 4GB stick or 500GB. It could hold all the books ever written or a video of someone's cat chasing a laser pointer or a buttload of ugly pornography.

Or it could contain the key to a trove of military and state secrets so hot that Carrie Johnstone would come out of the night and kidnap you to get them back. Only one way to find out.

The keyfile was less than 5K. It was just a long string of random numbers, and somewhere out there was the torrent file that they'd decrypt. But the keyfile itself was so small that I could have read it aloud to Ange on the phone, if I didn't mind reciting stuff like "I_?4Wac0'5_9'Ym4|PL" for an hour or so, and if Ange was willing to write it all down without getting a single letter, number, or weird piece of punctuation wrong.

Once I'd copied the key to my computer, I found myself sweating, my heart thundering in my chest. My hands shook as I typed the command that forced an immediate backup—I didn't want to wait ten minutes for the next scheduled backup. I didn't want to risk having Carrie Johnstone and her goons break down the door and stick a bag over my head and shove me into a waiting helicopter headed straight to Afghanistan. Of course, the *next* thing I did was start to download the torrent file.

If you haven't been paying close attention, you might just think BitTorrent = "pirate movie download," but there's plenty of cleverness in the way it works. Files are broken up into thousands of little pieces, and you can request any of the pieces you're missing from anyone who's got it. As you get more and more pieces of the file, you start to get requests from others, too—the whole thing is called a "swarm" and as you can see, the more people who are downloading, the faster the download gets. That's pretty cool, since in the physical world, the more people there are trying to get something, the harder all of them have to try to get at it. Imagine if food was like BitTorrent: every time you ate a meal, there'd be more food left over for everyone else to eat.

Of course, the downside of BitTorrent is that if only a few people have copies of a file, then there are only a few people who can share it with you. I typed "insurancefile.masha.torrent" into the search fields for a dozen BitTorrent search engines starting with The Pirate Bay, the biggest of them all. There were about ten "seeders"—computers that had whole copies of the file—out there on the net, and two other machines downloading it. That was interesting. Maybe they were evil government spooks who wanted to try to crack the files and find out what Masha had. Or maybe they were just random copyright-enforcement bots that downloaded *everything* and checked to see whether it contained anything worth suing over.

Either way, I wasn't going to use *my* IP address to download that file. My parents got their Internet through AT&T, a scumbag phone company with a track record of handing over their customers' data to the cops without court orders. Grabbing sensitive files off the net through them was like calling up the director of the DHS and saying, "Hey, are you missing any sensitive data? Because I'm small, defenseless, and unarmed, and I got 'em. Want my address?"

Which is why, no matter what, I always scraped up the money to pay for a subscription to IPredator, the proxy service operated by the Pirate Bay folks. IPredator was specifically designed to make it impossible for anyone else to tell what you've been downloading. It ping-ponged your data between Copenhagen and Stockholm, across an international border, and kept no logs or records of who was doing what. It was blazing fast—for a proxy, which are never as fast as a naked net connection—and it was run by some of the world's baddest-ass hacker antiauthoritarians, people who made me look like a goody two-shoes obedient toddler who could barely turn on a computer. If anyone could make my download anonymous, it was those cats.

While the file trickled in, I hit my email. I've never been much of an email user—it's not like my friends and I used it to figure out when to hook up, we all used Twitter and Xnet's Facebook overlay (which scrambled our updates and messages)—but all my profs had used it while I was at Berkeley, and then everyone I was hitting up for work expected me to give them an email address. God, but email was *tedious*. People expected you to answer all of it, and there was: So. Much. Spam. When it came to Twitter and Xnet, I could just take everything that had come in while I was at Burning Man and mark it as read, and no one would get pissed off at me. But people who sent you email took it personally if you didn't reply. It was just how email worked. Even I felt put out if someone didn't reply to my email.

Download download download. Spam spam spam. Delete delete delete. The stupid email ritual, so beloved of my parents. So boring. When I finally whittled down the huge log of crap to a little toothpick of actual mail, my eye jumped to one sent by "Joseph Noss." Of course, it was probably a fund-raising appeal, since my email address seemed to have found its way into the mailing lists of every political candidate in the state. But in my notebook, there was the email address for Joseph Noss's campaign manager, carefully copied after Mitch Kapor had written it on my arm with his Sharpie. The coincidence was . . . interesting.

I opened it.

> From: Joseph Noss <joe@joenossforsenate.com>

> To: Marcus Yallow <myallow271828183@gmail.com>

> Subject: Webmaster

> Dear Marcus,

> My campaign manager, Flor, tells me she heard from Mitch Kapor that you were thinking of coming on board to be our webmaster. Your name sounded familiar so I looked you up, and, well, you know what I found. From what I can see, you would be absolutely perfect for the job. Can you give me a call when you get this? We really need to make this happen, like, YESTERDAY. My personal cellular number is 510-314-1592.

> Joe

I read it twice and reached for my phone, everything else forgotten. After all these months of searching and begging, someone was *offering* me a job, and it was someone so cool his phone number was the first seven digits of pi. I mean, *woah*.

I dialed his number without having to look back at the screen—seriously, that was the coolest phone number I'd ever seen—and listened as the phone rang. Just before he picked up, I looked at the clock on my computer and realized it was nearly 11 P.M. on Sunday night. I fought the reflex to hang up the phone as he answered.

"Joseph Noss speaking," he said, and, yup, that was him all right. I'd heard his voice on TV and YouTube enough to recognize it instantly, a deep growly sound like the "This is CNN" guy or an old soul singer.

"Um," I said, and pinched my leg to make myself stop

saying *Um,* which is a trick Ange taught me. "Hello, sir, this is Marcus Yallow. You sent me an email? I hope it's not too late—"

"Not at all, Marcus, I was up late working. Sorry to say it, but 11 P.M. is prime time for me."

"Me, too," I said. "I've always been a night owl."

It's funny, but I liked him right off. Something in that voice—he sounded like someone who thought hard about things, and who was listening hard to everything he heard.

"I'm glad you called me, Marcus. I know you've been involved in little-p politics before, but as far as I can tell, you don't have any experience with the big-P kind, the kind that involves elections and so on. Is that right?"

"That's right, sir." I thought, *Ah well, it was worth a shot.* I didn't have the experience he was looking for after all.

But he said, "That's fine. We've got lots of experience with that sort of thing around here. Listen, Marcus, I want to give you a sense of the challenge we're up against here, and then maybe you can tell me whether you think you're the right sort of person to help us out.

"Now, California's got a reputation for being a little crazy, but we're trying to do something that's crazy even by California standards. You know I'm an independent candidate, right?"

"Yes," I said.

"The received wisdom here is that 'independent' is a synonym for 'unelectable.' The Dems and the Republicans have got all the major donors sewn up, they've got efficient machines, they've got close friends at every TV and radio station and newspaper in the state, and they've got national organizations they can draw on. Independents start with a huge disadvantage, and it only gets worse when push comes to shove, because if we gain even a little ground, well, the big boys bring in *their* big boys and crush us like bugs.

"I could have gotten the Democratic nomination. They

know me from my days at City Hall, they know that this district
is one where African-American candidates generally do well,
and I'm thought of as a decent sort who can be relied upon to
raise a decent amount of cash *and* stay honest and sober once
he gets elected, which puts me far ahead of most of the jokers
around these parts.

"I could have had the nomination. Between you and me,
they asked, several times, and in several ways. They seemed
pretty sure that a campaign for Joe Noss would be something
of a sure bet. But the more I thought about this, the more I realized that I didn't *want* the nomination. I've seen what it means
to be elected with major party support: it means that you have
to toe the line. By which I mean, when there is a vote where
your conscience tells you to go one way and party discipline tells
you to go the other way, well, you'd best tell your conscience to
sit that one out.

"That wouldn't be so bad if you could trust the party, but I
can't say as I trust either party in this country. You've got 'pro-
gressive' Democratic presidents who believe it's legal to assassinate American citizens overseas, who think that we should be
spying on phone calls and email without warrants—well, I
could go on, but I think you know what I mean."

"I do," I blurted. Maybe it was all the weird events of the
past week, but listening to Joe talk made me excited, made me
want to go out and man a barricade for him or something. It was
the way he talked, even over the phone; it made you feel like
whatever this guy was doing, it was going to work, and that if
you were lucky, you'd get to be a part of it.

"I believe you do, Marcus! But it's not just the Dems, of
course. I know many Republicans who are honorable, gener-
ous, thoughtful people. My father was one such Republican.
But there are power brokers in the Republican party who are
insane. I don't say that as a figure of speech. I mean it literally.

There are important movers and shakers in the RNC who believe that the Earth is five thousand years old. And these are
people who made their fortunes pumping sweet crude in Texas!
You think they tell their geoengineers to only pump oil in
places that accord with the Young Earth theory of creation?
Now, those people are hardly the worst—there's plenty who
think that torturing isn't just something you have to do when
there's no alternative, but something you should do all the time.
People who believe that anyone with ten million dollars is, by
definition, good, and anyone without ten cents to his name is,
by definition, a criminal. The thought of being beholden to
these—well, let's use the word my daddy liked, because Daddy
was a polite, well-spoken man, and he'd have called these people
dunces—these *dunces,* well, I never even considered it for a moment.

"No, I thought to myself, Joe, there's some smart people
who think you could win this election with their help. Maybe
you could win it *without* their help. Maybe if you took up positions that people believed in, positions that were grounded in
evidence and compassion, not ideology or lining your pockets,
you'd be able to beat the all-powerful party machines and show
up in the Senate without a single corporate logo sewn onto
your suit jacket.

"Of course, there was no way I'd be able to do this using
the old-fashioned methods—all the tactics we developed to win
elections in the last century. I knew that this campaign would
rise or fall on the strength of our technology use.

"Now, I might be over twenty-five"—he chuckled, a sound
as deep as the ocean—"but I know a thing or two about technology. Enough, at least, to know how much I *don't* know.
Finding the right tech people has been my top priority since I
started this thing, and I think I've found some good people who
can do top-level strategy and such. But I haven't found anyone

to be my special forces commando, if you will. A *doer,* not just a *thinker.* So when your name came up, well, it made me excited, Marcus. I think you could be the delta force ninja of our technology team. Does that sound like your sort of thing?"

My mouth was so dry I could barely talk and my palms were so sweaty I could barely hold the phone, but I managed to blurt out, "Yes, absolutely, that sounds like my *dream* job!"

"I was hoping you'd say that. Now, it's not my job to hire you, that's my campaign manager's job. But my recommendations do carry a *little* weight around here. I'm looking at her diary right now, and it looks like she's free tomorrow morning at 8:30 A.M. That's a little early for a night owl, I know, but if I were to put a meeting with you in her calendar, do you think you could make it?"

"Even if I have to stay up all night, Mr. Noss."

"Call me Joe. And I hope that won't be necessary. Get yourself some sleep and set an alarm. I'll tell Flor to expect you at 8:30. That's Flor Prentice Y Diaz. Let me spell it for you."

"It's okay, I've just googled her," I said.

"Of course you have," he said. "Do your research now, then get yourself into bed and don't forget the alarm!"

"I won't," I said.

I spent the next twenty minutes poring over everything I could find about Flor Prentice Y Diaz—parents were Guatemalan refugees, raised in the Bay Area, master's in public policy from Stanford, former executive director of a big homelessness charity. A photo showed a handsome but severe Hispanic woman in her fifties, wrinkles around her eyes and deep lines around her mouth, big dark eyes that seemed to bore straight through me. Then I noticed where the photo had come from: a profile in the *Bay Guardian* by Barbara Stratford. I checked the time in my menubar. It was coming up on midnight, which was probably too late to call Barbara and ask her to put in a good word for me. But I *did* send her an email asking her to drop my name to Flor Prentice Y Diaz if she got a chance. Email did have its uses.

I checked the status of my big torrent download. The file was halfway down, and there were eight more downloaders in the swarm. I wondered how many of them worked for three-letter spy agencies in the DC area.

There was a soft knock at my door. I opened it. It was Mom.

"Hey, you," she said. "How long have you been up?"

"A couple hours, I guess," I said. "I'm sorry I didn't come downstairs, but when I checked my email, I found a message from Joseph Noss asking me to call him about the job, so I called him and he wants me to go in tomorrow morning to meet with his campaign manager at 8:30 A.M. I think I've found a job!"

Mom smiled and reached out and stroked my hair, the way she used to do when I was a kid. It was a tell she had, whenever she was feeling especially proud of me. It made me happy all over. "That's wonderful news, love. How are you feeling, though?" Tentatively, she touched the tape over my nose. I flinched a little. The painkillers had worn off.

"Well, my nose is still broken, but my headache is gone. Apart from that, I feel fine. It looks much worse than it is. And it could have been a *lot* worse. As it was, I basically tripped and fell on my face." I shook my head. "There were lots of people who got hurt worse than me, caught right in the explosion."

She took her hand away. "I wish you'd called. We were—well, we were worried, Marcus." She didn't say anything about the *other* times I'd gone missing, like after the Bay Bridge blew up, when I was being held and humiliated on Treasure Island by Carrie Johnstone and her jolly friends from the DHS; or when I'd gone underground, run away with Zeb only to be caught by Johnstone again, this time for a round of simulated execution on her waterboard. Neither of those incidents had been very pleasant for me, but they'd been hell on my parents, too. I was a jerk.

"I'm sorry," I said. "I was fast asleep by the time we got back into cell-phone range. But yeah, you're right, I should have called."

We sat there silently for a little while, each of us remembering the bad times before. "How's *your* job search going, Mom?"

"Oh," she said, "oh, don't worry about me. There's little bits of contract work coming in all the time. Nothing earth-shaking, just a little freelance editing and such. But between that and the savings and Dad's severance, we're getting by."

I didn't bother to ask what they would do when Dad's severance ran out. I'd overheard them talking about that enough times to know that it was a sensitive subject—and the fact that they always shut up about it when I entered the room told me that they didn't want me to worry about it. Dad had sold his car the month before and they'd listed the parking spot in our driveway for rent on Craigslist, which I thought was pretty clever, even if it would be weird to have some stranger using our driveway. But yeah, I could see what they could see: first you lose your job, then your car, then what? Mom had torn up her flowerbeds in the backyard and planted vegetables, which tasted great, but I knew that taste had less to do with things than the grocery bill did. The drawer full of takeout menus hadn't been opened in months, and Mom and Dad had a tendency to disappear on the bus whenever Safeway had a big sale on meat, coming back with huge bags full for the freezer. I didn't have anything against saving money, but I couldn't help but wonder where it might all end. There were a lot of For Sale signs on our block, and one or two empty places with foreclosure notices taped to the door.

"Well," I said. "Got to get up early tomorrow!"

"Are you going to wear a suit?" Mom said. "I could get something out of your father's closet."

"*Mom,*" I said, "they're hiring me to be their *webmaster*— I'm pretty sure they don't want a dweeb in a suit."

She opened her mouth like she wanted to argue with me, then shut it again. "I'm sure you know what you're talking about," she said. "But just be sure to dress up smart, all right? No one likes a slob, even if he *is* the webmaster."

"Good night, Mom."

"I love you, Marcus."

"Love you, too."

Good thing I set three alarms. I managed to switch off both my phone and my alarm clock without even waking, but the raging music blaring out of Lurching Abomination's external speakers—Trudy Doo and the Speedwhores performing "Break It Off," which features some of the craziest death-metal screaming ever to be committed to MP3 by an all-girl post-punk anarcho-queer power-trio—was impossible to sleep through. It was 7:15.

I showered and peeled off the tape over my nose and grimaced at my beat-up face. Oh well, nothing to be done about it. Thinking of my mother's advice, I dug through my closet and found a white button-up shirt that I'd last worn to my graduation, and the gray wool slacks I'd worn at the same event. I even found the brown leather shoes that went with the outfit, and gave them a vigorous wipe with an old sock, bringing out a bit of a shine. As I buttoned up the shirt and tucked it in and got the line of buttons even with my fly, I found myself growing excited. Mom was right (as usual): dressing up made me *feel* competent, like the kind of guy you'd want to hire.

Dad was already at the kitchen table, eating oatmeal with sliced bananas and strawberries.

"Woah! You're looking suave, son," he said. I saw that he'd shaved off the stubble he'd sported the night before, and was dressed in his workout clothes.

"You going to the gym?" I said.

"Jogging," he said. "Just started. We're not using the gym anymore." *Translation: we can't afford the gym anymore.*

"That's great," I said.

"Yeah," he said, and I wished I hadn't said anything, because he looked embarrassed, which wasn't usual for him. "Your mother told me about your big interview. There's more oatmeal on the stove and there's sliced fruit in that bowl."

Dad hadn't made me breakfast since I was thirteen years old, when I started insisting that I was too old to have breakfast prepared for me and switched to grabbing some toast on my way out the door. I realized he must have gotten up early just to make sure that I went off to Joe's office with a full tummy. It made me want to hug him, but something held me back, like acknowledging what a big deal this was would have spoiled the illusion of normalcy.

I hadn't seen 8 A.M. in the Mission since I dropped out of school. I stopped in at the Turk's for a lethally strong pourover and let him fuss over me when I told him I was going in for a job interview. The Mission's always been a place with a lot of homelessness, but it seemed like things were worse than they'd ever been. At least, I couldn't remember seeing quite so many people sleeping on the edge of the sidewalk or in the doorways of boarded-up stores. I couldn't remember smelling quite so much pungent human pee-stink from the curbs.

I finished my coffee just as I reached Joseph Noss's campaign headquarters, between 22nd and 23rd on Mission, in a storefront that had been a huge discount furniture place for most of my life, but which had shut down the year before and had been sitting empty until now.

The big windows were plastered with orange and brown NOSS FOR STATE SENATE signs, neither Democrat blue nor Republican red. I checked my phone: 8:20. I was early. I tried the door, but it was locked. I rapped on the glass and peered in, trying to see if there was anyone inside. It was dark, and no one answered. I knocked again. Nothing. Oh, well. I stood by the door and waited for Flor Prentice Y Diaz, trying to project an air of employability.

She arrived at exactly 8:29, wearing blue jeans, a nice blouse, and a kerchief over her hair, and carrying a takeout cup from the Turk's. She had a serious, almost angry face on as she walked down the street, like there was a lot on her mind, but when she saw me, she smiled, then frowned as she took in my battered face. "Marcus?" she said.

I smiled back and extended my hand. "Hi there! Sorry about this—" I scrunched up my face. "I was at Burning Man last weekend and, well, a car exploded at me. It looks a lot worse than it is, really."

She shook my hand. Her grip was gentle, dry and warm. "I heard about that," she said. "Are you sure you're okay to be here? If you want to reschedule—"

I waved my hands. "No, no! Honestly, I'm fine. Besides, Joe—Mr. Noss—said that he was in a hurry, right?"

"Well, that's very true. All right then, let's get inside, shall we?"

She dug a big key ring out of her handbag and opened the doors, reaching out with one hand to hit a light switch. The fluorescents flickered on all around the cavernous space, revealing trestle-table desks with snarls of power strips beneath them. There were still signs advertising cheap sofas on some of the walls, and a long checkout counter that was now covered with silk-screening stuff. Someone had installed a big extractor fan over the table, but I could still smell the paint-y smell of the silk-screening station. Clotheslines hanging from the stained old drop ceiling were draped with shirts and posters in the campaign's orange and brown.

"This is where the magic happens," she said, crossing to a desk right in the middle of the floor. It had more papers on it than most, and a big external monitor. She slid a laptop out of her purse and connected its power cable and monitor cable and woke it up and entered her password. I politely looked away as she typed it, but I could hear that it was admirably long and complex—there was also the telltale sound of a shift key being depressed and several of those unmistakable spacebar *bang*s.

"Sounds like a good password," I said.

"Oh yes," she said. "Ever since I had my Yahoo mail compromised a few years ago and everyone I knew got an email saying I was stranded in London after being mugged and asking for them to wire money to help me out. I expect you've got your own little security rituals, right?"

I nodded. "Just a few. But as soon as you start looking into security, you discover that there's always more you could be doing."

She was staring intently at her screen as her email streamed in. I noticed she wasn't breathing, which was something I'd read about: email apnea. People unconsciously hold their breath when they're looking at their inboxes. I made a mental note to mention it to her later if I got the job.

"I like your taste in coffee," I said, as she slumped back and gasped for air. "The Turk is awesome."

"He's one of a kind," she said, sipping. She'd pulled some papers from her purse. I recognized my résumé. She tapped my address. "You live pretty close to here, huh?"

"Oh yeah," I said. "I went to Chavez High, just up the street."

"I sent my kids there, too. But that would have been before your time."

I was feeling good about the interview. We were bonding. We had all this stuff in common—Chavez High, the Turk . . . We hadn't even talked about Barbara Stratford.

She set the résumé down on her desk. "You seem like a very nice person, Marcus." Suddenly, I was a lot less confident. Her expression had turned into a professional mask. "But you don't exactly have a lot of work experience, do you?"

I felt my cheeks burning. "No," I said. "I mean—" I took a deep breath. "My dad got laid off from UC Berkeley last year and I had to drop out. No more discount tuition. So I've been looking for work ever since. But I've had some campaign experience, the Coalition of Voters for a Free America for two summers."

"Yes," she said. "Volunteer experience, right?"

"Right," I said. "We were all volunteers. But I'm very responsible. And I believe in Joe, and I believe that the Internet can change politics for the better—make it more accountable, more transparent. That's why I want to work here."

As I said it, it felt like exactly the right sort of thing to be saying. But when I was done, her expression was harder than ever. "Yes," she said. "I've heard all that before. I've been hearing it for twenty years now. But the fact is that elections are won by a lot of shoe leather and a lot of money and a lot of handshakes, the way they always have been. I know that Joe has lots of pie-in-the-sky ideas about reinventing elections *and* reforming politics, but I run the campaign and I think that reforming politics will be a big enough job to get through, and maybe we can leave the reinventing stuff for the next candidate."

I didn't know what to say to that. Some innate, primitive

sense of organizational politics told me I should just keep my mouth shut.

"We've got a lot of people around here with big ideas about how the world should be run. That's fine. That goes with the territory when you're running as an independent—you get independent-minded people working for you. But the bottom line is that this is a *campaign* to *elect* a *candidate.* It's not a lab for egalitarian, consensus-based organizational reform. It's not a high-tech start-up.

"Right now, this campaign needs a *webmaster.* That's someone who'll put up a website that doesn't get hacked the minute we stick it online. That website's got to help us raise money, it's got to help us mobilize voters, and it's got to help us win an election. I want to make myself clear on this point, because I've hired a few webmasters in my day, and I know a thing or two about some of the problems endemic to the trade. I'm looking for a website that gets the job done: nothing more and nothing less. I don't want it to be one micron prettier than it needs to be. I don't want it to be one quantum more technically elegant than it needs to be. And because our webmaster is also going to be our IT department, I need someone who can keep us all reasonably secure, keep our computers backed up, and keep the network up. Someone who's available on-call twenty-four-seven right up to election day.

"So, now that you've heard my little speech, I need to ask you, does that sound like you, Marcus?"

But Joe said he wanted a delta force ninja, is what I didn't say. I had already figured out enough to know that what Joe wanted and what Joe got was filtered through his campaign manager, who held the decision to hire me in her hands.

"I have done all those things in the past," I said. "I'm reliable. I'm a fast learner. I believe in Joseph Noss. I may not have had much work experience, but that's only because no one's given me the chance. There are lots of people in San Francisco who could be your webmaster, but how many of them have helped run an underground network that beat back the DHS and restored the Bill of Rights to San Francisco?" I spent most of my life telling people that M1k3y was just part of a movement, scuffing my toe when people told me how much they admired me. But something told me that this wasn't the right time to be humble.

Her smile came back. "Okay, that was well said." She finished off the Turk's coffee. "I've asked around about you. Barbara Stratford called me as I was on my way in to work this morning to put in a good word for you. There are lots of people who think the world of you as a leader and a techno-guerrilla. But none of them have ever employed you, and we have more than enough 'leaders' around here. Have you ever read *The Time Machine*, Marcus?"

"Yeah," I said. "I wrote a paper on it in AP English."

"Then you'll remember the Eloi and the Morlocks. The Eloi were the privileged surface dwellers, enjoying a life of high-tech sophistication and ease. But under the ground, there was an army of Morlocks, toiling away night and day in the subterranean engine rooms, making sure that everything was humming along tickedy-boo."

"You want Morlocks, not Eloi, right?"

She smiled. "Bright boy. Yes, exactly. It's not a glamorous job, but it's the job that needs doing. What I'm asking you to do now is look inside yourself and ask, 'Do I want to do the job that needs doing, even if it's boring and workaday and merely necessary and not at all exciting?' You say you believe in Joe—do you support him enough to join his army as a grunt and not a general?"

I could see why she was the campaign manager, and not Joe. Joe had made me want to take to the streets, but she made me want to prove I could get the job done. They must make a great team.

Which is not to say that I wasn't disappointed. I *had* hoped that I'd be greeted as a revolutionary hero and given a squadron of tough info-commandos to boss through a series of action-hero adventures. But the way that Flor Prentice Y Diaz pushed at me, implying that I was just a kid who wanted the spotlight more than he wanted to help, it was like a set of spurs in the belly. So even as I was thinking, *Man, that's an effective motivational technique,* I was also thinking, *I'll show her!*

I made a showy salute. "Yes ma'am, general, ma'am."

Her smile got wider. "All right, all right. I'm giving you a hard time this morning, because you come with a lot of advance recommendations, but there are also lots of warning flags. You're a bright young man, and bright young men are nice to have around, but in my experience, they need quite a lot of adult supervision. So I intend on *supervising* you very closely until I'm convinced that you have learned the difference between what we need and what you'd like us to have."

I blinked and replayed what she just said. "Does that mean I'm hired?"

She waved off the question. "Oh, Marcus, you've been hired since we sat down here. Joe loves you, or at least he loves your reputation, and he's as excited as a puppy about having you around here. But I needed to make sure you understood what working here entails."

I couldn't stop myself, I held my arms over my head like a quarterback after a touchdown: "All *right!*" I shouted.

She laughed at me. "Down, boy. Yes, you've got a j-o-b. Marian, our HR person, will talk over your pay and such with you later. But before we get started, there's one thing we need to discuss, and that's all this hacker business."

I composed myself. "Yes?"

"Don't. Do. It. You've done all sorts of clever things with computers, no doubt. You've outsmarted the feds and raided their data, you've gone wandering around computer systems where you had no business being. It's all in the grand old tradition of the Bay Area, but it has no place here. The first time I catch so much as a *whiff* of anything illegal, immoral, dangerous or 'leet' "—she made finger quotes—"I will personally bounce your ass to the curb before you have a chance to zip your fly. Do I make myself crystal clear?"

"You can really turn on and off the scary voice at will, huh?"

"I can. I find it's a useful way of indicating to my colleagues when I expect to be taken seriously."

"And you can do this really kind of stone-faced, severe facial expression, too. That's really amazing." What can I say? I'd just gotten a job. The joy was bringing out my inner weisenheimer.

"This face? This isn't my severe face. This is about gale force one. You do *not* want to be around for a force five."

"I'll keep that in mind."

Chapter 6

I spent the rest of the morning jumping straight into the
work with both feet. The previous webmaster, a volunteer, had
just gone back to school at Brown, but she'd left behind a neat
sheet of passwords and configuration data, as well as information on our network contracts. I figured the thing to do was to
conduct an audit of everything I'd be in charge of, checking
that it was all where it was supposed to be, doing what it was
supposed to be doing. I grabbed a stack of one-side-printed
paper out of a recycling box and three-hole punched it, then
snapped it into a used three-ring binder I found in a supply
closet. I could have used Lurch to take notes—I'd brought it
in, booted into its plausible deniability partition, with all that
deadly secret stuff locked away on disk sectors that were indis-
tinguishable from random noise. But I needed to be able to
walk and write, sitting down at peoples' desks and getting their
names and copying down their network cards' MAC addresses
and such, and paper is just easier for that sort of thing. I'd type
it all in later.

Every so often I'd look up and see Flor watching me from
her desk in the middle of the room. She'd catch my eye and then
nod in satisfaction—at my hustle, I assumed. It made me feel
good—like someone was noticing how I was busting my butt

to make a good impression on my first day. I may be a Morlock, but it was nice to know the Eloi were looking on in approval. After talking with Flor, I'd remembered that the Morlocks ate the Eloi, which made the whole analogy a little weird. I wondered if she'd intended that, and if so, what it was supposed to mean.

Joe had swept in around 10 A.M. with one phone pressed to his head and another in his hand and had been swarmed by about a dozen staffers and volunteers with urgent questions. He clamped one phone between his ear and shoulder and used his free hand to point at people in the mob and then at places they were to wait for him, all the while without losing his place in the animated conversation he was having. As the crowd dispersed, he said his good-byes and dropped his phone into one pocket, then did the same with the other one.

He was a tall, broad-shouldered black guy with his graying hair cropped short. His skin was somewhere between an americano and a macchiato, a few shades darker than the high-necked sweater he wore over comfortable-looking blue jeans and black Converse. I decided I could dress down for work the next day.

I was in the middle of going through every line of the WiFi router's configuration file, plugged straight into it at the very back of the room. Much as I wanted to jump up and introduce myself, I decided to play it Morlock and let him get on with all the urgent stuff he needed to do and try to find a quiet moment later to say hello.

But Joe scouted around the room, spotted me, and said, loudly, "Marcus, all right!" and half jogged straight to me, hand already out.

"Hello, sir," I said.

"Marcus, I can't *tell* you how glad I am that you're joining us. Flor tells me she's very impressed with you. I'm not surprised. I imagine you've got plenty to do to get up to speed, but please ask Flor to put you in my diary for tomorrow, whenever she can squeeze you in, so we can talk about strategy, all right?"

"All right," I said, making an effort not to stammer. In person, Joseph Noss just radiated charisma, and it made me tonguetied. Here was a guy who just felt, I don't know, *important* and *smart,* and I wanted to impress him, but everything I could think of to say felt too boring to burden him with.

"Good man," he said, and slapped my shoulder before turning on his heel to jog back to Flor's desk, pointing at the staffers he was ready to hear from as he went. They converged in a huddle at Flor's desk and I went back to work.

"Marcus?" someone said from behind me, a few minutes later.

I looked up, and into a semi-familiar face. It was a guy about my age, or maybe a little younger, with a scruffy beard, and he was grinning so widely I thought his head would fall off. I recognized him from somewhere, but I couldn't think where. I decided I'd try to fake it. I stood up and shook his hand. "Hey, man!" I said. "Great to see you again!"

He clapped in uncontainable delight. "Dude, I can't *believe* it's you. Are *you* the new webmaster? Really?"

"Yup," I said. "Sweet gig, huh?"

He shook his head furiously. "No. Way. I can't believe it! Marcus Yallow is our *webmaster*? Oh *man*!"

This was more familiar territory—someone going all gushy and me not knowing what to say in response. Been there, done that, still don't know what to do when it happens. "So, uh, what have you been up to?"

"I'm the swag barista," he said, thumping his chest. He was

wearing a SAN FRANCISCO NEEDS NOSS shirt, done like an old-timey sci-fi movie poster, with a giant Joe standing astride the Golden Gate bridge. "I design the T-shirts and posters. I try to do a new one every couple days, and screen them on demand. Keep it fresh, mix it up, you know? One thing I wanted to ask you about was whether you could put up a Threadless clone for the website so I could do a little shirt-community for all the Noss-ers out there?"

"Uh," I said, "yeah. Sure, why not?" We were running the site on OpenCampaign, which was a free mod of WordPress designed for election campaigns. It could run WordPress plug-ins with no additional work, and the one that was based on the Threadless user-generated T-shirt site was one I'd looked at before. It didn't seem like it'd be too hard to run.

"You are such a dude. God, I can't believe this! Wait until I tell Nate. He is going to flip out."

And that's when I remembered him. "Liam?" I said.

"Yeah, of course! Liam! I've been volunteering here all summer! Ever since I saw Joe's July Fourth video. That stuff was straight-up inspiring, yo."

I had friends who ended their sentences with "yo," but al-ways ironically, making fun of the people who were trying to talk all "street" and badass. Liam wasn't being ironic. He really did end his sentences with "yo."

"Yo," I said, then felt mean about it and gave him a friendly slug on the shoulder. "Liam, man, I didn't recognize you at first with the beard and all. How cool that we're going to be work-ing together?"

"Me too. Look, do you have lunch plans? Want to get a burrito? I know a great place up on Valencia—"

"Sure, burritos sound great," I said. I hefted my notebook and said, "I'd better get back to work if I'm going to get time for a lunch break, then."

He did a couple of dance steps on the spot, then gave me a surprise hug, a real crusher that involved lifting me a couple inches off the floor. "See you at lunch!"

Once upon a time, I'd been part of a tight foursome of awesomely close friends. Darryl, Jolu, Van, and I had done everything together since we'd been little kids. But after the whole Xnet thing, well, one thing happened and then another. Van and Darryl started dating, and Van didn't like Ange at all (and there was all the weirdness about the fact that she'd been secretly crushing on me, which loomed up like an invisible wall whenever we saw each other). Darryl went off to Berkeley, and we'd seen each other a little at first, but between classes, Van, and his psychotherapy for all the crazy nightmares and freak-outs he still had thanks to the horrors of Gitmo-by-the-Bay, we barely had time to say hi. Jolu, meanwhile, had graduated from his job at Pigspleen to a sweet gig as a programmer on a start-up that was commercializing municipal data, cranking out services based on the feeds put out by City Hall. He had a ton of new friends, including a bunch of intimidatingly smart civic hackers, and when they were all really going at it, I could only understand about half of what they said. We didn't see much of each other.

And then there was Ange, who was the world's most perfect girlfriend: funny, smart, exciting. She liked the same movies and games that I did, liked the same books and music, and was always up for keeping me company when she wasn't at school—she'd gotten into SFSU for communications studies and was acing her courses. So even though I missed my friends, it wasn't like I was actually *lonely* or anything—so somehow I never got around to calling them or IMing them or poking them and seeing how they were doing.

But it had been a long time since I'd had a regular gang of friends, a little posse of my own. And I missed that.

Liam's friend Nate joined us for lunch, taking BART
down from his mom's place downtown. He, too, gave me a
crushing hug, and then he and Liam exchanged one of the same.
These guys were as Californian as they came, and they *loved*
their physical contact. I'd been born and raised in San Francisco, but my mom was British, and so I just hadn't gotten into
the whole super-huggy scene ever.

We ended up at my favorite burrito joint, and I got tongue,
which Ange had convinced me to try and which turned out to
be amazingly tasty, provided you didn't think too hard about
the fact that you were, you know, *eating a tongue.* Liam ordered
one, too, and raved about how good it tasted and how he wished
he'd tried it sooner.

"I still can't believe you're our *webmaster,*" Liam said. "That's
like, I don't know, Bruce Lee being your bouncer or something."

"Or Jack Daniels being your bartender," Nate said. He had
the same beard as Liam.

"I think Jack Daniels is dead, or made up," Liam said.

"Okay, it's like Steve Wozniak fixing your PC," Nate said.

"Dude, old school," Liam said. "Woz is the guy who built
the first Apple computers," he said to me.

"Yeah," I said. "I know."

"Oh," Liam said. "Yeah! Of course you do! Listen to me,
huh?"

I wanted to find some way to politely say, "Hey, Liam,
don't worry about impressing me, okay? I already like you, and
all this stuff is just making you sound kind of desperate." But
every way I could think of saying that would make Liam feel
like a loser and make me sound like a dick.

"What are you up to, Nate?" I said, pointedly changing the
subject.

He shrugged. "Being unemployed. Polishing my nonexistent résumé." Another shrug.

"I know how that feels," I said. "I was unemployed until this morning."

They both boggled at me.

"No way," Liam said. "How could *you* be out of work? I assumed they'd poached you from some rad start-up or Google or something."

Now it was *my* turn to shrug. It seemed like unemployment talk always involved a fair bit of shrugging and looking away. "Dunno," I said. "I dropped out of school months ago, couldn't afford it anymore, and I've been looking ever since."

"Man," Nate said. "That's crazy. If you couldn't find work, what hope do *I* have?"

I didn't have an answer for him. I was starting to actually feel guilty about having a job, and I'd been employed for less than a day.

We finished our awkward lunch and went back to work, and I went back to mapping out the network and figuring out what needed fixing and what didn't, and I didn't even think about the torrent I'd downloaded the night before until I got home and rebooted my computer into my secret partition and the machine reconnected to IPredator and started seeding the file again.

The torrent contained a huge—HUGE—zip file that was encrypted. Of course, I had the key. And somewhere out there, Masha was being held captive—or worse—and I was pretty sure that she wanted me to dump the file *and* the key now.

I really wanted to talk this over with someone. Ange, of course. But she was still in class and wouldn't be out for hours. And this wasn't the kind of subject I wanted to talk about over the phone or email or IM or—well, I kind of felt like we should talk about it in a soundproofed room at the bottom of a mineshaft, but I didn't have either of those things.

I had been avoiding thinking about this for nearly thirty-six hours now. I'd had good excuses: I'd been blown up. I'd been doped up. I'd been asleep. I'd gotten a job. I'd had my first day at work. But I'd run out of excuses for inaction.

But wait! I just thought of a new excuse: it would be *insane* to have the decrypted file sitting on my drive, even on a secret partition. I couldn't get over the thought that a snatch team could break down my door at any time and haul me away. If I was loaded up on my "secret" partition at that point, it'd be easy for them to see what I was up to.

I decided I needed to build a few more layers of security into the system before I started to handle this info-plutonium.

First things first: go shopping for a virtual machine. Let me explain that, because VMs had become my best friends lately.

You can write a program that works just like your computer's microprocessor. You designate a file to act as your virtual computer's hard drive, and then you load it up with an operating system and any programs you want to run. When you "turn on the computer"—that is, when you run the program—it looks at the virtual drive and loads in the virtual operating system and follows all the instructions it finds there, passing them on to your *real* computer, which is running underneath all this.

It used to be that the main use for VMs was to simulate old computers on new ones—so you could simulate some ancient game console, an old Game Boy or whatever, and play all the vintage games. There's a megahuge games VM called MAME, the Multiple Arcade Machine Emulator, that can play pretty much every old game, ever.

The key word here is "old." That's because running a pretend computer inside a real computer is slow. But computers double in speed every eighteen months or so—this is called

Moore's Law, for Gordon Moore, who helped start Intel. That means a brand-new computer will be about sixty-four times faster than a computer you could buy for the same money six years ago, which means that so long as you're working with old VMs, you probably won't even notice the speed lag.

But lately, computer manufacturers have been figuring out how to design chips to run VMs more efficiently, so the gap between a VM and the real computer it runs on keeps shrinking. This means that it's easier than ever to try out new operating systems and new programs. If there's something you're *really* paranoid about, you can just run a free VM program, install a free OS on it, and run anything you want in that little sandbox. Nothing that happens in that VM can affect your real computer—not unless you give it privileges to see your real hard drive and real files. The VM is like a head in a jar, and you can tell it anything you want about what's going on in the world and it'll have to believe you.

You can download hundreds—thousands!—of VMs from the Internet and just fire them up as you need them. Want to turn an old computer into a router or a file server for an hour or a day or a year? Various sysadmins have bottled up perfectly tuned VMs that run any specialized function like that out of the box. There are even user reviews to help you figure out which ones are the good ones. And since it's all built on open, free code like Linux, anyone can modify, improve, and redistribute them.

I went hunting for an extra paranoid VM, and I found one. It started with a copy of ParanoidLinux, my own favorite distro, and nuked any programs and services you didn't need, to make it all the more bulletproof. ParanoidVM also stored its user files in TrueCrypt plausible deniability chunks, so there was no way to tell from the forensic examination of the disk how many users there were and how many files they had.

That was good for starters, but I wanted a dead man's switch: something that would cause the whole thing to lock itself and shut down if I didn't do something every fifteen minutes. So I wrote a little script that hit me up for a password every quarter hour. If I didn't enter it, it would issue a system-wide command to kill any VMs that were running, then erase itself. So if a snatch squad *were* to nab me, all the work I'd done on the files would disappear unless they could torture the password out of me in a quarter of an hour.

They'd still have the key and the torrent file, but they wouldn't know whom I'd shown anything to or what we'd talked about. All I'd have to do is key in my password every fifteen minutes, and not go off to the toilet or forget and go to dinner, or I'd lose everything I'd worked on up to the last save point.

There's a technical term for this kind of security work: yak-shaving—wasting time doing silly chores to avoid something harder and more important. There was an old essay I liked about working for Google by a hacker called Dhanji Prasanna, which talked about "shaving the entire yak pen at the zoo, and pretty soon traveling to Tibet to shave foreign yaks you've never seen before and whose barbering you know little about."

That's the territory I was heading into. It was time to decrypt the file.

It had been a while since I'd decrypted an encrypted ZIP file with a very long password. There was a specialized command you could use to specify that the password was in a file, and I couldn't remember it at first. I looked up how to do it. I did it. The list of files scrolled past faster than my eye could follow. Lots of files. *LOTS AND LOTS* of files.

810,097 files.

What had Masha said? *Eventually, you come across something so terrible, you can't look yourself in the mirror anymore unless you do something about it.*

That was a lot of dirty laundry, yo.

I could tell at a glance that they had human-generated file names—weird punctuation, weird capitalization, and both were all over the place. Computers might do weird capitalization, but every file would have been weird in the same way. Some had pretty descriptive names like "bribes paid to senate Def Cttee .doc" and others were more cryptic, like HumIntAfgh32533. There was a file called WATERBOARDING.PPT, a set of PowerPoint slides. My stomach curdled into a hard ball just looking at it.

I double clicked it. The first slide was just a title: "STRESS INTERROGATION SEMINAR 4320." The next slide was a long confidentiality notice, naming a bunch of private military contractors who, apparently, had been involved in producing this presentation. And the next slide—

—showed a boy, about my age, restrained in padded cuffs at the ankles, wrists, and chest, strapped to an angled wooden board that held his head lower than his feet, mouth covered tightly in Saran Wrap, having water poured down his nose in a splashing stream out of a bucket with a spout, held by two large, clean, white hands. The boy's body was arched up like a bow, straining against his restraints, pulling so hard that every muscle in his body stood out. He looked like an anatomical illustration.

No.

He looked like a torture victim.

The Saran Wrap was an evil touch. The water is poured down the nose, but it can't go into the lungs, because the body is tilted backwards. *His* body is tilted backwards. The body— *his body*—knows that there's water going into the windpipe and it's desperate for air. His mouth gasps, but the Saran Wrap only lets the air go out, because every time he tries to suck air *in,* the plastic makes a tight seal. The only place air could enter is his nose, and the water is pouring into his nose and so he can't breathe that way.

Eventually, his lungs empty out entirely, collapse like spent balloons, shrivel like raisins. His brain, starved of oxygen, begins to die. He may pull his bonds so hard he breaks his bones.

The government likes to call waterboarding a "simulated execution." It's not a simulation, though. They nearly kill you. If they don't stop, they will kill you.

One of the men at Guantánamo Bay, America's secret prison, was waterboarded more than 180 times. Nearly died 180 times. They say he planned 9/11. Maybe he did. But whatever he told them, they'd be crazy to trust it. When you're being slowly murdered, you will say anything and everything to get loose.

But I wasn't thinking about that. I was hypnotized by that boy, by the expression on his face, the veins standing out in his forehead, the terror in his eyes. I'd been there. I'd had that look in my eyes.

Time stopped.

And then the image disappeared. The window it was in disappeared. The VM that was in disappeared. My dead man's switch had been prompting me for a password, had run out of time, and had killed the VM and deleted itself like a good boy. I hadn't even noticed the password prompt. I'd been staring at that picture.

That picture was only one slide, from one file, out of more than 800,000 files. This was going to take a while.

Ange rang the bell around dinner time, and my mom sent her up to my room. She let herself in and snuck up on me and put her arms around my neck and kissed the top of my head. I pretended I didn't hear her or see her reflection in my screen. It was a game we played. We were adorable.

"Hey there, workin' man, how was your first big day at the office?"

"Pretty much like I said in my texts; I'm mostly trying to figure out what the job will entail, trying to get a handle on everything. I told you about that Liam guy, too, right?"

"Yeah, how weird is that? Small world, but I wouldn't want to paint it."

"Well, he got less sweaty about things by the end of the day, came by for a real chat, and it turns out he knows his stuff pretty well and had lots of good ideas for me, some authentication ideas I hadn't thought of for managing guest laptops."

"I think it's adorable that you've got a little groupie," she said, pulling up my spare chair and transferring the clutter of MakerBot parts to my bed before sitting down.

"It's embarrassing," I said. "How was class?"

She crossed her eyes. "I thought that after high school I'd get to start learning like an *adult,* without everything being about how many factoids I can regurgitate on cue during exams. But pretty much all of my courses give seventy-five percent of the grade based on exams."

"Well, you could always leak the exams," I said, and her hands were over my mouth before I'd gotten the words out.

"Don't. Even. Joke," she said.

Ange's deep, dark secret is that she stole and published the No Child Left Behind tests when she was in the eleventh grade, along with the answer sheets. The school board never figured out who was responsible for it, and they claimed that the stunt had cost millions. Served 'em right.

"Sorry," I said. "But there's worse ideas. And who better to do it?"

"Tell you what, let's figure out what to do about Masha's

little bombshell first. We can recycle anything we come up with for any final exams I should happen to find myself in possession of."

"That's why I love you; you're always thinking."

We joked a lot about love, but the truth was, I *did* love her, with a weird, scary kind of intensity. It probably had to do with drifting away from my gang of friends and dropping out of school—Ange was pretty much the only person I saw on a regular basis who wasn't a parent of mine. Every now and then, this freaked me out a little. I think it freaked her out, too—I was looking forward to getting a little more balance in my life from having a job with coworkers.

"So, what have you got?"

I felt that little paranoid shiver. You could eavesdrop on a room by bouncing a laser off the glass. The sound waves from the voices in the room made the glass vibrate, and the laser picked up the vibrations. I'd seen a demo of this in a YouTube video of a presentation from DEFCON, the big hacker conference in Vegas. The sound wasn't perfect, but it was pretty good. Good enough to pick out every word and recognize the speakers' voices.

"Um," I said. "Give me a sec, okay?"

I plugged a set of speakers into my laptop and then stretched out their wires until I could press them on the window glass. Then I used my computer's random-number generator, /dev/random, and requested some random white noise. The speakers began to hiss with staticky sound. I cranked them up to the point where I couldn't stand it, then turned them down a notch or two. I made sure the blinds were seated over the speakers again. Maybe a laser could pick up on the sound in the room, but I couldn't think of any way to subtract random noise from the audio signal. That didn't mean it was impossible, but at least we couldn't be eavesdropped on by anyone stupider than me.

"Huh," Ange said, observing this ritual. "Well, that's pretty intense."

"Yeah," I said. "It sure is." We moved the chairs so we could both see my laptop and I showed her my VM and the dead man's switch.

"Not bad," she said. "Okay, you've convinced me that you're worried about this stuff. Which, I suppose, means that you're sure that you saw Masha and Zeb get taken off the playa, and that means you think the explosion was deliberate." She closed her eyes and took a deep breath. "Back down the rabbit hole, here we go."

"Wait til you see." I brought up the VM, brought up the directory listing. Sat back.

"What is this? I don't even . . ." she said, staring wide-eyed at the listing. I handed her the mouse. She started clicking, beginning from the top. The first item was budget_8B5S.xls. It turned out to be a spreadsheet listing income and outgo. The titles down the left side were peoples' names. Across the top was a list of companies with bland names like "Holdings import/export" and "Property Management Ltd" and in the middle were dollar figures. None of them were very big—$1,001, $5,100—the biggest was $7,111.

"A lot of ones in those figures," I said.

Ange nodded. "Yeah. That's interesting, isn't it?" She stared at them for a while longer and got out her laptop. "You still like IPredator for anonymity?"

"Generally. But why don't you run it through Tor after IPredator." Tor—The Onion Router—would bounce the browser requests through a bunch of random computers, and none of those computers would know where the request came from and where it was going. It was slow—slower than IPredator, which was slower than the raw network connection. But there's a time to be paranoid, and this was it.

I stared at the mysterious spreadsheet for a while. The dead man's switch asked for a password and I entered it.

"There you go. I knew I'd read about this. The number one appears more frequently than other numbers in financial data."

"What? Why?"

She showed me the article, a summary of a paper at a security conference. "A lot more stuff costs between $10 and $19 or $100 and $199 than $20 and up, or $200 and up. Retail psychology: people are more likely to buy stuff that costs $9 than $10; it's a big jump. Ninety-nine dollars has less psychological weight than $100, but $999 is a lot less crazy than $1,000. So you get a lot of clusters of numbers with ones in them. But when people make up numbers, faking their finances or cheating on their taxes, you get a much more even distribution of numbers. It's one of the ways the IRS looks for tax cheats. I read about it in a book on data-journalism—tried to get my section's TA to read it last year but she said she had to get us ready for the exams and to show it to her again afterward.

"So all these ones, they're inserted by someone who knows he's making up numbers and wants to be sure that there's plenty of extra ones to make the statistical distribution look right. Someone who doesn't expect a human being to look at these numbers closely, but worried that a computer might spot them."

She peered at my spreadsheet and started to type again, but the dead man's switch wanted a password again and I didn't grab the computer in time to enter it. The VM disappeared.

"That's frustrating," she said.

"I'll teach you the password."

"What if you set the timeout to longer? Thirty minutes?"

I shook my head. "I think I could probably hold out against someone who wanted my password for fifteen minutes, especially if they were on a snatch team that broke the door down and didn't have any time to prepare. Thirty minutes, though . . ."

"Oh," she said.

"There's a presentation in there on how to do waterboarding. A PowerPoint. It's got bar graphs showing the time to brain damage based on age and general health."

"Oh," she said again. She knew that there were times when showering would give me uncontrollable shakes. Being executed will do that to you.

I brought up the VM and opened the spreadsheet again. Ange started to enter the names.

"They're all staffers for Illinois State Assemblyman Bedfellow. The logical next step is to look up which committees that Assemblyman is on, and what all he voted on. Data Journalism 101—or it would be, if there was a Data Journalism course in my program."

"Let's do it," I said.

"No," she said. "That's just one file. There's 800,000 more. We can't do this retail. We have to find a wholesale approach."

"We need Jolu," I said. **"This** is his thing."

We'd been brainstorming for hours. Ange was even more paranoid than I was. She had me clone the VM—easy, just copy the data file—and then set up a new TrueCrypt file that had one copy of the VM in its regular storage, and another copy in a hidden plausible deniability partition.

"Here's how it'll work: the snatch squad comes in, bags and tags you and grabs the computer. They start looking around, but before they can get very far, there's a password prompt. They start to rubber-hose you for the password, but you gut it out. *Whoosh,* the dead man's switch trips, the VM takes itself down, the data is scrambled.

"But *then* what happens?"

I chewed my lip. I had thought this through this far before and hadn't liked what came next. "They try to get the password out of me to decrypt the file."

"Right."

I said, "And if you're here, they can work on you, too."

"Which is why we're doing this. Because right away we can give them a password, and that password will unlock this copy of the VM. It's got a full set of the leaks. But that's not the copy we work with. That's the one we hide in the plausible deniability partition. And that's where we keep all our notes, any mailing lists of people who know about this and work on it with us. We never give them that password. Our story is, we kept the leaks on this encrypted VM, and we didn't keep notes on them. We didn't know what to do about them. It's believable. I mean, we *don't* know what to do with them."

We did that. We came up with two long, crazy passwords and practiced them on each other until we had them memorized. Then we stared at each other.

"Now what?"

"We need Jolu," I said again. "He's all about wholesale data these days."

Ange nuked the VMs, turning them back into random-seeming gibberish. "Those speakers are driving me crazy," she said. "Are you sure they'll stop this laser-listener stuff?"

I shook my head.

"Fine," she said. "Let's turn them down for a while, anyway."

"So, Jolu. You know that bringing Jolu into this is pretty much the same kind of dick move that Masha pulled when she brought *you* into it."

"I know. But it's different with Jolu. He's my friend. One of my best friends."

She chewed on some words for a while. "Marcus, no offense,

but is that still true? When was the last time you guys actually hung out? When was the last time you even *talked*?"

I squirmed. She was right. "Okay, point taken, but that doesn't mean we're not still friends. We don't dislike each other, we're just, you know, busy with our own things. I've known Jolu for most of my life, since I was a little kid. He's the right guy for this."

"I don't mean to make you all defensive, all right? It's just that you're about to put Jolu into a really hard spot, and it's the kind of thing that you should be really, really sure about before you do it."

"Jolu wouldn't turn me down. This is *important*."

Ange gave me a long, long look. Here's what she wasn't saying: *If this is so important, why didn't you drop everything to do something about it? Why didn't you go to the cops, or the press? Why are you screwing around with a new job instead of making this your top priority?*

It was a thought that I kept having, too, and of course, I knew the answer, and so did Ange. I was too scared to go public. The last time I spilled everything to the press, I'd ended up in a torture chamber. The stuff Masha had dumped on me was a *lot* more important and scary than what I'd had to say that time, too, if our small samples were anything to go by.

Besides, Masha hadn't told me to rescue her. She'd told me to get the material out. I would. Maybe if the material was out there, Carrie Johnstone would realize that snatching Masha would do no good and let her and Zeb go.

Maybe.

Chapter 7

I've always done my best work at night, and I knew all the tricks—combining careful doses of coffee, catnaps, and showers to get my tortured, sleep-deprived brain to perform during daylight, while still cranking away through the vampire hours, where inspiration lurked in every shadow.

Jolu was the same, and that was one reason we got along so well. I can't count how many 3 A.M.s I'd shared with him over Skype or IM, or in person as we snuck out of the house to go dingledodie around the streets of San Francisco. So even though it was 8 P.M. when Ange and I finally finished arguing, I didn't worry about whether he'd be free for the evening.

Though I *did* feel a little weird as my finger hovered over his icon in my speed dial. That thing, you know it: you haven't called someone in a long time, so it's weird to call them, so you don't call them, and more time goes by, and it gets weirder . . .

"Marcus!" he said. There was a lot of noise in the background, clinking bottles and glasses and loud talk.

"Jolu!" I said. "Look, man, I'm sorry to call you out of the blue—"

"One sec," he said. "Let me go somewhere quieter." I heard him navigate what sounded like a busy party. "Hey dude! Long time no speak!"

"I'm sorry to call you out of the blue—"

"No, no, it's cool. It's great, actually! Nice to hear from you."

Wonder if you'll feel the same way after I turn your life upside down.

"Can I meet you somewhere? It's important."

"Marcus?" he said. "Important how?"

"Important important. The kind of important I don't want to talk about on the phone."

I distinctly heard him say *Oh shit* under his breath. "Of course," he said. "Right now?"

"Yeah, now would be good."

"Um." A long pause. "What about the place where you met Ange?"

"You mean—" I stopped myself. Good old Jolu. Anyone listening in wouldn't know where I met Ange. He was more paranoid than I was, and that was *before* I told him what was up. He really was the right man for the job. "Okay, when?"

"Give me an hour?"

"Okay," I said. "And Jolu? Thanks."

I heard him snort, and I could totally picture the half smile that went with it, one bushy eyebrow raised in a quizzical expression. "No need. Anytime for you, man. You know that."

Friends. Nothing like them.

I met Ange at a key-signing party Jolu and I threw at Sutro Baths on Ocean Beach. The weird old/new ruins were spooky and dramatic, and the night was burned into my memory forever. Ange laughed when I told her where we were headed. She'd taken me there again on our first anniversary, with a picnic supper, and we'd watched the sun go down and necked on the blanket before we got too cold.

"I think we should switch off our phones," Ange said.

"Yeah," I said. That's the thing about paranoia—it's catching. But she was right—our phones would send our location to the phone companies, and if someone really wanted to snoop on us, it was always possible that they could find some way to tap into the GPSs on them. Then there'd be this really clear data trail: Marcus called Jolu, then Ange, Marcus, and Jolu all met up at Ocean Beach. Might as well get reflective orange vests and stencil COCONSPIRATOR on them. I took the battery out of my phone for good measure.

We were a quarter of an hour early—the buses were with us—and Jolu was ten minutes early. He hugged us both tightly, and Ange kissed him on the cheek. It had been months since I'd seen him—he'd dropped in on an open data lecture at Noisebridge—and he looked different. He'd grown a tidy little mustache and pointed sideburns, and had his hair styled in a short razor-cut that looked somehow grown-up, cool, and businesslike all at once. He'd always been better dressed than the rest of us, but he was particularly natty that night in a button-up shirt with slightly wiggly stripes that made my eyes cross when I stared at them, heavy old denim jeans with big rivets, and elaborate leather shoes. I was in my old thrift-store jeans, beat-up motorcycle boots caked with playa dust, and a hoodie, and I felt like a slob.

He had wine on his breath. "I hope it wasn't a totally excellent party," I said.

"Just a release party for a new traffic-predicting app," he said, shrugging. "We get users' anonymized GPS data at different times on different roads and try to predict traffic jams ahead of time, also looking at all the planned road maintenance and anything realtime from the DOT. You share your calendar with us and we look at where you're going and use that to give you advice on what roads to avoid to get there on time."

"Woah, creepy," Ange said. I'd been thinking it, but hadn't wanted to say anything.

Jolu wasn't offended, though. He just grinned. "Yeah, it is.

I mean, everyone is opt-in, and we anonymize the data when we get it so we don't know where *you've* been, just that *someone* has been there. But yeah, if we had a data leak, there'd be an awful lot of stuff there you might not want the world to know." He sat down on a rock and fished some gum out of his pockets, offered it around. It was black licorice gum, his favorite, the kind that turned your tongue and spit disgusting black. Just the smell of it made me smile and sent me spinning back in time to the old days.

"Or if the police seized your servers," Ange said. "It's so weird that we do all this Xnet stuff to keep our personal information from being captured by the government, but we give it to companies and the cops can just waltz in to their data centers whenever they want and just take it all."

"You don't know the half of it," Jolu said. "Get me to tell you about the lawful intercept stuff sometime, okay? It'll curl the hair on your toes."

"So, speaking of the police and servers," I said. "I've got an interesting technical problem I wanted to talk to you about."

"I figured you might."

"Before I start—is your phone on by any chance?"

He pulled it out of his pocket and removed the back, showed me the missing battery. "Dude, *estoy aqui por loco, no por pendejo*," which was the punch line to the funniest Spanish joke I knew. Okay, the only one. Google it.

Jolu listened attentively, asking a few questions as we told the story. I put in my theory about the explosion on the playa, and Ange didn't say anything about not believing me. When we were done, we both looked at him across the darkness and the gray no-color of the light leaking from the streetlamps on the cliff above us.

"So what do we do now?" he said.

"We?"

He shook his head. "Duh. Yes, 'we.' Did you think I wouldn't get involved?"

"The last time you sat where you're sitting and I sat where I'm sitting, you told me that it was different for you. You told me that the risk was bigger if you're brown than if you're white."

"Yeah, I said that. It's every bit as true today as it was, then, too."

"But you're in."

He looked out into the darkness and didn't say anything. I smelled his gum.

"Marcus," he said. "Have you noticed how *messed up* everything is today? How we put a 'good' president in the White House and he kept right on torturing and bombing and running secret prisons? How every time we turn around, someone's trying to take away the Internet from us, make it into some kind of giant stupid shopping mall where the rent-a-cops can kick you out if they don't like your clothes? Have you noticed how much money the one percent have? How we're putting more people in jail every day, and more people are unemployed every day, and more people are losing their houses every day?"

"I've noticed," I said. "But haven't things always been screwed up? I mean, doesn't everyone assume that their generation has the most special, most awful problems?"

"Yeah," Ange said. "But not every generation has had the net."

"Bingo," Jolu said. "I'm not saying it wasn't terrible in the Great Depression or whatever. But we've got the power to *organize* like we've never had before. And the creeps and the spooks have the power to spy on us more than ever before, to control us and censor us and find us and snatch us."

"Who's going to win?" I said. "I mean, I used to think that we'd win, because we understand computers and they don't."

"Oh, they understand computers. And they're doing everything they can to invent new ways to mess you up with them. But if we leave the field, it'll just be *them*. People who want everything, want to be in charge of everyone."

"So we're going to win?"

Jolu laughed. "There's no winning or losing, Marcus. There's only doing."

"Man, I leave you alone for a couple of months and you turn into *Yoda*."

"So what do we do?" Ange asked again.

"Well, we're not going to be able to look at 800,000 of these."

"810,097," I said.

"That. I think we need to build some kind of site for these things, something secure and private, where we can run searches on them, try to find the good stuff, leave notes for each other."

"And then what do we do with them?"

"We release them."

"Duh," Ange said. "But how do you think we'll do that? How do you put the information in a place where people will see it and care about it, but not a place that can be traced back to us?"

Jolu shrugged and stared at the ruins. "I don't know. I guess it depends on the kind of stuff we find. Maybe we google journalists who sound like they'd be interested in the story and email the docs to them from throwaway accounts. Something else, maybe. I don't know. But when you've got a problem that has two parts, and one part comes first, and you know how to solve that part, the best thing to do is solve that part and see if a solution to the rest suggests itself while you're working."

"That sounds right," I said.

"I suppose," Ange said. "But, Marcus, what about Zeb and Masha?"

"Yeah. Well, I don't know how we work that out. Maybe releasing the material will put them in more danger. Maybe it'll take them out of danger. We know who took them: Carrie Johnstone. That's got to be part of the story, however we release it."

"You're sure it was her?" Jolu asked.

"There are some faces I'll never, ever forget. Hers is one of them. It was *her*."

"Okay, okay. Let's talk about forward secrecy," he said.

It turned out Jolu had been hanging out with some heavy Tor dudes who were working on "darknet sites"—"hidden services" that could host files and message boards, sites that anyone could reach, providing they knew the address. But these were unlike regular sites: even if you knew the address, you couldn't figure out where the physical computer it led to was, who was running it, what server you'd have to seize to shut it down. Darknet sites were places you could visit but couldn't shut down.

"So you've got these rendezvous points, they're servers that know some other servers that know some other servers that know the way to reach the darknet site. You ask a rendezvous site to introduce you to the server and it does this dance with the other servers down the line, and creates a temporary circuit that bounces your connection through a one-off route to the darknet machine, so every time you visit the site, there's a different, random way to reach it.

"What I want to do is grab a cheapo server-on-demand VM and slap a ParanoidLinux install on it—nothing unencrypted, ever. Then we slap a copy of your data on it, and a clone of Google Spreadsheets. Grab a doc, put its title in the first field, a description in the next field, and a place where you can put some keywords. Smack together a script that runs every couple of minutes and searches for those keywords in the uncategorized documents, and automatically suggests possibly related ones."

"And then what? We look at 800,000 documents, us three?" I figured I might be able to do a hundred docs a night, depending on how complicated they were. At that rate, it'd take us three a year or so to get through them all. Too slow.

"No, not us three. With enough eyeballs, all bugs are shallow. We've got to bring more people in. People we can trust."

Jolu said, "Yeah, I know a few of those."

I was almost late for work the next day. After coming home, I'd stayed up for hours banging away at the document dump. I hadn't meant to, but Jolu's idea of searching for words in the dump gave me some ideas.

The first thing I searched for was "Masha" and "Zeb." I got a few documents with "zebra" and "mashallah," but nothing else. I tried "Marcus" and "Yellow." There were five Marcuses but none of them were me.

Then I tried "Carrie Johnstone" and hit the jackpot.

Carrie Johnstone had been a busy little soldier in Iraq. There were more than four hundred documents that mentioned her by name. I went after them alphabetically at first, but it was all confusing, until I had the bright idea of sorting them by date and starting with the oldest and reading toward the newest—a document that was just over a month old.

Reading those four hundred documents—some very short, some very long—kept me up to three in the morning, and the more I read, the more I learned about Carrie Johnstone's weird and terrible career in and out of the U.S. military.

The first documents dated from Johnstone's career at FOB Tikrit, Saddam Hussein's old palace. There was a memo she'd written describing the handover of a bunch of Iraqi prisoners to the Iraqi police. I didn't see at first why anyone would bother to save the document, but the next memo explained it. It was a memo explaining why they hadn't told the Red Cross about the transfer of prisoners, and hadn't gotten any kind of chain-of-custody receipts from the Iraqi cops. A little googling and I figured out what that meant: fifty-one men, women, and children had vanished into the custody of Iraq's police force, and no one knew whatever became of them. They had been arrested after anonymous tips, or snatched off the street for "suspicious behavior." And for all anyone knew, they were nameless and rotting in a jail somewhere, while their families wrote them off for dead. Or maybe they were dead, dumped in a mass grave.

Then she'd ended up at FOB Grizzly, working as an "intelligence officer" alongside the military police. She'd been reprimanded for unauthorized "stress interrogations" of suspected terrorists and had overseen an arrest sweep that brought in more than five hundred suspects, all of whom had been released over the coming months as it emerged that they had nothing to do with terrorism.

It was around then that she left the military, and though she'd written a letter of resignation, there was also a memo from a commanding officer to Army Human Resources Command saying that she'd been "shown the door" after an "incident" involving "materiel." Another memo was more explicit—she'd been involved in a plan that delivered American guns and ammo to private mercenaries working for a military contractor, and those guns and that ammo had been part of a massacre that killed over a hundred people.

From there, she'd gone private, working for the military "contractor"—hired killers, according to a quick search—and had distinguished herself with a very lucrative bid to take over the management contract for the FOB she'd been fired from.

It was ugly.

As I lay in bed with my thoughts swirling, I wondered if Carrie Johnstone had snatched Masha because the leaks file had so much embarrassing material about her, personally, or whether she'd been hired to retrieve them for the U.S. government. How could the Army fire her one day and then rehire her to do the same job at ten times her old salary a month later? Were they on crazy pills?

I couldn't afford to drag my ass around work the next day, so I didn't. I pounded the Turk's coffee and munched chocolate espresso beans and finished my inventory and network map. Joe surprised me by scheduling me for lunch. The first I heard of it was when he showed up at my desk at 12:30 and stood over it, smiling expectantly at me.

"Hi, Joe," I said.

"Lunchtime, Marcus?"

We went to a nice veggie place where they knew him by name and seated us right away. He knew their names, too, and greeted everyone from the waiter to the guy who filled up our water glasses personally, switching to Spanish as necessary and asking sincere, friendly questions about their wives and husbands and kids and health.

The sincere part was the weirdest thing. When I was really on fire and feeling very, very sociable, I might remember half of the names of the people I saw. I just sucked at names. And when people told me about their kids or parents or siblings or whatever, I tried to be interested, but I mean, how interested can you really be in the lives of people you barely know or have never met at all?

But Joe had the uncanny ability to seem really, genuinely interested in people. When he talked to you, you felt like he was also *listening* to you, carefully, thoughtfully, and not waiting for you to finish talking so that he could say whatever he was going to say next. It made him seem, I don't know, *holy* or something, like one of those people out of a religious story who overflows with love for his fellow man.

And the weirdest part? He didn't make me feel like a dick for not being that interested myself. Instead, he made me want to try to be more like him, more caring.

After our water glasses were full and we'd put in our orders, he said, "Thank you for making the time to see me today. I know you must be busy."

If it was anyone else, I'd have thought he was blowing smoke up my ass, but he really sounded like he thought being the webmaster/sysadmin/net guy was the hardest job in the world and he felt lucky that all he had to do was run around and try to get elected.

"You're welcome—I mean, it's a pleasure. I mean, it's wonderful. I'm so glad to have a job, and it's such a cool job, too. Everyone's really nice and interesting and I really believe in your platform, so, well, it's just great." I was babbling like an idiot and I couldn't seem to stop—and he didn't seem to notice.

"You remember when I spoke to you on the phone the other night, I mentioned how my campaign would need great technology to be successful. And I'm sure that when you and Flor chatted she had some pointed opinions about that and what her side of the campaign needed from you. You might be wondering who wins in a little struggle like that. I wanted to give you some context to help you resolve that.

"Flor is your boss—and she's my boss, too. She's in charge of the campaign from top to bottom, and I'm familiar with her ideas about what campaigns need vis-à-vis boots on the ground, knocking on doors, and raising money. She's right as far as she goes, and that's why I let her be my boss.

"But I'm the candidate, and I have some additional priori-
ties. I say 'additional'—not 'different.' Flor is right about need-
ing money, boots, and door-knocking. But once you've got all
that running to the best of your ability, there's more that I want
you to get thinking about. I want you to tell me how technology can help me reach people who would otherwise be beyond
my reach. I want you to tell me how technology can transform
the way that voters and their representatives collaborate to produce good, accountable government. Every wave of technology, from newspapers to radio to TV, has transformed politics,
and not always for the better. Some people think that the Internet is a tool for politicians to raise money or coordinate volunteers, but I don't think that's even one percent of what
technology can do for politics. I want you to help me figure out
the other ninety-nine percent."

Woah. "Okay," I said. "Do you want, what, an essay or a
website or something?"

He smiled. "Let's start with a chat, like this one, tomorrow at the end of the day. I'll have Flor put it in both of our
schedules."

It made me feel good and a little scared—I really didn't
want to let him down, but all I could think of was darknet sites
and leaked docs. I wondered what he would say if I told him
that I was sitting on more than 800,000 confidential, compro-
mising government memos. But I also remembered what Flor
had said: *The first time I catch so much as a whiff of anything illegal,
immoral, dangerous, or 'leet' I will personally bounce your ass to the
curb before you have a chance to zip your fly.*

I went over to Ange's after work. Jolu had already set
up our darknet site and grabbed a copy of the docs off BitTorrent. I'd handed him a USB stick with the key on it, and by the
time I got my computer up into a secure mode with a dead

man's switch and an anonymized, private network connection, the site was ready to go.

In fact, it was already going. Jolu had met with Van on his lunch break, and she'd plowed through more than fifty docs while I'd been bringing the Joe for Senate servers' patch levels up to date. I wondered whether Van had had a chance to talk to Darryl. He'd been my best friend, as tight as a brother, but I hadn't seen him in months. It was all too weird between us—the fact that he was with Van and that Van had confessed that she'd once had a crush on me; the unwordly fragility of his mind after his time in Gitmo-by-the-Bay; his constant struggle to keep up with even a half-time courseload at Berkeley. I thought of what seeing that nasty little waterboarding PowerPoint would do to Darryl.

It wasn't just Van working on the docs, either. Jolu had enlisted some of his other trusted friends, people with cryptic handles like Left-Handed Mutant and Endless Vegetables. I hoped Jolu was right to trust them. I hoped he'd been cagey about where the docs had actually come from. Out of curiosity, I googled the strangers' handles and confirmed to my satisfaction that they didn't appear to have been used before. It would have been such a basic mistake to recycle a nickname that you'd already used someplace that could be linked to your real identity.

Endless Vegetables was working his (or her) way through a gigantic pile of documents on student loans, judging from the tags and summaries. I vaguely knew that the government guaranteed student loans made by universities, which were sold to banks that collected on them. The darknet docs went into disgusting details—like a series of jokey emails between a congressman who'd gotten a tearful letter from a constituent who'd been hit with crazy penalties that turned her $20,000 loan into a $180,000 loan and an executive at the bank who'd assessed the penalties. The congressman sounded like he was pretty good friends with the banker, and they made it sound like this girl's problem was hilarious.

Jolu had added an "I'm feeling lucky" button to the spreadsheet that would bring up a random, uncataloged doc. I hit it and found myself looking at a cryptic set of numbers and acronyms. I tried to google the search terms but found myself getting nowhere, so I grabbed another, and then another. It was mesmerizing, like channel surfing on a massive cable network that only got heavy, strange programs about corruption, murder, and sleaze.

"Jeebus H. Christmas," Ange said. "Have a look at the doc I just checked in."

I resorted the spreadsheet by author and found Ange's latest contribution, loaded it up. It was an instruction manual for a "lawful intercept" network appliance sold to cops and governments for installation at an Internet Service Provider. The appliance monitored all incoming requests for updates to Android phones, and checked to see if the phone's owner was on a list of targets. If they were, the appliance took over the network session and sent a fake update to the phone that gave spies and spooks the power to secretly turn on the phone's GPS, camera, and mic. I stared in mounting horror at the phone on the bed next to me, then flipped it over and took out the battery.

"Keep reading," Ange said. She'd been following the autolinked documents and found a bunch of captured emails and phone sessions. One was a complaint from a DHS field operative about a target who'd installed "ParanoidAndroid" on his phone and couldn't be gotten at.

"What's ParanoidAndroid?" I asked.

"I'm reading up on that now," Ange said. "Looks like it's a fork from the CyanogenMod." I knew about Cyanogen, of course—hackers had taken the source code for Google's Android operating system and made a fully free and open version that could do all kinds of cool tricks. "It doesn't accept updates unless their checksums match with other users and the official releases. Lets you tell whether an update is real or a spoof."

"Well, what are we waiting for? Let's install it!"

Ange pointed at her phone, which was already cabled to her laptop. "What do you think I'm doing?"

"Do mine next?"

"Duh."

There was more. Other lawful intercept appliances would disguise themselves as iTunes updates for Macs and PCs, and another one worked by sending fake updates to your browser. Then there were the saved emails between a senior DHS IT manager who'd worked at one of these companies before going to Homeland Security. His old boss was explaining how they were using a shell company in Equatorial Guinea—a country I'd never even heard of!—to market their products in China, Iran, and other countries.

It just got worse. Logs of law enforcement requests to install spyware bugs on people involved in peaceful protest groups. Reports of break-ins by suspected criminals who'd used the systems to spy on their victims.

I was trying to figure out how all this stuff could possibly work. After all, software updates usually went over SSL, which used cryptographic certificates to verify the identity of the sender. How were they spoofing connections from Apple and Google and Microsoft and Mozilla?

Oh, that's how. A search on "certificates lawful intercept" brought up another email exchange, this one with a huge American security company that had one of the "signing certificates" that were trusted by all browsers and operating systems. They'd been supplying blank certificates to the DHS for years, it seemed—certificates that would give the government the power to undetectably impersonate your bank or your company, or Apple, Microsoft, and Google.

Ange and I split up the remaining lawful intercept docs, getting deeper and deeper into the terrifying secrets of snoops and spies. Before I knew it, it was 2 A.M. and I could barely keep my eyes open.

"Want to stay over?" Ange said as I yawned for the tenth time in five minutes.

"I think I already have," I said. We'd started staying over at each other's houses that summer, and while it had been weird at first (especially over breakfast with the parents!), everyone had gotten used to it. My parents had more important stuff to worry about, and Ange's mom was just one of those cool grown-ups who seemed to have an instinctive grasp of what mattered and what didn't.

Chapter 8

Once upon a time, terrorists blew up a bridge in my city and killed over four thousand people. They told me everything changed. They told me that we didn't have the same rights we used to, because catching terrorists was more important than our little freedoms.

They say they caught the terrorists. One of the guys, who had been killed by a drone in Yemen, supposedly thought the whole thing up. I guess I'm okay with him being dead if that's the case. I hope it's the case. No one would show us the proof, of course, because of "national security."

But "everything is different" turned out to be a demand and not a description. It pretended to describe what the new reality was, but instead it demanded that everyone accept a new reality, one where we could be spied on and arrested and even tortured.

A few years later, everything changed again. It seemed like overnight, no one had jobs anymore, no one had money anymore, and people started to lose their houses. It was weird, because now that it was *obvious* that everything had changed, no one wanted to talk about how everything had changed.

When the streets are full of armed cops and soldiers telling you that everything is different, everyone can point at one thing, a thing with a human face, and agree, "It's different, it's different."

But when some mysterious social/financial/political *force* upends the world and changes everything—when "everything is different now" is a description and not a demand—somehow, it gets much harder to agree on whether things were different and what we needed to do about it.

It was one thing to demand that the armed guards leave our streets. It was another to figure out how to demand that the silent red overdue bills and sneaky process servers with their eviction notices go away.

I was nearly late getting to work the next day, but I just squeaked in. I'd stolen back one of my T-shirts from Ange's laundry pile (she liked to steal mine and sleep in them), and it smelled wonderfully of her and put me in a good mood as I came through the door and made a beeline for my desk.

"Dude!" Liam said, practically bouncing in place by my chair. "Can you believe it?"

"What?" I said.

"You know! The darknet stuff!"

All the blood rushed out of my head and into my gut and swirled there like a stormy ocean. My ears throbbed with my pulse. "What?" I said.

"You didn't see?"

He leaned over me and moused to my browser, went to the front page of Reddit, a site where you could submit and vote on news stories. Every item on the front page talked about darknet leaks. Feeling like I was in a horror movie, I clicked one of them. It was a story on wired.com about a file that had been anonymously dumped into pastebin.com, instructions for using a lawful intercept appliance to take over Android phones and work their cameras. Whoever had dumped the file had sent an email to a reporter at wired.com saying that there were more than 800,000 documents like it on a darknet site and that volunteers were combing through them, and there was a lot more to come. It didn't say where they'd come from or who the volunteers were.

I went back to Reddit and checked the others. How many darknet docs had leaked? It seemed like everyone had the same story, in different variants—800,000 docs, darknet, more to come, but nothing more. I started to calm down.

"You've got an Android phone, right?" Liam said.

"Yeah," I said. "I do. But I run ParanoidAndroid—it's an alternate OS that resists that kind of spyware."

"Really?" Joe said. He'd walked up on us on cat's-paw feet while we were talking, and I jumped in my seat. "Woah, sorry, calm down there, Marcus. I've got an Android phone, too. Tell you what, I'll order in pizza for lunch if you'll give us a workshop on keeping our phones secure. Sounds like the kind of thing we should all know about."

"Yeah, sure," I said. "Of course." Though as soon as I saw the *Wired* story, I'd started scheming to take lunch off and find a WiFi network with weak, crackable WEP security so that I could hop on, tunnel into the darknet, and try to figure out what had just happened. I mean, I knew better than anyone that there was no such thing as perfect security, and I understood that it was likely that someone, someday, would get a look at the darknet docs who we hadn't invited in. But I didn't think that day would be the day after we set up the darknet!

But I couldn't screw up my job. I'd been desperate for work for so long, and it was such a cool job. The fact that I might now be the target of a ruthless mercenary army didn't mean that I didn't have to help Joe get elected.

So I did my job, and when the pizza came, I stood with a slice in one hand and a whiteboard pen in the other and sketched out a little flowchart of how your phone could be taken over, and what could be done with your phone after it was pwned.

Joe munched thoughtfully at a slice, wiped his fingers and his mouth, and put up his hand. "So you're saying that the police could take over our phones?"

"No!" Liam said, vibrating in his chair. "He's saying *anyone* could—"

I put up my hands and Liam calmed down. "What I mean is, once the intercept appliance is installed at the phone company's data center, anyone who has a login and password for it could use it."

"But who has that login and password? The police, yes?"

"Probably not, actually. The leaks suggested that these appliances were managed by the phone company or ISP. So a police officer calls up the lawful intercept technicians and they set it up for him. So the list of anyone who could break into the ISP's network, anyone who could bribe or blackmail someone at the ISP, anyone who can convincingly pretend to be a police officer to the ISP, anyone who can get a *real* police officer to give him access, or anyone who can pay someone to do any of the above."

"So you're saying that turning anyone's phone into a superbug is as easy as fixing a parking ticket?"

"I've never fixed a parking ticket," I said. "I don't drive. Is it hard to fix a parking ticket?"

Joe drummed his fingers on the table. "Not if you're rich or well connected. Or so I'm told."

"Yeah," I said, "rich or well-connected people could turn any phone into a mobile bug. In theory there's no reason this is limited to Android phones. It could work by pushing out updates to iTunes, or Firefox, or any app. They'd just need a signing certificate and—" I stopped talking, because I'd just remembered that there hadn't been anything about the signing certificates in the leak. "And things like that. So theoretically, any computer, any phone, anything that updates itself automatically could be turned into a bug once these things are installed."

My hands were sweating. Joe and the rest of the office may not know what a "signing certificate" was, but Liam did, and he looked like he was committing every word I uttered to memory. "Uh," I said. "Also, once your computer is infected with this stuff, it's possible that people other than the police or whoever bugged you will start to watch what you do."

Joe put his hand up again. "Explain?" he said.

"Oh, well, here's how it would work. Say I pay someone to bug your computer. Now your computer has some malicious software on it that can, I don't know, look out your camera, listen to your mic, watch your keystrokes, snatch files off your hard drive, the whole thing. The bug will have some kind of control software, a program that I run to access your computer. Maybe that program lives on a server somewhere else, in which case anyone who breaks into that server can then break into all the infected computers and phones and stuff. Or maybe it lives on your computer, so if I take over your computer, I can jump from it to all the infected computers. But also, if someone figures out that your computer is running the bug, maybe they can connect directly to your computer—like they could hang around outside your house and crack your WiFi password and wait for your computer to log on, and then snag it, or maybe they don't know who you are and they just sit at Starbucks all day waiting for *anyone* with the bug to join the network and then they grab the computer's controls."

Flor put up her hand. "How realistic is this? I mean, this all sounds pretty scary, but can you give me an idea of how many computers have been infected this way? In the real world, is this something I need to worry about? Or is it like being struck by lightning?"

I shrugged. "I guess I'm the wrong guy to ask about that. I've never used this stuff, never shelled out a hundred grand for one of these boxes. I'm guessing if the police buy them, they must use them. I mean, you could think of this as HIV. Your computer has an immune system, all the passwords and so forth that stop it from being taken over by parasites. Once it's bugged, it's got a compromised immune system. So parasites can come in and infect it." I thought a moment. I was calming down. No, that's not right, I was just excited now, and not scared, because it was kind of cool that everyone in the office was hanging on my every word. It made me feel important and smart. "Actually, it's like the *network* has an immune system, including things like Internet Service Providers who don't conspire to trick your computer into downloading malicious software. When your ISP's router tells you a file is coming from Google or Apple or Mozilla, your computer assumes that that's where the packets are coming from. But once you start monkeying with that, once you create a procedure that tells ISPs to start secretly lying to their customers, well, it seems to me like you can expect that to start happening."

"So what do we do?"

"Oh," I said. "Well, for Android, that's easy. It's open and free, which means Google has to publish the source code for the operating system. A group of privacy hackers have created an alternate version called ParanoidAndroid that checks a bunch of places every time it gets an update and tries to figure out how trustworthy it is. It used to be really hard to install, but it keeps on getting easier. I've made up a little installer script that you can download from the intranet that makes it even simpler. Just plug in your Android phone and run the script and it should just work. Let me know if it doesn't."

"But how do we know we can trust your script?" Flor said. "Maybe you're bugging us all."

Liam practically leapt to his feet: "Marcus would *never* do that—"

I had to laugh. "No, she's right. You're right, Flor. You've got no reason to trust me. I've only been here a couple of days. I mean, you guys asked me to work here, so it's not likely that I'd have planned to take over this place with malicious software, but maybe I'm the kind of guy who goes around doing it all the time." I thought about it. "So, you could google everything I just told you and download ParanoidAndroid yourself— but maybe I planted all that information there for Google to find. I guess it all depends on how paranoid you're feeling."

"I'm feeling moderately paranoid, with a side of prudence and common sense," Joe announced, getting a laugh. "I'll install it. Then what do I do?"

"Nothing, unless your phone throws a warning about an update. Then you can google it or ask me, or rely on your own judgment. There's a paranoia flag for Ubuntu Linux, too, if any of you are running that—it'll tell you if an update doesn't match up with the fingerprints on the public servers. Sorry, but I don't know about anything comparable for Mac or Windows." I stood with my hands folded again. "Is there any more pizza?"

Jolu threw a little instant browser chat app up on darknet for us, and started it off with

> ALL RIGHT, WHO SPILLED THE BEANS? FIRST RULE OF DARKNET IS NO ONE TALKS ABOUT DARKNET —Swollen Rabbit

"Swollen Rabbit" was the handle he'd chosen for himself— he'd also put up a nickname generator to help us all choose random, single-use, cool-sounding handles for the system.

I felt like he wasn't taking this very seriously—all those

caps and the jokey tone. We were dealing with a plutonium spill and he was treating it like a minor nuisance.

> This is serious folks. Swollen Rabbit, are you sure it was a leak from one of us and not a break-in? —Nasty Locomotive

> it's impossible to be sure but yeah. I've been over the logs and I don't see anyone except us. Maybe someone's got a screenlogger infection or something? —Swollen Rabbit

Oh yeah, of course. Maybe *we* were bugged. That'd be a weird form of humor: to use a bug to spy on someone who'd found a leak about bugs and then leak the leak to the press using the bug. . . . It was weird enough that it made me feel dizzy if I thought about it enough. I decided to fall back on Occam's Razor. The idea that someone blabbed was a *lot* simpler.

> I know I can trust you and the rest of our crew and Tasty Ducks

—that was Ange—

> but what about all your friends? —Nasty Locomotive

> Wait why should we trust YOUR crew? Who died and made you infallible? —Restless Agent

That was one of the people Jolu had brought in, though I didn't know anything else about him (or her). Jolu and I had decided it'd be better if we kept everything on a need-to-know basis. I didn't need to know who Restless Agent was, just that the handle represented someone Jolu trusted utterly.

But Jolu or no, I found myself getting ready to clobber this Restless Agent person. How *dare* anyone call Darryl and Van and Ange and me into question? Ange, meanwhile, had already read the message on her screen. She was sitting cross-legged on my bed, hair in her eyes, bent over her laptop. As soon as my fingers began to pound angrily on the keyboard, she said, "Woah there, hoss. Calm down."

"But—" I said.

"I know, I know. Someone is wrong on the Internet. Count to ten. In ternary."

"But—"

"Do it."

"One. Two. Ten. Eleven. Twelve. Twenty. Twenty one. Twenty two. One hundred. One oh one. One oh two." I stopped. "Wait, I lost count. Is one oh two ten or eleven?" I could count in binary when I was angry, but counting in ternary— base three—took too much concentration. "Fine, you win. I'm calm."

> You're right, you can't. —Tasty Ducks

> You don't know us and we don't know you. And we can't keep this up if someone here is showing off by letting blabby writers into the darknet. So what do we do? Shut it down? —Tasty Ducks

> I could turn on logging and make it visible to everyone. Then we'd know who got to see every document. If a doc leaked we'd have the list of everyone who saw it. If enough docs leaked we'll be able to narrow down the list and find the one person who saw everything —Swollen Rabbit

> Assuming only one person is blabbing —Nasty Locomotive

> Yeah maybe we're all running our mouths —Poseidon Snake

That was another of Jolu's buddies.

> Logging sounds like a good plan. If we can all see what everyone's done, it'll keep us all honest —Nasty Locomotive

> Unless I'm the rat in which case I could be
editing the logs and you suckers would never know
—Swollen Rabbit

> Ell Oh Ell. You're such a comedian. If you're the
rat we're all dead meat. Don't be the rat, dude —Tasty
Ducks

"All right, fine, that's settled for now," I said. "Thanks for keeping me from turning into Angry Internet Man."

"Any time. It was kind of weak for you to just say 'how can we trust your friends' where everyone could see it."

I wanted to argue, but it wasn't really an arguable point. After all, I'd lost my cool when Restless Agent did exactly the same thing.

"Yeah, okay, fine." I paged up and down through the monster spreadsheet with its 800,000-plus rows. "So what are we going to read through today, anyway?"

"More of the lawful intercept stuff, I guess. There's hundreds more suggested docs. Since the story's out there, it'd make sense to find out more."

"Okay," I said. "You take suggested docs from the first half, I'll take the ones from 400,000 onward. My mom says you're welcome to stay for dinner, by the way."

"Deal," she said, and we got to work.

One thing about the darknet docs I should probably mention: they were mostly unbelievably boring. Rows of numbers. Indecipherable memos written in bureaucratic jargon, laden with acronyms and names of people and agencies I'd never heard of. It was tempting to skip over these and look for juicy ones—or at least ones I could understand—but every so often I'd find something that made some other doc make sense, a piece of the puzzle falling into place, and I'd be glad I'd read it.

For example, there was a list from the San Francisco Unified School Board about schools that had participated in a "laptop anti-theft trial" that had run the year before. It used some kind of phone-home software on all the school-issued laptops that checked in with the school district every day or two. The district used it to track down stolen laptops—getting IP addresses from the software and turning them over to the cops. I noted without much interest that Chavez High was on the list of trial sites, the name standing out immediately, seeing as how I'd carried a backpack with the school's name through four years of attendance.

But ten or fifteen documents later, I found myself looking at a brochure for a product called LaptopLock, which was the product used in the trials. I wondered why Jolu's algorithm had tagged this stuff as relevant to the lawful intercept documents—which keywords had made it jump out. It turned out that the matching words were "covert activation" and "webcam." "Covert activation" was self-explanatory—if you had software that phoned home after a laptop was stolen, you wouldn't want it to advertise that that was what it was doing. "Attention thief: I am about to tell the police your IP address. Do you want me to continue? [OK] [CANCEL]."

But why would you want to activate the webcam on a stolen laptop? I paged through the brochure. Oh, right, to take pictures of the thief. The software could covertly activate the webcam—turn it on without turning on the little "camera on" light—take a pic and silently send it back to the school board. Well that *was* creepy. I wondered if any students had ever found a password and login and used that little "feature" to spy on other students. My laptop sat open on my desk all the time—when I was sleeping, when I was getting dressed, when Ange and I were—

Yikes.

So then I went digging for more docs. I had a product name now, something I could use to search on, and hoo-boy were there a *lot* of hits for LaptopLock in the darknet docs. I did my sort-by-date trick and found myself reading through emails from a worried IT manager at the San Francisco Unified to her boss about the fact that there was a principal who was using LaptopLock's administrative interface to watch students—not laptop thieves—at all sorts of hours, including early in the morning (when they might be getting dressed) and late at night (when they might be sleeping).

The IT manager had looked at the principal's shared-drive folder and found thousands of pics of students and their families, sometimes naked, sometimes asleep. There was also audio and video of students and their parents having private conversations. The IT manager's boss was furious—because the IT manager wasn't supposed to be "snooping" on school principals. The argument got more and more vicious, as the IT manager pointed out that her snooping was nothing compared to this principal, and ended with the IT manager's resignation letter. I felt bad for her—she was an honorable geek, and it wasn't easy to find new jobs in this bad old modern world of ours.

It wasn't just the San Francisco United School District where a principal got a little power-crazy with the old LaptopLock control panel. It turns out that pretty much every school district had someone (or a few people) in positions of power who felt that spying on students was part of their job. But in the case of the San Francisco Unified School District, that someone was a certain school board member named Fred Benson.

Once upon a time, Fred had been a vice principal at Chavez High, and from that lordly height, he'd presided like a warden or a king, doling out harsh justice against anyone who offended his delicate sense of conservative morality.

Such as, ahem, me.

But old Fred had "retired" when it became clear that San Francisco and California were no longer going to put up with a city occupied by the forces of "law and order"—that is, the torturing, kidnapping, lying paramilitary who'd taken the city hostage in the name of "protecting us from terrorism." It had been *so* sad to see him pack up his desk and hit the bricks, just another casualty of the war on the war on terror.

But Fred was a retired athlete, the kind of thrusting, vigorous guy who just can't take it easy. He'd run for the school board—unopposed, except for a crank candidate who'd been convicted of three counts of felony fraud in a real estate swindle, who nevertheless got nearly half the vote—and had been collecting a tidy public salary and enjoying his ascent to the exalted pinnacle of the education system by bossing around teachers and trying to impose his "leadership style" on the whole school district.

In case you didn't catch it, I don't like this guy.

But even I was surprised to discover that old Fred was such a prolific user of the district's LaptopLock system. After all, he wasn't responsible for students at all, but look at that, he requested so many specific LaptopLock activations that the district's IT department had given him his own login, to save on work. Someone in that department wasn't happy about it, and that person had helpfully logged Fred's many, many, *many* uses of the system.

Did I say uses? I mean *abuses*.

"Come on, we've *got* to leak this," I said. "I mean, come *on*, Ange. Seriously? You don't think I should go public with this?"

"No, Marcus, I think it's a really stupid idea. You've just got through yelling at everyone about a leak. Once you do it, everyone'll do it. We agreed that we'd catalog the whole dump, decide on the highest priority stuff, then publish it in a way that kept us all safe. If you get us all busted tomorrow, Masha and

Zeb are doomed. Hell, *we're* doomed. You don't have any right to put us all in jeopardy just to settle a score with some vice principal you have a hate-on for."

"He's a Peeping Tom! It's not just a personal vendetta. People have the right to know that this guy is spying on their kids. That could have been me, Ange. I've still got friends at Chavez High, kids that Benson *hates*—you can bet he's all over them, night and day."

"You're just picturing him sitting in his house and rubbing his hands and getting off on all his power and secrecy, admit it. Benson's not the worst monster in these files. Look at what the others have been up to. Look at 439,412."

I scrolled to the line, read the summary:

STATE DEPARTMENT BILL OF LADING. FREIGHT FORWARDING FOR LAWFUL INTERCEPT APPLIANCE TO SYRIA. SEE 298,120

And 298,120:

EMBASSY STAFF INTELLIGENCE REPORT ON TORTURE-MURDER OF DISSIDENTS CAUGHT WITH LAWFUL INTERCEPT APPLIANCE

"Oh," I said.

"Yeah," she said. "Oh. So cut it out. Maintain discipline. This isn't kid's stuff, it's the big leagues."

And before I had a chance to get angry with her—really angry, the kind of angry you get when you've been totally wrong and someone calls you out and you don't have any excuse so you get mad instead—my mom called up the stairs, "Marcus, Ange, time for supper!"

There'd been a time when we'd had "family dinner" practically every night—either something that my mom or dad cooked in a huge frenzy of pots, pans, clatter, and smells, or, if everyone was too tired, something from a delivery restaurant.

I'd even been known to cook from time to time, and I liked it, though it took a lot of energy to get started. Facing down the empty kitchen always seemed like a major chore. But I made a mean rack of lamb, and when I cooked pizza, there weren't ever any leftovers, no matter how much I made.

Family dinners had evaporated along with my parents' jobs. The contract work they got in pieces sometimes kept one or another away at suppertime, but the real reason was that they were trapped in the house together all day, and half the time I was there with them, and so no one much wanted to spend an hour at the table playing pass-the-peas. There just wasn't much small talk available to us. "How was your day?" was a painfully stupid question when the farthest apart you've been since getting up is about five yards.

But everyone put in an effort when Ange came over. My parents really liked her. Hey, so did I. Plus it was fun to watch her eat.

"Smells great!" she said as she came into the kitchen, as she always did. She already had her mister in her hand. When I'd met her, she was mixing up her chili oil at about 200,000 Scovilles, as hot as a mild Scotch Bonnet Pepper. But she was always in training, working her way up to higher heights of culinary daring. She mixed up a new batch of oil once a month, starting with a lethal, tight-stoppered bottle of crushed Red Savina Habanero in a few ounces of oil. She diluted this a little less every month, playing with the levels until it was just right. For Ange, "just right" was the temperature that made sweat appear on her upper lip within a minute of putting a drop of oil on her tongue.

A couple times a year, she'd actually taken the temperature of her oil, mixing a little alcohol in with her month's dose, then progressively diluting it in sugar water until she could barely taste the heat. The last time she checked, she'd been up to 320,000

Scovilles. It was around then that I started insisting that she brush her teeth between her eating and us kissing. I was starting to get chemical burns on my lips.

"It's just chips and sausages," Mom said. "Proper British comfort food, you know."

"Cooked by an American, no less," Dad said from the stove.

"Oi! *I* put the chips in the oven, didn't I?" Mom said. When Mom says "chips," she's speaking British and means "fries"—specifically the sweet potato oven fries she makes herself and freezes. I have to admit, they're pretty awesome.

"Yes, my dear, you certainly did. Plus, you supervised."

Dad set down the platter of faintly sizzling meat on the table. He once did some freelance work helping an organic meat cooperative with its data mining and ecommerce tuning, and when he'd written to them asking if they had anything else for him, they'd taken pity on him and offered to sell him some meat at employee rates. So we had all the emu, venison, and buffalo sausage we could want, as often as we wanted. I especially liked the venison, which tasted very good, assuming you didn't think too much about Bambi while you ate it.

Dad went back to turn off the stove's extractor fan, which had been humming loudly while it sucked out all the delicious meaty smoke and steam. Then he smacked himself in the forehead. "Wait, Ange, you're a vegetarian, aren't you?"

I hid a smile. Ange had gone veggie at the start of the summer, but Burning Man had brought out her inner carnivore—especially the trips to camps where they were handing out kick-ass barbecue.

"It's okay," Ange said. "Beef is just a highly processed form of vegetable matter."

"Riiiight," Dad said, and forked a couple of sausages onto her plate before sitting down himself.

It felt curiously wonderful to be having dinner as a family

again, with a big plateful of food in front of me and my parents making bright conversation as though they weren't in a mild, continuous panic about the mortgage and the grocery bill.

But it couldn't last. I had to say something stupid.

"I saw the coolest thing the other day," I said. "It was from a history of crypto in World War II and there was this chapter on the history of cipher machines—Enigmas and such—at Bletchley Park, in England."

"Which ones were they again?" Mom said.

"The ones the Nazis used to scramble their messages," Dad said. "Even I know that."

"Sorry," Mom said. "I'm a little rusty on my Nazi gadgets."

"Actually," Ange said, swallowing a huge mouthful of buffalo sausage, "the Enigmas weren't exactly 'Nazi.' They were developed in the Netherlands, and sold as a commercial product to help bankers scramble their telegrams."

"Right," I said. "And all the Axis powers used them. So the first generations of these were, you know, *beautiful.* Just really well made by some totally badass engineers, copying the Dutch models, but after adding a bunch of cool tricks so they'd produce harder-to-break ciphers. There were about ten iterations of these things, the Enigma and its successors, and they kept on adding rotors and doing other stuff to make them stronger. But at the same time, they were using up all their best raw materials on killing people. So by the end of the war, you've got this box with twelve rotors, up from the original three, but it's made of sandwich metal and looks, I don't know, boringly functional, without any of that flair and craftsmanship of the first generation. I guess they were in a pretty bad mood by then. They probably spent half their time overseeing slave labor or tending the death-camp adding machines. So, basically, everything elegant and beautiful in these things was just sucked out by the war, until all that was left was something you wouldn't call 'beautiful' unless you were totally insane."

"Woah," Ange said. "Symbolic."

I play-punched her in the shoulder. "It *was,* doofus. It was like a little illustration of the collapse of everything good in a society. I'll show you the pictures later. Those first-gen machines were *awesome,* just amazingly made. They were like works of art. The last versions looked like they'd been built by someone who was absolutely miserable. You'll see."

Mom and Dad didn't say anything. I didn't think much of it, then I saw a silent tear slip down Dad's cheek. I felt weirdly ashamed and embarrassed. Dad got up wordlessly from the table and went to the bathroom, came back a few minutes later. None of us said anything while he was gone, and the silence continued after he got back, his face freshly washed and still slightly damp.

He ate a few mouthfuls and said, quietly, "Amazing how a society can just slide into the crapper, huh?"

Mom gave a brittle laugh. "I don't think it's as bad as all that, Drew."

He put his fork down and chewed and chewed and chewed at his food, chewed like he was angry at it. The words that came out after he swallowed had a choked, tight feel. "Isn't it? There were three more foreclosures on our street today, Lillian. *Today.* And as for slave labor, just think about how much of what we own is stamped 'Made in China,' and how much of our 'Made in the USA' came out of a prison somewhere."

"Drew—" Mom said.

"Marcus, Ange, I'm very sorry," he said.

"It's okay, Dad," I began.

"No, I mean I'm *sorry* that you've inherited such a miserable, collapsing old country. A place where rich bankers own everything, where you've got to be grateful for a part-time job with no benefits and no retirement plan, where the most health insurance you can afford is being careful and hoping you don't get sick, where—"

He clamped his lips shut and looked away. I'd seen a bill on Mom's desk from a health insurance company warning us that we'd lose our coverage if we didn't make a payment. I'd tried not to think too hard about it.

"It's okay, Dad," I said again. His skin had gone pale beneath his beard, and it made the wrinkles at the corners of his eyes and in his neck stand out. He looked twenty years older than he had at the start of dinner.

"Cheer up, Drew," Mom said. "Honestly, it could be much worse. There's plenty who'd be grateful for our problems. Let's have a glass of wine and watch *The Daily Show,* all right? I PVRed it." When my parents got rid of their cable box, I'd built them a cheapie PVR using MythTV and an old PC. It only worked with the few HD broadcast channels that aired in San Francisco, but it automatically converted the files so they could play on our phones and laptops, and snipped out all the commercials.

Dad looked down and didn't say anything.

"Come on, Ange," I said. We were pretty much through with dinner anyway. And there were darknet docs to plow through.

Chapter 9

If you ever want to blow your own mind, sit down and think hard about what "randomness" means.

I mean, take pi, the ratio of a circle's circumference to its diameter. Everyone who's passed sixth-grade math knows that pi is an "irrational" number. It has no end, and it never repeats (as far as we know):

3.141592653589793238462643383279502884197169399375105820974944592307816406286208998628034825342117067982148086513282306647093844609550582231725359408128481117450284102701938521105559644622948954930381964428810975665933446128475648233786783165271201909145648566923460348610454326648213393607260249141273724587006606315588174881520920962829254091715363436789259036001133053054882046652138414695194151160923 . . .

And so on. With a short computer program, you can compute pi all day long. Hell, you can compute it to the heat-death of the universe.

You can grab any thousand digits of pi and about a hundred of them will be 1s, a hundred will be 2s, and so on. But there's no pattern within those digits. Pick any digit of pi—digit 2,670, which happens to be 0. The next digit happens to be 4, then 7, then 7, then two 5s. If you were rolling a ten-sided dice and you got these outcomes, you'd call it random. But if you know that 047755 are the values for the 2670th—2675th digits of pi, then you'd know that the next "dice roll" would be 5 (again!). Then 1. Then 3. Then 2.

This isn't "random." It's *predictable*. You may not know exactly what "random" means (I certainly don't!), but whatever "random" means, it *doesn't* mean "predictable," right?

So it would be crazy to call pi a "random number," even though it has a bunch of random-like characteristics.

So what about some other number? What if you asked your computer to use some kind of pseudorandom algorithm to spit up some grotendous number like this: 27182818284590452353 60287471352662497757. Is that random?

Well, not really. That *also* happens to be a number called "e," which is sometimes called "Napier's constant." Never mind what "e" means, it's complicated. The point is that e is a number like pi. Every digit in it can be predicted.

How about if your random-number generator gave you this number:

2222222222222222222222222222222222222222222222222
2222222222222222222222222222222222222222222222222
2222222222222222222222222222222222222222222222222
2222222222222222222222222222222222222222222222222
2222222222222222222222222222222222222222222222222
2222222222222222222222222222222222222222222222222
2222222222222222222222222222222222222222222222222
2222222222222222222222222222222222222222222222222
2222222222222222222222222222222222222222222222222
2222222222222222222222222222222222222222222222222
2222222222222222222222222222222222222222222222222
2222222222222222222222222222222222222222222222222
2222222222222222222222222222222222222222222222222
2222222

Is that random?

Well, duh. No.

Why isn't it random? Because if I said, "What's the one hundredth digit of a number that consists of a thousand twos?" you'd know the answer. You wouldn't be *surprised*.

It turns out a lot of people have spent a lot of time trying to come up with a decent definition of "random." One of the best definitions anyone's ever come up with is "A number is random if the simplest way to express it is by writing it down."

If you just went lolwut, don't panic. This is hard, but cool. So, take our friend pi again. You could write a program to print out pi in, like two hundred characters. Maybe less. Pi itself is infinite, which is a lot more than two hundred characters long. So the simplest way to express pi is definitely to write the "print out pi program" and not to write out all the infinite digits of pi.

And if pi is easy, "222222222222222222222222222222222 2222222222" and so on is really easy. In python, it'd be: "print ''.join(['2']*42)." Perl's more compact: "print 2×42." But even in verbose old BASIC, a programming language that's so flowery and ornate it's practically Shakespearean, it's:

10 PRINT "2" 20 GOTO 10 30 END

That's thirty characters, which is shorter than 22222222222 22222222222222222222222222222 to infinity. A lot shorter. So if we mean a random number is a surprising one—one that has no easily expressed pattern or structure, then we can say that:

A number is "random" if the shortest program you can write to print that number out is longer than the number itself.

This has a neat compactness to it, the ring of a good rule: short, punchy, and to the point. A guy named Gregory Chaitin came up with this neat rule, then he came up with a hell of a twist on it. He was so proud of this feat that he mailed a paper

to one of math's great mad geniuses, a guy called Kurt Gödel
(pronounced "Girdle," more or less) and messed everything up
by asking, "How do you know whether you've come up with
the shortest program for printing out a number?"

Which was a good point. Programmers are always coming
up with novel ways of solving problems, after all. And there
may be some hidden pattern to a number you didn't even realize was there. Say I asked you to write a program to print out
this number:

64641260024379684543777339026472512819416320076848
73625176406596754069362175887930785591647877272747392
72002910342949562447661308200729250734529170764226621
04767303786316995423745511745652202278332409680352466
76631908610112067458562873174135111622920788651329412
44815471628182079877168346341322362234117788231027659
82510935889235916205510876329808799316517252893800123
78174348968321515905624933473702068322321001186373957
70567473867102173212375224325241626358034376253606808
66916357159455152781780392177432282343663377281118639
05118930759016666507429527583840085446354193171905313
63659724905158409106582201814734799022359067138146905
11605192230126948231611341743994471483304086248426913
95023367134124251238640266572581309439676219396554073
86524229897879782198637918299709557924747320303239116
41044590690797786231551834959303530592378981751589145
76504080251094791234217584828418819501385461656803017
55035580054944894884871351605375593402345748979516602
44233832140603009593710558845705251570426628460035

Look all you want, you probably won't find any pattern at
all (if you do, it's a product of your imagination). So is it random?
Nope. It's part of pi: digits 100,000–101,000, to be specific.
Now you can write a *very* short program to print out that number: just add a line to the "print out pi" program that says,

"only start printing when you get to the 100,000th digit, and stop 1,000 digits later."

What Chaitin realized was that no one could ever know for sure whether a sufficiently long, interesting number could be printed out with a program shorter than it. That is, you could never tell whether *any* big number was random or not. In fact, maybe there were *no* random numbers. He called this "incompleteness," as in "You can never be completely sure you know if a number is random."

Gödel was already famous for the idea of "incompleteness," the idea that mathematical systems couldn't prove themselves. Chaitin saw incompleteness in the way we thought about random numbers, too.

As far as anyone knows, he was right. We basically can never know whether something is random or totally predictable. He is one of mathematics' great smartasses.

Fun fact: Gödel went crazy at the end of his life and became convinced that someone was trying to poison him. He refused to eat and ended up starving himself to death. No one knows exactly why he went crazy, but I sometimes wonder if all that uncertainty drove him around the bend.

I didn't leak the docs on LaptopLock. Neither did Ange. Neither did Jolu. According to the logs, we were the only ones that had touched them.

But they leaked anyway.

Of course, Liam knew about it before I did. He pretty much *ran* over to my desk as soon as he saw the story on Reddit. "You went to Chavez High, right?"

"Uh, yeah?"

"Did you know this Fred Benson skeeze?"

He didn't have to say anything else, really. By that point, I knew exactly what this had to be about. But it was worse than that. The pastebin dumps of the stuff about LaptopLock were all headed "DARKNET DOC ———" with the number of the document. The highest numbered LaptopLock document happened to be 745,120, and several people had already noted this and concluded that somewhere out there, there was a site called "darknet docs" with at least 745,120 documents on it.

We were blown.

"It's amazing, right? I mean, can you believe it? I wonder what else they've got?"

"Yeah," I said. "Huh. Wow."

Liam dragged a chair over to my desk. He put his head close to mine. He smelled of Axe body spray, which may just be the most disgusting scent known to humankind.

"Marcus," he said, in a low voice, "dude. You remember yesterday, when you were talking about root certs and stuff? It sounded like maybe you knew more about the subject than you were letting on."

"Did it."

"I mean, look, you're *Marcus Yallow*. If there's a darknet, you've gotta be all over that shit, yo. I mean, seriously, dude." He seemed to be waiting for me to say something. I never knew what to say when someone ended a sentence with "yo." They always seemed to be acting out some script for a bromance comedy movie that I hadn't had a chance to see. But Liam was so excited he was shaking a little. "Come on, hook me up, man."

Ah, there it was. Liam wasn't stupid. He was enthusiastic and a little immature, but he listened carefully and knew that 10 plus 10 equaled 100 (in binary, at least). His heart was in the right place. And Jolu had brought his friends into the darknet clubhouse. But I couldn't just randomly start signing up over-enthusiastic puppies like Liam without talking to everyone else. Especially as there appeared to be someone in our base, possibly killing our doodz.

"Liam, I seriously, totally, honestly have no idea what you're talking about. This is the first I've heard of it."

"Really? Like pinky-swear really?"

"Cross my eyes and hope to fry. I don't even have a Reddit account. I can't believe how much stuff they've dug up on the administrators who were using LaptopLock."

"Oh, that's nothing," Liam said, already forgetting his conviction that I was the ringleader of some leak-gang in his excitement at the awesome power of the Internet hivemind. "You should see what happens when Anon d0xxes someone."

I knew about Anonymous—the weird nongroup that was an offshoot of /b/, the messageboard on 4chan where everyone was anonymous and the name of the game was to be as humorously offensive as possible. I knew that they kept spinning out these subgroups that did something brave or stupid or vicious (or all three), like getting thousands of people to knock PayPal offline in protest of PayPal cutting off WikiLeaks. I knew that they had some incredibly badass hackers in their orbit, as well as plenty of kids who drifted in and out without knowing much about computers or politics, but who liked the camaraderie or the power or the lulz (or all three).

But I can't say as I spent a lot of time on them. I'd had my time in the cyberguerrilla underground and I had decided I didn't want any more to do with it, especially when it came to crazy, impossible-to-describe "movements" that spent as much time squabbling among themselves as they did fighting for freedom and lulz.

"D0xxes," I said, trying to remember what it meant.

"Yeah, they get really righteously pissed at someone and they d0x them, dig up all the documents they can about them that they can find—court records, property records, marriage, birth and death, school records, home address, work address, phone number, news dumps . . . everything. It's insane, like the

DHS turned inside out, all that weird crap all the different agencies and companies and search engines know about you, just, like, *hanging out there,* all of it where the search engines can find it, forever. The stuff they found about your douchey old vice principal is *nothing,* man. If Anon gets on this tip, *bam,* it's going to be *sick.*"

Now I remembered what d0xxing meant. Yikes. "Do you ever wonder if there's anyone else who can do that sort of thing?"

"What do you mean? Like the cops or the FBI or something?"

"Well, I mean, sure, yeah, of course they can do all this stuff." *And more,* I thought, imagining what you might dig up with a lawful intercept appliance. "But what about, I don't know, some CEO? Or a private military contractor?"

"You mean, is there someone like Anonymous out there, but doing it for the money instead of the lulz? Like hackers for hire or whatever? Oh, man, I'm totally sure there are. It's not like you have to be an angel or a genius to learn how to do an SQL injection or crack a crappy password file. I bet you half the creeps who used to give me noogies at recess are laughing it up at private intelligence outfits these days."

"Yeah," I said. I wondered how many of those particular kinds of creeps were drawing a paycheck from Carrie Johnstone and whether any of them might be hanging out in our darknet, messing with our heads.

I took a long lunch (feeling like a total slacker for grabbing extra time off on my third day at work) and asked Ange and Jolu to meet me in South Park, which was about the same distance from Ange's school and Jolu's and my offices. It was a slightly scuzzy little park right in the middle of SoMa—south of Market—but it had been ground zero for a whole ton of dot-com start-ups and tech companies and it was always full of the right kind of nerds. I felt comfortable there.

Jolu arrived first, looking cool and grown-up as usual. A couple of the people eating their lunches on the benches around us recognized him and waved at him.

"How do you do it?" I said when he sat down.

"What?" he said, smiling like he and I were in on some enormous joke together.

"I don't know; how are you so cool? I'm crapping myself over this darknet stuff, I look like I dressed myself in the dark, I can't figure out how to cut my hair so I don't look fifteen years old, and you, you're so totally, I don't know, you know, *styling*."

He gave me that easy smile again. "I don't know, Marcus. I used to be kind of anxious all the time, did I look 'cool,' was I going to get in trouble, was the world going to end or whatever? And then one day, I just thought, *You know, whatever's happening, I'm not going to improve it by having a total spaz attack.* So I decided to just *stop*. And I did."

"You're a Zen master, you know that?"

"You should try it, pal. You're looking a little freaked out, if you don't mind my saying so."

"Well, you know: 'When in trouble or in doubt, run in circles, scream and shout.'"

"Yeah, I've heard you say that before. I guess what I'm asking is, how's that working out for you?"

I closed my eyes and rubbed my hands on my jeans. "Not so good."

"Why don't you try just cooling it down for a minute or two, see if you can't get your head right before this all kicks off?"

If it had been anyone except Jolu, I might have been offended, but I'd known Jolu forever, and he knew me as well as anyone in the world. I remembered that feeling I'd had in the temple that time I'd lain in the dust among the gongs and the Omm, the total peace and calm that had washed over me like a warm bath. I could *remember* how that felt, but I couldn't *feel* it—the harder I chased it, the more elusive it felt.

Jolu put his hand on my shoulder and gave me a gentle shake. "Easy there, hoss. Don't sprain anything. You look like you're getting ready to kung-fu my ass. This is about relaxing, not stressing out. If it's hard, you're doing something wrong."

I actually felt really bad, like I'd failed at something. To cover up for it, I kind of hammed it up, putting my face in my hands and acting like I was experiencing some kind of artistic torment.

"Don't sweat it, Marcus. Just something to keep in mind, all right? There's the stuff that's happening out there in the world, which we only have limited control over, and the stuff that's happening in our heads, which we can have total control over—in theory, at least. I've noticed that you spend a lot of time trying to change the outside world, but not much energy on changing how the outside world makes your inside world feel. I'm not saying you should give up on changing the world, but you might try doing a little of both for a while, see what happens."

He was smiling when he said it, and I knew he wasn't trying to be a dick, but it still made me feel ashamed. I guess because I knew he was right. All my life, people had been telling me to chill out, calm down, take it easy, but for some reason, taking it easy was *hard,* while freaking out came naturally.

He looked worried now. "Okay, forget I said anything. I only brought it up because you asked. Let's talk about the current situation, right? As in, what the hell's going on with the darknet? Who's reading over our shoulders? What are they up to?"

"Good," I said. I was relieved by the change of subject.

"Start with the process of elimination, because we need to start somewhere. The logs say no one but me, you, and Ange accessed those docs. Are you *sure* Ange didn't leak them? Don't get mad, okay? It's just about covering all the bases."

"Yeah, I get that. No, I can't imagine why Ange would do that. She practically tore my throat out when I suggested that we should go public with the stuff about Benson."

"So *you* wanted to leak them?"

"What? No. I mean, yeah, of course my first reaction was to nail all those bastards to a wall, but Ange told me not to be an idiot and I reconsidered it. Besides, all I wanted to do was talk to everyone else about it, not go rogue and do it myself. I don't even know how I'd leak it if I wanted to—whoever's doing it is good. They stick it up on pastebin, and Reddit goes crazy and the press follows."

Ange arrived then, looking absolutely beautiful in a chunky black sweater with a pixel-art Mario/Cthulhu mashup worked into the front, black-and-white striped tights, and a red skirt. She topped it off with ancient, cracked motorcycle boots the color of old cement and a 3D-printed plastic bracelet on each wrist. Ange was basically the most perfect woman I'd ever known, and my best friend in the whole world, and every now and again I'd see her coming down the street or walking through the park and I'd realize that I was pretty much the luckiest man that ever lived.

There's no way Ange had been leaking stuff behind our backs.

She gave Jolu a warm hug and then gave me a warmer one, with a big long kiss that ended with me burying my face in her neck and breathing in the heavenly smell of her collarbones.

"Hey, guys, so have you solved all our problems yet?"

"Not yet, but we're working on it."

We unpacked our lunches. I'd made myself a sack of PB&Js

and thrown in an apple, some cookies, and a little bottle of cold brew before leaving the house that morning. I'd realized I'd need to start brown-bagging it when I started thinking about how little of my paycheck would be left over if I blew eight bucks every day on coffee, a burrito, and horchata. Ange, like always, had made herself a perfect and awesomely cute bento box with rice and vegetables and cold tofu and beef arranged in precise, colorful patterns. Jolu had one of his badass homemade energy bars, big as a two-by-four and twice as dense with all kinds of nuts and seeds, studded with bits of smoked bacon and dusted with his secret mix of spices. I'd seen him live off one of those for a whole day while on a camping trip, having a casual gnaw at it whenever he got a little peckish.

"Before we go any further," Ange said, around a dainty mouthful of rice and marinated eggplant, "Jolu, you're not the leak, are you? I mean, no offense, but—"

He laughed. "Yeah, I know. You should have seen Marcus here when I asked if he thought it could be you."

"Well, you've got to start somewhere. I'm not the leak, for what it's worth. I wish I was, because it would mean that no one was inside our security, messing with us. But Jolu, you haven't answered the question yet—are *you* the leak?"

"No, Ange. I wish I was, for the same reason. Because I don't like the alternative, either. I mean, either someone's really seriously compromised the security of my server, which would be pretty goddamned hard because there isn't a single byte of cleartext going in or out of that box, or—"

"Or someone's rooted your computer, or mine, or Ange's."

"Yeah."

That was the possibility that had been going through my head all morning. Someone with total control over my computer, someone with the power to light up the camera and the mic, to grab text off my screen or files off my hard drive. It wasn't a possibility I liked to think about. The darknet docs showed that Fred Benson had grabbed over eight thousand photos of *one* student alone, some poor kid the old bastard had a hate-on for.

How many times had my computer been compromised? Zero? Or eight thousand?

And more important: if my computer *had* been pwned, had it been "random"—someone scanning for vulnerabilities discovering my computer in a rare, unpatched moment and grabbing control over it—or had it been "special"? That is, had someone targeted me? Like Gödel, I wasn't sure I knew the difference between random and special anymore.

I don't know what Jolu told Restless Agent and the rest of his buddies, but there was no darknet chat accusing me or Ange of being the leak. I still didn't know who Jolu's people were, and didn't want to know, but I kind of assumed that they were people he worked with and that he'd gone back from lunch and had a little chat with them—hopefully away from any computers that might be covertly running their mics and cameras.

But of course, no one wanted to do much chatting at all on darknet, not without knowing who and how someone or someones were eavesdropping on us.

Long after the last person—Liam—had left Joe's campaign office, I sat at my desk, staring at my computer like it might have a live, venomous snake hiding inside it. I had stayed late at my desk, theoretically to finish up the day's work and make up for my little lunchtime face-to-face meeting, but also because I didn't want to try to deworm my laptop at home, not when I had an office filled with so many spare and useful computers lying around.

In theory, it should be easy to secure (or resecure) my laptop.

Find another hard drive and create an encrypted filesystem on it. Boot up my computer—or any computer!—with a boot disk downloaded fresh from the Internet, after carefully validating the checksum to make absolutely, positively certain that I was using a clean, uninfected, pristine version of ParanoidLinux. Then I'd install a fresh build of ParanoidLinux on the new drive, copy over the user data from my old disk to the new one, and I'd essentially have given my computer a fresh brain with all the memories of the old one, but with a high degree of certainty about the brain's reliability and trustworthiness. It all worked best if you had a couple of spare laptops and hard drives lying around, which the Joe campaign had—old laptops are one of those things that no one really wants to throw away, so we'd accumulated a lot of semiantique machines that had been donated by Joe's supporters.

Figuring out whether the old machine had been infected at all was a harder, more subtle problem. If someone had infected the machine and altered the kernel—the nugget at the middle of the operating system where you'd hide the most vicious spyware—I'd either have to go through it line-by-line looking for something out of place (which might take a hundred years or so), or try to build an identical kernel from known good sources and compare the checksums and see if there was any obvious dissimilarity. The problem was that I'd patched and tweaked my kernel so many times over the years that if the new one didn't match, it would almost certainly be because I'd built the new one wrong, not because I'd been taken over. At the very least, I wouldn't be able to tell the difference.

My computer sat there, staring at me from its little webcam, a ring the size of a grain of rice. The mic was a pinhole-sized hole set into the screen's frame. The first thing I'd done after getting back to the office was grab a roll of duct tape from the supply cupboard, thinking I'd tape over the camera and mic.

But I hadn't done it. It felt paranoid. I *was* paranoid. If there was someone inside my computer, that person knew more about me than anyone. But so far, all that person had done was carefully, effectively release docs that I'd been planning to leak. Maybe that person wasn't a bad guy (or girl). Maybe that person was on my side, in some twisted way. I found myself imagining the snoop: a seventeen-year-old like me a couple years ago, glorying in the thrill of being where he shouldn't be. Or maybe an old, crusty FBI agent, sitting in a cubicle in Quantico, making careful notes on my facial expressions and my kissing techniques with Ange. Or some thick-necked mercenary saving screengrabs of the most embarrassing moments so that Carrie Johnstone could laugh at them later.

It was eerily silent inside Joe's office. The street noises were washed out by the air-conditioning's hum. I looked straight into the webcam and started talking: "You're in there, aren't you? I think it's pretty creepy, I have to say. If you think you're helping me, let me tell you, you're freaking me out instead. I'd much rather that you *talk* to me than sneak around spying on me. And if you're one of the bad guys, well, screw you. Nothing you do to me now will stop the darknet docs from going public, and if I get scared enough or disappear altogether, I'll just dump the whole goddamned pile. Do you hear me? Are you there?"

Boy, did I feel stupid and awkward. It was like the one time I'd tried praying by my bed, when I was about ten or eleven and I'd been seized by a weird, sudden terror that if there was a God, He'd be really pissed off at me and my family for our total disbelief in Him. I didn't actually *believe* in God, but I had this wobbly cost-benefit analysis moment that went like this: *It costs nothing to believe in God. If the tiny likelihood of the existence of God turns out to be the truth, then He'll punish a failure of belief with eternal damnation. The consequences are terrible, but the risk is low. Wouldn't it make sense to take out some sort of insurance policy to protect against this tiny possibility?* My dad had just changed our household insurer and an adjuster had come over to look at the house and talk about whether we'd need flood and fire and lightning and earthquake insurance, and how much, and Dad and I had geeked out on the math together, which had been codified by Richard Price, a British mathematician who had been the patron of Thomas Bayes, my dad's all-time math hero. So I had insurance on the brain.

That was weird enough—but the really weird part was that once I got this idea, it got me, too. I couldn't let go of the feeling that I hadn't bought the right kind of insurance—I was believing in the wrong God—or that I wasn't sending my premiums to the right place—I wasn't praying right. I spent about a week in a low-grade panic about my religious incompetence, and it was always worse at night, when I was lying in bed, waiting for sleep to come.

So one night, I'd gotten out of bed and, feeling incredibly dumb and self-conscious, I'd gotten down on my knees beside the bed, folded my hands together, bowed my head, and closed my eyes. I'd seen kids praying this way in old cartoons—I think Donald Duck made his nephews do it, or maybe that was Popeye—though I'd never done it myself.

I had searched for the words. "Please, God," is what came out. "Please, God, please don't kill us. Please make us happy and healthy. Please tell Darryl's dad to let him have a sleepover with me this weekend. Please help me do good on my history assignment—" Once I started going, it turned out that there was a whole litany of stuff I hadn't known that I was worried about, things that I wanted some invisible, all-powerful sky-daddy to solve for me. It came pouring out. I started out in a low conversational tone, but I dropped to a whisper, and then just moved my lips, the way I did when making a birthday-candle wish.

And then, after I'd run out and said, "Amen," I opened my

eyes. My knees hurt. It had felt good to unburden myself of all those worries, and it had been surprising to discover them there, but at the same time, I couldn't help but feel absolutely, totally ridiculous. If there was a God, why would He care about whether I had a sleepover that weekend?

But what cinched it was the absence of any feeling of a *reply*. I'd spoken all my secret fears and worries, words so secret I hadn't even known they were inside me. I'd sent them into the air and into the sky, and the words had floated away, but no words had come back. No feeling of presence. No feeling of being listened to, or heard, or understood. I had spoken to the universe, and the universe hadn't given a damn. I stopped worrying about my "insurance premiums" that night, lost the nagging worry that I was meant to be praying to Allah or preparing for my bar mitzvah or joining the Hare Krishnas. In the space of an hour, I went from an anxious agnostic to a carefree atheist, and I'd stayed that way forever after.

That night, in Joe's office, I spoke words again into the air, sent them out to the universe.

That night, the universe answered.

> ooohhh busted

Unseen hands had dragged my computer's mouse pointer to the dock and clicked on the LibreOffice icon, making a new text document window appear on my screen with an inaudible mouse click. It was so spooky that the hairs on the back of my neck actually all stood up, and I shivered down my spine. I tried to keep a poker face, staring into the eye of the camera over my screen as one of my biggest fears in the world came to life before me.

I tried to think of something to say or do, but my mouth felt like it was full of ashes and my hands were trembling on the desk in front of me.

> you worry too much dude

With a deliberate effort, I got my arms to move, got my hands onto the lid of my laptop. I slammed it down, then I stood up so fast that my chair went over backwards. I found myself standing in the middle of Joe's office, shaking and goosepimply, and all I could see were the other screens in the room, with their webcam eyes, and imagine the ghostly, distant eyes staring out of them.

Willing myself not to run, I brisk-walked back to the wiring closet, seized with an animalistic need to tear the building's Internet connection out of the physical router, to turn us into a little lightless island of no-man's-land in the great glowing spiderweb of the planetary network. But once I got back into the humming, air-conditioned room with its server rack and its router and network switches and blocky uninterruptable power supplies, I found myself calming down, catching my breath. This room was full of computers, sure, but they didn't have cameras and mics. There was only one keyboard, a little clickety number that sounded like machine gun fire when you rattled out commands on it for checking or rebooting routers. There was one screen, a nine-inch flat panel with burned-in text from the password prompt for one of the routers. Everything in this room was familiar, and safe, and reassuringly technological. In this room, I was invisible to webcams, and in this room, I could program my routers to generate enormous, voluminous logs, whole libraries' worth of data about every packet in or out of the building. From this room, I might be able to set a trap.

The laptop sat back on my desk, the document window staring me in the face:

> you worry too much dude

"Are you there?"

Are you there, God? It's me, Marcus. A hysterical giggle welled up in my throat and I swallowed it.

Nothing. The air-conditioning hummed. Back in the wiring closet, the router was streaming a few extra million bits into its solid-state storage, the work of it all creating a tiny bit more heat than usual, making the air conditioner work just a tiny little bit harder. A puff of extra carbon wafted into the atmosphere.

I stared into the beady glass eye of the webcam, thinking of the unknown party or parties who may or may not be watching on the other end. I wondered how the bug worked. Did it phone home every time I signed onto a network, telling the snoops that I was online and available for watching and spying? Did it store up pictures of me and logs of my keystrokes when I was offline, waiting for an opportune moment to dump all this stuff?

Did someone's phone just get a discreet SMS? "MARCUS ONLINE NOW" and a cheerful ringtone? Maybe "La Cucaracha"?

"Hello? Anyone home?"

Nothing.

"Come on, you chickenshits, I know you're out there." Now I had the paranoid sensation that I was being recorded, that anything I said or did might end up on YouTube in ten minutes. I tried to butch it up, be as tough and cool as a superspy so that I'd be able to stand tall when the world saw how I reacted to the news that I was on candid webcam. "There's no point in hiding now. I know you've got root. I'll be shutting down this machine and reinstalling the OS just as soon as I'm done. Last chance to chat before I patch your back door."

I stared at the screen. It stared back.

"Fine," I said, and reached up to close the lid. For a second, I felt like I might be insane, like I might have hallucinated the whole thing. Just as my hand reached the lid, a word appeared on the screen:

> **wait**

I sat back.

"Nice to see you again. Do you have something you'd like to say?"

> **were on ur side dude**

"You've been spying on me," I said. I heard the tremor in my voice.

> **privacys dead get over it**

I felt the tremor now. These bastards had been spying on me and they had the nerve to tell me to "get over it"?

"You're not—" My voice caught. I swallowed and took a couple of breaths. "You're not on my side if you believe that. Do you have any idea how totally evil it is to do what you're doing?"

> **what a homo**

> **shut up**

> **felch me dickcheese**

> **ur sister said you like that**

I started to get offended, and then I noticed something. This wasn't a string of insults directed at *me*. Two or more people were arguing in my text window. One was a much faster typist than the other, and smoother.

"Are you like twelve years old or something?" I said. "That's it, isn't it? You're children, right?"

> **born same year as you marcus edward yellow 1320 rhode island drive san francisco ca 94107 . . . .**

> **. . . . . hey were both aquariuses. . . .**

> **. . . . . . . fish in tha hizouse"**

Hizouse was right up there with ending sentences with *yo* on my list of linguistic crimes. These *were* kids, even if Mr. Aquarius wasn't lying about his age. Emotionally, at least, these guys were children.

"I just want you to know that there's two people who might die because of what you've done. Those docs were given to me by someone who's been kidnapped since. You might have gotten some lulz out of it, but you've seriously screwed up the work we were doing to help our friends."

> we did it 4 zeb/masha you fag////// got tired of waiting around for you

For a second I thought they must be part of Masha's group, maybe her multicolored-hair friends. But then—Occam's Razor—I figured they must have learned about Masha and Zeb by eavesdropping on me.

"That wasn't your call to make."

> no? oppps. our bad. now what?

"What do you mean?"

> now what are you going to do? the docs are getting out there. you can't change that. are you going 2 help or wot?

"Am *I* going to help? What do you think I've been doing all this time? I mean, when I wasn't running around trying to figure out how all the leaks got out. When I wasn't wasting time on you pindicks."

> flattery will get you nowhere

> sorry d00d it needed doing

> you r soooooooooooooooooo slow

> what u waiting 4? carrie johnstone is pure evil

> btw u shld c wot we got on johnstone

> shes a very naughty girl

> worse than youd imagine from ur little docs diving

> the kind of person makes you want to believe in 92nd term abortion

> she will be fun to destroy

> bet she goes total apeshirt

> apeshirt

> apeshirt

> eff you eff ay gee ess
> marcus

"Yes?" I'd been watching the typing. I thought there were three of them. Maybe four.

> u need 2 dump everything now now now what u waiting for a rainy day? What you think masha/zeb are doing right now? enjoying a beach holiday? smokin fatties in a hot club? more like experiencing batteries strapped to their nipples

With normal chat, you get the whole message in a blip— there's a pause, then some text. But this was different. I could watch the typist on the other end typing, the hesitations and the backspaces, even a couple spots where another mysterious typist broke in and tried to interrupt, only to be furiously deleted. There was a lot of *texture* in this text, and it made it somehow less spooky. These were squabbling people, not all-powerful gods, and the fact that they'd pwned me wasn't an indication of their omnipotence or their moral superiority.

"I want to dump it all, but I don't want to go to jail. And I want it to make a difference, to put it into stories that people can make sense out of and care about. You've been watching what we're doing, you know why we're doing it." My fear was turning into anger. "What's more, we'd be a lot further along if we weren't screwing around trying to do damage control after you decided to start posting without talking to us."

> srsly? yr pissed that we leaked yr leaks? weak
> masha trusted u, u didnt have da stones. we do. suck it.

"So, what, you just happened to root my computer just in time to get on this little campaign? You only started spying on me at the very second that I started doing something you disapprove of?"

> when we pwned u is irrelevant. stop changing the
subject. u r 2 scared 2 do what needs doing. time 2
man up

"Or what? I make one call and all the darknet passwords'll
be changed. Give me an hour, I'll have my computers cleaned
off. You've got nothing, you little pricks, and without my co-
operation, you'll have nothing."

> thats what you think.

I kept my face as still and expressionless as I could. Of
course they didn't have "nothing"—in some sense, they had
everything. Depending on how much they'd been logging, they'd
have my passwords, my email, video of me, audio . . . and
they'd have Ange, too—her name, her discussing the leaks with
me, our makeout sessions.

"Yeah, you could ruin my life, but then no one will be in a
position to help Masha. Is that what you want?"

I had the sense that there was just one person typing now,
someone I started to think of as Final Boss, the über-snoop in
this little posse.

"We're going nowhere with this. I'm going now, going to
rebuild everything, change all the passwords. You want to talk
to me like people instead of stalkers, you know where I am."

> we certainly do

It took two hours to rebuild Lurching Abomination,
almost all of it consisting of painfully slow file transfers from
my backups and tedious verification of checksums as I downloaded my OS and all my apps all over again, making sure each
time that I had clean copies that hadn't had a single byte changed.

I dragged a chair into the wiring closet and did the rebuild
there. That gave me direct access to the router and its voluminous, verbose logs. I'd grabbed every packet going in and out
of the building's network, a senseless tsunami, a packetstorm, a

flood. Trying to make sense of the raw feed would be as pointless and brutal as trying to make sense of every mote of dust floating in the air. But dust is analog, and packets are digital. The router couldn't do much by way of large-scale statistical analysis, but it didn't need to—that wasn't its job.

VMWare had a fine catalog of virtual machines, preconfigured for heavy data crunching. With two clicks, I loaded one onto a cloud VM loaded on Amazon S3, ticking off the "private/ encrypted" box. I booted the VM with another click, then switched to VNC, a screen-sharing app, and now I was looking at the desktop of my virtual machine on that little flatscreen with its burned-in ghost characters. I had the router throw its monster logfile at the machine, and in about two minutes, I had all the pretty charts and graphs you could ever want, courtesy of hadoop, a free data-munging package that did to large blobs of data what Photoshop did to graphics.

I knew just enough hadoop to be a danger to myself and those around me, but by mousing around a lot, I managed to pare away all the traffic except for the streams that were being used to snoop on my laptop. It was hard to tell from a single session, but it looked like the spyware waited a short interval after the machine found a new network, then sent out a little encrypted blip that I figured meant "Here I am." A few milliseconds later, my computer got some bits back ("I see you"). Then, blam, an encrypted stream erupted from the machine. It was encrypted, so I didn't know what it was, technically, though I was moderately certain it was a feed from my screen, my camera, and my mic.

Hadoop had a handy traffic-analysis library that went further, hazarding a guess that some of the packets were from Kphone, a free Skype-style phone app that did video, and the rest were from VNC, the same program I was using. Which all made sense: if you were going to put together a trojan to take over peoples' computers, your fastest and most reliable method would be to just smush together a bunch of highly reliable, well-tested, best-of-breed apps. You could even keep it up to date with the bug fixes the apps released, piggybacking on their development, leaving you with more time to get on with invading peoples' privacy. I'd be willing to bet that the lawful intercept stuff detailed in the darknet dumps did exactly the same thing. Cops and robbers all using the same screwdrivers, and civilians in the middle, getting screwed.

Then I noticed something I should have seen from the start: the "I see you" message, the screen grabs, and the camera feed were all going to different IP addresses. I punched each one into Google and, of course, they were Tor exit nodes. My snoops weren't just encrypting the traffic from my machine, they were bouncing it all over the Internet so that I couldn't see where it was going. Somewhere out there was a server like our darknet dump except it had buttons labeled "View from Marcus's camera" and "Sound from Marcus's mic" and "Marcus's screen" and "Marcus's hard drive."

In other words, they'd taken the technology I used to protect my privacy on the net and used it to protect *their* privacy while they snooped on me. The irony, it burns.

That wasn't going to get me anywhere. Meanwhile, Lurch was back up to nominal. I'd even nuked its BIOS, the part of the computer that tells the rest of the computer how to turn on; a tedious process, but I felt like I'd be nuts not to do it. It was considered insanely hard to poison a computer's BIOS remotely, but if I was going to rebuild a computer that had been fatally pwned, ignoring the BIOS would be like changing all your house locks after losing your keys but leaving all the windows unlocked.

BIOS flashed, computer restored, trolls locked out, I shut off all the lights at Joe for Senate, shrugged on my jacket, set the burglar alarm, and stepped out into the cool night of the Mission.

And straight into the arms of the goons who'd been waiting for me in the parked car across the street.

I've been snatched twice. This was not the roughest of the lot (that would be when the DHS grabbed us off Market Street the day the Bay Bridge blew and clubbed us in the head when we asked what the hell was going on), nor was it the scariest (that would be when I puked into the bag Carrie Johnstone's squad cinched around my neck, convinced I was going to choke to death on Dumpster-dived pizza). It was so smooth and professional, I would have given them a customer service award if I wasn't so busy freaking out.

They stepped out of the car in perfect synchrony just as I came through the door. Two guys, big and beefy, with the "cop" vibe that always made my neck muscles go as tight as a tennis racket. One of them stood at the curb, covering me and watching who was around with a regular, predatory head swivel. The other closed the distance between me and him in three quick steps, coming right into my personal space, flipping a laminated DHS ID out of his pocket. Before I could look at it, he'd put it back in his pocket, as neat as a magician vanishing a card.

"Marcus," he said. "We'd like to talk to you for a moment."

When in trouble or in doubt . . .

"I'd like to have a lawyer present," I said.

"You won't need a lawyer, it's just an informal chat." He smelled like Axe body spray. It was the perfect gag-worthy aroma for a huge, looming goon.

"I would like to see your badge again," I said.

"You don't need to see my badge again. Let's go."

Run in circles . . .

I took one step up Mission Street, away from the goon, already looking around for passersby to call out to. A hand like a bar of iron wrapped itself around my bicep and *lifted,* and I felt like my shoulder might separate as my toes dangled over the pavement.

Scream and shout . . .

"FIRE!" I screamed. No one in the Mission is going to come running if you scream "Help!" but everyone likes to get a good look at a fire. That was the theory, anyway—what they told you in self-defense classes. "FIRE!" I screamed again.

The goon's other hand covered my mouth and nose with an airtight seal, his thumb hooked under my chin, clamping my jaw shut.

Maybe I should have tried "HELP!"

They did that cop thing when they put me in the car, pushing my head down with that weird rough/tender gesture so that I wouldn't brain myself on the door frame. But I was 110 percent certain that these two were not cops, or DHS, or any-one else on a government payroll. It was the gear in the car: none of your scarred, scratched, rubberized cop laptops like you got in the SFPD cruisers I'd been handcuffed in. These guys had computers that screamed "tactical," that matte black finish and those rugged matte black steel corner reinforcements, screens fitted with polarized privacy filters that made them ap-pear black unless you were sitting right in front of them. They looked like they'd been designed by someone who'd never seen a modern computer, but had had one described to him by some-one who spent a lot of time in muscle cars or Hummers.

They didn't just have a GPS: they had a crazy militarized one, with a hedgehog bristle of stubby, rubberized antennae and a street map display that showed the familiar streets of the

Mission using blocky, eight-bit-style graphics that looked nothing at all like any commercial GPS or Google Maps. They had these crazy armored USB ports set right into the dashboard, each with a pair of LEDs set under hardened glass. There was a strong new-car smell, like they'd ordered some kind of fresh spookmobile that morning to stalk me with, something they could douse in gasoline and roll off a cliff when they were through with it.

These guys looked like they had money, a lot of it, and weren't afraid to spend it. They didn't look like the sort of people who had to fill in a lot of crazy paperwork to get reimbursed, the way my dad had had to do for the books he'd bought for his department at UC Berkeley. The guy who'd been on lookout slid into the backseat with me—I noticed that there were no door handles on the inside of the back doors and wondered how he'd get back out again when he was through with me. This was a distracting thing to wonder about. It took my mind off what "through with me" might mean.

"Hi there, Marcus," the man in the back said. He *also* smelled like Axe body spray, which must be the national scent of Douchesylvania. He had a disarmingly friendly look: his tight, smooth-shaved face had all kinds of smile lines and wrinkles around his eyes. He projected this air of total relaxation and confidence, like the grown-up version of the Most Popular Kid on the Football Team character from a bad teen movie. "You can call me Timmy." If we were about to play good cop/ bad cop, Timmy was most definitely the good cop.

"I'd like to consult an attorney," I said.

He smiled wider. "I like that," he said. "That's exactly what she said he'd say, isn't it? She even got the voice down. Man, she really knows you well." "She" must be Carrie Johnstone, squirreled away in some lair somewhere, eating popcorn and regaling her underlings with stories of my weakness and patheticness.

These guys were here to shake me up, get me to say or do something, give them something: the names of the people who had access to the leaks, the passwords or keys, the locations of all the copies. They wanted to scare me. They *had* scared me. I felt like I could throw up at any second. I felt like I could piss myself.

No. You know what I felt like? I felt like I was *drowning*. Like I'd been strapped to a board, tilted backwards with Saran Wrap over my mouth, and had water ladled down my nose, so that it filled my windpipe. My choke reflex had come to life, sucking hard to try to bring air into my lungs. Each time I coughed, the Saran Wrap belled out, pushing out some of the precious sips of air left in my lungs. Each time I breathed in, the Saran Wrap formed a tight seal around my mouth, and the suction drew more water down my windpipe. My lungs began to empty and collapse. My brain began a kind of awful fireworks display, the last lights and noises of a panicked organ about to wither and die and rot.

That.

I was sweating now, all over my body, and had the feeling of a terrible weight on my chest. It was the weight of the knowledge that I was in the power of someone who believed that he could do anything he wanted to me and never pay a single consequence.

"Marcus, buddy, calm down, all right? We're not here to hurt you."

I hated myself for the weakness I was showing. I'd once slept badly, pinching a nerve or a vein or something in my leg, and when I'd stood up in the morning, my leg had given way like it was made of wood, and I'd pitched forward on my face.

Now I felt like something else—my inner strength, the place I'd gone to that moment on the playa at the temple—had let me down when I least expected it.

"I would like," I said, voice a gasp, "to consult—"

He slapped me. Not hard. In fact, he was almost gentle. But he was *fast,* so fast I didn't even see his hand move, and had to reconstruct what had just happened from the way that his body shifted, leaning forward a little, then relaxing back, his arm a blur in between. My face stung, but didn't hurt.

"Marcus," he said, and now his voice was stern and paternal. "Enough of that. We're not here to hurt you." *But you slapped me, didn't you?* Of course, he hadn't slapped me hard. And I had no doubt that he could have, had he chosen to. He was a good six inches taller than me, broad-shouldered, and the muscles on his forearms and wrists stood out in cords and masses like a superhero drawing. "We just want to talk to you. If you want to get this over with, you should listen to what we have to say."

I stared fixedly ahead of me.

"There's something you have, Marcus. Something important. Something that you've been gossiping about to certain urinalists in the big old world.

"The thing you have, it's not yours. It's our job to get it back. Once we're confident that we have secured it, there will be no further need for us to communicate with you and no further need for you to communicate with us."

I thought about asking for a lawyer again, but couldn't see the point. I kept up my fixed staring.

"I understand that a certain party has asked you to publish this material." What? Oh, right, Masha. "That party has changed her mind."

I was trying to keep my poker face on, but I suck at poker faces. He saw something change in my expression.

"You think that we beat her up or something? Forced her to change her mind?" He laughed (a full-throated laugh, like someone hearing a funny joke) and his friend in the front seat laughed, too (a mean little bark of a laugh, like someone enjoying the sight of a stranger tripping and falling painfully). "Marcus, buddy. That little girl was plain worn out from all her rough travel. She was tired of living on tortillas and beans, tired of hiding out in the badlands. She wanted what she'd had before, three hots and a cot, a big-screen TV and a minifridge full of Twinkies, all the luxury stuff. Living large. She didn't want to spend the rest of her life as a refugee, sleeping under a newspaper and eating out of the trash. And hey, we need people like her. Our group, we know her, some of us have worked with her before. We like what she does. She's good at it. We didn't beat her up, we didn't pull out her fingernails or drip candle wax on her skin. We just *offered her a job* and she took it."

This was so obvious a lie I nearly laughed myself. Whatever else Masha was, there was no way she'd sell out to these sick assholes.

But, well, how well did I know Masha, really? I'd only met her three times, after all. Only knew her by reputation, mostly, and it wasn't like her reputation was particularly spotless.

Zeb, though. No way Zeb would have gone for it. And I'd seen Masha and Zeb together. They were a unit. Or they seemed like it, at least.

"That little old man of hers," said Timmy, reading my mind—or my crappy poker face—again. "He doesn't really have much we need. We told her we'd keep him around though, if she wanted him. It's not like he takes up a lot of room or eats a lot of chow. Everyone's entitled to a pet. But she was through with him, not that I was privy to the, you know, intimate details. But they had words, is what I'm saying, and he went his way.

"I bet you think we're the bad guys. We're not, though. We're no monsters. We're good guys, Marcus."

Yeah, because good guys do a lot of kidnapping. Good guys blow up art cars in the middle of the desert and put a whole load of people in the hospital. You're a pack of angels. Thinking it, but not saying it.

"What if we take you to see her? We could do that, you know. It's a bit of traveling, though. Could take a while."

"You got all your shots?" said the guy in the front seat with a voice full of morbid cheer. "You don't wanna go there without all your shots, Marcus."

"That's very true. But if that's what it'll take to convince you, we'd be happy to. Who knows, maybe there'd be something you could do for us, too. Kid like you, you're at least half smart, which is smarter than most of the sheep out here. But I don't think you wanna go on a long trip right now, do you?"

The guy in front started the car and eased out onto Mission, and the guy in back put a gentle hand on my chest before I'd had a chance to move. A pane of opaque glass slid up between the front and back seats, and something happened to the rear windows, rendering them black. The only light came from the little dome light on the car's ceiling.

"Where are we going?" I said, and I sounded like a scared little kid, which is exactly what I felt like.

"Just somewhere more private, Marcus. Glad to hear you're up for a little chat, though. So, let's talk."

If I were a superspy, I'd have spent the ride counting hills and listening for the telltale cues of San Francisco traffic and figured out exactly where we were headed. But San Francisco is full of hills, and if you can tell one from the other while you're scared to death in a blacked-out box, you're a truer San Franciscan than I am.

Timmy hummed softly to himself while we drove. He had

taken my jacket and bag and he methodically went through the
pockets of both, taking out every bit of electronics—laptop,
phone, ereader, a little circuit tester I had stuck in my pocket so
I could check on the Ethernet wiring in the office—and removed the battery from each device, then put the device and its
battery in a heavy-duty freezer bag and set it to one side. Everything else got a fast but thorough examination and then went
back into the bag, except for my multitool, a cool little Leather-
man Skeletool that I'd coated in candy apple–red enamel using
the gear at Noisebridge. He turned that over a few times,
brought out the blade and tested it on his thumb—I kept it
razor-sharp—and smiled and nodded approvingly. "Nice," he
said, and I felt stupid pride that this badass ninja goon approved
of my knife. Maybe that's the feeling that Masha had felt when
she went to work for the DHS the first time around, or when she
joined up with Carrie Johnstone and tossed out Zeb—if that's
what she'd actually done.

The knife went into a baggie on the seat beside him, with
the electronics. He felt carefully around the seams and edges of
my bags, and I realized that he was doing the kind of bag search
that you would get at the airport if the people at the airport
actually gave a crap about finding stuff, instead of putting on a
little puppet show about security.

The car came to a stop. We'd been driving for a few minutes, or a hundred years, take your pick. The divider between
the front and the back of the car slid down with that kind of
purring near-silence of a really well-engineered mechanism.
The guy in the front, whose ultrashort hair revealed a gnarly
knob of scar tissue that ran from the crown of his head to the
tendons standing out in the back of his neck, turned around to
look at us. I looked past him, trying to figure out where we'd
come. There was water, some dark shapes that might be boats,
some industrial-looking buildings. I thought it must be China

Basin, a landfill neighborhood that was a mix of abandoned warehouses and factories and trendy condos and offices built into former abandoned warehouses and factories. Judging from the boarded-up windows and the plastic bags and other ancient trash caught in the trees, this was the actual abandoned part.

"Well, here we are," Timmy said, and rubbed his hands together. He and the other man exchanged a long look. "Marcus," Timmy said, turning back to me. "You know what the deal is now. We need what you've got back. We'll take whatever steps you make us take to convince you that that's the right thing to do. If you need us to take you to where your little friend is so she can explain the facts of life to you, that's what we'll do.

"I don't think you want that, do you? I think you'd like to have this unpleasantness behind you quickly and with a minimum of mess."

The other man twisted his face into an ugly smile. "You don't want a mess, buddy. You *really* don't want a mess."

I knew he was saying it to intimidate me.

But it worked.

"On the other hand," Timmy said, accepting a little bottle of mineral water from his friend and sucking back half of it in one go, "you could just give us what we want and we'll give you a ride to anywhere you'd like to go. You'd be out of this business, we'd get to knock off early and hit the strip bars, and you'd even get a free taxi ride out of it. It's up to you. Are you a smart guy, Marcus, or are you a stupid guy?"

I tried to find peace and calm, but it wouldn't come. So I looked for anger, which is an easy place to get to from scared, and yeah, there it was. "You guys are so full of it," I said. "You must think I'm a complete tard. I open up my laptop and nuke the file, and then what, you believe that's my only copy and you let me go? Please. If that file is so important to you, you're never going to trust me."

Timmy laughed and thumped the car door. "Oh, Marcus. Come on, we're pros. We know how to do this kind of thing. We don't want to take you along with us if we don't have to. Where we're headed, it's a nice place, it's a reward and an honor to get assigned there. The people there, they're elite. You wouldn't fit in. If we have any choice in the matter, we'll leave you right where we found you."

I tried again for a poker face. Yeah, sure they'd leave me. In a garbage bag at the bottom of the San Francisco Bay.

"Or maybe you think we want to off you? Now *that* wouldn't make any sense. Smart guy like you, you'd have lots of copies where we couldn't find them, but where they'd be sure to come to light some day if you weren't around. We want your co-operation, and we can only get that for so long as you're alive."

"And so long as you've got something to lose," the other guy said. Bad cop.

"Show him," Timmy said. The guy in the front seat got out and walked around the car, closing the door behind him with another well-engineered *thunk*. The car rocked a little on its suspension as he opened it and got something out. His shoes crunched softly on the ground as he came back around and opened the passenger-side door and slid in. He was holding a heavy-duty ballistic plastic equipment case, another tactical black number, with big, chunky latches that had worn away a little to show glints of silver metal beneath the matte black paint. He thumbed the latches and opened the case, which made a little gasketty, rubbery sound as it opened. It had been filled with foam rubber with precise cutouts to accommodate a little black box, some wires, assorted discs of plastic and clips.

"Polygraph," the man said. It was such a pleasant surprise that I found myself on the verge of laughter.

"Polygraph" is the fancy, semiscientific name for a "lie de-tector," a machine that's supposed to be able to tell whether you're fibbing by measuring things like "galvanic skin response" (another science-y word, meaning "sweatiness") and your heart rate. They were invented in 1921, and, like many science-y things, people decided they were so complicated that they must work. This, of course, is an insane reason to believe something.

Lie detectors are crap. What they tell you is whether the person they've been hooked up to is sweaty, or whether his pulse has gone up, but that doesn't mean he's lying. Courts don't admit lie detector evidence for a reason.

But they're still made and they're still used—for much the same reason that people still wear crystals around their necks to cure their diseases or buy "homeopathic remedies" to get better. It's a combination of two distinct flavors of stupidity. I call the first one "It's better than nothing." I call the second one "It worked for me."

These delusions are why many big corporations, the U.S. military, and the FBI subject their people to lie detectors. Imagine that you're some kind of millionaire big-shot company executive, the founder of a chain of successful convenience stores. You need to hire a regional manager, and if you hire the wrong person, he or she might rob you blind and ruin you. You need to get this right.

So you pay some expensive "executive recruiting" company to find the right person. They have a big sales pitch: we're smart, we've been doing this for years, and best of all, we're *scientific*. We have "scientific personality tests" we'll administer to make sure you're getting the right person. And before you hire that person, we'll wire her up to our lie detector and ask her some important questions, like "Are you planning on robbing the company?" and "Are you a secret drug user?" and so on.

Science is awesome, right? A scientific recruiting company's going to be totally badass at finding you the right person, using the science of hiring-ology, and their science lab must have a bunch of Ph.D. hire-ologists. But you've heard that the polygraph is, you know, kind of sketchy. Does it really work?

"Oh, sure," the consultants tell you. "Not perfectly, of course. But nothing's perfect. Polygraphs, though, *sometimes* tell you when someone is lying, and isn't that better than nothing?"

(The correct answer is "probably not." Flipping a coin or sacrificing a goat would "sometimes" tell you if someone was lying, if you had enough lies and enough goats and you did it for long enough.)

Now, imagine you're a section chief at the FBI. You got your job by passing a lie detector test. You'd been wired up, you'd been asked if you were a secret communist islamofascist terrorist dope-fiend. You'd said "no," and the machine agreed. It works! Now, some people out there say that the machine's a piece of crap, but what do they know? After all, it not only worked on you, it worked on everyone you work with!

(Of course, everyone it didn't work on wasn't hired, or was hired even though they're snorting lines of meth through rolled up pages of *The Communist Manifesto* while they strap on their suicide bombs.)

The world is full of science-y crap. You probably know someone who wears a copper bracelet to "help with arthritis." They might as well burn a witch or cover themselves in blue mud and dance widdershins under a full moon. There's a chance either of those things will make them feel better, because of the placebo effect (when your brain convinces itself to stop feeling bad), but there are an alarming number of people who insist that because something "works" it must not be a placebo, it must be "real."

These guys wanted to wire me up to a lie detector and sacrifice a goat and figure out if I'd lied to them. They were big and tough and rich, they were faster than I was and infinitely better armed, but they'd let a witch doctor sell them a magical lie-catching talisman, and so I was going to absolutely pwn them.

They were total dicks about it, too. They watched me enter my password on my computer, making a show of recording it with yet another black rubber tactical gizmo (it was like these guys had an infinite supply of grown-up Tonka toys): a webcam with a white LED that lit my fingers with harsh, uncompromising light as I entered it. They watched as I fired up TrueCrypt and brought up my hidden partition, watched as I did a directory listing and showed them the files, watched as I nuked them.

"Okay, that's fine. But what about your backups, Marcus?"

Maybe they weren't totally stupid.

"I've got a lot of backups," I admitted. "But I think I can solve that problem for you."

"Yeah? Tell me." Timmy was smiling again, all his smile lines crinkling, making him look like he was really enjoying himself and wanted me to enjoy myself, too. I started to get the feeling that Timmy might wear exactly that smile if he was cutting off my fingers or taping electrical wires to my nuts.

"Well, I encrypt all my backups, of course."

"Of course."

"And I need a key to get at the backups, right?"

"Sure."

"So what if I delete the key?"

"Haven't you backed up the key?"

"Yeah," I said. "I'll need to get online and erase it in a few places. But once it's gone, everything is gone. It might as well be random noise."

The other guy—Knothead—was holding the webcam with its bright light shining at me, and I couldn't make out his face. But when Timmy shifted his attention to him, he lowered the

light and I saw he was wearing a (tactical) earpiece. I wondered
how many times these guys dropped something small and important on the floor and lost it forever as its black paint job
rendered it invisible. I wondered if any of them had been goths
in an earlier life.

Probably not.

Knothead raised one thick finger. He was listening to someone on the earpiece. So the webcam must be streaming over
the net to someone else, a technical expert who was watching
everything I did, helping them figure out what to do. He nodded
twice, said, "Check that," and turned to us. "Do it," he said.
"We'll polygraph him later."

Timmy said, "I'm about to give you a WiFi password for
the car. You're going to get a chance to do what you say you're
doing. We're going to see what you do. We're going to verify
what you do. If we can verify it, you get to go home. It's that
simple. Do we have a deal?"

Before I'd been afraid. Now I was afraid they'd see how
happy I was. That was important, because what I was about to
do depended on them believing that I was very, very nervous.

I keyed in the WiFi password and waited while I connected. I wondered what sort of link I was on. I figured if I
were them, I'd be running everything through an SSL tunnel
to a Tor router somewhere on the net, so that everything came
through nicely anonymized. Why not? If it was good enough
for paranoid freaks like me, it'd suit them just fine. That was
the thing about this stuff. It worked equally well for everyone—
people who had leaks, people who worried about leaks, people
who leaked leaks. We were all smart enough to keep our
paranoid packets bouncing around the net like hyperactive
superballs.

Certainly, the connection was slow enough. I waited inter-
minably as my computer logged into the backup at home. "This

is my home drive," I said. I typed in the passphrase that unlocked the key on my hard drive and caused it to be sent to the disk on my desk at home. I let the camera see my fingers enter the commands to securely delete the leaks file from my primary backup drive, overwriting them with three successive passes of random (or "random") data, then did a search on the drive to show that that was the only copy. "That drive synchs up to one at the hackerspace, Noisebridge." I logged out and logged in to Noisebridge's open shell, pwny, the connection crawling over its layers of misdirection and encryption. "I'm nuking it here." I did. "Noisebridge backs up to the cloud. It's not a drive I can control, but Noisebridge resynchs every five minutes, and here's where the process logs." I opened the log-file with the "tail -f" command, which let us see new lines as they were being written to it. We waited in stuffy silence for the next synch, then watched as the log showed the Noisebridge server being compared to the remote copy, noticing that I'd deleted the leaks files and keys, and instructing that they be deleted on the other side as well.

I logged out. "Done."

"Do we believe him, Timmy?" said Knothead, in a teasing, mean way.

"Oh, I believe him, but you know what they say: 'Trust, but verify.' Your turn, buddy."

Knothead came around and opened the back door and swapped places with Timmy. He brought out each piece of his high-technology lie detector, examining it minutely, making sure I saw him do it. Back in the days of the Spanish Inquisition, the torturers had a thing called "showing the implements" where they showed the heretic the weird cutlery they had on hand to lift, separate, and disconnect all the moist, tender, painful places in his body. Knothead would have made a great inquisitor, and he even had the science background for it. It's a shame he was born five hundred years too late to get the job.

He fitted me with a blood-pressure cuff—yeah, it was a tactical cuff, which clearly made this guy as happy as a pig in shit—and then started in with the electrodes. He had a lot of electrodes and he was going to use 'em all, that much was clear. Each one went in over a smear of conductive jelly that came out of a disposable packet, like the ketchup packets you get at McDonald's. These, at least, were nontactical, emblazoned instead with German writing and an unfamiliar logo.

That was when I started puckering and unpuckering my anus.

Yes, you read that right. Here's the thing about lie detectors: they work by measuring the signs of nervousness, like increases in pulse, respiration, and yeah, sweatiness. The theory is that people get more nervous when they're lying, and that nervousness can be measured by the gadget.

This doesn't work so well. There's plenty of cool customers who're capable of lying without any outward signs of anxiety, because they're not feeling any anxiety. That's pretty much the definition of a sociopath, in fact: someone who doesn't have any reaction to a lie. So lie detectors work great, except when it comes to the most dangerous liars in the world. That's the "It's better than nothing" stupidity I mentioned before, remember?

But there're plenty of people who start off nervous—say, people who're nervous because they're taking a lie detector test on which depends their job or their freedom. Or someone who's been kidnapped by a couple of private mercenaries who've threatened to take him to their hideout if he doesn't cooperate.

But sometimes, lie detectors *can* tell the difference between normal nervousness and lying nervousness. Which is why it's useful to inject a few little extra signs of anxiety into the process. There are lots of ways to do this. Supposedly, spies used to keep a thumbtack in their shoe and they could wiggle their toes against it to make their nervous systems do the Charleston at just the right moment to make their "calm" state seem pretty damned nervous. So when they told a lie, any additional nervousness would be swamped by the crazy parasympathetic nervous system jitterbug their bodies were jangling through.

Thumbtacks in your shoe are overkill, though. They're fine for supermacho superspies for whom a punctured toe is a badge of honor. But if you ever need to beat a polygraph, just pucker up—your butt, that is.

Squeezing and releasing your butthole recruits many major muscle and nerve groups, gets a lot of blood flowing, and makes you look like you're at least as nervous as a liar, when all you're doing are some rhythmic bum-squeezes. As a side bonus, do it enough and you will have BUNS OF STEEL.

One of the reasons Noisebridge is such a cool place is that people experimented with stuff like this all the time. Someone heard about the butt-squeezing attack for polygraphs and told someone else, and before you knew it, we'd found a couple models cheap on eBay and were merrily hooking them up to one another and squeezing. You'd think that you could tell if the person you were talking to was clenching, but you'd be wrong. A little bit of practice and you can be a perfectly covert anus flexer.

"What day is it?" Knothead said.

"Wednesday," I said, clenching. This was how you started a lie-detector session, by getting the answers to a bunch of questions you knew the answer to, so you could see what the normal, nonlying state looked like.

"Is your name Marcus Yallow?"

Clench. "Yes." Clench.

"Am I wearing a black jacket?"

Squeeze, squeeze. "Yes." *And a black shirt and black pants and black socks and a black belt.* Clench, clench.

"Were you given the tools to download and decrypt a file containing confidential documents by a confederate at the Burning Man festival in Nevada?"

"Yes." Squeeze. I was going to have an ass you could bounce quarters off of by the time this was done.

"Were you born in San Francisco?"

Clench. "Yes."

"Do you speak Latin?"

"No." Clench.

Knothead went on in this vein for quite some time. It was clear that he was going to be ultra-sure that he had precisely calibrated his gizmo before he got to the good stuff.

Then: "Did you delete your copies of this file?"

Squeeze. "Yes."

"Have you got any remaining copies of this file?"

"No." Clench.

"Is there any way for you to retrieve a copy of this file or its decrypted components?"

"Yes. Some of them have been published already. I can access those."

He snarled, but Timmy laughed. "He's got you there, buddy."

"Excluding the documents that are already in the public's hands, is there any way for you to retrieve a copy of this file or its decrypted components?"

"Yes. I assume I can still download the encrypted torrent file."

Knothead jabbed a finger that was as hard as a steel rod into a spot below my ribs and a scorching ball of pain radiated outward from the spot and I pitched forward, gasping, gagging, feeling like I'd puke.

"Puke on me and I'll twist your head off and shove it down your neck," Knothead said, in an absolutely conversational tone.

I kept gasping, but the air didn't want to come back in. Sip by sip, I refilled my lungs. I hadn't thrown up.

"Is that going to decalibrate the polygraph?" Timmy said, sounding slightly irritated at the thought. I didn't for a second think that he was irritated with his partner for hurting me.

"Nope," said Knothead. "Watch." He reached out and gave me a firm, but not hard, smack across the face. "Hey, Marcus, you ready for more questions?"

"Yes," I said, and squeezed automatically.

"Are you sorry you were such a smartdick?"

"Yes." Squeeze.

"Have you deleted all the copies you possess of the documents you were leaked?"

"Yes." Squeeze.

"Do you still have access to the keys to decrypt any other copies you might find?"

"No." Squeeze.

"Have you told anyone else about these documents, or given copies of them to anyone else?"

"No." I squeezed. This was the big one. This was the one that determined whether they hunted down Ange or Jolu or my other friends and gave them the same treatment I got—and did to them whatever would be done to me. I kept squeezing and releasing.

He showed Timmy the screen. Timmy cocked his head and listened to the voice in his headset briefly. "Roger," he said. Knothead turned off the gadget. "It's all good, buddy. Nice work. Let's take our little pal here where he wants to go. Where you want to go, Marcus? The malt shop? The drive-in? You got a Bible-study class we could take you to? Eagle scouts?"

"I can walk from here," I said. I was bathed in sweat, and

wanted desperately to get out of the car. My eyes kept darting back to the handleless doors, my brain kept thinking, *This isn't a car, it's a rolling prison.* I was half certain that they were still planning to fill my pockets with rocks and chuck me into the Bay. That's what mercenaries did, right? Kill people.

"Now, don't be like that, sweetie pie," Timmy said. "We were friendly enough, weren't we? We're just guys with a job to do. And by the way, that job is protecting your butt from some really bad guys who'd love to blow up your house and put your mama in a burka. You've done your country a service to-night. You should be proud of yourself."

I didn't say anything. Everything I could think of saying was the sort of thing that would earn me another slap, another punch. Maybe worse.

"Where are we taking you, Marcus? Want to come to the titty bar with us?"

"I'll get out here."

He looked disgusted. "Suit yourself," he said.

Knothead ripped the electrodes off me and popped the door. I began to repack my bag, just throwing things in. As I reached for my multitool, Timmy snatched it up and dangled it. "You don't mind if I keep this, do you? As a memento, you know? Of our time campaigning together for truth and justice?" His eyes glittered with lunatic merriment and he suddenly looked more dangerous than Knothead. I shook my head.

"Keep it."

"Gosh, that's very nice of you, Marcus," he said. "Isn't that nice of him?"

Knothead laughed. I grabbed my bag and zipped it up, then shrugged into my jacket and set out walking. I didn't know exactly where I was, but it wasn't hard to figure out that walking away from the water would take me toward SoMa, and from there I could find Mission Street and walk all the way home, or catch a bus, or hop on BART. I got about twenty steps before I heard the car's big engine gun, and then I jumped to one side as the car roared past me, nearly clipping me. It was a final dick-move screw-you from Knothead and Timmy, a last reminder that I was a little pussy and they were big, tough guys. It was so petty it should have been laughable, but if it was so funny, why did I start crying?

Real, big, wet sobs, too, and snot running down my face. My hands were shaking, and my legs wobbled under me. I felt like my backpack weighed a million pounds, and I slipped out of it and let it drop to the ground, not caring about my laptop.

I felt . . . *beaten.* Like I counted for nothing. Like I *was* nothing. I tried to comfort myself with the fact that they were stupid enough to believe a lie detector, the fact that I'd out-smarted them. It didn't matter. They were bigger, stronger, better funded. They believed in lie detectors because they'd taken lie detector tests and so had everyone they knew, so they "knew" that the tests worked. It was no different from people who believed in astrology or faith healing because everyone they knew believed, too. It didn't stop these guys from being more powerful and stronger than me.

I made myself stop crying, squeezed my eyes shut, and tried to get rid of that scratchy, weepy feeling. I shouldered my bag again. I started walking. I needed to get home, get in touch with Ange and Jolu, tell them about this. Tell them about *everything.* My broken nose ached. It was nearly midnight and I was supposed to be at work in a few hours, with a proposal for turning Joe's campaign into "Election 2.0." I had no idea what I was going to tell him.

Maybe I'd just tell him the mercenaries ate my homework.

I didn't make it home. Halfway to Mission Street, I kept going to Market, kept walking to Hayes Valley and Ange's place. I stood at her door, dithering. It was late and every light was off in the house, and the battery on my phone was dead so I couldn't even call. I was going to have to ring the bell and wake up the whole house. Or I was going to have to go home and spend the night alone. I couldn't face that.

I realized I could sit down on the front step, get out my laptop, log on to Ange's WiFi, and use Skype to call her phone and wake her up. It was a perverse way of making a phone call to a person who was about ten yards away from me, but it was also how I made my cell phone ring when I couldn't remember where I put it. Ange's window must have been open a crack because as the Skype call rang, I could hear her ringtone—the *Doctor Who* Tardis *whoosh-whoosh* sound—floating out over the street.

"Who is this?" Skype calls came up UNKNOWN NUMBER.

"It's me. I'm downstairs. Let me in."

"Downstairs where?"

"Downstairs here. Like, right below you." I heard movement over my computer's speakers and through the window and the bones of the house: Ange getting on a bathrobe and coming down the stairs. A moment later, the chain scraped on the door and the dead bolts snapped open and the door opened and there was Ange. My computer started to play a feedback squeal as Ange's phone got too close to it and I flipped the lid shut as she stabbed at her phone's screen with a finger to hang it up.

"Marcus?"

"Let me in, okay?"

I love Ange. She kissed me hard on the mouth, grabbed my hand, and pulled me inside the house. We went upstairs together, tiptoeing, and before I went into her room, I whispered, "Is your computer on?"

She cocked her head at me. "Yeah."

"Go shut it off, okay?"

I waited outside her door while she went into her room and moved around. She opened her door, holding her laptop in one hand and its battery in the other.

"I think you'd better tell me what's going on."

I thought I'd have the biggest news of the night, but I was wrong.

"How sure are you that your computer is safe?" Ange said, when I was finished telling her my story. It wasn't exactly what I was expecting her to say at that juncture.

"Yes, I'm fine, just a little shaken up, thank you for asking," I said.

"Forget that for now. Do you think your computer is clean? Do you trust it enough to get into the darknet?"

Only now did I notice what I should have seen right away. Ange was freaked out, too, and not just because of what I had to tell her.

"What is it?"

"Do. You. Trust. Your. Computer—"

"Yes, yes," I said. I woke it up and started typing and clicking.

"Search the database," she said. "Look for Zyz. That's zee-why-zee."

"What's a 'zyz'?"

She gave me a "don't ask stupid questions" look. I typed.

Chapter 10

2y2 wasn't always called 2y2. It was once called Fireguard Security, and it was founded by an exec at Halliburton, a giant military contractor that sucked a bazillion dollars out of America's bank accounts selling pricey, underperforming military services to our troops all over the world, then followed up by helping to build a couple of semidefective, way-over-budget oil wells, including one that may yet be responsible for the sterilization of the Gulf of Mexico.

Halliburton had a "dynamic, thrusting young VP" (seriously, that's what *Fortune* magazine called him) named Chambers Martin, who quit the company in 2008 to found Fireguard, which immediately began to make major bank by taking U.S. Army contracts to guard Halliburton supply convoys in Iraq and Afghanistan.

So far, so normal. There are plenty of companies who bled out the taxpayer by providing bloodthirsty mercs. They guarded truckloads of Twinkies around Kandahar Province and Fallujah to restock the Forward Operating Bases that were a cross between an armed fortress and a minimall. The Army paid them enormous fees to have soldiers' clothes laundered and to supply Internet access and Pizza Hut.

But Fireguard had bigger plans. Rather than simply sucking

up tax dollars for substandard services, they decided to be-come . . . a bank. Specifically, they began to issue bonds based on their anticipated future U.S. government contracts. The sim-plest bonds are basically loans: I sell you a bond for $100 with a five percent return and then I pay you $5 a year over the term of the bond (say, five years), and when the bond runs out its term, say, five years, we're done. Of course, if I go broke before the bond runs out, I go bankrupt and you're screwed.

Fireguard was selling its debt left, right, and center, paying top interest rates, telling everyone that the gravy train could never end, because every year they were taking in bigger mili-tary contracts, which meant that every year, they'd have more money on hand to make their bonds' payouts. It worked great, until the military drawdowns started to reduce their annual revenues, and they needed to branch out.

So they started trading bonds, instead of just issuing them, beginning with bonds issued on student loan debt. It turned out that every dollar I borrowed to go to Berkeley got turned into a bond—someone with money bought the right to get paid every time I made a payment on my debt. This made big bucks for Berkeley and for other universities and companies that "gave" students the loans they needed to get their magic diploma paper. Student debt bonds are even better than skeezy military con-tractor debt bonds because a skeezy military contractor can go bankrupt, but students can't.

Bet you didn't know that, huh? If you borrowed money to go to college and you someday find yourself so flat broke that you have to go bankrupt, all your debts will be wiped off the books—credit cards, car notes—but your student debts are im-mortal. And whenever you miss a payment, the scuzzy finance companies that buy the debts from universities are allowed to jack your debt up with monster fees and penalties, so if you owe $30,000 for college and $50,000 in credit card debt and you go

bankrupt, you'll find the credit card debt reduced or elimi-
nated, but your student debt might grow to *$150,000* after all
the missed-payment fees are tacked on. The way student debt
bankruptcy laws are set up, they can take money out of your
Social Security check to pay the student loans you took out as
a teenager, even if you've already paid *millions* in fees and
penalties.

Zyz liked the sound of this. So they took the money that
was coming in from the sale of their bonds and started buying
up student debt. But not just any student debt: desperate, miserable student debt. Debt carried by the poorest people in America, who had put themselves into permanent hock just to try to
get a better job than their parents had by getting a degree.

These people were in trouble. Getting a college degree (or,
ahem, dropping out of college) hadn't led to them getting great
jobs. They were unemployed, or working a ton of crappy part-
time jobs to make rent, and they were missing payments like
crazy. They had debts that they could never, ever pay off.

Enter Zyz. They had a dynamic, thrusting plan to get people
to pay: straight-up thuggery. Zyz knew a lot about scaring,
hurting, and chasing people. They had deep connections with
Homeland Security, which meant access to databases of who
lived where, who they were related to, what their tax returns
said, how much income their parents, ex-spouses, grandparents,
cousins, and school pals made. Zyz was . . . aggressive . . . about
using this information. Thrusting, even.

So far, so sleazy. But it got worse. People who owed money
to Zyz started to do things that were pretty out of character for
them: a couple armed robberies, some burglaries, a little blackmail. A bunch of them joined the military, only to be dis-
charged for being grossly unfit for service.

Why were they doing this? Because Zyz was providing them
with "financial advice." As in "You'd better find some way to

pay your bills, pal, or things could get very, very bad for you and the people you love." Zyz wasn't just a private military service, and they weren't just high-flying financial engineers: they were the mafia.

All this was contained in a series of memos, including a bunch of letters from attorneys general and district attorneys who'd gotten complaints from Zyz's "clients." Zyz, of course, denied everything, while simultaneously getting friends of theirs in state and national government, law enforcement, and the DHS itself to keep everything calm and easy.

The most damning memo came from a San Francisco city attorney who'd heard too many nearly identical stories from Zyz clients, and had painstakingly built a case against them, with mountains of supporting documents (all also included in the docs), only to have her boss tell her to forget about it because "there wasn't sufficient evidence to justify an additional investigation at this time."

Well, this lady—I cheered her on as I read—wasn't going to take this lying down. She continued to collect stories from Zyz's victims, and to pick away at Zyz's finances, trying to find the "sufficient evidence" that would convince her boss. This continued right up to the time that her bank foreclosed on her house, citing payments in arrears. Being woken up at 6 A.M. and thrown out of her house with her husband and two small children turned her into a full-time, professional prisoner of a bureaucratic nightmare, trying to clear her name and credit and get her house back.

That's where her story ended, but not Zyz's. Zyz had hired lobbyists in every state capital in America—which must have cost a fortune, and gave me an idea of the kind of money they were sucking in from buying and selling their dirty bonds—to push for legislation that allowed them "greater leeway" in going after the assets of parents and even grandparents of ex-students who owed money, especially when the ex-students were living at home. Translation: if you owed for your student loans and were so broke you had to live with your parents (ahem), they wanted to go after your folks' house, their wages, and their pension. They didn't just want to wait to raid *your* Social Security check; they wanted to raid your grandma's Social Security.

These lobbyists had been busy everywhere, but especially in California, where youth unemployment was leading the country, and where, thanks to skyrocketing tuition in the UC state system, there were also record numbers of dropouts like me, whose student debts had come due early, and Zyz wanted our parents' dough.

Now that elections were coming up, Zyz was spreading around a lot of money. They had dozens of subsidiaries for doing this, but once again, some hardworking whistle-blower (his or her name was scrubbed out of the memo) had compiled a list of them and pointed out that they had donated to every "serious" candidate in every race, often backing opposing candidates—anyone who stood a chance of ending up on an important committee if she or he won the election.

Once the darknet team had known to search for Zyz, they'd uncovered a *mountain* of stuff like this. Including something that jumped out at me: Zyz had hired a top-notch head of security with years of DHS and military experience: Carrie Johnstone.

"Holy crap," I said.

"Yeah," Ange said. "This is why they're so freaked out. This is their big push. They've been buying up all this debt—cheap bonds backed by student loans from really broke-ass kids. If they can go after those kids' families' houses, they'll make millions—hundreds of millions."

"So what happens if we go public?"

"*If* we go public? What do you mean, 'if'?" She was looking at me like I'd grown another head.

"Ange," I said, putting up my hands. "You know. These guys, you've read about them. They know who I am. They know I'm the guy who got the leaks from Masha. If this stuff gets out, they'll—"

"What? Marcus, they're insane criminals. You're not going to keep yourself safe by going along with them. If it suits them, they'll come after you again. And what about Masha? Those hacker creeps might've been total dicks, but they're right about her. She trusted you to be her insurance policy and instead you've spent your time cataloging the evidence—"

"Wait, what? I've spent my time? You've spent your time, too, Ange. We all agreed that we needed to go through the darknet docs before we put them out, find out what we had, decide on a strategy—"

"Marcus, that's what *you* wanted, so that's what we did. There was no reason you couldn't have just tweeted the torrent name and the key and said, 'DOWNLOAD THIS NOW. IT'S FULL OF CRIMINAL STUFF.' You've got what, ten thousand followers? Once you did that, the file would be unkillable."

"Masha's not unkillable," I shot back.

"You don't even know if she's working with those creeps—"

"Ange, come on, you're not making sense. A second ago, you were telling me how evil I was because I hadn't released the docs to save Masha. Now you're saying it doesn't matter if we put Masha in danger because *she* might be evil? Which one is it?"

Ange shook her head. "It doesn't matter. What matters is that you could be doing something here, and instead you're doing your run in circles, scream and shout act."

"I just want to have a *plan* before I do something, Ange. What's wrong with that?"

"I've got a plan for you, Marcus. Step one: tell everyone how to get to the docs. Step two: there is no step two."

I felt trapped. Our voices kept getting louder, and I was worried that we'd wake up Ange's mom and sister. If we'd been arguing in public—in a park or something—I might have gotten up and walked away to cool off. But it was going on 2 A.M. Where was I going to go? And of course, all this only made me *more* angry.

"Sure, it's that easy. Especially if you're not the one getting kidnapped and threatened."

She was ready for that one. "You don't think they've figured out who I am? You don't think I'm next on the list if we publish this stuff? Marcus, I don't *care* what happens to me. This is too important to let my safety come first. This is bigger than me."

"Nice of you to volunteer me to give up my safety, too."

"I didn't think I had to volunteer you, Marcus. I thought that M1k3y would be right there, ready to fight for what was right, rather than screwing around with getting everything perfectly organized and *safe* before he took action."

There it was. Pretty much everything I'd been afraid of, laid out by the one person I loved, trusted, and needed more than anyone else in the world. There's only one thing worse than being shredded unfairly by someone like that: being shredded when you deserve it.

"Ange—" I began.

"Forget it," she said. "Let's just go to sleep."

We lay in bed next to each other, like two marble statues, rigid, not touching. I kept replaying the discussions I'd had that day and that night, the anonymous hackers who'd been in my computer, the thugs from Zyz, and Ange, furious and disappointed with me. Around and around they went, a chorus of shame and accusations.

When they got too loud, I stood up and started putting on my clothes, fumbling in the dark. I heard Ange hold her breath, expel it, start to say something, stop.

Half-dressed, shoes undone, my bag hastily restuffed with my crap, I stepped out of Ange's room and let myself down the stairs and out the front door.

At least I'd had the foresight to charge my phone. I scrolled through the speed dial. I suppose I could have called my parents, but what could I say to them? How could they help?

There were two people in my speed dial I hadn't called in months and months. They'd been autosorted to the bottom of the list. Only the fact that I'd manually favorited them kept them from being dropped altogether.

Darryl and Van.

I let my thumb hover over Darryl's picture for a long second as I walked down toward Market Street, thinking of how awkward it had been to talk with him, knowing that Van had confessed her crush on me and not knowing whether Darryl knew it, knowing that Van and Ange had hated each other for years and that this couldn't have made it any better, wondering all the time whether Darryl hated me for being his rival or hated my girlfriend for whatever grievance Van held. The days between our talks had turned to weeks, the weeks to months. The longer the gap between conversations and meetings, the weirder and more uncomfortable it would be to get back in touch—the more it would seem like some special occasion.

It was cold now, and I was shivering, and once I started shivering, it felt like something inside me was giving way and then I was shivering for reasons other than the cold, and I pressed the button. It was after three in the morning. It rang and rang.

"Hi, this is Darryl. Leave a message, or better yet, send me a text or an email."

I hung up.

It was funny how I could feel all alone and under surveillance at the same time. I had ParanoidAndroid installed, but that didn't mean that my phone wasn't rooted—just that it would be harder to root. Had it been in my line of sight the whole time I'd been in the car with Knothead and Timmy had control over it? Had the creeps who'd taken over my laptop taken a run or two at my phone?

It was all for the best. Waking someone up at three in the morning while you're having a meltdown is no way to restart a friendship—

My phone rang. Darryl.

"Hey, man."

"Are you okay, Marcus?" He sounded so genuinely concerned I wanted to cry again.

Sorry, dude, just pressed the wrong button—butt-dialing. Sorry. Go back to sleep. The words were on the tip of my tongue. They wouldn't come.

"No," I said. "No, I'm not." A siren screamed past me, a fire engine, and I jumped and gave a little squeak.

"Where are you?" he said.

I looked up at the street signs. "Market and Guerrero."

"Stay there," he said. "Be there in fifteen."

Friends.

Darryl's dad hadn't lost his job in the Berkeley layoffs, though he'd taken a "voluntary" pay cut. But things weren't so bad that they'd sold their car, a ten-year-old Honda that Darryl had his own keys for. It was fugly and held together with bondo and good thoughts, but it was a car, and capable of getting from Twin Peaks to downtown in fifteen minutes at 3 A.M., though I'm guessing that Darryl blew through a few yellow lights and maybe a red or two to make that time.

It pulled up to the curb and the locks popped, and I opened the door and slid in, my nose filling with the familiar smell of the car, which I'd ridden in a million times before: old coffee, a hint of McDonald's breakfast sandwich, the baked/mildewed smell of a vehicle that had spent a lot of time with its windows rolled up in the alternating scorching heat and misty cool of the Berkeley campus.

He was wearing track pants and a T-shirt, and his feet were bare in his unlaced Converse, big toe poking through a hole in the right one. Darryl had humongous feet, and his shoes were always going out at the toes.

The first words he said weren't "What's wrong?" or "Do you know what time it is?" or "You owe me, buddy, big time."

The first words he said were, "It's great to see you again, bud."

It was the best thing he could have said. "Yeah," I said. "Yeah, it's great to see you, too."

I tried to find some words, some place to start the story. He knew about the darknet, had been going through the docs. Presumably, he'd seen the Zyz docs, helped to assemble them. But there was so much to say, and I couldn't figure out where to begin. I closed my eyes to think and the next thing I knew, he was shaking me awake. I ungummed my eyelids and looked around. We were outside his dad's place, which had once been as familiar to me as my own home.

"Come on, bud," he said, "up you go."

I stumbled after him, scuffing my boots on the ground,

kicking them off in the doorway, trailing after him up to the bedroom.

I barely registered that Van was in his bed, sitting up in the dark, wearing a T-shirt, hair in a crazy anime-spray. "Hey, Van," I said, as Darryl steered me to the narrow camping mattress that was already laid out at the foot of the bed. I flopped down on it, eyes closing before my head hit the pillow. Someone— Darryl—tried to make me roll off the bed so that he could pull the spare blanket out from under me and cover me with it, but I wasn't budging. I was made of lead. My body knew that it was somewhere safe, with people I could trust, and it was not going to allow me to keep it awake one second longer. A half-formed thought about setting an alarm so I wouldn't be late for work crossed my mind, but my hands were as heavy as cinder blocks, and my phone was a million miles away in my pocket. Besides, I was already asleep.

I woke to the smells of bacon and eggs and toast and, most of all, coffee. The bedroom was empty, filled with gray light filtering through the heavy blinds. I pulled them aside and saw that it was broad daylight. I checked my phone, noting the ache as I pulled it out—I'd slept on it—and saw that it was 11:24. I was incredibly late for work. My adrenals tried to fire and fill me with panic, but I was empty. Instead, I felt a kind of low-grade anxiety as I had a quick pee and headed downstairs into the sunny kitchen.

The light dazzled me and I shaded my eyes, provoking laughter from Darryl and Van, who were dancing around the kitchen in a clatter of pans and plates and glasses and mugs.

"Told you that'd get him up," Darryl said. "The boy thinks with his stomach."

Van giggled. "That's a good six inches higher than most

boys' thought-centers." They smooched. Were Ange and I this sickening? Probably, I decided.

"Guys," I said. "I really, really owe you, but I can't stay for breakfast. I'm late—"

"For work," Darryl said. "I know. Which is why I called your mom and she called your boss and told him you were feeling poorly and would work from home for the morning and try to come in this afternoon. You're covered, bro. Sit and eat."

Friends! Did it get any better? I poked my nose toward the stove where a little caffettiera was starting to bubble. If you have to make coffee, a caffettiera isn't the worst way to do it, but they're tricky to get right. They're basically a double boiler: you fill the bottom part with water, the top with ground coffee, and you put it straight on the stove. The water heats up and expands and the pressure forces it through the coffee and into the top of the pot. But they have a tendency to get too hot, and the super-hot water extracts all the worst, most bitter acids, making a cup of strong, nasty coffee that needs a gallon of milk and a pound of sugar to drown out the ick.

"Let me in," I said, twisting the burner off, grabbing a kitchen towel and running it under the cold tap and then wrapping it around the boiler, cooling down the water and stopping the extraction. I gave it a three-count, then unscrewed the top section. Ideally, you'd want to cool it all off even faster, but caffettiera have a tendency to crack if they change temperature too fast. I'd found that out the hard way in an adventure involving a bowl full of ice water, a caffettiera, and a mess that took most of the day to clean up. At least I didn't blow my hand off when the cast-iron boiler shattered.

"Marcus," Darryl said, "it's only coffee."

"Yeah," I said. "It's only coffee. What's your point?" I reached for the cupboard where the little espresso cups I'd given Darryl for Christmas years ago were kept, automatically remembering which cupboard that was, and I fished down three cups and poured out the coffee. I tasted mine. It wasn't terrible. It was almost good.

Darryl grabbed another and had a sip, then nodded. "Okay, that's better than anything I make."

Van tried hers. "Darryl, that's *amazing*. Come on, give the man credit where credit's due."

Darryl faked a little bow at me. "Sir, you astound me with your coffee prowess. Prithee, place thine butt in yonder chair so that I might proffer you a repast of finest fried victuals."

Van swatted him on the ass and I sat down and food appeared before me, with knife and fork and Tabasco—which reminded me of Ange and sent a knife through my heart—and even a multivitamin.

Darryl and Van sat, too, and we turned food into dirty dishes and then I turned the dirty dishes into clean ones while Darryl found some tunes and put them on and Van had a shower, coming back down with her hair wrapped in a towel, dressed in a little skirt and a loose, floppy cotton top that hung down as low as the skirt. She looked amazing, and I found myself staring for longer than was polite. She caught me at it and gave me a weird look and I looked away.

"You ready to talk about it?" Darryl said.

"Not really," I said. "But I guess I'd better."

Telling it again, the day after, with a full stomach, felt a little like I was recounting the plot of a movie I'd seen and less like I was telling the story of something that had happened to *me*. I found myself discoursing on weird details I'd noticed, like the Zyz guys' tactical gear obsession, which provoked comforting hoots of laughter from Van, making it all seem more like a well-worn story of my life, rather than a source of imminent doom. Darryl and Van knew about Zyz, so I was able to skip over that part of my talk with Ange, which left me with the part where she'd told me I was a coward and a jerk for not putting my life at risk. Or at least, that's how it came out.

They made sympathetic faces and noises, and I felt better in a way that was also kind of bad. Like I knew that I'd made myself to be the hero of a story that I didn't deserve to be the hero of.

"Jesus, Marcus, what a frigging *nightmare,*" Van said.

"So what are you going to do?" Darryl said.

Van gave him an impatient look. "What do you think? He's going to walk away from this. He's right: this is too risky for him. It's not his fight."

Darryl had been holding her hand, and he let go of it. "Come on, he can't do that. For one thing, there's other people involved now. Even if he stops, they won't."

Van folded her arms. "Jolu will shut it down if Marcus tells him to. Problem solved."

It was amazing. They'd gone from being a cuddly couple to furious in seconds. It made me realize how infrequently I bickered with Ange, and how little I knew about their relationship. I tried to say something, but Darryl was already speaking.

"No, he won't. He can't and he shouldn't. The stuff about Zyz, all that other stuff, it *needs* to come out."

"Oh really? And why does it *need* to come out? Is it going to solve anything? Don't you think that everyone already knows that the whole system is rotten? Do you think a bunch of anonymous, unverified Internet rumors are going to make people rise up and take action? Throw off their chains and free the world? Come on, Darryl. After everything you've been through—"

Darryl stood up abruptly. "Going for a walk," he said. He was out the door before I could say anything. Darryl had had it worse than me, had been in Gitmo-by-the-Bay for *months.*

They'd held him in solitary, messed with his mind, hurt him in ways that showed and ways that didn't. He'd spent a month in the hospital under observation before they let him out. No one ever said it out loud, but I knew they'd had him on suicide watch.

Van had tears in her eyes. "He is such an *idiot* sometimes," she said. "What's wrong with wanting to be safe? Where does he get off making *you* take the risk for someone else's principles?"

I didn't have anything to say to that. Of course, they weren't someone else's principles, they were mine. Or they had been, before I'd had the principles terrorized out of me. How was it that Darryl had gone through so much more than I had but had emerged so fearless? Was he the broken one, or was I?

Van was crying now. I gave her a half-assed hug and she put her face on my shoulder and really cried, hard. She'd kissed me, just once, hard on the mouth, when she'd come through for me and helped me get a message through to Barbara Stratford at the *Bay Guardian*. That's when she'd confessed to me that she had a thing for me, and we'd never spoken about it since. At that moment, it was all I could think about. Between the fight with Ange and the events of the past few days and the strain, I felt like I was about to do something really, really stupid, like kiss her again.

I let go of her and stood up. My shoulder was wet with her tears. She looked up at me, tears streaking her face. I felt like I might cry, too. "I'm going to go find Darryl," I said. "He shouldn't be alone."

It was only once I was out the door that I wondered how Van felt about being alone.

I found Darryl exactly where I expected to find him: a little dog run up the hill from his house that had a commanding view of a valley bowl that swept back up the hills on the other side, to more hills, set below the weird semihuman shape of Sutro Tower, the broadcast antenna that looked like an alien with its hands held up in surrender. It's where we'd always snuck off to when we were up to no good—a covert joint or an illicit bottle of something, even a couple of epic firecracker experiments, which had miraculously failed to blind or maim us. Judging by the number of times we'd found roaches, bottles, and used-up firecrackers up there, we were hardly the only ones.

Darryl was sitting on the graffiti-carved bench looking down at the valley and the cars below, staring into the middle distance and seeing nothing, I guessed. I sat down next to him.

"I don't know how you can be so brave," I said. "I really don't. I wish I could do it."

He made a noise that sounded a bit like a laugh, but with no humor in it. "Brave? Marcus, I'm not brave. I'm *pissed*. All the time, do you understand that? A hundred times a day, I feel like I could beat someone's head in. Mostly *hers*." I didn't have to ask who "her" was—Carrie Johnstone, the woman of my nightmares. Darryl's, too. "I get *so* angry, so *fast*. It's like I'm watching myself from outside myself.

"You got to *do* something. I was locked away. I couldn't do anything. I couldn't help spread the Xnet, or go to big demonstrations, or jam with the other Xnetters. I sat in that room, naked, alone, for hours and hours and hours, nothing in there but my thoughts, my voices."

I'd never really thought of myself as *lucky* for being where I had been after the DHS took over San Francisco, but now that I looked at it from Darryl's point of view, I had to admit that yeah, it could have been a lot worse. I tried to imagine what it would have been like to be totally helpless and alone, instead of with all these amazing friends and people who looked up to me and hailed me.

"I'm sorry, D," I said.

"It's not your fault," he said. "I don't want to put this on you. It's my own damned problem." He swallowed a couple times. "It's partly why I hadn't been around much for you lately. Didn't want to say something, you know, ugly. Because I know you did what you did for me." Had I? Maybe a little. But I also did it for me, for the humiliation and suffering and fear, to try and get past all that. "But when Jolu told me about the darknet, when I saw those documents, I felt, like, all right, now it's my turn. Now I can finally *do* something about all the nastiness and corruption and evil in the world.

"But Van, she's not down for that. She just wants me to be safe. I get that. But she doesn't understand how being 'safe' means that I can't be *whole* again, can't get demons out of my head. I need to make something right, I need to be the star of my own movie for a change."

"Jeez, D, man—" I couldn't really find the words. I guess I'd suspected some of this, but I don't think I'd ever imagined that Darryl would ever say these words to me. It wasn't the kind of thing that guys said to each other—not even guys who were as close as brothers, the way we had been.

"Yeah," he said. "It sure is a bitch, isn't it?"

"So what do you want to do?" I said.

"What do *I* want to do?"

"Yeah," I said. "Yeah. What do *you* want to do? Not 'What do you think I should do?' or 'What do you think is the safest thing to do?' What does Darryl Glover want to do, right now, today?"

He looked down at his hands. His fingernails were chewed ragged, his cuticles dotted with little scabs from where he'd chewed them bloody. He'd done that as a kid, but he'd stopped when we were both fourteen. I didn't know he'd started again.

"I want to release the whole thing. Today. Now."

"Yeah," I said. "Yeah, that sounds about right. Let's fucking do it."

Van didn't like it, but she got in the car with us. Darryl drove carefully and slowly, but I was in the passenger seat and I could see how his hands were shaking. We snarled in traffic in SoMa, and Darryl showed off his encyclopedic knowledge of the alleyways of the neighborhood to beat it, popping out on Market Street from an alleyway that was so narrow we scraped up a couple of plastic recycling wheelie-bins on our way out. He was in Hayes Valley a few minutes later, pulling up in front of Ange's house. I knew she didn't have any classes that afternoon, but she hadn't answered her phone when I called her. I thumped on her door.

She came down in track pants and the T-shirt she'd slept in the night before, her eyes swollen and red. She folded her arms when she saw me and glared. "Get dressed, okay?" I said. "You can be pissed at me later. Get dressed." She looked over my shoulder at Darryl, who waved at her. Van gave a half-assed, unenthusiastic wave, too.

"You're kidding me," she said.

"Get dressed," I said. "It's happening."

She gave me a long, searching look. I looked back at her, thinking, *Come on, Ange, argue later, do this now before I lose my nerve.* My heart was fluttering in my chest like a pigeon trapped in a store, beating against the windows and trying to break out.

She turned on her heel and disappeared into the house. I heard her run up the stairs to her room. A minute later, her little sister, Tina, appeared in the hallway. "You remember when I told you if you broke her heart I'd pull your scrotum over your head?" She was two years younger than Ange, and tall and skinny where Ange was short and curvy, but they were unmistakably sisters, with nearly the same voice and facial expressions.

"I remember, Tina. Can we save the scrotal reconfiguration for later? We're kind of into something more important than me or Ange or any of us."

She cocked her head. "I'll think about it."

Ange came pelting down the stairs, toothpaste on the corner of her mouth. She was wearing a long electric-blue raincoat I loved and hand-painted Keds and huge, squarish Japanese pants she'd sewn herself from a pattern, all clothes that had been strewn on the floor of her room the last time I'd been in it, a hundred years ago, the night before.

"Tina, enough with the scrotums, already," Ange said as she reached us. Tina made an exaggerated, monkeylike face at her and then gave her a kiss on the cheek. "Come on," Ange said to me, whisking past me toward Darryl's car, hesitating for a second before yanking open the back door and sliding into the seat next to Van. I brought up the rear and got into the passenger seat, checking out whether Van and Ange were ready to kill each other while trying to look like I wasn't checking it out at all.

Inside the car, the tension was as thick as the fog on a wet night on Twin Peaks.

"You know where Jolu's office is, right?" I said to Darryl.

"We're going to see Jolu?" Ange said.

"I told you," I said. "It's happening. And if it's going to happen, we should all be there, in person. Better than worrying about our computers or phones being tapped."

Ange took her phone out of her purse and switched it off. I did the same, and so did Van. Darryl dug his phone out and handed it to me, and I did the same for him.

"Okay," Ange said.

Darryl said, "Yeah, I know where he works." We were halfway there already. Darryl had an almost mystical knack for beating San Francisco traffic. He could have been the world's greatest cab driver or getaway man.

"What's the plan?" Ange said as we got closer.

Van said, "They don't have a *plan*. They just got in the car and started driving."

I looked over my shoulder at Ange, who was nodding. "Yeah," she said. "That sounds like them."

The two women looked at each other for a moment. I tried not to hold my breath. They'd disliked each other since eighth grade, and while I'd never gotten the whole story, I assumed that it was one of those old grievances that takes on a life of its own, so that the reason you don't get along is that you don't get along.

They stopped looking. I turned back around. A few seconds later, Van said, conversationally, "You got a lawyer?"

Ange said, "Not really. There was the public defender and that guy from the ACLU, back in the Gitmo-by-the-Bay days, but no one who's really *my* lawyer."

"Yeah," Van said. "Did you have the woman from ACLU, or the guy?"

"Both. But the woman really seemed like she knew her stuff. What was her name?"

"Alyssa? Alanna?"

"Elana," Ange said. "She was great."

"So I was thinking we should write a lawyer's number on our arms, you know, just in case. One phone call, right? Don't want to waste it calling directory assistance."

"I'm pretty sure I've got her number in my email." I heard Ange open her computer, enter her password.

"Here's a Sharpie."

There was some mutual arm-scribbling.

"Not so big," Ange said.

"If I write it this big, the rest of us will be able to read it from across the room, even if ours has been washed off or, you know, whatever."

"Good point," Ange said. "Here, roll up your sleeve."

"You really think if we get busted anyone's going to let us talk to a lawyer?" I asked, secretly pleased at how civilized the two of them were being to each other.

"You shut up," Ange said. "Wouldn't you feel like a total moron if we *did* get a phone call and you didn't have a number? Idiot."

"Yeah, dude," Darryl said.

"You shut up, too," Van said. "And hold your arm out at the next red light."

I rolled up my sleeve and twisted to stick my arm into the back seat. Ange's fingers grabbed around my wrist and yanked painfully. I yelped, and she made a disgusted noise. "Silence," she said, and I felt the tickle of the Sharpie moving over my arm. It seemed to be taking an awfully long time. When I finally got my arm back, I saw that she'd made sour faces of the 0s and skulls out of the 8s. I decided that this was a gesture of affection. At least, it comforted me to think of it that way.

Jolu's little startup was three guys and a woman sharing two desks in the back of a bigger, richer startup, crammed together with four broken-down Aeron chairs that looked like they'd been in continuous use since the dot-com boom of the last century, more duct-tape than original mesh. Jolu noticed us as we threaded our way down the office, past the desks of people from the bigger startup—some kind of analytics company that I'd vaguely heard of—toward him. He took a moment to assess the fact that all four of us were together, and quietly tapped one of his coworkers, the woman, on the shoulder, stood and moved to intercept us.

"Let's go to the meeting room," he said, pointing back the way we'd come.

The meeting room was barely big enough for all of us to fit

in, and the meeting-table was a converted ping-pong table (there was a net and paddles tucked onto one of the room's crowded shelves). But it had a door, and Jolu closed it.

"Everyone, this is Kylie Deveau," he said, pointing to his coworker, a pretty black woman a little older than us, with short hair and red-framed round-lensed wire-rim glasses. She smiled and shook hands all around.

"You must be the darknet," she said. "Pleased to meet you in the flesh."

"Kylie started the company," Jolu said. "I couldn't do darknet without letting her in on it."

"Yeah," I said. "I guess it wouldn't be fair."

"No," Jolu said. "Well, yeah. But I told Kylie because I figured that she was smarter than the rest of us put together." Kylie made a small pretend-bow. "She's the one who found the Zyz stuff in the first place. I assume that's why you are all here, right? Or is there some other enormous, terrible conspiracy I'm about to expose that I should know about?"

"No," I said. "Just that one. Nice to meet you, Kylie. Let me tell you about some people I ran into last night. Well, I say people, but the first batch could have been ghosts or super-intelligent LOLCats for all I know, and the second batch were more like gorillas or possibly hyenas."

"I can tell this is going to be good," Jolu said, and sat down.

ḥylie said, "Well, I can see why you want to get this out now."

Darryl said, "You do? Because I keep feeling like it's suicidal." I winced when he used the word, thinking of all the shrinks who'd felt the need to keep Darryl under observation for all that time.

Kylie smiled. "It just might be. But doing nothing is entirely suicidal, isn't it? It's not like these characters are going to ignore the fact that you're still out here, not forever. I'm guessing that they only let you go because they'd had to act fast and hadn't had a chance to figure out how to put you away without sticking out their own necks. But from what we've seen, they've got a lot of juice with a lot of different agencies, enough to take away city attorneys' houses, anyway. I don't suppose it'd be hard for them to figure out a way to get the police to take a special interest in you."

"You know," I said, "I hadn't even thought about that until now. I'd only gotten as far as them putting a bag over my head and sticking me in a plane to Yemen or something."

Kylie said, "That sounds expensive. You know what jet-fuel costs, these days? Much cheaper to get someone else to bear the expense. These guys are the world's biggest welfare queens, after all—suck up government money in military contracts, use it to issue bonds, get the government to pass laws that make your bonds into safer bets, then go after even bigger and better laws. I'm guessing they never spend a penny if they can get Uncle Sucker to foot the bill.

"No, I bet last night was all about making sure that if they *did* send the law after you that you wouldn't somehow get out of it, say, by revealing a giant trove of documents about all kinds of illegal activity. Which is why I think it's right for you to act now, because the next thing that's going to happen, I bet, is that someone from some law-enforcement agency is going to get an important phone call, maybe just about you, or maybe about you and all your friends, because they *know* who your friends are from last time around, and when that happens, it's going to be much harder for you to get the truth out there—"

I put my hands up. "I get the picture." I looked around at my friends—my oldest, best friends. Ange was looking a little pale, her hands clasped in front of her on the table, white-knuckled, the lawyer's number written in Van's familiar hand-writing on her arm. Darryl, too, was looking sick and scared.

Jolu, as always, was as cool as a movie star, though I could recognize the subtle signs around his eyes and the corners of his mouth, the vein that stood out faintly on his forehead and the pulse thudding in his throat. But Van—well, she looked grimly determined, and not at all scared. "So we'd better do it, right?" she said.

Jolu nodded. "It's time, all right. I wrote a script that would nuke our chats on the darknet site and erase all the logs and scrub our handles from the notes in the database."

"You wrote that script, huh?" Van said.

Jolu smiled his movie-star smile. "Yeah, the first night. I figured that there was a good chance we'd have to open up the site in a hurry, so I figured what the hell, better beat the rush. Stitch in time saves nine."

"That's a great motto, Jolu," Ange said. "Beats the shit out of 'When in trouble or in doubt, run in circles, scream and shout.'" I winced.

Jolu shrugged. "I don't want to get in the middle of whatever you two are into, Ange, but you know, there's a time and place for running in circles, too. We all got our own superpowers."

Darryl laughed nervously. "Yeah, he wouldn't be Marcus if he didn't do that scream and shout thing, right?"

"Guys," I said, "I'm here. I can hear you."

"Shut up, sweetheart," Ange said. But she leaned across the table and took my hand and gave it a squeeze. I squeezed back and she hauled back, dragging me across the table to her and she grabbed my head with her other hand and gave me a ferocious kiss. "You're an idiot," she said, when we were done. "But you're my idiot. Don't you ever run out on me after an argument again or I'm going to start sitting on you whenever you lose a fight until I'm sure you won't turn rabbit."

"*Daww,*" Jolu said. "Isn't young love *sweet?*"

"Actually," Van said, "it is." And Darryl got up and came around the table and wrapped her up in his long arms and hugged her so hard I heard her ribs creak.

Kylie said, "Children, love is sweet and important indeed, but we've got a job to do. Mr. Torrez, I believe you mentioned a script you have ready to run?"

Jolu thunked at his keyboard. "Done."

Darryl stuck his hand up. "So what I was thinking, you know, is that we should start by getting in touch with those weirdos who'd been spying on Marcus. They sure seemed to have a good idea about how to get people to notice what they had to say."

I bit my tongue. If I hadn't been kidnapped by two totally evil mercenaries after my run-in with the ghosts in my machine, I think my head would have exploded in rage at the suggestion that we should work with those total creeps. As it was, my creepiness scale had been radically recalibrated in the last day or so, and while the spooks who'd rooted my machine might have rated a nine the week before, now they were about a six, and falling fast.

Ange spoke up for me, though. "I don't think that's fair to Marcus, Darryl. They were spying on *him,* after all. They violated his privacy all the way, from asshole to appetite. I don't think that's the kind of people we want to work with."

I relaxed a little. Good old Ange.

"So what do you propose?" Darryl said. His body language was noticeably more on edge than it had been a second before. I remembered his confession in the park, his desire to get a chance to be the star of his own movie for a change. I'm sure it sucked to have someone else second-guess his awesome action-hero plan. But screw it, those guys were still creeps.

"We tell it to the press. Mail a link to Barbara Stratford, anonymously, tell her how to access the darknet. Of all the journalists in the world, she's probably the most likely to be able to figure out how to use a Tor darknet site. And if she can't figure it out, she'll know lots of hairfaces who can help her out." Barbara Stratford was a muckraking journo who wrote for the *Bay Guardian*. She was an old friend of my folks, and had led the effort to spring me from the clutches of Carrie Johnstone's torturers. But she was a traditional print journalist with a lot to lose, and she moved with a lot of plodding caution.

"That sounds *slow*," Darryl said. "What's she going to do, read all those docs, call up a second source to corroborate them, run it past legal, write a story, and file it for publication in next week's issue? We need this stuff to go live *now*."

Ange opened her mouth to argue, but Jolu held a hand up. "No reason we can't do both. We tell your reporter friend about it, but we also post the darknet address where anyone can find it."

"How?" I said. I'd been thinking about this. How do you publicize something while staying anonymous?

Jolu shrugged. "Create a new Twitter account, use it from behind IPredator. Create a new WordPress blog, do the same thing. Make a new Facebook identity, put it there, too."

I shook my head. "That'll never work. Who pays attention to a Twitter account that's just been created?"

"Well, you could retweet it, you've got thousands of followers. Or I could."

"Yeah, and I could just make a blinking EL wire sign that says 'That anonymous account? It's really me.'"

"Good point," Darryl said. "So we find someone we trust, and ask that person to ask *their* friends to big it up, link to it, retweet it, friend it, whatever. Make it hard to trace it back."

Now Jolu was shaking his head. "Sorry, dude. Remember that they'll be doing this on social networks—you know, places where they've conveniently laid out lists of all their friends for

the whole world to see. All you do is, slurp up all those contacts, check to see which contact *they* have in common, and
there you go, a convenient list of high-probability suspects to
spy on or assassinate with your aerial drones."

Darryl shut up and glared at the table. Jolu stayed cool.
"Sorry, man, but you know, it's just *reality*. It's not convenient,
but it's real."

Through this all, Van had been hanging back a little, not
really seeming to be engaged with us. Now she said, "Kylie,
Jolu says you're the smartest person he knows, and he's a smart
guy. So what do you think we should do?"

"Well, let me start by saying this is a hard problem. Maybe
the hard problem today. You've got the same problem anyone
who wants to attract attention to a product or a cause has. This
is what every politician faces, everyone who makes soda-pop or
opens a restaurant, everyone who wants to sell a record or get
people to come to their little league games. It's the reason that
ad agencies and marketing companies exist, it's the basis for bil-
lions of dollars in business every year. And you've got the additional complications of wanting to make this stuff happen in
a hurry, and of not wanting anyone to know who's behind it.
What I mean to say here is, you're doing something *hard*.

"Now, all that said, there's at least two important things
going for you here: first, you're *good,* you know a lot about
computers and networks and people and technology. And second, you've got a great 'product' to 'sell'. I've been in those
docs, I know the kind of dynamite you're sitting on. You're not
trying to get people to give a damn about yet another flavor
of sugar-water. You want to tell people about a trove of some
genuinely explosive materiel, a pile of information plutonium
that you've dug up in the government's backyard. There's a certain intrinsic interest in this stuff, you know, and it's the kind of
thing that people might enjoy telling each other about.

"I think our best strategy is going to be sending out messages from our new account, messages to anyone we can think of with any political clout or a lot of followers or a big platform of some description. Your basic 'Hey mister, look what I've got' message. Most of these people are going to ignore us, initially at least, because they get a bazillion of these every day, from con artists and spammers and PR people and nutcases. But we've got to think like dandelions here."

"What do you mean?" Van said. I could tell that she liked Kylie, saw her as a potential ally in her role as designated grownup and worry-wart. I liked her, too—she talked like I wished I could talk, saying the stuff I thought better than I could.

"Well, we're mammals, so we tend to think of reproduction as being expensive and precious. When we want to copy ourselves, we take ourselves out of commission for months, then commit years of more-or-less full-time work to making sure our copies survive." I wasn't sure if I liked being talked about as a "copy" of my parents, but I couldn't deny the underlying truth. "But look at a dandelion: by the time it's seeding, it's made thousands of potential copies of itself, all those little bits of fluff that make up the puffball. When a gust of wind comes along, the dandelion doesn't follow all its children to make sure they get steered in the right direction and have their mittens and a packed lunch with them. Almost every seed a dandelion tosses into the wind is going to die without taking root, but that's not what matters to a dandelion. Dandelions don't care that every seed survives: they care that every opportunity to take root is exploited. A successful dandelion is one that colonizes every crack in the sidewalk, not one that successfully plants all its seeds.

"Sending out messages about the darknet shouldn't cost much. It's probably worth tailoring each message a little to the people we're spamming—put their name in the message, mention some kind of fit with what they do. But keep it down to less than a minute for each message, dandelion style. The important thing isn't to make sure that everyone we hit repeats the story, but rather to make sure that everyone who *might* give us a little signal boost knows that the story is out there to be boosted."

"And if that doesn't work?" I said. It all seemed a little too easy, too pat.

"We try something else," she said.

"And if a snatch squad takes us away and throws us in the ocean with weights around our ankles before we can try something else?" Kylie gave me a look down her nose.

Van leapt in. "Marcus, I know you've got a reason to be worried, but honestly, what else can we do? It's not like you've got a better idea, right? You and Darryl decided it was time to do this, and we're all going along with it, but don't just shoot down everything—that's not fair."

I briefly reconsidered trying to get in touch with the creeps who'd been spying on me, but I didn't want to do that—and I didn't know how, either. Half of me wanted to just say screw it, and start shouting it all from the mountaintops, using my own accounts, which had plenty of followers. It'd probably cost me my job, but hell, if it was a race to make this well known before Zyz could come after me, that was more important than a paycheck I might never get to cash. The other half of me was, well, *scared*. The thing about Kylie's suggestion was that it sounded a lot safer.

"Fine," I said. "But when we all get sent to a secret prison in Afghanistan, don't come crying to me."

Darryl gave us a ride back to Ange's place. We flopped around her room as we had a million times before, perching with our computers on our laps, quickly researching people who might pick up our message, tailoring it for each one, and firing it out using the anonymous accounts that we'd cooked up at Jolu's office. We used both IPredator and Tor to do the research and messaging, which slowed us down somewhat—so to compensate we each targeted several people at once, using multiple tabs, cycling from one to the next. Jolu had offered to whip up *another* darknet site where we could all coordinate who we were spamming and what the response had been to avoid double-dipping, but Kylie had just said, "You're not thinking like a dandelion, Jolu," and he'd dropped the idea.

Ange and I had been on edge when we got back to her room, still smarting from the fight we'd had the night before, but we both quickly lost ourselves in the work and forgot about the fight. Soon we were joking and teasing the way we usually did—Ange started it when I got too engrossed in reading the bio of the Woz, the legendary engineering wizard who'd co-founded Apple, who had millions of Twitter followers. I was in a real Wikipedia clicktrance, following link after link to information about his achievements and career and all the awesome hacks he'd pulled off.

Ange threw a pencil at my head and said, "Hey, mister, I don't hear any typing. Are you thinking like a dandelion or a mammal?" I snorted and gave her the finger, but I also stopped screwing around and sent off the message.

We ate dinner in her room—PB&J sandwiches that we'd made together in the kitchen, and yeah, Ange even put hot sauce on that, which actually tasted pretty good, like Indonesian curry—and then she kicked me out. "You've got to go to work tomorrow," she said. "You can't afford to miss two days in a row."

I let myself be pushed out and spent the whole bus ride home reloading a search for links to our darknet site on my phone. There were a few, a couple dozen, but of course it was *hard* to figure out the darknet—you had to install Tor on your computer, and then you had to figure out how to use it, installing something like Torbutton in your browser. Even I forgot how to get it installed and had to look up the docs every time I set up a new computer. I swore to myself that if I made it out of this mess alive and intact, I'd throw myself into the work of the Noisebridge hackers who were always messing around with making Tor easier to use.

I was bone-tired. I'd hardly slept the night before, and my adrenals had been bashing my body around like a punching bag for the past seventy-two hours—plus I still had my stupid, aching broken nose and assorted bruises from Burning Man, not to mention the lasting effects of a week spent in the desert. It's a good thing Mom and Dad were so caught up in their own problems—if they'd been paying the kind of attention they used to give me back when I was sixteen, they'd have had a total freakout.

And yeah, that made me feel pretty rotten too—lying there in my bed, setting the alarm on the glowing bedside nixie-tube clock I'd built, aching and stupid-feeling, and the stupid voices in my head kept whispering that my parents didn't even care enough about me to have a meltdown over my absence, which was as stupid as stupid could be.

It's a lucky thing I was so close to total exhaustion, because even the voices in my head couldn't fight the biological necessity of sleep and the next thing I knew, the alarm was yanking me back from murky dreams and I was staggering into the bathroom for a pee, a shower, and a tooth-brushing.

By the time I got out the door, I was half convinced that it was all over. After all, the last time I'd done this, Barbara Stratford had put my face on the cover of the *Bay Guardian,* and the events had more or less unfolded from there. The closer I got to the office, the more certain I was that I'd step through the door and the first thing anyone would say to me would be, "Man, can you believe all that darknet stuff? It's all anyone's talking about."

But no one even looked up when I got in. No one seemed to know that the world had turned on its head. I sat down at my desk and tried to concentrate on putting together my briefing for Joe, who'd emailed me that he was sorry I was feeling under the weather but that he looked forward to hearing my ideas when I got back into the office.

I felt like I should be putting together some kind of Power-Point presentation, but every time I loaded up LibreOffice Impress, the free equivalent, I felt like a total tool. I *hated* Power-Point. Besides, all I could think about was the darknet.

I told myself I'd just spend a minute or two googling it and seeing what came up. Yeah, right.

An hour later, I was furious. Oh, there were a few promi-nent places that had published our link, some cracks in the sidewalk with dandelion stalks sprouting from them. But every single one of these was flooded with sarcastic, dismissive com-ments. Some people insisted it had to be a hoax. Others said there was nothing there. Hundreds claimed that it was impos-sible to reach and don't bother trying. All of these were from different IDs, and they all seemed to have been written by dif-ferent people, but I found it hard to believe that everyone who looked at the darknet docs would be so convinced that there was nothing to them.

Worse: if *I* had just happened upon this stuff for the first time, I'd probably figure that anything that attracted all this negative attention and people saying "hoax" and "nothing to see here," was just junk. As Kylie pointed out, I spent most of my day trying to figure out what *not* to pay attention to, so that I could free up my attention for the good stuff, and one of the ways I figured out which stuff to ignore was by paying attention to what was said by the people who'd already gone and looked.

I dragged myself back to hopeless PowerPoint fiddling, and was incredibly relieved when Liam came by to pester me, thus putting me out of my misery.

"What do you think? Is the darknet stuff a hoax?"

I wasn't surprised that Liam had found out about it already. It would have been a surprise if he hadn't—this stuff was totally up his alley.

"Did you actually check it out?" I asked.

He looked a little embarrassed. "Naw," he said. "I mean, I used to have Tor on my machine, but then I upgraded the OS, and I hadn't gotten around to reinstalling it, and, well, with all those people saying it was a hoax . . ." He trailed off and shrugged.

"It's pretty weak to dismiss it as a hoax until you've seen it yourself, don't you think?" I said. "I mean, why would you take some random Internet idiot's word for it instead of checking it out with your own two eyes? Don't you have a brain? Don't you know how to *think*." Even as I said it, I knew how unfair it was, not least because Liam didn't make a secret of how much he looked up to me. He shrank as I pummeled him with words, looking like he wished the ground would open up and swallow him. The part of me that wasn't feeling like a total dick felt good about that, because he *deserved* to be humiliated and miserable for not going off and looking at the stuff we'd sweated so hard to make available to him. I mean, if *Liam* couldn't get worked up about the darknet docs, who would?

"So you've seen them?" he said in a small, hurt voice. "You think they're real?"

Yeah, I'm not just a dick, I'm an idiot. I hadn't planned on admitting that I'd seen the darknet docs to anyone, at least not until they were all over the front page and the evening news, because I didn't want to be known as a guy who was suspiciously interested in them. But now I couldn't say, *No dude, I didn't look either,* because that would make me look like even more of a dick.

"Yeah," I said, kicking myself. "I saw them. They're incredible. Explosive stuff. You should really, really have a look."

"Okay," he said. "Totally. You're right, I really should make up my mind for myself, not let other people tell me what to do."

And then he went off and did what I'd told him to do. I am a total dick.

Chapter 11

What if you threw a blockbuster news event and no one showed up? We'd just dumped one of the biggest troves of leaked documents in the history of the human race all over the net, and no one really gave a crap. Some critical combination of the sheer size of the dump, our sketchy promotions strategy, the pain in the ass nature of Tor, and the fact that the net was full of people saying that they were hoaxes and stupid and that there was nothing juicy there—it all added up to a big, fat yawn.

Joe finally came by my desk at 3:30, just as I was falling into the post-lunch slump, wherein my blood-sugar troughed out so low that I felt like I could barely keep my eyes open— probably as a result of all the horchata I'd guzzled at lunch, the sugar sending my blood-sugar spiking to infinity so it had nowhere to go but down.

"Hello, Marcus," he said. He was dressed in his campaigning uniform, a nicely tailored button-up sweater over a crisp white shirt, slacks that showed off the fact that although he was pushing fifty, he still had the waistline he'd had as a college varsity sprinter, a JOE FOR SENATE badge on his lapel. He had like eight of those sweaters, and he kept a spare in a dry-cleaning bag by his desk, just in case a car splattered him or a baby got sick on him between campaign stops.

"Joe," I said, feeling like I was about to be sick. "Look, I'm sorry I wasn't in yesterday, I was really under the weather. And well, today, you know, it's just been crazy. I've just about got the network here sorted out, but the website—" I waved my hands in a way that was meant to convey that it was a total disaster.

He looked grave. "I thought that the website was all in order. I remember you saying something to that effect. Or did I misunderstand?"

I was sinking lower with every utterance. "Well, yeah, it looked okay, but when I started doing a code-audit I found a bunch of potential code-injection vulnerabilities so I've been doing what I can to reduce the attack-surface of the site, you know, so I can get it all down to a manageable scale, and—"

He held his hands up to stop my torrent of technobabble. "My, it certainly sounds like quite an undertaking. I really thought that Myra was better than that."

And now I *really* felt like a jerk. Myra, my predecessor, had done an awful lot with very little, and here I was, dumping all over all her hard work to cover my own useless butt. "Well, yeah, I mean, she did, but things move really fast, and the patch-levels were super lagged, and you know, the last thing we want is someone hijacking our donors' credit card numbers or passwords, or using our site to install malicious software on visitors' computers, and, well—"

"I get the picture. Well, you sound like you've got important things to do here, Marcus. But I want you to remember that this campaign needs you for more than your ability to patch our software and keep our computers running: we need fresh approaches, ways to reach people, motivate them, bring them out to the polls. I'm counting on you, Marcus. I think you're the right person for this job."

Well, I would be if I wasn't spending all my time trying to leak a mountain of confidential documents that contain the details of thousands of criminal conspiracies—while being kidnapped by mercenaries and spied on by weirdos who probably buy their Guy Fawkes masks by the crate.

"I won't let you down, Joe."

"I know you won't, Marcus. Remember: you're not here to be a grunt in the information troop, you're my delta force ninja. Get ninj-ing. In two months, we're going to have an election, and win or lose, that will be the end of the road for the Noss for Senate campaign, our sites, servers, and all the associated whatnot and fooforaw. We need technology that will last us until then and no further. Keep that in mind while you're managing your time, and I'm sure you'll find room in your schedule to get past the station-keeping work and on to the important stuff. The *fun* stuff, right?"

"I'm sorry," I said. He was right. As important as the stuff I had been obsessed with was, I had taken a job, and I wasn't doing it. I could tell he was disappointed with me, and that was just a brutal feeling. I had a moment's premonition of what it would be like to get *fired* from this job, to go home and admit that to my parents. The world seemed to spin away from beneath me. "Tomorrow, okay? I promise."

He squeezed my shoulder. "You don't need to look so gutted, son. Remember, this is an *independent* campaign. We're *supposed* to be scrappy, exhausted, and overextended."

I smiled a little at that, and noticed that Joe had some pretty serious bags under his eyes. On impulse, I said, "Have you been getting enough sleep?"

He laughed again, that amazing, deep laugh that was his trademark. "You sound like Flor. And you look like you might be burning the candle at both ends, too. How much sleep did you get last night?"

"I decline to answer that question on the grounds that it might tend to incriminate me," I said.

"Spoken like a good civil libertarian. A good, *tired* civil libertarian. I tell you what, I'm damned busy tomorrow anyway. Take an extra day to get your thoughts in order. And get a good night's sleep. All right, Marcus?"

"It's a deal."

Have I mentioned that Joe was a really good guy and that he'd make a hell of a California senator?

When he left my desk, I found my spirits lifted. Knowing someone like Joe had confidence in me made me want to be a better person. And soon, ideas began to flow—not always good ones, but ideas. Stuff I'd seen done before, new things too. A way to use free voice-over-IP to let kids call their offline parents and grandparents to ask them to vote—"Have you called your mom today?" A browser plugin that would do a popup with the names of the large corporate donors to Joe's opponents, every time you loaded a page that mentioned their names, a reminder that the other guys were all bought and paid for.

And I had a killer idea. Or maybe a really stupid idea. I kept putting it out of my head, but it kept coming back and insisting that I put it down in the long file I was brainstorming into (ditching the PowerPoint was really helping, too). So I wrote it down and added THIS IS A KILLER STUPID IDEA right next to it, so I wouldn't forget.

At the end of the day, I caught Liam slinking out of the door, not making eye contact with me. God, I was such a dick sometimes.

I called out to him and dragged him back over by my desk and apologized, and before I knew it, I'd invited him out for a cup of coffee after work and I was shutting down my computer and throwing it in my bag and heading out the door with him.

On the way home, I passed a Guatemalan grocery with a bunch of mouth-watering fresh California produce out front.

I had a few dollars in my pockets and I was suddenly seized with a desire to cook my family an amazing, fresh dinner, sit my mom and dad down at the table and have a rollicking discussion, the way we once had. I blew some money on the makings of a big salad and a fruit salad for dessert, then stopped in at a Vietnamese grocer for fresh noodles and some tofu and chicken for pho, the Vietnamese noodle soup. I'd only cooked it once before, but it wasn't that hard, and it was filling and cheap.

When I got home, I tied on an apron and googled some recipes and started washing the dishes and putting them away. Mom heard the rattle and clatter and came into the kitchen, carrying a mug of cold tea.

"Goodness, Marcus, have you contracted a brain fever?"

"Har. Har. You're not invited to dinner now. And it's going to be a good one. Pho."

"Fa?"

"Yes. Pho. It's pronounced 'fa.' Not 'foh.' Fun fact. And now you know."

"Indeed I do. What has precipitated this uncharacteristic burst of activity, dare I ask? I'm certain you haven't wrecked the car, as we no longer own one. Is there some sort of terrible news you plan on breaking to us? Are we to be grandparents?"

"Mom!"

"Inquiring minds want to know, Marcus."

"I just felt like a good supper, and thought you might enjoy one, too. And it's the least I could do, right? After you carried me about in your womb for nine months, endured the pain of childbirth, the long years of childrearing—"

"So you *were* listening all those times we explained the ways of the world to you."

"—I figure I'll make you some soup and salad and we can call it even, right?"

She picked up a soapy dishcloth from the counter and threw it at me, but it was a slow, easy toss and I caught it out of the air and wound up like a baseball pitcher, making her squeal and run out of the kitchen. "Dinner's in an hour!" I called after her. "Wear something nice, would you?"

She made a disgusted shriek and I heard her telling my dad about the weird thing their kid was doing now.

Yeah, I was in trouble, and it was only going to get worse. But in the previous week, I'd been blown up, had my nose broken, gotten a job, been kidnapped and freaked out, nearly broken up with the love of my life, and screwed up at the job I could hardly believe I'd landed.

I needed a night off. And I was going to enjoy it. I got one of my dad's beers out of the fridge and cracked it. Technically, I was still two years too young to be doing that, but screw it, it was time to unlax like a boss.

Mom treated me to a raised eyebrow as I set out the food and clicked my second beer in place in front of my plate. "Oh really?" she said.

"What, you want me to use a glass?"

Dad snorted. "Forget it, Lillian, it's not going to kill him. And if it does, we can collect on his life insurance policy."

And then there was no talking, only the sound of soup being blown upon, the sound of noodles being slurped, the sound of Dad trying not to slurp his soup, Mom teasing him about eating like a barbarian. I couldn't remember the last time we'd eaten like this: normal and funny and not freaking out about, well, *everything*. It felt insanely great.

My phone rang while we were working our way through the fruit salad I'd made for dessert, garnishing it with chopped mint and drizzling it with spiced rum. I looked at the faceplate: 202-456-1414.

I knew that number, but I couldn't place it at first. 202 was Washington DC, right? Why was that number so familiar. The ringer went off again. Hum. Oh, yeah, right. It was the White House's main switchboard.

(Don't ask me how I knew that—just let it be said that I had friends who had weird ideas about what constituted a funny crank call in the eighth grade, which is how my junior high got a visit from the secret service: it had been scrawled on half the bathroom walls in school, with FOR A GOOD TIME CALL above it.)

"Excuse me," I said, getting up from the table so fast I nearly knocked over my chair, hustling up the stairs with my thumb over the green button. I pressed it as I passed into my room and closed the door.

"Hello?" I said.

There was a long, weird, flat silence, with a couple loud clicks.

"Hello?" I said again.

"Marcus?" It was a computer-generated voice, and not a very good one. Needless to say, it wasn't the president, or the White House. Spoofing caller ID was a pretty basic trick, a one-google query job.

"Yeah."

A little pause. Someone was typing. "You haven't been checking your email."

"What, in the last two hours? No. I haven't."

"And you're not on IM."

"No. I had dinner. Is there something you needed to say?"

"In the darknet docs, there's a procurement order and brochure for a product called 'Hearts and Minds.'" The text-to-speech engine was stupid enough that "hearts" came out "heerts" and I had to try to recalibrate my brain to understand what it meant.

"Okay, I'll take your word for it. What about it?"

"You should be checking your email." Somehow, the robot voice managed to sound peeved. "It's all in the email."

"I'll check my email," I said. "But I've had a lot of IT crap to wade through lately. Some total jackasses have been using my computer to violate my privacy and creep me right the hell out. I don't suppose you'd know anything about that, right?"

A pause. "Stop changing the subject."

"Look, I've got plenty of stuff I could be doing here. In case you didn't notice, I released all the docs, just like you were whining at me to do. For all the good it's done. No one gives a damn. In case you didn't notice."

"Hearts and Minds"—*heerts and minds*—"just you have a look. And check your email more often."

The line went dead. So much for my night off.

ᒲ5ᒪ **had its fingers in a** lot of pies, and liked to spin off new divisions for each of its special projects. RedCoat was the name of the "security software" contractor that did a lot of gross lawful intercept work for various branches of the U.S. government, and governments overseas.

Hearts and Minds was one of its flagship products, though it didn't exactly show up on the company's website. But there it was in the darknet docs, and the more I read about it, the more angry I became.

It looked like Hearts and Minds started with a procurement order from the United States Air Force Air Mobility Command, which was looking for "persona management" software. What's persona management? I didn't know either. It's the kind of weirdness you couldn't make up.

You've heard of "grassroots" political movements, right? That's when ordinary people start to care about a political cause, and start to demand justice and action.

The bizarro-world version of "grassroots" movements are "astroturf" movements. These are fake grassroots movements started by political groups, governments, ad agencies, marketing companies, crooks, intelligence outfits. I wasn't sure at this point whether, practically speaking, there was any difference between these sorts of organizations. In astroturf movements, you get hundreds or even thousands of "ordinary" people writing letters to the editor, showing up for demonstrations, writing to their congresscritters or town assembly or school board, all the stuff that people do when they care about a cause. But in an astroturf movement, the "ordinary people" are, in fact, paid operatives—the cast of a giant theatrical production in which people are paid to pretend to be ordinary citizens who just happen to want to see a park turned into an oil field, for example.

Now, getting all those phonies to pretend to be real people with real passion costs a lot of money. A handy-dandy way to save on this unfortunate expense is to use "sock puppets"—that's when one person operates several online identities, each pretending to be a different person, each one vigorously agreeing with the rest. Sock puppetry can get seriously twisted—you can even create a sock puppet to *disagree* with your cause, but in such a disagreeable, stupid, oafish fashion that they make the other side look like dolts.

But being a sock puppeteer isn't easy. You've got to keep all your identities separate, remember what each one has said about its life and beliefs. The last thing you want is for your fake suburban housewife to start talking about the stuff that only your fake long-haul trucker should know.

If you want to run more than a couple fake people at a time, you need good tools to help you keep track of who's who in your imaginary world.

That tool is called "persona management."

Hearts and Minds was developed for the USAF, but Red-Coat sold lots of copies elsewhere. The product brochure boasted that it was used by "reputation management" companies, "marketing and communications" and "strategic communications" outfits. It was clear from the testimonial quotes that these were all fancy names for companies that helped other companies discredit people who complained about their products and services online. If you were selling crappy food, or had rude staff, or if your strollers had a tendency to collapse and squish the babies inside them, it was cheaper to hire someone with a Hearts and Minds license to help "manage your reputation" by making your dissatisfied customers seem like lone whiners than it was to actually fix your shit.

The product literature boasted about how Hearts and Minds was more efficient than the 50 Cent Army, the name for the legion of fake commenters employed by the Chinese government to discredit anyone who complained about official corruption or crimes. They made fun of the crudeness of paying badly educated thugs 50 cents per post to smear their targets.

Hearts and Minds could let a single operator pretend to be dozens of people. All of a sudden, I had a pretty good idea where all those messages about how the darknet docs were just BS and hoaxes and irrelevant had come from. All of a sudden, I wondered how much of the stuff I thought to be "true" had been made true by some creep with a sock-puppet army and a copy of Hearts and Minds. It was an ugly feeling.

I did a lot of work on the darknet spreadsheet, unpicking the threads that documented Hearts and Minds (which I kept thinking of as "Heerts and Minds"), adding tags and cross references. Now that we'd told the world about the darknet docs, the spreadsheet was more important than ever, as it was the only index to the massive trove. We'd dropped signing our edits with individual IDs, and now we all shared a single admin account that let us all edit the sheet without letting the public vandalize it or add weird conspiracy theories to it (we had enough of those among ourselves). We'd indexed over 3,000 documents between us now, which only left, uh, well, basically 800,000 more to go. It was going to take a while.

When that was done, I dragged my exhausted ass into bed, barely getting my shoes off before I hit the sack. But a few hours later I woke up with a jolt from a claustrophobic dream, my mouth pasty and tasting of the ginger in the pho. I slopped into the bathroom and gulped a cup of water and swiped at my teeth with a toothbrush and at my face with a facecloth and went back to bed, put my head on the pillow, and closed my eyes. But now sleep wouldn't come. Why would anyone go to all that trouble to tell me about Hearts and Minds? It wasn't like I could do anything about it.

It was stupid, is what it was, and every time sleep stole over me, I'd feel a kind of full-body pucker of outrage that these dinks had made such a point of calling me up just to tell me that I was the target of powerful, highly resourced attackers who had me outgunned in every way. I mean, duh. I knew that already.

Not being able to sleep sucked mightily. I needed to sleep. I had a job to do tomorrow, and I needed a clear head, and it had been so long since I'd had a real night's sleep, it was starting to turn me into a member of the living dead. The more I worried about this, of course, the harder it was to find sleep. Finally I counted down slowly from one hundred, taking a breath at every number, trying to find that place I'd gone to in the temple on the playa, and I was just about there when a thought occurred to me:

If all the Hearts and Minds messages were being generated and

managed by a single piece of software, maybe there was a way to auto-
matically figure out whether someone was using Hearts and Minds to
post—a fingerprint, a signature, a trademark. I had a moment's excitement at this, a sketch of a plan for a program to analyze
Hearts and Minds messages and find the connection, and then
sleep *did* come, and bash me over the head with a sledgeham-
mer, knocking me into a deep, dark dreamless place that my
alarm-clock dragged me out of just a few short hours later.

I was at my desk when Liam came over, still looking a
little wounded, but with that kind of worshipful look that
made me so awesomely uncomfortable.

"So," he said, "uh, you going to go to lunch soon?"

I nodded. I'd packed another PB&J that morning before
blearily going out the door, sprinkling a handful of chocolate
espresso beans in the sandwich, which seemed like a good idea
at the time but which I'd probably regret.

"'Cause I thought I might go to Civic Center for the occupation."

"Is there another one of those today?" It seemed like there
were new occupations springing up every month, like putting
up tents and taking over some public square had become the
default way to show that you were pissed off about something.
Sometimes they were huge, and sometimes they were just a few
hardcore people, but I kind of felt like we'd all gotten to the
point where news-footage of pepper-spray-happy cops in Darth
Vader suits waging chemical warfare on vomiting, weeping
protesters had lost its shock value. I mean, I was sympathetic to
the victims of course—I'd ridden the Scoville Express myself—
but I just couldn't get as worked up as I'd been a couple years
back when it all kicked off.

Liam's eyes bugged out, as though he couldn't believe that
someone as amazingly cool as me didn't know about every-

thing going on everywhere in the world. I always hated those people, people who always said, "Oh yeah, I heard about that," no matter what it was, even when you knew they were lying. The kind of people who'd never done anything for the first time. But hanging around Liam was going to turn me into one of them if I didn't watch it.

"It's *huge,* yo! A bunch of different Anons are way pissed about this darknet stuff, they want to get at Zyz." He put on a menacing robot voice. "We are Anonymous. We are legion. We don't forget. We don't forgive. Expect us." I squirmed. You used to hear a lot about Anonymous, a kind of tribe of Internet people who would pull off these daring raids and denial-of-service attacks. But then the price for botnets crashed and any-one could be a denial-of-service terrorist, and then there were a ton of big stupid Hollywood movies where the good guys or the bad guys or the serial killers or the stoners were running around in Guy Fawkes masks, and well, it just all got kind of lame and played out. There were still real anons out there, hanging out on places like 4chan and being deeply weird and offensive in the way that no Hollywood movie would dare to come close to, but the image of Anonymous has been turned into even more of a cartoon than it had been when they started. And as for this "We are legion" business, it had been the chorus of a summer pop song so awful you'd icepick your own ear to escape it. Any menace it had once held was now offset by the fact that it was the modern successor to La Macarena and the Chicken Dance.

"So it's a bunch of Anons in tents?"

"No, dude. Anons kicked it off, but it's, like, *everyone.* It's *huge.* There's students from all over the city, even high school kids playing hooky. Teachers, too! Even parents."

I dug around my bag for my sandwich and stuck it in my coat-pocket. "All right," I said. "You've convinced me." And truth be told, he *had*. Maybe the darknet docs weren't on the front page of every newspaper, but here was a bunch of people who were protesting because of them, sort-of-kind-of. If that was all I was going to get out of this, I'd take it. For now, anyway.

"We don't have to wear masks, do we?" Those plastic *V-for-Vendetta* masks were even more played out now. Plus the last thing I wanted was to be in a crowded, volatile situation with no peripheral vision.

"Naw," Liam said. "These are better." He reached into his pocket and pulled out a couple of worn black bandannas, screened with elaborate patterns. He shook one out and held it out. It was a cotton kerchief, silk-screened with the Guy Fawkes face right in the middle of it. "Watch," he said. He folded it in half diagonally, making it into a big triangle, and tied it around his neck like a cowboy. Then he pulled it like a bank robber, and the way he had it folded, his whole lower face was the Guy Fawkes face. Then he untied it and shook it out again and took off his baseball hat and fussed with the kerchief, tucking the top edge under the hat and then retying the corners at the back of his head, so that now it covered his whole face, with only his eyes looking out through the eyeholes he'd cut out of the cloth. "It's a transformer," he said, muffled by the cloth. "Choose your level of covertness and tie accordingly. Plus it's treated with stuff that's supposed to help with pepper spray. I got 'em from a guy on eBay. Want to take one? We could both wear them!"

He sounded so enthusiastic I wanted to hide in the toilet. One thing I did *not* want was to show up looking like the dork twins. "That's okay," I said. "I'll just keep it in my pocket, you know, in case."

"Cool," he said, crestfallen. I made a show of carefully folding the kerchief and tucking it into my pocket. Who knew, maybe I would need to blow my nose—or soak up some blood.

I heard the protest long before I saw it, the unmistakable drum-circle, whistle-blowing sound. It made something inside of me cramp up a little, a reminder of the Xnet concert in Mission Dolores park, the gassings and beatings that had followed it. But Liam was clearly energized by the noise, started to pogo a little as we came up out of the BART station and headed toward it. The streets were lined with SFPD cruisers, and the sidewalks were thronged with beefy SFPD officers, ostentatiously sporting thick bundles of zip-strip handcuffs at their belts. They all had goggles pushed up on their foreheads, masks pulled down around their collars. For the gas, of course. And yeah, there were a couple officers wearing what looked like SCUBA tanks, except I knew they were filled with pepper spray, connected to spray-nozzle hoses that were clipped to their chests. I didn't make eye contact with them, but their body language told me they were playing plenty of attention to me and Liam. I wondered if it was the Guy Fawkes bandanna around Liam's neck.

The tents filled the area in front of City Hall, spraypainted with old slogans from old occupations. This left very little room for the demonstrators, so we spilled out into the street, holding hand-lettered signs about student debt, corrupt politics, joblessness. The news was always full of stories about homeless camps being moved along, and big lengths of Shotwell Street had turned into tent cities, the whole sidewalk full of tents and mattresses and piles of cardboard. There was a big billboard by the Powell Street BART advertising the services of a security-through-occupation company that would move its employees into abandoned or foreclosed houses to keep squatters out.

Off to one side, a woman had climbed up on the high concrete base of a lamp post. She had cut off her long, fluorescent pink dreads, and it made her seem a lot older and wiser, but I'd recognize Trudy Doo anywhere. The frontwoman for Speedwhores and founder of Pigspleen.net was a San Francisco icon, and she'd been Jolu's boss until her ISP went out of business the year before. She shouted, "Mic check!"

Around her, people echoed the cry: "Mic check! Mic check!" This was the People's Mic, another fixture of occupy protests. At first, people did it because their cities wouldn't give them "amplification permits" to use megaphones, but even in cities where the authorities didn't play stupid amplification gotcha-games, the People's Mic was preferred. Something about having everyone cooperating to help each other be heard really felt *right*.

"We have the best government—"

She shouted with her gravelly punk-singer voice, making each word good and clear and loud. The crowd echoed it, with some grumbles. "We. Have. The. Best. Government," shouted the people around Trudy Doo. Then people around them repeated it. Then the people around them, and so on, in concentric circles that finally reached to the other side of Van Ness Ave, which was now thronged with people.

"Money can buy."

There was laughter near Trudy Doo, and it took a few moments before the laughter subsided enough for the people near her to repeat the punch line.

"I have been out at a million of these things.

"And we always say the same things.

"And sometimes it feels hopeless.

"But we keep coming out.

"Because the reasons we come out haven't changed.

"Because the corruption, the brutality, and the unemployment are still there.

"So we're still here."

There was applause here—occupy style, with hands in the

air, fingers wiggling—but Trudy Doo wasn't done yet. She called out, "Mic check!" and everyone went silent.

"They tell us we overspent.

"They tell us we were greedy and we lied on our mortgage loans.

"They tell us it's a global world and we can't get paid more than they're paying in India or China.

"They tell us this is the new normal.

"No jobs.

"No schools.

"No libraries.

"No houses.

"No retirement.

"No health care.

"But somehow, there's enough money for wars.

"Somehow, there's enough money for banks and bonuses.

"Somehow, it makes economic sense to give war criminals the power to take our houses.

"But they haven't passed their dirty laws yet.

"Now we know about them, thanks to the darknet.

"And we know that any politician who votes for this is bought and paid for.

"So we're here.

"We're here to say that our country is no longer for sale.

"We're here to say we're watching."

She hopped nimbly off the base and people applauded again, both ways, and it turned into a chant, "We're watching, we're watching, we're watching." There were some people in Fawkes masks and they pointed to their eyes and then to City Hall, making a little dance out of it, shuffling back and forth funkily in their thrift-store three-piece suits. Liam was pretty much in heaven.

Trudy Doo was surrounded by a crowd, part of an intense

discussion, explaining to people who hadn't heard of the dark-net what it was. She spotted me and shouted, "Marcus, come here a sec!" Liam almost fangasmed right then. I admit I was a little bit pleased with myself to be called out by Trudy Doo.

But then she said, "Marcus, you've heard of the darknet docs, right?"

My mouth went dry. "Um, I guess," I said.

"Good. Gimme a sec."

She hopped nimbly back up on the base. "Mic check!" she bellowed, cupping her hands around her mouth.

"Mic check!" the crowd roared back.

"Listen up! Marcus here, some of you know him as M1k3y, right?"

All of a sudden, there were about a million pairs of eyes on me. I squirmed and made a half-assed wave.

"You want to know about darknet, right? He's the guy to ask.

"Get up here, Marcus!"

She hopped down off the base and there was a polite round of applause. She gave me a rough hug, smelling somehow of the power supply of an overheated computer, like she was wearing Eau du Server. "Knock 'em dead," she said, right in my ear, and gave me another squeeze, then shoved me toward the base. I hesitated a second by the base of the plinth and she grabbed me by the back of my jeans with one hand, put the other under my butt, and basically wedgied me up onto it.

I looked out at the crowd. They looked back. It wasn't all strangers. There were familiar faces there—people I knew from Noisebridge, a couple girls I'd seen around the Mission, some people I knew from high school. I even spotted John Gilmore, the EFF guy, wearing a tie-dyed shirt and flat cap, smiling imp-ishly within his long beard, light glinting off his round glasses.

"Wow," I said, before I could stop myself. The crowd around

me said, "Wow," People's Mic style, and there was laughter all round. Ah yes, the old "repeating stuff that wasn't meant to be said" gag. Har.

And now I had no choice: I was about to give a public lecture to a couple thousand people on my top-secret leaks site. Way to keep your cover, Marcus.

Once upon a time, I helped invent a network called Xnet, because we ran it on top of hacked Xbox Universals, a games console that Microsoft gave away for free one Christmas so that they could sell more software. Naturally, there'd been a lot of interest in figuring out how to get *other* games to play on the Xbox, so someone went out and hacked it to accept a new OS: GNU/Linux, the free operating system made out of free and open code that anyone could improve and republish. There are a zillion flavors of Linux, and one of them, ParanoidLinux, was the desktop equivalent of ParanoidAndroid: an OS that assumed you were being spied on and did everything it could to keep you private.

Jolu and I tweaked ParanoidLinux so that it was ready to crack other peoples' WiFi out of the box, and then share it around, so if one Xbox was within range of a cracked WiFi link, all the Xboxes in range of it could share its connection. We used ParanoidLinux's built-in Tor stuff to create our own secret servers, chat, and games, routing some of the trickier stuff through Pigspleen, Trudy Doo's old ISP.

By the time I got picked up by the DHS, Xnet was already showing its age. The ParanoidLinux project was always being patched as new security issues were found and clobbered, and keeping the Xnet version up to date was a lot of work for us. We handed over control of the project to a volunteer committee who ran it for a few more months before they folded it back in with ParanoidLinux, which was, by this time, a boot-disk that set up Tor, secure versions of Firefox and a chat program called Pidgin, and other security tools right out of the box, so you just stuck it into any computer and rebooted it and you were locked down tight and secure, assuming you could manage all the complexity of your keys, and understood how darknet sites worked, and, well, a lot of other stuff that most of the world didn't get. Yet.

So the darknet was just the latest version of the Xnet—in the same way that humans were just the latest version of chimps. I could use it, sure, but could I even explain it anymore? I was about to find out.

"Darknet sites run on Tor.

"That's The Onion Router.

"It's a tool that bounces your traffic around the net.

"Making it harder to trace and censor you.

"A darknet site is a normal website.

"Except that your computer never knows its address.

"And it doesn't know your computer's address.

"There's a darknet site.

"It has over 800,000 leaked memos on it.

"No one knows who put them there.

"No one knows what's in them.

"But a few thousand have been cataloged.

"And they're scary as hell."

I took a deep breath.

"You probably saw a lot of comments.

"About how it's all BS.

"A hoax.

"Nothing there.

"Well, if you check the darknet.

"You'll find a ton of memos about something called Hearts and Minds." I managed not to pronounce it "heerts."

"That's a product developed by Zyz.

"To help them spam discussion forums.

"With fake people.

"And now there are a whole crapton of people.

"You've never heard of.

"Flooding message boards.

"Saying that the memos that show that Zyz is really evil.

"Are all BS.

"I think that's pretty suspicious."

Finger-wagging applause. That made me feel a little better about the fact that I was on the verge of outing myself as the darknet docs guy.

"The easiest way to get to the darknet.

"Is to install a free browser plugin called Torbutton.

"Then visit est5g5fuenqhqinx.onion.

"I know that's a long number to remember.

"I'll say it again."

A voice from the crowd—one of the Anonymous guys, muffled by his mask—said, "I have a bunch of flyers explaining all this with the address on it."

I waved at him. He waved back, all jaunty body language to match the wide, sardonic grin on his mask. "That guy has the address on flyers." He executed a showy bow over one leg.

"I hope you'll go and see the darknet docs yourself.

"And make up your own mind.

"Well, thanks, I guess," I finished, and hopped down off the base, my pulse going *whoosh-whoosh* in my ears. The crowd was clapping politely, which was more than I had any right to expect. It wasn't as if I'd riled them up, given them marching orders, and sent them to fight the powers of evil. I'd given them tech support. There'd been a million cameras on me, of course, and some of them would have been streaming live to the net, and the rest would be grabbing footage to upload to YouTube and whatnot later on. And then there were three clean-cut guys in blue SFPD windcheaters with little camcorders who circulated endlessly through the crowd, making sure to get long shots of every face, especially anyone standing on a piece of street furniture and yelling out instructions, like me. I swallowed. Well, they knew who I was already, right? I'd been gassed and busted by them before. As the old saying went, it was the equivalent of a formal introduction.

The Anon guy with the flyers came over and handed me one, then shook my hand. "Nice to meet you, sir," he said.

"You, too." He was about my age, as far as I could tell from his eyes and the way he held himself. I looked at the little quarter-sheet of paper in my hand, hastily sliced into an off-kilter rectangle. It had all the basic info: an address for downloading a ParanoidLinux disk image that would boot any computer, the darknet docs address, some URLs for tutorials. It was liberally decorated with Guy Fawkes masks and funny slogans, and it had a fingerprint you could use to verify that your ParanoidLinux disk image hadn't been interfered with during the download. For a second, I thought that the numeric address they'd listed was wrong, and I spun off on a paranoid fantasy that these guys were part of some kind of disinformation campaign and maybe the ParanoidLinux fingerprint was no good, maybe it went to a poisoned version that spied on everything you did? Then I realized I'd been reading the address wrong and decided I needed to calm the hell down. "This is good," I said. "Thanks for doing it."

The Anon cocked his mask at me. "No problem—it was the least I could do. Seemed like it needed doing. I jumped on the darknet docs as soon as I heard about 'em, saw that BS this morning about Hearts and Minds, figured people needed to know the truth, so I wrote it down and made some copies. That seems like the best way to do stuff these days: make a *lot* of copies."

He said it with such hilarity I had to laugh. "Works for the bacteria," I said.

"Yeah," he said. "You think we could get some biotech freak to encode it all in a bacteria? Leave it in a petri dish overnight, make a trillion copies?"

"Viral marketing," I said.

Liam said, "*Bacterial* marketing."

Anon guy laughed some more behind his mask. I wondered if it itched. "This is my friend Liam," I said. "He brought me here today." They shook, and the Anon guy fingered Liam's bandanna with admiration. Liam slipped it on and I could see he was grinning behind it.

"Dude," Anon guy said.

"I know, right?" Liam said.

Trudy Doo flung an arm around my shoulders from behind. "You look like you're doing good, Marcus," she said.

"I haven't slept properly in weeks, I broke my nose last week, and I'm kind of a nervous wreck, but that's nice of you to say," I said.

"Just like I said. Looks like you're keeping really busy, which means you're doing good. Better than being a tube-fed zombie waiting for the grave." She shook my shoulders.

"How are you doing?" It seemed like a rude thing to say to someone who'd just lost her company, but I didn't know what else to say, plus I was kind of basking in the envious looks I was getting from Liam and didn't want Trudy Doo to go away before I'd finished showing off how cool I was.

She shrugged. "Pissed off," she said. "Pissed off is *good*. I'd rather be pissed off than resigned and peaceful. All the stuff that's gone down, all the money the super-duper richie-richies took out of the economy, all the shenanigans from the big phone companies that nuked Pigspleen . . . Every bit of it's made me ready to fight and fight some more."

The Anons clustered around her as she spoke, clearly enjoying her rant. I wished I could talk like that.

I had another paranoid moment: maybe Anon guy was the person who'd been spying on me through my computer. Maybe he and his buddies were the ones who'd staged that ghostly argument in my word-processing window the other night. For some reason, I'd pictured them living thousands of miles away, in a small town where there was a lot of spare time. But maybe they were practically my neighbors. Hell, maybe I hadn't flushed them out of my computer after all and they'd been watching me all along, had rushed down here when they saw Liam come and drag me off to the demonstration.

I couldn't go on like this. I was going to have to get my head straight. If I could only get a decent night's sleep, I could sort it all out. I'd felt that way for years, I realized. If I could only get a normal day, a day when my parents weren't freaking out about money and jobs, a day when I was just a regular student or a regular coder, or something else regular—

Was there ever going to be a "normal" again? Since we'd arrived, the crowd had been growing. And growing. And *growing*. I'd been in some big demonstrations in San Francisco before, but they were generally the kind that had permits and marshalls and were very orderly. This wasn't like that. I'd been vaguely aware all summer that occupy demonstrations had been growing, mobilizing more people each time. But I hadn't quite figured out what that meant, not until I realized that the nearly painful roaring in my ears was just thousands and thousands of people all *talking* in very close quarters.

"Holy crap," I said, and Liam grinned, looking around, then showed me his phone, which had a live feed off someone's UAV, one of several that were buzzing the demonstration. Some had police markings, other had news-crew logos, and some were more colorful, with rainbows and slogans and grinning skulls.

But most of them were eerily blank, and could have belonged to anyone. The one that was feeding Liam's phone was flying a lazy figure-eight pattern over the crowd, which, I saw now, stretched all the way down to Grove Street and all the way up to Golden Gate Avenue, and there were people with homemade signs converging on the crowd from side streets.

Liam was practically dancing a jig, and he was showing his phone's display off to everyone else—Trudy Doo, the Anons, anyone who'd hold still. Meanwhile, I was fighting panic. There was one big, unscheduled crowd I'd been in, the thousands of people who'd streamed into the Powell Street BART station when the air-raid sirens went off, a crowd so dense it had been like a living thing, a boa constrictor that strangled you, an enormous dray horse that trampled you to death. Someone in that crowd had stabbed Darryl, a random act of senseless violence that I had often laid awake at night wondering about. Had that person just freaked out? Or had they been secretly waiting for the day when the opportunity to stab strangers with impunity would arise?

The crowd pressed in on all sides of me, moving in little increments, a sixteenth of an inch at a time, but moving, and not stopping, and growing closer every moment. I tried to step backwards and landed on someone's toe. "Sorry!" I said, and it came out in a yelp.

"Um, Liam," I said, grabbing his arm.

"What is it?"

"I got a bad feeling, Liam. Can we go? Now? I want to get back to the office, and we're not going to do that if we go to jail." *Or if we get crushed to death.*

"It's cool," he said. "Don't worry about it."

"Liam, I'm *going,*" I said. "I'll see you at Joe's."

"Wait," he said, grabbing hold of me. "I'll go." Then, "Wait. Shit."

"What?"

"Kettle."

I bit the inside of my cheek and swallowed hard against the rising knob of vomit coming up my throat. "Kettling" is when the police surround a protest in a cordon of cops with riot shields, facemasks, batons, and helmets, and then *tighten* it, reducing the amount of space for the crowd, shoving them in together like frozen peas in a bag, often with nowhere to sit or lie down, with no food or water or toilets. Tens of thousands of people—kids, sick people, pregnant women, old people, people who needed to get back to work. For some reason, kettles had to be airtight— no one was allowed to get in or out until the police decided to let you dribble out in small numbers. Anyone who tried to get out was treated as a desperate criminal, which is why "kettle" had become synonymous with protesters on stretchers, blood streaming from their head wounds, eyes red with pepper spray, twitching with the effects of the gas and their injuries.

"Liam," I said. "We need to get out of here now." On his screen, I could see the skirmish line of SFPD officers with all their tactical crap, helmets and shields, like the wet dream of some Zyz mercenary or mall ninja. "Before they tighten the cordon."

To my amazement, he started *singing* and smiling. "Polly put the kettle on/Sukey take it off again!" Meanwhile, his fingers flew over his phone's screen. "Don't you know it?" he said, seeing my puzzlement.

"What?"

"Sukey? Like the old poem? 'Polly put the kettle on/Sukey take it off again'? No? It's a nursery rhyme. I thought everyone knew it!"

"I don't know this nursery rhyme, Liam. Why does it matter, precisely?" I was struggling not to bite his head off. No one should look that thrilled about being in a kettle.

"Sukey's an open source intelligence app. It gathers reports on kettles from people in the crowds, UAVs, webcams, SMSs, whatever, and overlays them on a U.S. Geographical Survey map, so that you can easily see what routes are still open. There's no way they could block *all* the side streets off in a space this big."

He handed me his phone and I peered intently at it. Angry, thick red lines denoted the police lines, with arrows showing the directions that reinforcements were arriving from. Thin green lines showed the escape routes.

"Dotted lines are unverified. Solid lines are verified, but they fade into unverified dots if they're not regularly refreshed. That one looks good." He pointed at a pedestrian walkway between two civic buildings, a few hundred yards down the street.

"That one's unverified," I said. "What about this one? It's verified and it's closer."

He shook his head. "Yeah, but someone needs to go verify that one. And if it's shut off, look, there's another verified route just past it. It'd be doing our part for the cause."

"I just want to *go,* Liam," I said.

He gave me a look of such utter disappointment that I was literally unable to set off, pinned in place by his gaze and the crush of bodies around me. The Anons had climbed up on the base and were impossible to read beneath their masks' gigantic grins. Trudy Doo had moved off into the crowd and I'd lost sight of her. But I felt like she was watching me, along with the Anons, and Liam, and the whole crowd, all watching "M1k3y" lose his nerve. Like they were already tweeting it.

"Forget it," I said. "Let's go check the Sukey route."

Liam smiled uncertainly and we set off. It was like walking through molasses, and while there was plenty of happy chanting and discussion, there were also far-off cries that might have been screams. I began to shiver as I inched through the press of bodies. But Sukey was right: the little walkway was unguarded, and people were slipping in and out of it. We followed them, going single file, and when we reached the end, Liam tapped his screen and verified the route. "Job done," he said, and we headed down Market Street. I made Liam take off his bandanna. We passed plenty of cops, both stationary and moving toward the demonstration. There were also plenty of demonstrators, and the police were stopping some of them, searching them and their bags. We passed a pair of girls about our age in plastic handcuffs, one looking furious, the other looking like she might cry any second, being led into a police cruiser. We hurried past.

We descended into the BART station and rode in uncomfortable silence. The oppressive feeling of being watched crowded in from all sides.

As we came up onto Mission, Liam said, "I can't believe how many people came out."

"Yeah."

"Like, no one wanted to come out until they found out that everyone else was. And once everyone started to come out, everyone else came out, too."

Unspoken, hanging in the air between us, was the question "So why aren't we there now?"

I finished the day at my desk, flipping back and forth from my work to newsfeeds and streams and tweets from the monster demonstration. According to Sukey, people were still escaping the kettle, but from what I could tell from the overhead shots, more people were joining the demo than were leaving. The UAV shots were like some kind of monster rock show. Ange texted me after class to say she was heading to one of the satellite demonstrations that had formed on the other side of the kettle, turning the police line into a stupid joke. Later, I found out that Jolu, Darryl, and Van had all been there separately. I didn't go back. Just before I fell asleep, I checked my phone and saw that the kettle had lifted and most of the demonstrators had gone home—except for the 600-plus who'd been hauled off to jail, and the couple dozen who'd gone to the hospital. I went to sleep.

Chapter 12

I got up the next morning before my alarm sounded, lurching out of bed and into the bathroom in a mild panic over all the work I had to do that day. I pulled on a T-shirt that passed the sniff test (barely) and decided I could get away with the same socks I'd had on the day before. I was about to open my throat and tip a bowl of muesli down it when I saw the fat newspaper sitting on the kitchen table where my mom had left it. Thick as a hotel-room Bible: the *San Francisco Chronicle,* a newspaper that had thumped down on our doorstep every Saturday morning since time began.

Every *Saturday* morning. I put down my muesli mid-guzzle and flumpfed into a kitchen chair, all the get-out-of-the-house adrenaline leaving my body with an almost audible *whoosh.*

Five minutes later, I was still sitting there, contemplating the question of what I should do with my weekend. The last time I'd had a real *weekend* was back in high school, and even then I'd had all that homework. I decided it'd be good to make a big ole weekend brunch, something for Mom and Dad, with proper coffee (not the swill they normally drank) brewed up with my little AeroPress. Then I could have a leisurely shower, tidy up my room, stick a load of laundry in the machine, and meander down to Noisebridge and dust off Secret Project X-1 and see about getting my 3D printer going in time for *next year's* Burning Man.

It was the best plan I could have made—for a change. I did crazy-ass 3D pancake sculptures (I cook a mean pancake AT-AT), and the coffee was "brilliant" (a direct quote from my mom). The parents were duly impressed with my room-cleaning, and by the time I shoved Lurch into my backpack and jumped on my bike, I was feeling like maybe I'd found some of that "normal" I'd been missing.

There weren't too many Noisebridgers around by the time I rolled in at 10:30. I went to my shelf and grabbed down my box-o'-stuff, making puffs of playa dust rise off all the broken crap I'd brought back from Burning Man. I found a free workbench and nodded at the girl with the shaved head who was teaching her little sister how to solder at the next bench over. I got a can of compressed air and some soft cloths and started blowing out the dust and getting ready to wrestle with my printer anew. I slipped into an easy reverie, punctuated by Club-Mate breaks—this being the official drink of hackerspaces around the world, a sweet German soda laced with caffeine and maté tea extract, a jet-fuel–grade stimulant.

When the cleaning was done, I grabbed a multimeter and started testing all the circuits in X-1, starting from the power supply and working my way through the system. Partway through my checks, I thought I found the problem, a spot where it looked like a stepper motor had been mounted backwards, so I grabbed Lurch and went hunting for a diagram to see if I was right, thinking, *Jeez, if it turns out that this was all that was wrong, I'm going to feel like a total derp.*

Of course, once my laptop was open on the workbench beside me, it was inevitable that I'd have a sneaky peek at my email—looking at my laptop without checking in would be like going to the cupboard and not snagging a cookie.

```
To: <marcusyallow@pirateparty.org.se>
From: Leaky McLeakerpants
Subject: carrie johnstone d0x
2 use as u see fit
```

It was signed with a little ASCII-art Guy Fawkes face made out of punctuation marks and letters, and attached to the email was a gigantic ZIP file.

I had a pretty good idea what that was: every single fact and fantasy that could be had about Carrie Johnstone and what she was up to. I'd seen d0xxes that went back to second-grade report cards, ones that included the subjects' kids' medical records, everything. Nothing was off limits when you were being d0xxed.

I closed my laptop's lid and closed my eyes.

A big part of me didn't want to see the docs in that folder. I had plenty of secret docs in my life already. And I knew what it was like to be totally, absolutely invaded. Carrie Johnstone had done it to me. So had the jerks who'd rooted my laptop. Somewhere in the world, someone might be staring at an email whose subject line was "Marcus Yallow d0x."

The thing was, I *knew* I was going to open that ZIP file. Of course I was. Who wouldn't? Carrie Johnstone was a monster: kidnapper, torturer, murderer. War criminal. Power-tripping mercenary. Scumbag and commander of scumbags. She was hunting me, too. Let's not forget that. Now that the story was out, wouldn't Zyz be back? How long until I met Timmy and Knothead again? Would I end up at the bottom of the Bay this time?

I *had* to open it. It was self-defense. In fact, I'd bet the only reason Carrie Johnstone hadn't had me whisked away to some private torture chamber was that she assumed that I'd been sneaky enough to gather this kind of dossier and had it ready to dump, on a dead man's switch, if I got disappeared. People like

Carrie Johnstone always assume everyone else thinks like them.
Not like people like me. People like me are good people. We
deserve to read other peoples' dirty laundry. Especially bad
people.

I was such a coward.

I unpacked the folder and started browsing the docs.

You would have done it, too.

"Marcus?" a voice said, some eternity later. It was
Lemmy, the Noisebridger who'd given me and Ange our ride
back from Burning Man. He was in his forties, an old ex-punk
with stretched-out ear piercings and blurred tattoos up and down
his arms. He was a demon in the machine shop, and was the
first person I'd ask any time I had a question about something
big, fast-moving, and lethal. I always got the impression that he
thought my little electronics projects were cute toys, fun, but not
serious like a giant piece of precision-machined metal.

I had the feeling he'd been talking to me for a little while,
and that I hadn't heard him.

"Sorry," I said. "Engrossing reading, is all."

He smiled. "Look, I was going to go join the rest down at
the big demonstration, bring some UAVs along. Want to come
along and be my crew?"

"There's a big demonstration?"

He laughed. "Come on, buddy, take a break every now and
then, will you? You know that big one that happened yesterday? Well, it looks like everyone who went yesterday's come
back again, and they brought all their friends. Downtown's *shut
down*. I've been playing with my quadcopters, think I can get
them to produce some killer footage. They're all rigged to act
as WiFi bridges, too, each on a different 4G network, so we
should be able to supply some free connectivity to the crowd.
I've also got a software-defined radio rig in three of them that

can triangulate on police and emergency bands. I think I've got it set so they'll home in on any clusters of dense police-radio chatter, which should be pretty interesting. But you know, I'm not really much of a coder, so I thought I could use a pit crew to help me debug the code on the fly during the inaugural flight."

Lemmy was also a UAV nut, though, again, I think he'd have preferred unmanned autonomous tanks or ATVs, anything with a lot of shiny, heavy metal. I looked at my screen, and my screen looked back at me, with everything I could have ever wanted to know about Carrie Johnstone and a lot more.

I couldn't stop looking at it, but I didn't want to keep looking at it.

"Let's go," I said, putting my lid down and sticking Lurch in my bag. "You can't write code for shit, dude."

"Yeah," he said, cheerfully. "Code's just *details*. I'm a big-picture kind of guy."

Lemmy wanted to drive—it being hard to carry four miniature quadcopters the couple of miles to the periphery of the demonstration—but we probably could have crawled in less time than it took to beat the frozen traffic leading up to the march. I spent the time getting familiar with Lemmy's control software, which built on some standard libraries I was already familiar with: systems for steering UAVs and for running software-defined radios, mostly.

Software-defined radio is hot stuff, and it's kind of snuck up on the world without us noticing much. Old-fashioned radios work with a little quartz crystal, like the one in an electrical watch. Quartz vibrates, buzzing back and forth at a rate that's determined at the time that it's manufactured. You choose a crystal, build a circuit around it, and the radio is done—it can tune in to any signals that are inside the vibrational frequency of the crystal. One radio works for tuning in to GPS satellites, another to CDMA cellular phone signals, another for FM radio, and so on.

But SDR is *programmable* radio. Instead of a crystal, it uses a fast analog-to-digital converter, a little electronic gizmo that takes any analog signal off a sensor (say, light patterns off an electric eye, or sound patterns off a microphone) and turns it into ones and zeros. You connect the converter to a radio antenna and tell it what band to listen in on, and then you use standard software to make sense of what it receives.

What this means is that the same box can be used to read air-traffic signals, police band, CB radio, analog TV, digital TV, AM radio, FM radio, satellite radio, GPS, baby monitors, eleven flavors of WiFi, and every cellular phone standard ever invented, *all at once,* provided the converter is fast enough, the antenna is big enough, and the software is smart enough. It's the radio-wave equivalent of inventing a car that can turn itself into a bicycle, a jumbo jet, a zeppelin, an ocean liner, or a performance motorcycle just by loading different code into its computer. It's badass.

Lemmy's UAVs had some off-the-shelf SDRs he'd bought from an open-source hardware company called Adafruit in New York. Adafruit sells electronics that come with full source code and schematics, complete road maps for remaking them to do your bidding. Everyone at Noisebridge loved their SDRs and other gear. And since there were thousands of hackers and tinkerers around the world who worked with the Adafruit SDRs (and all the other versions that Adafruit's competition made from the same plans), there was a lot of very clean, very well-documented code for talking to them.

I dove into this in the passenger seat, vaguely aware that the car was lurching from stop to start, turning corner after corner, as Lemmy sought out a spot close to the protest.

"What's the verdict, doc?" he said, as he engaged the parking brake. "Is my code going to live?"

I shrugged. "Looks about right to me. Am I right in thinking you've just pasted in the code examples from the tutorials with a couple of lines tying each module in with the last?"

He grinned. "Yup. I treat writing code like making a cake from a cake mix: pour it into a bowl, add an egg and a cup of water, stir, and throw it in the oven. It's not always pretty, but it's always a cake."

"Well, let's see if we've got a cake, then."

I got out of the car, a tricky feat since we were parked on the upslope of a steep hill. I didn't immediately recognize the neighborhood, but when I did, I was surprised. "Are we on the *other side* of Nob Hill?"

"Yup. It's the closest I could get to the protest. That thing is *huge*."

"But we must be, I don't know, a mile away?"

"Oh, less than that. Plus the protest is getting bigger, from what I can tell. It might reach here before the day's out. Something's *happening*. People are *pissed*. I've been living here since the eighties and I've never seen anything on this scale."

He dug around in the trunk and pulled out his quadcopters. Each one was an X of light, flexible plastic, with helicopter rotors at the end of each leg of the X. A round pod in the middle carried the battery and the electronics, radios, and control systems. Without the battery, each one weighed less than a pound, but the batteries doubled their weight. He handed me two of them, and I held one in each hand, awkwardly fitting my fingers around the sensors and antennae in the center disc, trying not to bend anything or smudge any of the lens covers.

Then he handed me one more, being much rougher with it than I'd dared to be (but then, it was his quadcopter to break, not mine). I stuck it awkwardly under one arm. He perched the remaining one on his hand and thumbed at his phone with his other hand. The four rotors spun up with a dragonfly whirring, the quadcopter wobbled twice on his palm, then lifted off straight into the sky in a vertical takeoff that was so fast it seemed like the quadcopter had simply vanished like a special effect.

He took back the extra copter from me and showed me his phone, which was showing the view from the copter's lower camera, a receding landscape with the tops of our heads in the middle of it, shrinking to two little dots as the copter clawed at the air and pulled itself into the sky.

"Well, that works," he said. "Thought it'd be useful to have a little overview as we got close. Here, I'm going to web-cast the feed." He thumbed some more buttons.

"Nice," I said. This was exactly what I loved about tech-nology: when it just *worked* and turned individuals into forces of nature. We'd just put an eye in the sky that anyone could tune in to. "What's the link?"

"It automatically tweets the URL from my account when I start it up. Do you follow me?"

"Yeah," I said. I got out my phone and punched up the Twitter client, found the tweet with the link, and retweeted it, tapping in, "Heading to the #sanfrancisco #occupy #protest. Bringing quadcopters. Aerial video here."

We walked laboriously uphill to the top of Nob Hill, the copter hovering a hundred feet above us, high enough to be clear of any overhead wires or trees. From Lemmy's phone screen, we could see the hairy edges of the protest, where people were still arriving. Farther in, it looked almost like static, all these little dots—peoples' heads—moving in tiny, quick blips, packed as densely as oranges in an orange crate.

"Holy crap," I breathed, as the copter rose higher, revealing the size of the crowd, which spread from Fell Street to Market

Street, spilling out over the side streets, filling them back for blocks and blocks.

"Day-umn," Lemmy agreed. "Want to buzz 'em?"

"Can you do that from here?"

"Yeah," he said. "It'll take the copter out of direct radio range, but we'll still get its feed off the net. And we can check out the software, see if it really works." I watched as he tapped out a flight pattern on his phone, tracing a zigzag over the crowd with his fingertip. Then he pressed GO. Over our heads, the copter zipped off toward the crowd, keeping its altitude for most of the journey, then gently descending to a mere five yards off the ground.

At this height, I could make out individual faces in the crowd, read the slogans on the signs. Then the flight path kicked in and the point of view swerved nauseously, tracing that zigzag with mathematical precision, sometimes shuddering as the copter got caught in a gust of wind. We stopped walking and just watched the feed for a while. I shouted "Look out!" at the phone's screen when the copter nearly collided with another UAV, this one covered in markings from MSNBC. Either it had some kind of automatic avoidance routine built into it, or there was a fast-fingered human operator nearby, because it banked hard and barely missed the midair collision.

"Uh, Lemmy, what happens if that thing crashes? I mean, I don't want to turn someone into hamburger."

"Well, yeah, me neither. In theory, any two rotors can give it enough lift to slow its descent, and it makes a lot of noise if it goes in for an emergency landing, which should help people get out of the way."

"Unless it's so noisy that they don't hear it."

"Yeah. Well, that's life in the big city."

I wasn't sure I agreed. Crashing the quadcopter into someone's head would really, really suck. On the other hand, the knowledge that this might happen certainly gave watching the footage an air of extreme danger, which made it that much more compelling. As if it wasn't compelling enough, watching the video of all those faces, thousands and thousands of them, ripping past at speed.

"Let's get down there," he said, and I agreed.

The demonstration was even louder than the one the day before, a roar like a PA stack that I could hear from two blocks away, over the honking horns of the cars trying to find their way around it. The sidewalk was too jammed with people to walk, so we joined the hundreds who were threading their way through the stuck cars, dodging the bikes and motorcycles that were doing the same. Soon we could barely move, and I realized we were now *in* the demonstration, even though there were stuck cars all around us. I looked in one, saw a harried-looking woman with two little kids in the backseat who were losing their minds, one hitting the other with a toy car, both of them screaming like banshees, silent gaping mouths through the closed windows.

I locked eyes with the driver, who was looking resigned and frazzled. I wondered about all the other people who were stuck around me, wanting to get home and feed the kids or get to work and not get docked for being late or wanting to get to the hospital or the airport. I entertained a brief fantasy of directing traffic, helping all those people get unstuck and turn around and head away from the protest, get moving again, but there was no way I could do that. (Later, I read reports of other people doing just that, and of the crowds making way to help this happen, and I felt both proud of my fellow human beings and ashamed of not having the guts to try it myself at the time.)

Now we couldn't move without a lot of "excuse me"s shouted into the ears of people who were shouting the same thing into the ears of the people ahead of them.

"This is insane," I said.

"Pretty amazing," Lemmy said, and smiled hugely.

Suddenly, it felt like the world was flipping upside down. It *was* amazing. Hundreds of thousands—millions?—of my neighbors and friends had taken over the city of San Francisco because they were pissed off about the same things I was pissed off about. They'd come and put their lives and liberty on the line because, well, because stuff was *messed up*. It wasn't just the darknet docs, it wasn't just the lobbying to make the deal over student loans even worse, it wasn't just the foreclosed houses and all the jobs that had vanished. It wasn't just the planetary devastation and global warming, it wasn't just the foreign dictators we'd propped up or the private prison industry we supported at home. It was *all of it*. It was the fact that there was all this *terrible stuff* and no one seemed to be able to do anything about it. Not our political leaders. Not our police. Not our army. Not our businesses. In fact, a lot of the time, it seemed like politicians, police, soldiers, and businesses were the ones *doing* the stuff we wanted to put a stop to, and they said things like "We don't like it either, but it has to be done, right?"

Here was a big slice of my city that had turned out to say *WRONG*. To say *STOP*. To say *ENOUGH*. I knew that these were all complicated problems that I couldn't grasp in their entirety, but I also knew that "It's complicated" was often an excuse, not an explanation. It was a way of copping out, saying that nothing further could be done, shrug, let's get back to business as usual.

I'd never seen this many people in one place. From the copters' point of view, it was like the city had come to life, the streets turning from lifeless stone and concrete into a living carpet of

humanity that stretched on and on and on. It was scary, and I had
no idea how it would turn out, but I didn't care. This was what
I'd been waiting for, this was the thing that *had to happen*. No
more business as usual. No more shrugging and saying "What can
you do?" From now on, we'd do *something*. Not "Run in circles,
scream and shout," but "March together, demand a change."

I also realized that my stupid idea for what to do next for
Joe's campaign wasn't so stupid after all.

Lemmy's copters just kept buzzing the crowd, and
our Ustream channel kept picking up viewers, up to a couple
thousand now. No doubt a lot of them were in that crowd, but
plenty were from all over the world, to judge by the realtime
stats.

Every so often, we'd deploy the three copters with the
software-defined radio scanners to check for high concentra-
tions of police-band chatter. The police had recently started to
encrypt their signals, but that didn't matter: we didn't care *what*
they were saying, we only wanted to detect places where a lot
of police communications were taking place. In other words,
we were interested in the fact that they were talking, not what
they were talking about.

When the three detected police-band spikes, they sent the
fourth copter to home in on it and take some video. That way,
we caught a lot of footage of arriving convoys of militarized cops
and then the National Guard. Hundreds of them, and dozens of
police buses—the kind they took masses of prisoners away in—
and even little clusters of police quadcopters that were sending
their signals back and forth in the same encrypted band.

Two of these copters latched on to our scout and started to
follow it around.

"Uh-oh," Lemmy said.

"Why uh-oh?"

"Well, even with these new power-cells, that little guy's going to run out of battery soon enough, and I'm going to have to bring him in for a fresh power pack, and they're going to know exactly who we are and where we are."

"Uh-oh," I agreed. "Is flying a UAV illegal?"

He shrugged. "Probably. I mean, no, not in general, but is there some kind of freaky, 'conspiracy to abet civil disorder' BS charge they could whomp up against anyone they don't like? I'm pretty sure there is."

"Uh-oh," I said again.

"I guess I'll just ditch it," he said. "Man, this sucks."

"How much time is on the power pack?"

He looked at the telemetry streaming off the scout. "Maybe twenty minutes."

"Can you tell it to land somewhere out of the way, maybe a rooftop, and we can try to collect it later?"

"Yeah," he said. "Good one."

I used Google Earth to scout out the nearby roofs and found a likely looking spot, which I showed to Lemmy, and he took over steering the scout to it—it was away from the main body of the protest, and who knows what the SFPD crew who were piloting our tails thought we were up to. I got to steer the remaining three, staying away from the police copters. Mostly, I just tried to zoom in on any place where things looked interesting. I found one spot, right by civic center, where a bunch of parents with small children had made a kind of kindergarten, an open circle of people with a bunch of playing kids in the middle. Boy, was that cool—made me think that my fellow humans were really basically great.

I got a call from Ange, who, of course, was already in the thick of the crowd, blocks away from me within the mass. I told her where I was and she told me to stay put and she'd come and meet me.

"Okay, we're down," Lemmy said. "You bookmarked that location, right?"

"Got it," I said.

"Roger that, mission control," he said.

"Yeah, that." I flicked from one copter feed to the next, watching as a cam soared over our heads and I saw that we weren't on the edge of the protest anymore—it now stretched for two blocks behind us, and there were lots of people still arriving.

I was still taking in this fact when a large, firm hand clamped my shoulder and I had a momentary panic, sure that this was someone from Zyz come to snatch me out of the crowd. Before I was even conscious of what I was doing, I had started to move into the thick of the crowd, turning sideways to eel my way through the small gaps between bodies. But then a familiar voice said, "Marcus!" and I stopped and turned around. It was Joe Noss, in his usual campaigning clothes, sweater and all. He was grinning like a bandit.

"Joe!" I said. "Sorry, you startled me!"

"Ah, I know no one wants to run into the boss on the weekend," he said. "Isn't this something, then?"

"It's amazing," I said, thinking as I said it that maybe he wasn't someone who supported this kind of thing and wondering if I'd said the wrong thing. "I mean, I think it's incredible, right?"

"Marcus, in all my life I've never seen anything like this. If there was ever a time to be an independent candidate, it's now. These people are just plain *fed up* with the way things work in government. And so am I; so there we are, all in this together."

"Preach, brother!" Lemmy said, and Joe smiled his thousand-watt smile at him.

"Hello there," he said. "I'm Joseph Noss."

"Oh, I know it! I'm Lemmy."

"Lemmy's a friend of mine. From the hackerspace."

Joe shook his hand. "What a treat. Marcus has told me about your space. It sounds, well, extraordinary. Like you're some kind of superheroes of science. From what he tells me, you folks can build just about anything you set your mind to."

Lemmy nodded vigorously. "Yeah, pretty much. And if we can't build it, someone at some other makerspace or hacker-space will help us out. We have a Friday night drop-in—you should come by and see what we're up to."

"I'd love that, though perhaps I might have to wait until after election day, as I'm a little preoccupied." He scanned the crowd again. "I can't get over this," he said. "All these people."

"Look at this," Lemmy said, and showed him his screen.

"Is that from one of the news networks?" Joe asked.

Lemmy laughed. "Yeah, HNN, Hackerspace News Net-work. It's coming off some unmanned quadcopters I built. Up there." He pointed at the sky. Joe looked up, looked back at him.

"You're joking. You're flying *helicopters* by remote control?"

"Oh, they only weigh a couple pounds and they're the size of dinner plates. Little guys, nothing fancy. Maybe fifty bucks' worth of parts in each of them. Most expensive thing in them are the batteries, and I hand-built them from salvaged cell phone battery packs."

Joe put his hands on his hips and cocked his head at Lemmy, as if wondering whether he was pulling his leg. Then he shook his head in admiration. "Incredible," he said. "Just amazing."

"Want to fly one?" Lemmy said, tapping at his screen. "There's about fifteen thousand people watching the feed off this one, go nuts. Just use the keypad."

Joe looked at the phone in his hand as if it were radioactive. "I don't think I'm qualified to operate an aircraft."

"Oh, you're not *operating* it. It operates itself. You just tell it where to go."

I thought Joe was going to balk, but he prodded tentatively at the screen, then more forcefully. "Amazing," he said, after a little time. "Just . . . *amazing.* What's this red icon flashing for, though?"

Lemmy took the phone. "Low battery," he said. "Better bring the gang in for a battery swap. Luckily I brought a ton of charged spares."

He disappeared down the rabbit hole, all his attention focused on his phone, doing that classic nerd-focus thing, radiating a cone of "I'm busy, don't bug me" as his fingers danced.

There was something I wanted to tell Joe, but I was scared to. My mouth had dried up, but my palms were wet. The crowd noise around us was loud, but I could still hear my heart in my ears.

"Joe," I said. He looked at me with those eyes that seemed to bore straight into my soul.

"Yes, Marcus?" he said. His whole body language shifted into a posture of thoughtful listening, one of those politician magic tricks that seemed to set him apart from the rest of us. Part of my mind wondered if he even knew he was doing it, while the rest of my mind was calming down and responding to it. Minds are weird.

"I think I've got an idea for your campaign. It's a bit, um, ambitious, though."

"Ambitious is good. I like ambitious."

"What if we give our supporters a vote-finding machine, a little app they can run on their PCs. First it goes through your contacts lists on Facebook, Twitter, email, and whatever, and gives you a one-click way to send a message to each person in your neighborhood who you think you could recruit to support your campaign. We could give them some checkboxes for issues that they think each contact cares about, and automatically create a pitch note with your positions on each. Every new supporter is then asked to do the same thing with *their* contacts list. Then we go after everyone in the local campaign donor records, cross-checking to see if any existing supporters have a connection to them that we can use to pitch them for money. And then it moves on to voters and people you could register to vote.

"But we don't just use a static pitch. We start with what we think our best talking points are, write several variations, and test them to see which ones perform best. A/B testing—is this one or that one more effective? We can tweak the pitch several times a day, if we get enough volume, all through the campaign, like polling but *fast*. And anyone who recruits a friend gets points, and we do leaderboards, and invite the best performers every week to a big beer-and-pizza party at HQ, make it all into a game, a championship.

"Meanwhile, we use mapping software that knows where every voter is to calculate the optimal places to hold events around the state. The press database is blasting them out—and the press is coming, because they're actually fun. Instead of sober speeches about random words, they're much more like stand-up or *The Daily Show*—full of great, witty sound bites that work perfectly in an evening newscast or a newspaper story. And because they're so entertaining and always a little different, they bring quite a following; they become events."

Joe's eyes were wide. "You can build this?"

I shrugged. "Probably. I mean, most of it sounds like it's just a quick tweak of some of the free/open campaignware out there. But I don't think anyone's done it for elections yet. I could build something, get it running."

"So if you could build it, then my opponents could, too?"

"Can't see why not. But that sounds like a reason for you to build it first."

He laughed. I had an idea, though.

"So, but I've also been thinking of ways you can use the net that your opponents can't."

"Go on."

The same remote part of my mind wondered why he didn't say, "Can't this wait until Monday?" But then, he was Joe. He was the candidate. He didn't get weekends. He was here, with one of his campaign workers, and that meant that he was, fundamentally, *at work*.

"You know the darknet docs, right?" It took everything in me not to look around at that moment to see if anyone was watching.

"I'm familiar with them," he said. His face was unreadable, the same mask of *listening* he'd slipped into when I started talking.

"Well, they're hard to get at right now. You have to do a lot of stuff with Tor, which is this anonymizing technology that's kind of tricky. On the plus side, it's really hard to take them down or even figure out where they are. On the other hand, they're hard for normal people to go and see. That's because no one's hosting them on a regular, boring old Internet site, as a collection of documents that anyone with a web browser can see and link to."

"Yes," he said. "I think that's right. The main reason *I* didn't go and look at them myself is that it seemed altogether too complicated for someone who wasn't a dedicated techno-ninja."

I started to say, *It's not that hard*—and was about to launch into a little tutorial about how to use Tor, but I stopped myself. It didn't matter, and besides, if Joe *felt* like it was too complicated, it was important to acknowledge that he had the right to feel that way.

"Well, I *have* looked at these documents, and from what I've seen of them, they're full of corruption, crime, and sleaze. And by and large, this corruption, crime, and sleaze has been committed by the big parties and their pals. So it seems to me that if you want to convince people that they should risk voting for an independent candidate, it'd help if you could show people that they're not 'wasting their votes' when they vote for you, because any other vote is going to give power to the same dirt-bags who did all this bad stuff."

"You think we should host all the darknet documents," he said. He didn't look like he thought it was the worst idea in the world, but he also didn't throw his arms up and give me a bear hug and shout, *Marcus, you've done it!*

"Yeah."

"From what I understand, only a small percentage of these documents have been examined. What if we put all this stuff on our site and it turns out that its full of lies or dirty jokes or peoples' bank details?"

Damn, I liked Joe. That was a really good question. "Well, there's the darknet spreadsheet, and that lists all the docs that have been combed over by the darknet team, whoever they are"—I made a conscious effort not to look guilty—"so we could just slurp those in. I could write a script that checks the spreadsheet several times a day and grabs anything that's been described."

He looked thoughtful. "Well, that's better than putting it all up, but, Marcus, we don't know who these darknet people are. What you're talking about is fundamentally giving them the ability to put anything they want on the Joe Noss campaign website, just by adding it to their spreadsheet. That seems like a big step to me. And a big risk."

That was frustratingly true. I hate it when people are right at me. "Um," I said. "Well, what if we set up a requirement that everything has to be looked at by a human in our office before it goes live?" I thought for a moment longer. "I could put up all the titles of the docs that we haven't approved yet, and let visitors to the site vote for which ones they want reviewed first. So if they started pouring in by the thousands, we'd prioritize the ones that Joe Noss supporters were most interested in."

He started nodding midway through this, and by the time I finished, he was smiling. "That's a very interesting idea. Not at all what I had in mind, I have to say, but it's pretty interesting. Being the best place in the world to find out about the corruption of traditional politics is a smart move for a reforming, independent political candidate. And you think you could build this?"

I thought about it for a moment or two, mentally sketching out the way I'd stitch together off-the-shelf parts from various software libraries that already existed for Drupal, the industrial-strength system we were using to manage our website. "Yeah," I said. "It should be pretty straightforward. I've done most of that stuff before, it's just a matter of doing it again, but gluing it together in a different way."

He nodded again. "Do it," he said. "Do both. Build me a demo and I'll show it to Flor and my advisory committee. I might get you in to help with that. If they sign off on it, we'll make it happen. Can you have something for Monday?"

It was Saturday. Theoretically, I could do this on Sunday. He'd said a demo, right? I could nail up a demo in a couple hours. "Yeah," I said. "I can do that."

"You are my delta force ninja, Marcus!"

Lemmy straightened up from his work on the quadcopters' batteries and laughed. "That sounds about right."

My phone rang then—it was Ange, lost in the crowd nearby, and I talked her in, waving my hands in the air so she could spot me. She gave me a giant hug, and I introduced her to Joe.

"Marcus thinks you're pretty awesome," she said to him, by way of hello.

"It's entirely mutual," he said, and the way he said it, it was like he meant it, not like a mere formality. I could actually feel my head swelling. "And I'm sure you're something special, given what I know about him. You should come by our office sometime and say hello, watch Marcus do his magic."

"I'd like that," Ange said, and I could tell she felt the same immediate trust and bond with Noss that I'd felt. It was like magic—scary and wonderful at once.

Ange crouched down to say hi to Lemmy and went to work with him getting the quadcopters ready to go again. She'd tuned in to our feed—following my tweet—and was itching to do some flying. I could tell that Lemmy would have a hard time getting the controller away from her.

"I imagine you go to these all the time," Joe said to me.

"Um," I said. "Not really. Liam and I went to one yesterday, but I have to admit I don't get down to protests very often."

"I see," he said. "When I was a young man, it seemed like all we did was protest—the Reagan years were pretty turbulent in San Francisco. Haven't been out to many since. I keep wondering when something's going to *happen,* though. We used to have speeches and such."

"Well," I said. "You can do a speech if you want. I think a lot of people would like to hear what you have to say." I told him about the People's Mic, which he'd heard of but never seen.

"It sounds like a microphone that only works if you can convince the people around you that you've got something to say," he said. "I like that."

"Want to try?" Having been shoved in front of the People's Mic the day before, I was eager to do it to someone else. After all, Joe was a real, no-fooling politician, with that spooky ability to make you trust him with a look and a few words.

He looked around at the crowd, considering it seriously. "I do believe I would," he said.

"Right now?"

He grinned. "Oh yes, certainly—before I lose my nerve and go home."

I put my hands around my mouth, and feeling a little self-conscious, hollered, "Mic check!"

A dozen or so people picked up the call. I repeated it, and again, until a few hundred people around us were saying "Mic check" and waiting for Joe to start.

Joe, meanwhile, had struck up a conversation with the driver of a nearby parked car, who had climbed out of the driver's seat and perched on the car's bumper. "This gentleman's volunteered the hood of his car for a stage," Joe said. The driver, an older Asian guy in a sportscoat and aviator shades, was looking interested and good-tempered. The whole thing was remarkably cheerful, really—for a gathering of hordes of pissed-off people, we were all in very good spirits. Must have been discovering how many of our neighbors felt the same way we did.

Joe stepped nimbly onto the car's hood, wobbled once, caught his balance.

"My name is Joe Noss and I'm running as an independent for the California senate, but that's not why I'm here today."

This was *waaay* too long for the People's Mic, and the words got jumbled in the repetition. Joe didn't look flustered, just did his thoughtful face again, and started over. "Sorry about that."

"Sorry about that," the People's Mic said.

"My name is Joseph Noss.

"I'm running as an independent candidate.

"For the California senate.

"I could have had the party nomination from the Democrats.

"And probably from the Republicans.

"But I decided to go independent.

"Even though everyone says you can't win in this country.

"Unless you're part of a party.

"And they may be right.

"But I've been a Democrat all my life.

"And the spying, the wars, the banksterism.

"It's not the Democratic Party I joined.

"And the Republicans don't offer anything better.

"Because there's something *wrong* with our country.

"There's something wrong with our *world*.

"Somehow, the ideals of fairness, neighborliness, and justice have vanished.

"To be replaced by a cult of greed, shortsightedness, and whatever you can get away with."

He had the rolling tones of a preacher, and a voice like a bullhorn. He had to wait a long time between sentences, because there were rings and rings of people repeating his words, far down the street in every direction. The guy whose car he was standing on wasn't looking mildly amused anymore. He was looking enraptured. After every sentence, while he was waiting for the mic to finish, he had a look on his face of serene confidence.

"I don't have the answer.

"I don't think anyone has the answer.

"But I think we're only going to find the answer when we stop making it all worse.

"We need politicians who stand for people, not money.

"Which is what I have been.

"And what I plan on being.

"We have an office on Mission Street, right by 24th.

"It's open every weekday.

"You can drop in any time.

"Tell us what you hope for from your government.

"And we'll tell you what we plan on doing.

"And you can visit our website of course.

"Just google Joe Noss." He flashed me a smile. I'd noticed that he always made a point of spelling out double-you-double-you-double-you-dot-joseph-noss-for-california-senate-dot-org every time he finished his speeches, which made him sound like a time traveler from the 1990s, and I'd pointed out that he was the top three results for his own name on every search engine.

"Thank you."

He got a lot of Peoples' Mic–style cheers, fingers wiggling in the air so as not to drown out the speaker, and people crushed in around him as he stepped down and thanked the guy whose car he'd been using. The guy gave him a surprise hug—this was California, after all!—and Joe took it like a pro and gave him a hearty, back-slapping bear hug in return.

"That was most remarkable, Marcus," he said. "Thank you for that opportunity."

"You did great," I said, feeling a little silly telling this guy who was a total pro that he'd done well by the lights of a pip-squeak like me, but he seemed genuinely happy.

We chatted a while longer, and then someone else stood up and did a People's Mic about her student debts, which had grown by over $200,000 in fines and penalties when the loan company lost one of her payments. There were a few more of these, and I was getting hungry. Ange had some cold pizza in tinfoil in her pack, so we moved off a ways and ate, and when we rejoined Lemmy, Joe was gone.

"Said he wanted to see what was happening elsewhere," Lemmy said. "Seems like a good guy."

"He is," I said, vicariously proud to have been the guy who introduced Joe to Lemmy.

Crowds have moods, like people, and these moods are more than the sum of the moods of everyone in the crowd. It's possible to be a happy person in an angry crowd—but not for long, because either you leave or you get angry yourself.

The mood of the crowd when we arrived had been happy, if a little nervous. As the day wore on and the crowds grew and grew, the mood got more excited, with tinges of holy-crap-can-you-believe-this and man-we-should-do-something and how-long-are-we-going-to-get-away-with-this?

The three of us—Lemmy, Ange, and me—moved around some, getting deeper into the crowd and then off into its sub-branches, using the copters to spot places where interesting stuff was happening. We visited a place where a marching band was playing ragtime and people were dancing and whooping; another where a gigantic group of drummers was beating out a wall of polyrhythmic sound, a few makeshift stages where People's Mic talks were going on. One was a really interesting talk about the Federal Reserve, the other an embarrassing conspiracy theory about the government being secretly behind the bombing of the Bay Bridge. The speaker claimed he'd worked on the rebuilding project and had been officially-secretly told not to save anything that might help figure out who was behind the attack.

I'd heard that theory a few times and it just didn't hang together—it seemed like the kind of thing you'd only believe in if you were looking for an excuse to distrust the government. I didn't need any excuse to distrust the government. I didn't need to speculate about the unlikely possibility that they'd blown up the Bay Bridge to find a reason to believe that there were people in power who were just *waiting* for the chance to set up a police state. I distrusted the government because when the Bay Bridge blew, the city of San Francisco became a police state in the space of hours. Either that meant that some evil genius had attacked the Bay Bridge in order to send in all his authoritarian thug henchmen, *or* it meant that there were people out there who were just *waiting* for *any* disaster, standing by with a whole well-developed plan for unleashing their goons on people who've just lived through some kind of terrible emergency.

Call me a skeptic, but I think it's even *creepier* to see someone who's just suffered disaster and think, *Hey, great, they're vulnerable and I can screw 'em over,* than to actually *plan* the disaster. So I just don't see the point in trying to make some kind of case proving that the Bay Bridge was an inside job—it's ever so much more evil if it *wasn't* an inside job.

Thinking this stuff, talking it over with Ange, I started to feel like, somehow, the crowd's mood was changing. It was getting dark, and the temperature was dropping—it had started off as one of those San Francisco September days that are as hot as a July day anywhere else, but it was turning into one of those foggy San Francisco nights that makes you cold right to your marrow. The day's excitement was giving way to more anger and more fear, and it seemed to me that I was hearing a lot more crackling police radios, seeing a lot more helicopters and UAVs overhead.

We were stopped in a particularly dense spot near McAllister Street, so I got out my phone and watched Lemmy's copters' point of view for a while. There were a *lot* more cops, it was true. One of the copters was off at the fringe of the protest and as it swung around, I saw a line of police and military buses stretching out to infinity, seemingly all the way to the Embarcadero. Either those buses were there to bring about a zillion cops to the protest, or they were there to take a zillion protesters away in handcuffs. Or both.

"Lemmy," I said, showing him my screen. Ange pulled my hands lower so she could see, too—I was so freaked that I'd forgotten to take her height into account, which is pretty freaked, all right. Ange wasn't kind to people who were oblivious to the world of short people.

"Time to get out of Dodge," Lemmy said.

"Yeah," I said. "Let's go." We looked around, trying to figure out the shortest path out of the protest, starting to feel a little fear. As I scanned the crowd, I saw that I wasn't the only one getting wild-eyed. There were probably lots of other people who'd been tuned in to feeds from overhead and noticed the massing horde.

I looked back at my phone. "Something's weird."

Ange yanked my arm down, stared at my phone. "Can you be more specific?"

"No," I said. "I can't. But something's weird."

Lemmy peered intently at my screen.

"No police UAVs," he said.

We all looked up at the airspace over the protest. The density of UAVs—gliders and quadcopters—had definitely fallen off. "How do you know it's the police UAVs that are missing?" I said.

"They're the lowest flying," Lemmy said. "Better for getting face shots."

My mouth had gone dry. "Why would they ground all their UAVs?"

Lemmy looked at me with a crazy eye-roll. "Maybe they don't want to get any video of what's about to happen."

"Or maybe they're about to do something to the electronics," Ange said.

Lemmy and I both looked at her. She had a pitbull look of determination on her face and she was digging through her bag. She pulled out two pairs of swim goggles and a stack of paper painter's masks. She pulled one pair of goggles over her eyes and passed the other to me, then used her free hand to produce a quart of milk of magnesia that she used to douse the painter's masks. She put one on, I put one on, and I handed one to Lemmy, but he wasn't paying attention. Instead, he'd crouched down and buried his face in his backpack and he was all but throwing its contents on the ground as he dug for something.

"Lemmy," I said, shaking the dripping mask under his nose. The liquid would neutralize some of the sting in any kind of pepper spray, and if they used some other chemical agent, the wet mask would trap more than a dry one. "Lemmy!"

He stood up so fast he caught me on the chin a little and would have sent me backwards on my ass if there'd been room for it. As it was, the people behind me caught me and steadied me, and I waved a quick thanks at them and turned back to see Lemmy holding a silver zip-lock bag.

"Phones," he said. "Quick!"

I recognized the bag: a Faraday pouch, the kind of thing you put your RFID-emitting ID, transit pass, toll road transponder, or passport into if you didn't want strangers to be able to read it.

But Faraday pouches weren't just good at keeping the stuff inside from communicating with the outside world: they were also good at keeping radio waves from the outside world from getting *inside* them. I yanked out my phone so fast I turned my jeans pocket inside out and scattered small change on the ground around our feet. Ange already had hers out. We dropped them in the bag and Lemmy shoved his in and sealed it and dropped it back in his backpack, then he took the mask from me and dug out his own goggles and pulled them on.

The people around us had seen this weird behavior and some of them were following us. Others were starting to push and panic, trying to get out, and I thought *Oh god, there's going to be a stampede, we're going to die—*

And at that moment, there was a *crack* like the sky was a

sheet of paper being torn in two by enormous, divine hands, and every electronic device in the vicinity sputtered and died.

They'd HERFed us.

HERF stands for High Energy Radio Frequency, and it basically means a big, nasty pulse of raw radio energy. You can build a HERF gun that will tune the power from a standard car battery, focusing it into a pencil-beam of ugly brute force by means of a mini satellite dish and use it to kill a laptop at twenty paces. The whole thing'll cost you under $200 if you're smart about parts.

Of course, if you're a big government or well-equipped police force, you don't need to homebrew anything like this. You can just go through a paramilitary mail-order catalog and buy some ginormous pulsed-energy appliances from off the shelf. From a law-enforcement perspective, they're like a friendly nuclear bomb, one that leaves all the people and buildings intact, but preserves that wicked electromagnetic pulse that turns anything more complicated than a 1975 diesel engine into a paperweight.

I figured that the police had HERFed the crowd, but that wasn't quite right. Later on, during the hearings on the September 24th Protest, police crowd-control specialists testified that they aimed the pulse weapon 100 feet over the crowd, instantly killing every UAV in the sky. These plummeted to the crowd below, and represented the first wave of casualties of the night. No fatalities, but one person was in a coma for six months, and another lost her left eye.

The specialists who testified swore that the mobile phones that they took out were unintentional, as were the firmware on all the cars that caught the edges of the burst. And the six people whose hearing aids died, and the twelve whose pacemakers stopped—entirely accidental and *most* unfortunate.

But they had to "preserve operational security," which is police-ese for "make sure no one could watch what they did next." And after all, they *had* given a "lawful order to disperse," though I can't say as I heard it. Stuff happens, I suppose. All part of life in the big city.

I put my masked mouth right up to Lemmy's ear.

"Lemmy."

"Yeah?"

"You know that copter we landed on the roof, the one with the low battery?"

"Yeah."

"You think it's still able to fly?"

"Dunno. Maybe. Why?"

"I think you should get it in the sky and start streaming video with infrared *right now*."

"Yeah."

He broke the seal on the Faraday pouch and spilled out the phones, handing me mine and Ange's, prodding his handset. The cellular towers had all been switched off at SFPD request a moment before the HERF detonated, but Lemmy's phone included a 900Mhz direct radio link to his UAVs. 900Mhz was a good frequency, great for penetrating walls and other structures, but it was also a *busy* band, noisy with baby monitors and walkie-talkies and RC toys. Of course, all of *those* were pretty much toast at the moment, so Lemmy had the airwaves all to himself.

He grunted in satisfaction. "It's up," he said. "Maybe twenty-five minutes on the battery." A moment later: "It's got 4G, too. Must be picking up towers farther away from us—it's the altitude."

"Great," I said. "Get it over us."

"Yeah."

Ange, meanwhile, was hitting reload-reload-reload on her phone's wifinder, waiting for the moment that the network the copter was retransmitting became available to her. "Got it," she said.

"Can you tweet out the URL for the livestream off the copter?"

"Derp. What do you think I'm doing?"

"Sorry."

I had my phone out, too, and signed on to the UAV's network, sent out my tweet.

"Can you shut down its network bridge?" I asked Lemmy. "There's going to be a zillion people trying to get online and none of the video'll make it out if they do."

"Yeah," Lemmy said. "Yeah, done."

"Okay," I said, and looked around for the first time since the pulse. "Holy mother of Zeus." It was as though all the light in the area had been sucked into the Earth, leaving us in a realm of shadows. All I could see, for as far as I could make out in every direction, were silhouettes, moving uneasily like stalks of wheat in a gathering storm. Here and there people had found flashlights or headlights, and these created pinpricks of illumination that stood out like searchlights.

Then, a wailing sound, a sound I hadn't heard since the day the Bay Bridge blew. It was the San Francisco air-raid siren, a sound like an effect from an old war movie. They used to test it every Tuesday afternoon, but after the trauma of its actual use following the attack on the bridge, they'd discontinued the tests. Too many people reacted to the sound with post-traumatic-stress freak-outs—crying jags, an uncontrollable urge to hide or get out of doors—or indoors—and various other low-grade psychotic reactions. There'd been a long debate and finally the city had settled on testing the alarm by playing three long beeps, three short beeps, and three long beeps—Morse code for SOS.

But now the siren blared, and it was louder than I remembered, though I couldn't see the nearest PA pole. It was so loud it felt like it was *inside* my head, so loud it made my teeth clench as it howled up and down its waveform, a sound that every cell in my body knew meant "Bad stuff is happening."

The silhouetted stalks of wheat began to waver more forcefully, colliding with one another as they tried to find some place away from that punishing sound.

Suddenly, the sound cut off, leaving behind a ringing silence that was almost as scary. Then, an echoing, giant voice broke out over the PA system. It was the voice of pure authority, like something engineered in a lab or coming off a text-to-speech library designed for maximum intimidation and terror.

"THIS IS AN UNLAWFUL GATHERING."

The words bounced around the precincts of the protests, blocks and blocks of it, like a tasteless parody of the People's Mic.

"YOU ARE SUBJECT TO SEARCH AND BACK-GROUND CHECKS."

I thought of the copter zipping over our heads, streaming all this live to the Web. I wondered how many people were tuned in.

"THOSE WHO COOPERATE AND WHO HAVE NOT BROKEN LAWS WILL NOT BE ARRESTED."

There was pushing and shoving from nearby. I looked around and saw that one of the pools of light belonged to a husky protester with a headlamp. He was taking off his baggy coat, revealing a windbreaker emblazoned front and back with block-cap letters: SFPD. I looked around from side to side and back and front and saw that there were more SFPD windbreakers coming into view as burly guys dotted around the crowd like raisins in rice pudding revealed themselves.

But they weren't the only ones revealing their secret identities. A dozen yards away, a trio of guys in all-tactical black, wearing goggles and face masks, arranged in a flying wedge, forced their way through the crowd, knocking people aside as they bulled in a straight line. They snapped to a stop in front of a pair of young guys with scared-pale faces and eyes wide enough to show the whites. With no preamble or windup, two of the officers stuck them with Tasers, and they fell to the ground like stunned oxen, twitching and thrashing. One of them brushed a bystander with his hand and she screamed and her head whipped back and hit the nose of the man behind her, which began to gush blood.

The three guys in the flying wedge took no notice. They knelt down and bound the two guys hand and foot with plastic cuffs, cinching the bindings tight with savage yanks, looking like they were trying to start balky gas mowers, then tossed the guys over their shoulders like rolled-up rugs and bulled their way back out of the crowd.

It was around then that the screams and the pushing started.

At first, it was a distant sound, sounding like it might be a block away, and the pushing was just rippling waves back and forth through the crowd, the person behind me taking a half step back to absorb the shock of the person who'd just taken a half step into *her*, banging into me, me taking a half step back and colliding with Ange, who steadied me and took a half step back.

But the next wave was much stronger, not a half-step push, but a step and a half, and I got an elbow in the solar plexus that drove the wind out of me and would have doubled me over if there were room to double over. And the wave after that was like a mosh pit, and the wave after that was like an earthquake, and the wave after that was like—it was like being in a crowd of hundreds of thousands of people where panic had seized the night and was driving us insane.

Then someone had a brilliant idea.

"Mic check!"

I was irritated at first. Who the hell thought giving a speech at this juncture was going to improve things? But of course, it wasn't about giving a speech, it was about getting through the crowd's animal nature and to its human brain, the part that knew that pushing and shoving was a disaster waiting to happen.

"Mic check!" I called back, and others joined it.

"Mic check!"

"Mic check!"

The call rippled out in concentric circles through the humanswarm, and where it was heard, calmness came. A police snatch squad barreled past me, so close I could have stuck out a foot to trip them, but I did nothing, didn't even flinch. There was a calmness descending on me now, that calmness from the temple, the calmness I'd always sought in moments like this but found so rarely.

One of the husky SFPD guys was heading my way, various pieces of gear clipped to his belt, stuff that I found myself eyeing up curiously despite myself, wanting to know what all those gadgets were about. He stopped a few people away from me, facing a woman and a man who looked like they could have been my parents' friends, the sort they sometimes met for dinner and a show, back in the good days.

The policeman spoke to them authoritatively, and they both produced IDs. The policeman held up a PDA and snapped a photo of each, the ID briefly illuminated in a grid of red laser light, like a supermarket checkout. He stared at his display for a moment, then put it away. Next, they talked intensely for a few minutes, and then the couple handed over their phones, tapping out unlock codes first. They must have been in a radio-frequency shadow, shielded from the HERF blast, leaving their phones in working order. The officer stared at the cable jacks on the phone's underside for a minute before he pulled out a matching cable and inserted it. The cable ended with one of those intriguing boxes on his belt, and I thought I understood what was going on: the police were checking people, logging them, and *copying all the data off their phones* before letting them go.

I was agog. Somehow, this was worse than the snatch squads who'd taken people out of the crowd without so much as a word. Those phones would have so many intimate details of their owners' lives. Passwords. Address books of friends and family. GPS logs of all the locations they'd visited. Browser logs of all the websites they'd loaded. Their IMs, wall updates, tweets. I couldn't believe it.

When the officer was done, he took a pen out of a little arm-holster and scrawled something on the back of each of their hands. The couple were looking glazed-over and horrified. The officer smiled at them and explained something in detail, and they nodded in stunned silence.

The officer gave them a friendly slap on the shoulder and pointed, sending them off through the crowd. I moved to intercept them.

"Hey," I said. "Hey, wait!"

They stopped.

"What did he say to you? The cop, I mean."

The man—about sixty, with a friendly face and a neat little mustache and a soft Southern accent—said, "He said we could show this to anyone who stopped us and they'd let us through." He held up his hand, showed me the mark. It looked like a graffiti tagger's mark, a scribble. Maybe it was his initials. "Special ink," the man said.

"Did he make a copy of your phones?"

The woman nodded. She was about the same age, with a good haircut and chunky wooden jewelry around her neck and wrists, like an old hippie maybe. "Yeah. And he deleted our photos." She frowned. "I had some pictures of my grandchildren on there." They both spoke like they were in a dream or a nightmare.

"Thanks," I said.

"Yeah," they said, and moved off.

The officer had moved on to someone else. He scanned the ID, took the phone. This time, he searched the guy. The guy was black. Maybe that had something to do with it. The cop searched his bag, his pockets. By then, the guy's phone had locked up again and the cop made him unlock it. The guy looked like he wanted to cry—or hit the cop. The cop was clearly enjoying this. He scribbled on the guy's hand and sent him on his way.

Ange and Lemmy had been watching, too. We exchanged horrified looks. Another snatch squad sent a shock wave rippling through the crowd, and this time I did fall over, scraping my palms a little on the ground. The pain seemed to wake me up. I knew what I had to do.

"Mic check!" I called.

Ange gave me an alarmed look.

"Mic check!" I called again.

Ange repeated it. So did Lemmy. The call went around.

"The police are recording IDs.

"And copying the data off your phones.

"And erasing the photos.

"Without a warrant.

"Without charges.

"This is illegal.

"It's a crime.

"It's still a crime when the police do it.

"The police don't get to make up the law as they go."

The officer caught this and looked up at me. I resisted the temptation to speak faster. The People's Mic required slow, measured speech.

"Don't comply.

"Demand a lawyer.

"Refuse to allow them to break the law."

The cop was moving toward me now, plowing through the crowd, reaching for something on his belt. Pepper spray? A Taser? No—a long plastic handcuff strip.

"I think he's going to arrest me now.

"For telling you to uphold the law.

"Think about that."

The policeman was close enough to reach out and grab me when a guy stepped out of the crowd and interposed himself between me and him. I only saw his back—a green Army-surplus parka with a head of long hair protruding from it. He had three earrings in his left ear and two in his right. I saw it all in photographic clarity, limned with the light from the officer's flashlight.

The policeman tried to sidestep him, but two more people stepped in his way. Then more. I took a step back and people closed ranks around me. The officer shouted something. No one repeated it. He didn't have the People's Mic.

"You can go now."

I don't know what possessed me to say it. It just popped out.

"You can go now." The crowd repeated it, the sound rippling out.

"You can go now." It became a chant. "You can go now."

Four little words. Not "Screw you, pig!" or "This is what democracy looks like." Instead, it was a group of people asserting that they were capable of looking after themselves, and dismissing the "public servant" who'd come along to send them off to bed like naughty children.

"You can go now."

The cop stopped. His expression had changed from the

confident, condescending friendliness with which he'd ad-
dressed the people he'd searched to something between rage
and terror. His hand moved toward his belt, which was hung
with all sorts of things that had pistol grips or aerosol buttons—
"nonlethal" weapons he could use to shock us, gas us, immobi-
lize us. More people joined the crowd between the cop and me,
and I had to stand on tiptoes to see that behind him, the crowd
had parted, leaving a clear walkway for him to turn around and
leave.

"You can go now."

Hundreds of us were chanting it now. We weren't angry
anymore. And we weren't laughing, either. There was no
mockery in this. *We've got this. You're not needed. Go do something
else.* That's what it meant.

"You can go now."

The cop turned on his heel and walked slowly away, his
head held high, chin out, shoulders rigid. Even though he had
been on the verge of gassing me a moment before, I felt a
moment's pity for him. All he had was authority, and we'd taken
that away from him. Now he was just a man in a kid's dress-up
future-soldier costume, retreating from the "civilians" he was
supposed to be guardian and master to.

A sound is just a shock wave, vibrating at a certain pitch and
frequency. In thin air, there aren't many molecules for the shock
wave to push ahead of itself, so the sound travels slowly and dies
quickly. But in dense substances—steel and stone and water—
sound travels fast and for a long, long way, because the shock
wave has so much material to work with as it pushes forward
and out.

We were packed in dense and thick, and our ideas traveled
like sound vibrating along a steel beam. *You can go now* was
rippling away from us like rings in a pond. The crowd lurched

toward Market Street: one step, two steps. After a day of gathering—gathering our numbers and our strength—we were on the march. We were going to go somewhere.

Ange twined her fingers with mine, and I threw my arm around Lemmy's neck. We must have looked like Dorothy, the Tin Man, and the Scarecrow setting off down the Yellow Brick Road. Another step. *You can go now.* And so can we. Another step.

I had just a moment's warning—a general commotion, angry shouts, an elbow in the back as the person behind me was shoved forward—and then the snatch squad had me.

It was just a confusion of hands at first. Strong hands, all over my body. Then a meaty arm put me in a headlock, squeezing hard on my neck, choking so hard I couldn't get a sip of air down my throat. The hands on my arms yanked them behind my back, twisting them painfully in some kind of martial arts come-along hold that made me feel like they would be torn off at the shoulders.

The plastic handcuff bit cruelly into my left wrist and I'd have screamed if I'd had the breath for it. I thrashed instead, and there was a red-black haze creeping in around the edges of my vision. I registered screaming—Ange, other voices—and was lifted off my feet briefly and shoved this way and then that.

And then I was on the ground, gasping for breath, and the hands were gone. Ange was beside me, and she grabbed my goggles and pulled them over my eyes and pulled my mask up over my mouth, her fingers shaking with haste and desperation. I brought my hands up to help her and saw that the plastic cuff was still fastened to my left wrist—but not my right. I levered myself to my feet, feeling like I might retch at any minute. Lemmy was standing beside me, his jacket torn, seeping blood from an ugly, swelling bruise on his cheek. He pressed one hand to the wound and gave me a quick thumbs-up with the other.

"What happened?" I said.

"You were de-arrested," Ange said, matter-of-factly. I looked around. A guy with wild dreadlocks beside me was wearing what looked like a police-issue gas mask and carrying what was definitely a police-issue riot shield. Behind him, a short woman was wearing a police helmet. A few more police helmets bobbed around the crowd.

"What did they do to the cops?" I said.

Lemmy shrugged. "Not much. Took their stuff as they retreated. Don't worry, no one beat up a cop or anything."

We were still on the march. The crowd took another shuddering step toward Market Street. The mask over my face made it hard to breathe, and my goggles were fogging up. I was just about to clean them when the gas fell.

They were dropping it from nearly invisible, nearly silent black aerostats, little toy blimps that used whispering electric motors to keep themselves in place. I'd helped build some at Noisebridge once, a side project of the space-program team, who had also launched a lighter-than-air weather balloon with two cameras into the upper atmosphere, snapping pictures of the planet below it, curving away like the ball we knew it to be but could never see. The aerostats were as light and flimsy as a dry cleaner's plastic suit bag. The way they hovered in place was eerie—prod one with your finger and it would waft away like dandelion fluff, then return to the exact same location with tiny, precise bursts from its little fans. The ones I'd played with had reminded me of jellyfish, and not in a good way. They were like brainless, drifting aliens, and I'd instinctively feared them. Like they might have a sting waiting for the unwary.

The gas canisters slung under their bellies released their payloads with little near-synchronized *pops*, popcorn kernels detonating in a pan, and we all looked up at once, then—

—Panic.

The gas had been released from four or five yards over our heads, far enough up that it formed a drifting cloud that you could actually watch for a moment, which we did, and then as the reality of the falling chemical poison sank in, we all tried to simultaneously hit the ground *and* run away, anything to get away from the floating, descending toxin.

I was jostled this way and that, knocked to the ground, stamped on—one hard boot landed on my head, another got me in the kidney—dragged to my feet by anonymous hands, shoved, knocked down again, picked up again.

Then the choking started, and with it, choked screams. Then vomiting. Maybe there was something in the gas to make you puke, or maybe it was its victims' bodies trying desperately to expel the noxious foreign substance from every orifice. I was splashed with puke from all sides, and I slipped in it as I got to my hands and knees, then to my knees, then to my feet.

I'd caught some of the gas through my painter's mask, but not much. I was having a little trouble breathing, and my eyes were watering inside my goggles from the irritants that had climbed up my sinuses. I was half blind and it was dark, and there was only one thing I could think: *Ange*.

I scanned for her, but couldn't find her. A few other people had gotten to their feet, and I heard and then saw quadcopters and gliders start to crisscross the airspace over our heads again. I was sure they had their nightscopes on and were getting lots of footage. I supposed they'd be able to get nice, long, clear pictures of anyone who showed up with goggles and masks—"troublemakers" who'd come expecting that the police would deploy chemical agents against them for having an opinion.

I called Ange's name through my mask, and it came out muffled, and when I breathed deep to shout louder, I caught a mouthful of the chemicals clinging to the mask's outside, sucked through its pores and around its sides, and doubled over coughing, swallowing hard to keep from vomiting. I did *not* want to vomit into my mask, and I did *not* want to take my mask off and show my face.

I started grabbing the people on the ground around me and helping them to their feet. I had no idea where Ange was, but if she was one of those people thrashing in their own vomit on the ground, I hoped that someone was helping her up.

I reached for a big guy with a short, military brush cut who was holding his head and groaning, and something stopped me, rooted me to the spot with an irrational icicle of fear stabbing me right in the spine. I squinted at the man, and then it hit me—an ugly gnarl of scar tissue that ran from the crown of his head to his thick neck. I'd seen it before, in the back of an all-black luxury car whose back doors had no handles. It was Knothead, the Zyz goon.

Chapter 13

He was only a few yards behind where I'd been. Close enough to keep a good eye on me, if that's what he'd been doing there. Far enough away that he couldn't have quite reached out and grabbed me, if that was his goal.

I took a step backwards, landing on someone's fingers, jerking my foot up, nearly skidding on a slick of used food and toxic chemicals. I caught my balance, took another step. Knothead hadn't spotted me yet. He wasn't wearing tactical black, but I saw that his blue jeans had a couple of bulging cargo pockets, and there were a few little bulges around his waistline.

I took another step and looked carefully around me. Would Knothead have been here alone? Would he have had Timmy with him? Zyz didn't strike me as the kind of organization that sent its goons out on their own. I looked all around me, finding new reservoirs of panic and fear, searching the crowd for guys who could be Timmy, wondering if he might be wearing a wig or some other disguise. I didn't see him, but I *did* spot Lemmy helping an older guy who was limping, his arm around Lemmy's shoulders. I started to move toward him, and then I felt a hand take mine. For a glorious moment, I thought Ange had crept up on me and grabbed my hand—somehow, I could feel that these were a woman's fingers.

Then the fingers grabbed hold of my thumb and did something awful and painful to it, something that made my head snap back in pain. I cried out, the sound muffled by my mask, and tried to squirm away from the terrible, wrenching pain. That only made it worse. I went up on my tiptoes, in agony, and managed to twist around and see who was the author of my suffering.

It was Carrie Johnstone, dressed like a sitcom housewife doing the grocery shopping in track pants, a loose SFSU sweatshirt, her hair tied back in a scrunchie. It was such a great disguise, so utterly unlike her efficient, ruthless persona, that I couldn't figure out where I knew that stern face from at first. When I did, I gasped harder. "Hello, Marcus," she said, and relaxed her grip on my thumb, just a little, so that I could catch my breath and focus for a moment. She watched my eyes carefully and when she was convinced that I was paying full attention, she brought her other hand out from beneath her sweatshirt. In it, she held a little two-pronged, pistol-gripped tactical black gizmo. A Taser.

"I'd prefer not to use this," she said. "Because then I'd have to carry you. That would be conspicuous. And I might have to drop you. You wouldn't like that. Am I being clear?" I nodded and swallowed a few times behind my mask. She made the Tazer vanish. "Smart boy. Come along now. We've got to move."

It was full night now, and as the people around us regained their feet, there was chaos—shoving and pushing in the dark, crying and some screams and retching. Every now and again, I'd hear someone shout, "Mic check," and some weak echoes as people tried to establish order, but Carrie Johnstone always steered me away from those places, pushing me ahead of her like a battering ram, still gripping my thumb but hardly twisting it. Instead, she pulled it this way and that, steering me with it as if it were a joystick.

Somewhere behind us, I could hear the police bullhorns giving orders to sit down and put your hands on your head, and then I heard Johnstone curse, and she started pushing me faster.

The night blurred past, but something was nagging at me. Carrie Johnstone and Knothead had been at the protest, looking for me, I suppose, and they'd have been caught in the HERF burst. They were all about tactical this and tactical that, but would they have thought to put their clever devices inside Faraday pouches? Johnstone said the reason she hadn't Tased me was that she didn't want to carry me, but really, would it be that hard for her to drag me out of the crowd? Would it be that conspicuous? I was willing to bet that Johnstone could bench-press a water buffalo.

And the million-dollar question: was there enough electronic circuitry in a dumb little Taser to make it vulnerable to a HERF blast?

I crashed into an old man whose face was streaked with dirt and tears, his face looming out of the night, eyes wide and surprised. He barely had time to register the fact that I was about to collide with him before we were going down in a tangle. As we fell, I felt Carrie Johnstone's grip tighten on my thumb, try to wrench it into that special configuration of torment, and slip.

I coiled my legs under me and sprang into the night like a jackrabbit, scrambling to get away, using hands and feet to get through the crowd, running blindly in the darkness. Behind me, I heard outraged cries and wondered if they were from the people I'd hurtled past, or from people who were being tossed aside by the vengeful hands of Carrie Johnstone. I ran so hard I lost my breath and couldn't catch it, couldn't get even a sip of air to pass my throat, but I forced myself to run on, even as my vision blackened around the edges, telescoping again.

I had been running west, and something about the buildings around me made me think I was getting away from the protest's center, out toward the edge. Soon I might escape to the real world, a place away from relentless pursuers and gas and crowds. Keeping that in my mind, I forced one foot in front of the other, gulping like a fish in my wet, claustrophobic mask.

It wasn't going to work. I wasn't going to make it. Any second now, I was going to fall to my knees and a second after that, Carrie Johnstone would have me. Even without the Taser, she was going to have to carry me—things inside me were wearing out, bursting, breaking, and once I stopped moving, I wouldn't be able to start again.

But there was the edge of the crowd, I could see it. See the place where the wall of people ended and the city began. Just a few more steps. The lights ahead glittered in my foggy, steamed-up goggles. I was so fixated on them, I didn't even see the police line that divided the protest from the real world, a line of helmeted men wearing bouquets of plastic handcuffs at their waists, hard-faced, hands encased in black gloves. I almost stopped myself then, but I didn't. Maybe I couldn't have. In any event, I was pretty sure that Carrie Johnstone couldn't kidnap me from jail.

One step, two steps, and then I was crashing into a policeman—I actually smelled his cologne and the hamburger on his breath as he absorbed the weak momentum of my last stumbling rush. He steadied me, took in my mask and goggles, spotted the plastic handcuff around one wrist, grabbed hold of the loose cuff, jerked my arm around, grabbed my other arm, and cuffed it. I was handled as impersonally as a sack of potatoes as another cop stepped forward out of the line and directed me to one of the waiting buses I'd spotted from the sky.

Before he put me inside, he patted me down, reaching for my phone, then stopping when his gloved hand encountered some of the vomit I'd been spattered with. He said, "That a cell phone?"

"Yeah," I said. "It's dead, though."

"Right," he said. "They'll take it from you when you get processed anyway."

There were already a couple dozen people in the darkness and quiet of the bus. Some were young, some were old, some were brown or Asian, some were white. It was laid out like a school bus, the kind of thing I'd ridden a thousand times on school trips, except for the steel mesh separating the driver's seat and back of the bus from the rest of the interior. Each seat held two people, and they were loading us from the back forward. I was halfway down the bus's length, and I had a seatmate, a guy in black jeans and sweatshirt. He was unconscious and breathing shallowly. The officer who led me to him didn't say anything as he guided me down into the seat, with an impersonal air that was neither hostile nor friendly. I jostled the guy and he made a whimpering noise, like a hurt animal.

"I think this guy needs medical help," I said, squirming in my seat to find a comfortable way of sitting with my arms lashed together behind me.

"He'll get it," the cop said. "Soon as he's processed."

There were murmured conversations around me, the voices tight and scared, like the voices of kids hiding from a killer in a slasher movie. I stared out the windows, looking for any sign of Carrie Johnstone or Knothead—or Ange or Lemmy, for that matter. At five-minute intervals, I remembered that I had forgotten to write a lawyer's phone number on my arm and thought about what an idiot I was. Against all odds, I actually drifted off to sleep for a while, leaning forward with my head against the back of the seat in front of mine. I guess my body had used up so much adrenaline that there just wasn't anything left to keep me awake. On top of everything else, I had the mother of all caffeine-withdrawal headaches. I would have happily eaten a pound of espresso beans and asked for seconds.

I woke up when someone was plunked down in the seat in front of mine. I looked up groggily and saw that it was a girl about my age. She was Middle Eastern–looking, with designer clothes and long hair that had mostly escaped from its ponytail. She had a look of utter, grim determination.

"Hey," I said to the cop. "Hey, are we going to get to go to the bathroom soon?"

"After you're processed," the cop said.

"When's that?"

"Later."

"Come on, we've been in here forever. Could you at least take my cuffs off?"

"No." The cop turned on his heel and left. The weird thing was how impersonal the whole thing had been. The guy could have been telling a panhandler that he didn't have any spare change.

"How long have you been in here?" the girl said.

"I don't know," I said. "I nodded off. A while. Do you know what time it is?"

She shrugged. "I think it must be after eleven."

"What's going on out there?"

"Oh," she said. "They're questioning everyone. If they don't like your answers, you go behind the fence."

"The fence?"

"You didn't see it? There's a big area, a block square. All fenced in with movable barriers. They don't like you, they put you there. Then they talk to you some more. If they still don't like you, they bring you here. You didn't go to the fence, huh?"

I thought about explaining that I'd been chased into a cop by a psychotic war-criminal merc. I said, "Nope. Just got grabbed and put here."

She shook her head. "Not me. They grabbed me, checked my ID, penned me in, checked my ID again, put me here. Bastards."

"Why do you think they grabbed you?"

She shrugged again. "I don't know. Racism? These days, having an Egyptian last name is like being called Jasmina Bin Terrorist Al Jihad. Or maybe it's because I belong to ECWR."

"What's that?"

"Women's group," she said. "The Egyptian Center for Women's Rights. Solidarity with women in the Middle East. The women came out for the revolutions, helped overthrow the dictators, spilled their blood. Then the new 'revolutionary' governments sent them back home, started running around talking about 'modesty' and 'a women's place.' So we talk about it here, have discussion groups, produce literature about what the Koran actually says about women. We call them out for their bullshit." She shrugged again. "So maybe that's it. I don't know. I tried to call my family when I was in the fenced area, but my phone didn't work. No one's did."

Huh. "Do you have a lawyer you could call?"

"No," she said. "But my mother would know someone— once she got over having a heart attack about me being arrested. What does it matter, though?"

I dropped my voice to a whisper. "I have a working phone."

The unconscious guy next to me stirred. He cracked one eyelid and said something indistinct.

"What?" I said, leaning in.

"415-285-1011," he said. "National Lawyers Guild number for San Francisco. If you've got a phone, I'd appreciate it if you'd call them for me."

There was a guard sitting at the front of the bus, on the other side of the heavy wire mesh that enclosed us. He wasn't paying much attention. Or maybe he had a hidden mic and was listening to every word through a headphone in the ear I couldn't see.

"Right," I said. "Do you think you could get your fingers in my pocket if I move around so you can reach?"

He shifted, made a hissing noise like a teakettle. "Don't think so. I expect my arm's busted."

I looked more closely. The arm closest to me was definitely at a funny angle. He must have been in agony. I turned back to the girl ahead of me. "Do you think you could get the phone out of my pocket?"

She craned around to look at me. "Maybe," she said, doubtfully. "How are we going to dial it?"

"Dunno," I said. "Let's burn that bridge when we come to it."

I twisted around to get my hip to stick out in the vicinity of the girl's bound hands. I jostled the guy with the broken arm in the process and he made another hissing sound, but didn't say anything when I said "Sorry."

The next part was really hard. We had both moved so we were sitting on the seats with our legs in the aisle. My phone was in my front pocket, so to get it close to her, I had to turn around so I wasn't facing her anymore and scootch backwards to where her hands had been. Then she had to find my pocket with her bound hands, working blind, facing away from me.

"Ew," she said.

"It's not mine," I said. "Someone puked on me."

"That's so much more comforting, thanks."

She got her thumb and forefinger into my pocket, pushed in farther, gripped my phone, started to tug it out of my pocket. She got it most of the way out and lost her grip and I thought the phone was going to fall on the floor, but I kind of twisted my hip so that it ended up slipping back. She tried again and this time, she got it out.

"Give me a sec," she said. "These cuffs are so tight I can barely move my hands, and wriggling like that didn't help."

"Take your time," I said. "Can you get the phone into my hand?" I backed up until my fingers brushed hers and she pressed the phone into my hand.

While she flexed her fingers and wrists, trying to get the blood to circulate, I turned my phone around in my hands behind my back. I remembered the days when phones had actual buttons you could find by touch and dial without seeing them. I could feel the phone in my hand, in its familiar grip, my thumb over the power button. I turned it on and ran my finger over the screen, feeling the familiar haptic buzz—the little vibrations the phone emitted each time my finger brushed over a "hot" region on the screen to let me know that I was in a spot that could make the phone do something. Running my fingertip up the screen, I carefully counted out the four buzzes from bottom to top, and the three from left to right, trying to figure out where the number pad layout was drawn. This was the lock screen for my phone, which I'd configured to take a superstrong eight-digit password. Because, you know, I'm paranoid like that.

Gee, thanks, paranoid me. I was going to have to try to key in eight numbers correctly, blind, with half-numb hands. Without alerting the police.

"What are you doing?" the girl in front of me asked.

"I *think* my finger is on the number one. Is that right?"

"I don't know, you're holding the phone upside down."

Oh, this was going to be great. I rotated my wrists around so that the screen was facing her. Incidentally, this also made my fingers feel like I was trying to do the world's stupidest and hardest magic trick.

"Your fingers are on the one, the nine, the three, and the six."

Now I rearranged my hand again so that only one of my index fingers was on the glass. So now I had my hands in the stupid-magic-trick pose, *and* was gripping the phone only by its edges.

"Now your finger is on the one."

I moved it. "Three, right?"

"Right, but you got the two on the way."

I bit my tongue and started to count in my head. When I got to twenty, she said, "Okay, it's reset."

It took six tries. After the fifth try, the phone locked itself and we had to wait for ten tense minutes until it unlocked itself. Security is awesome.

"Okay, you've done it," she said. I could barely feel my hands.

"Who do we call first?"

"My mom," she said. "She knows a crapload of lawyers."

It took more fumbling to press the button that brought up the dialer and then an eternity to get her mom's number keyed in correctly. At least the dialer let me press the backspace button when I screwed up.

"You've done it!" she said, loud enough that people in the other seats shifted and looked around. I closed my hand around my phone, trying to hide it without inadvertently pressing any of the buttons. We waited until everyone had gone back to their solitary misery, and then I said, "Okay, how do we do this?"

"Do what?"

"I'm going to call your mom, right? How are you going to talk to her from up there, when the phone is down here?"

"Oh."

"Yeah."

"How high can you get your arms?"

I tried. It actually felt good to lift them some, working the kinks out of my shoulder blades, but I was left wishing I'd gone to more yoga classes with Ange. The woman—I still didn't know her name, isn't that funny?—shifted behind me, and I felt

her prod the call button with her nose or tongue, and then my
fingertips tingled with the sound of the phone ringing. From
where I sat, I saw several of my fellow prisoners watching with
expressions ranging from bemusement to delight to fear. I heard/
felt someone answer, a kind of *buzz-buzz?* that my fingers
translated as *Hello?* and then the girl whispered, "Mama," and
started to talk in a low, urgent whisper, speaking a language
I didn't know—Arabic, I guess? Is that what they speak in
Egypt?

The bus was brightly lit, but we had been locked in it for
ages—hours, it felt like—since the last prisoners were brought
in. Surely the guard at the front was half asleep or bored stupid,
or maybe he was stupid to begin with. Either way, I felt a welcome sense of superiority. They might be heavily armed, they
might be able to arrest us and stick us in their plastic cuffs,
they might be able to jail us and try us for crimes they'd invented just for the occasion, but they couldn't control us utterly
and totally. Here we were, right in the belly of the beast, and
we'd cooperated to establish a channel to the outside world.
Between the gas and the violence and the sleep deprivation, I
felt a strange madness creep over me, a sense that I was invul-
nerable and invincible, that I was destined to win, because I was
able to do the things that the hero of a story would do, and don't
heroes always win?

The first clue I had as to my total vincibility, my utter vulnerability, was when the eyes of the prisoners behind me on the
bus widened in unison, turning to comical expressions of horror that made them all look like they were somehow related,
cousins in a family of genetically frightened people.

The next clue was the terrified squeak from the girl behind me, and then the final clue a bare instant later: the phone
knocked out of my hands, my wrists grabbed by a gloved hand
and yanked so high and so fast that I barely had time to lever

myself out of the seat, bending almost double, forehead impact-
ing painfully with the floor as I sought to escape the wrenching, tearing agony in my shoulders.

Then there was a face beside mine, so close I heard the
click of its teeth in my ear, so close I could smell the gum on its
breath. It belonged to my tormentor, who said, "Kid, no one
likes a smart-ass." My hands were released and I whimpered as
my arms snapped back, my fists kind of bouncing off my butt,
my face grinding into the dirty floor of the bus.

Before I could get my breath, the same hands had my ankles
and the familiar, dread sound of plastic handcuffs being ratch-
eted along their closure mechanism ripped through the air as
one ankle, then the other, were cinched tight enough to hurt.
The hands kept moving. My wrists were jerked back as the
plastic between them was caught and hauled back up, the man
working over me grunting softly—a curiously tender sound—
and another set of cuffs were attached to the plastic between
them. Then my ankles were hauled up toward my wrists and
my fogged-over brain realized that I was about to be hogtied.

I kicked and bucked and shouted something, I don't know
what—maybe not even words. Just a kind of howl, a *NO* that
ripped from my guts to my throat. I began to worm my way
down the length of the bus, trying to get away from the tormentor and his hands. The other prisoners got their feet out of
the way, giving me passage, and I heard them shout things at
the guard who was pursuing me: "Shame!" in a dozen voices.

I reached the cage at the back of the bus and squirmed and
wormed my way around on it, turning to face back up the aisle.
The police officer—a young white guy whose hat had been
knocked off, a look on his face like a vengeful god—was trying
to come after me, but the other prisoners on the bus had stretched
their ankles back into the aisles, making a forest of legs that the
cop had to bull past. He reached for the nightstick on his belt,

had it halfway out of its ring, when he seemed to think better of it and shifted his grip to his can of Mace.

He lifted it up like bug spray, shifting the mask around his neck over his face as he did, settling the goggles around his eyes with gloved fingers. The prisoners who saw what he was doing retracted their legs, one by one, until the way between the guard and me was open.

He blinked twice at me.

"It's okay," I said. "I'll sit quietly. You don't have to tie me up—"

He took two steps toward me, holding the Mace in front of him like a vampire hunter holding up a crucifix. Like a vampire, I shrank away from it. My world telescoped down to the nozzle of the Mace bottle, the square aperture with the little round nozzle within. "Please," I said. His finger tightened on the trigger. The bottle was inches from my face, aimed right at a spot midway between my mouth and nose.

"Tom," a voice called from the front of the bus. "What the hell is going on here?"

The guard's finger froze. He slipped the bottle back into its pouch on his Batman belt, turned around on his heel, looked up the length of the bus at an older cop with a couple stripes on his shoulder, an inspector.

The guard walked the length of the bus to his boss and the two of them had a quiet, intense conversation. Every pair of eyes on the bus was glued to them, every ear cocked for them. Tom's back was to me, and I could see from where I stood that his shoulders were as tight as a tennis racket. It was clear to me that he was getting some kind of dressing-down. I confess that I felt a little smug to see this guy get told off, but mostly I was still crapping myself with residual fear.

Tom got off the bus, and the inspector marched down the bus without a word, grabbed me by the arm, and half dragged me back to my seat, while I tried to keep upright by shuffling my bound feet in a frantic penguin-gait. He pushed me impersonally into my seat and turned on his heel without a word.

"You should have called the lawyers first," the guy beside me said.

I didn't say anything. The lights in the bus went off and the engine roared to life and we were off.

The girl in front of me apologized over the bump and the growl of the bus as we rattled through the night. The irony was that her mom had been so freaked out that the girl hadn't managed to convey anything useful to her. On the plus side, the girl—whose name was Dalia—managed to retrieve my phone after Officer Friendly knocked it out of my hands. She'd managed to drop it into one of her boot cuffs, and promised to get it back to me as soon as she had the chance. I wasn't too optimistic about such a chance coming up, being bound hand and foot as I was, but I appreciated the thought. In the meantime, I gave her my name and told her that if she wouldn't mind googling me and getting my email address to get me the phone back when the time came, I'd appreciate it an awful lot.

The bus wasn't going very fast or very far. Out the window, it was all a confusion of traffic—lots of other police buses—and long delays. Several times we stopped for long periods—it felt like hours, and certainly my arms and shoulders told me it was an eternity—before moving on. I dozed several times, once flopping onto the guy with the broken arm, who made a weak whimper that was worse than a scream.

We got to where we were going just as the sun was coming up. It was a nondescript warehouse-type building, swarming with cops. They took us off the bus two at a time, spaced out by ten or twenty minutes. I guessed that this must be "processing." They left the people who couldn't walk until last. Two burly cops carried me off the bus like a sack of garbage, then went back for my seatmate. I shouted that he needed medical attention. They pretended they didn't hear.

No one asked me why I was bound at the ankles, and no one moved to release me. I was hefted from one station to the next. First I was propped up in a chair in front of a trestle table where a couple of bleary cops with ruggedized laptops—about one millionth as cool and military-looking as the ones that Timmy and Knothead had—fingerprinted me, retina-scanned me, swabbed my cheek for DNA, and then took my name and address and Social Security number. I told them I declined to answer any further questions. I told them I wanted to see a lawyer. I told them I needed to pee. I asked them what I was under arrest for. (I'd drilled this routine a zillion times, but it was a lot harder to do in handcuffs than it was in front of the bedroom mirror when I was having what Mom called *collywobbles* about the thought of being arrested some day.)

They weren't impressed. Their responses, in order, were "Spell Yallow again?" "We don't have any further questions," "Later," "Later," and "Disorderly conduct and conspiracy to disturb the peace."

They called out to someone else and then I was picked up—the whole chair came with me this time—and taken to a fingerprinting station.

Then they took me indoors and led me to a cold, bright room that looked like it had once been a supervisor's office, or maybe a foreman's room, and strip-searched me. At least they cut loose my cuffs for this. I chafed at my wrists and ankles, doing my best not to whimper as the blood started to flow to them again. There were fifteen or twenty other guys in there, and we avoided one another's eyes as we stripped off our clothes and stood shivering and naked while more bored cops went from one person to the next, searching our clothes with hands clad in surgical gloves, like we were infected with some kind of vermin or virus. They looked in our armpits, under our testicles, up our butts. It was one of the most humiliating experiences of my life, partly because it was so bored and clinical. These guys had nothing personal against us. They could have been government health workers inspecting beef on the way to market.

It's surprising how philosophical being shivering, terrified, and naked in police custody can make you. If you'd have asked me how I'd have felt about these guys beforehand, I would have told you that I hated them, thought they were gutless cowards and worse. They were traitors to humanity, people who made their living defending the interests of the wealthy and corrupt and powerful from everyone else. I'd seen them commit violence, seen them arrive at a peaceful protest dressed up like science fiction super-soldiers, seen them bristling with (supposedly) nonlethal weapons and treating people who were scared and upset about the world like vermin.

But there we were, two groups of human beings in a cold room, one group naked, one group wearing overblown Halloween costumes, and none of us wanted to be there. We had parts we'd been given by some weird, unimaginable authority, "the system," and now we had to act them out. I could see that the cops in the room would rather have been pretty much anywhere else, doing pretty much anything else. But there they were, looking up our buttholes and getting ready to throw us into cages.

There was a knife-edged moment where I felt like I could just pull on my underwear and walk up to the nearest cop and say, "Come on, dude, let's be reasonable about this," and we could have talked it over like real people who lived in the same city with the same problems. This guy might have kids who were going to get stuck paying off a quarter million bucks' worth of student debt or he'd lose his house; that guy was young enough that he might actually be living with his parents and trying to pay off that debt.

The moment stretched and broke. Our clothes were patted down and shaken out, then we were allowed to dress again. They cuffed us again, too. I silently begged the universe to keep me free from ankle cuffs and thought I'd made it, when the cop who was trussing me up seemed to remember that I'd been ankle-cuffed and reached for his belt again.

"It's okay," I said. "You don't have to do that."

He pretended he didn't hear me, but grabbed one of my ankles and started to cinch the zip strip around it.

"Come on, man," I said, wheedling and whining now, hating the sound of it in my voice. "It's really not necessary."

The guy made eye contact with me and grunted. "You did something to earn those cuffs. Not my job to figure out whether it's time to get rid of 'em."

I squeezed my eyes shut. This guy had no idea why I'd been cuffed, but because I'd been cuffed, I obviously deserved to be cuffed. Tom was long gone, and so was the inspector who'd rescued me. I could imagine wearing leg cuffs all the way to the courthouse and the judge, and being denied bail because I was the kind of dangerous offender who got leg bindings.

I shuffled out of the foreman's office and into the main building. The cavernous space had been fitted with mesh cages, stretching in corridors as far as I could see. The cages were made of chain-link and steel poles, the poles bolted to the floor and ceiling at precise intervals, slicing the room into little pens. Each one had an electric lock fitted to its hasp, an open-air chemical toilet, and a collection of grim-looking prisoners. Men were on one side of the central aisle, women on the other.

One by one, the cops tossed us into different "cells," following instructions on their hardened, tactical handheld computers. I decided that "tactical" was the world's most boring fashion statement. Sometimes, they put guys into cells that were so full there was no room to sit, other guys went into cells where they were virtually on their own. Several cells sat empty. Whatever sorting and packing algorithm was being used to incarcerate us, it had a sense of humor.

I ended up in one of the nearly empty ones, and was glad that my hands had been cuffed in front of me, because I was finally able to take the piss that had been trying to batter its way to freedom for the past several hours, sitting down on the exposed toilet and hunching over for privacy, then fumbling my underwear and pants back up.

Within a few hours, the cell had gone from empty to full. Yes, I said hours. More hours went by. It felt like we'd been there for a day, though there was no daylight, and everyone had had their watches and phones confiscated. I got to know some of the guys in my cell, and someone tried a mic check and gave a little speech about how much it sucked that we were being held this way and asked the cops to uphold the law and give us our phone calls and food and water. He got cheers from the other protesters in the cells, and the cops pretended they didn't hear.

Hours oozed past.

People had come and gone for so long that I stopped paying attention. I was hungry and thirsty, and the toilet was overflowing and making revolting smells and starting to ooze a sickening chemical slick that reduced the space in the cell. Finally, I realized that the whole place was quieter and emptier than it had been before. More people were going than coming. They weren't coming back. So they were going *somewhere,* possibly to get their phone calls and their hearings.

Finally, officers came for me, two of them. They sliced the middle of the cuffs around my ankles so that I could walk, and I saw that nearly all the cells toward the front of the building were empty. A tingle of hope came into my belly, joining the hunger growls and the pasty, parched thirst.

We came out to the same foreman's room where I'd been searched. A woman police officer, older, black, took my finger-prints again, read notes off a screen, typed, didn't say anything. It's a good thing she didn't, because I kept forgetting that I wasn't going to say anything to *her* unless I had a lawyer present.

She nodded at the guys who'd brought me out and they gripped my arms and walked me to the door. I emerged to cold, gray daylight and a light drizzle. There were thousands of people standing across the street, holding signs and chanting. The officers brought me to the curb, then let go.

"You're done," one said.

"What?" I said.

"Go," the other one said. "You're done."

"What about the charges?"

"What charges? You want us to press charges?"

After all that, they were just going to let me go. Some part of me wanted to say, "Hell yeah, I want you to press charges. Otherwise, what the hell just happened here? A kidnapping?"

The people across the street with the signs and banners were angry. Now I understood why.

"What a load of bullshit," I said, with feeling.

The cops' faces slammed shut. I stood my ground. I was scared as hell, but I stood my ground. Let 'em grab me, chain me up, arrest me, put me in jail, waterboard me, try me, find me guilty, send me up for life. That *was* a load of bullshit, and I had every right to say it.

We stared at each other like dogs about to fight. I noticed that the people across the street had gotten quieter, then louder.

I was peripherally aware of a lot of people with a lot of camera-phones maneuvering into position near me. I guess the cops were, too. One of them turned and walked back. Then the other one.

I was shaking, my fists clenched so hard my fingernails ac-tually broke the skin on my palms in a couple of places.

The protesters patted me on the back. It seemed that they knew what I was freaking out about. There was a table laden with free food—someone had brought down a whole crapton of lentils and rice and PB&J sandwiches and hot pizzas—and five different people asked if I had any money to get home and whether I needed to talk to a doctor.

I sat down on the curb amid the shouting, jostling people and wolfed down about a hundred thousand calories' worth of food, eating mechanically, stopping only once I'd run out of food. Then I got up, dusted off my filthy clothes, and walked away, finding my way home, though I couldn't even tell you how I got there.

Chapter 14

Mom and Dad were gray-faced when I knocked on the door. I tried to make a joke of it. "I'd have thought that you guys'd be used to this by now." My voice cracked a little on the last couple words, and they gave me enormous hugs. They'd figured out where I was, and confirmed it by calling my phone, which Dalia had answered, telling them all about what had happened on the bus. Mom and Dad had dipped into their line of credit to pay a lawyer to start shouting at the SFPD about me, but she was only one of hundreds of lawyers so employed and my parents had had no idea that I was released until I stumbled up the walk.

I wanted to shower for a hundred years. I wanted to sleep for a millennium. But before I did anything, I wanted to find Ange.

"She got home ten hours ago," Mom said. "But her mother said she went right back out to the chicken farm." That was what the press was calling the place we'd all been held, down in South San Francisco, the name coming from the cameraphone photos that had already appeared online, making the place look like some kind of nightmarish poultry factory.

No doubt Ange was waiting for me there and I'd missed her in the horde. How the hell did people live before phones?

"Can I borrow your phone?" I said.

Mom handed it to me, and I spent a couple moments un-fogging my brain enough to get it to cough up Ange's phone number, which had been my first speed-dial for years. "Have you heard from him?" she said as soon as she picked up.

"Kind of," I said.

"Where the hell *are* you?"

"Home," I said.

"What the hell are you doing *there*?"

"Preparing to estivate," I said. Estivate is a very handy verb: it's a kind of hibernation, "a prolonged state of torpor or dor-mancy." Just where I was heading.

"Not until I get there. How *dare* you get out of jail without my finding you?"

"I know," I said. "I'm a rotter. Sorry, darling."

"Have yourself bathed, waxed, perfumed, and put into bed. I'll be there in thirty-five minutes."

"Aye, aye, Cap'n."

The reunion, when it came, was just what I needed and then some. Both of us had been hurt. Ange had been gassed and trampled, arrested and freed, and while her story had some minor variations in its specifics, it came out to about the same thing as mine. She'd been with Lemmy through most of the process—they'd stayed together somehow, Lemmy bodily lift-ing Ange free of the crowd at one point when the crushing started, holding her over his head like a freaky circus act. She'd seen him again after they were released, and promised to call him as soon as she found me.

We talked about it for a few minutes, kissing each other in the places where we were bruised or hurt, holding each other, murmuring to each other, until sleep took us.

———

And the next day, I went to work.

Well, of course I did. It was Tuesday, and the election was coming up, and someone had to get Joseph Noss elected, and it was going to be me. A hundred times on the way to work, I reached for my phone—to make a reminder for myself, to send a text to Ange (who was still sleeping in my bed; her first class didn't start until after lunch), to check the weather for that night, to read what my tweeps had to say. Each time, I thought, *Crap, I've lost my phone.* Got to call it from my laptop and talk to Dalia and arrange to get it back from her. Then I thought, *Huh, I should really make a note about that, now, where's my phone?* And it began again. It was so funny I forgot to laugh.

I came through the door of the Joe for Senate office and stopped. Something was different. I couldn't put my finger on it at first, and then I realized what it was.

Everyone was staring at me.

Every single person in the office was watching me with owl-eyed intensity, giving off a mixture of awe and fear. I gave a little half wave and took off my jacket and headed for my desk, plunked down in my seat, pulled out Lurch, and plugged in my monitor and keyboard and mouse and started entering the passwords that got my disks mounted and my network connection going. There was near-total silence as I did this, and it was so unnerving that I fatfingered my password twice before getting it.

I sat down at my computer and started going through my start-of-day routine: downloading my email, checking the server log summaries to see if we were in danger of running out of bits, kicking off my own personal backups—stationkeeping stuff I could have done while half asleep.

I started off half asleep—or half distracted—and so it was only after a few minutes that I pounced on my mouse and started unclosing the browser tabs I'd just closed, hammering on crtl-F12 with a series of *whaps* so hard I actually felt the spring under the key start to lose its sprungedness. I clicked and clicked again.

Then I got up from my desk and looked into the sea of stares. "Can someone please explain to me what the hell's going on?"

As one, the whole office turned to look at Liam, who got up and came over to my desk.

"You wanna get a cup of coffee?" he said.

I realized that that was exactly what I wanted, more than pretty much anything in the entire goddamned universe. I let him steer me up to Dolores Park, stopping at the Turk's to get a cup to go and a thermosful for after that. We perched on a bench and Liam waited patiently while I drank my first cup and poured myself a second one. Then he raised his eyebrows at me, silently asking if it was time to hear what he had to say. I nodded.

"Joe came into the office on Monday breathing fire. He kept asking where you were, getting Flor to call your phone, getting me to send you email. He had something he really, *really* wanted to talk to you about, and he couldn't reach you, so finally, he came and got me. He said I got computers and the Internet and stuff and asked if I had access to our 'web thing.' Well, I knew where you kept the sealed envelope with the admin passwords, so the answer was technically yes.

"Then he told me about what you'd suggested at the protest, hosting all those darknet docs. He couldn't believe that there were all these people in the streets of San Francisco pissed off about the kind of thing that was in those docs, but that they'd gotten practically no mainstream media publication and no one had made a political issue of it. He said that the Dems and the Republicans didn't want to start everyone thinking about how corrupt the system was, how money bought policy, how scummy the whole Sacramento scene was at the state house.

He'd been thinking about it all weekend and had decided that this was going to be the thing that made him different from the regular candidates. Flor tried to argue with him, but you know how he gets when he's sure about something. He was *sure.*

"So he tried to explain to me what you'd suggested, some kind of voting system or something? He couldn't really explain it. After a while, I said, 'Look, I can pull down all the darknet docs and put them up on our server in a couple hours, but I have *no* idea how to do all this other stuff, and if I tried, I'd probably leave the whole thing in such an insecure mess that someone'd take us down and replace the whole site with pictures of penises in about ten seconds flat.'"

I winced. "So what did he say?"

"He said that he'd rather beg forgiveness than ask permission, and told me to just put all the docs up, now, and he'd take care of the rest. The next thing I knew, he was calling in the press team and the next thing I knew after that, they were all checking to see if we could handle the capacity if, like, *millions* of people all came to download the docs at once. I was like, erm, yeah, I *think.* I mean, I knew we were on a cloud machine that could expand if we needed it. I tried calling the data center, but I didn't have your passphrase, so all they would tell me is that their servers could handle anything up to and including the entire state accessing us at once."

"Is that what happened?" The server logs showed that our traffic had hit over a million simultaneous connections overnight, and the rate was climbing.

"Oh no," he said. "Worse. I mean: 'more.' There was a *lot* of interest from out of state. At this rate, it's like the whole *world* wants to know about it. I mean, you've seen the news, right? It was the lead on every broadcast yesterday, and it's been trending on Twitter since about ten seconds after it went live. We've all been waiting for you to come in and get some decent analytics for it. I tried, but . . ." He shrugged. "Well, I'm just the T-shirt guy, right?"

I took a really, really deep breath. "I've been in jail."

"I figured," he said. "That was the leading theory. Joe was going to try to find your parents today if you didn't show up. What happened to your phone, by the way? I've been calling and calling."

"It's a long story," I said. I wondered why Dalia wasn't answering the phone anymore. Maybe she was answering calls where the return number showed up as "Mom," and ignoring the rest. Maybe the battery was dead. If that was the case, I wasn't going to be able to get my phone back until she got in touch with me. Great. "Where's Joe?"

"He's doing a press conference about this at Rootstrikers," he said. "They're an activist group that does something with getting the money out of politics. They're pretty excited about all this."

"Huh," I said, and reviewed what I'd just been told in my head. I mean, basically they'd taken my idea and *run* with it, and it had worked out *well*. So far, anyway. I wondered how long it could last, and decided that wasn't my job. My job was to keep the website online while Joe was off being Joe. The coffee was in my veins now, turning my thick, sluggish blood into quicksilver. It was time to go make some technology work. I was good at that.

Meantime, though: "What about the other thing, the vote-getting machine?"

"Yeah," Liam said. "That. He told me about it, but I couldn't really figure out what he was talking about. Something to mine your social-media contacts?"

"Basically," I said, and ran it down for him.

"Oh," he said. "That is awesome. And we could use the whole thing as a decision-making process, any time some big campaign issue comes up, or after he's in office, get the whole Joe for Senate machine to have instant runoff polls to see what we should do. That sounds *wicked*. Are we doing that, too?"

"That depends on whether we can find the time, now that the darknet docs are live." It's funny, even though the darknet docs had basically taken over my life, I was a lot more excited about this vote-getting machine, and half wished that I could just focus on that. I'd have to find some time to do it.

But first, I had to harden our infrastructure.

I figured the first thing to do was get us spanned out across a *lot* of cloud servers. My predecessor had gotten us hosted on Amazon's cloud, which was as robust as they came, an inconceivable network of humming racks in data centers all over the world, overseen by labcoated priests who could diagnose and swap out a faulty component in two minutes flat, fed by twisted fiber-optic bundles as thick as my arm, and cooled by enormous chillers with carbon footprints the size of cities. Amazon was a great choice if you wanted to get hosted by someone who'd keep your servers online no matter how popular they got.

However, they were a *terrible* choice for hosting your data if you were worried about the police going bugnuts on you. You see, the police don't necessarily know how to seize just one customer's data from a global network of server racks. If you're doing something with your data that was going to *really* interest the cops, then you had to be prepared for someone powerful calling up Amazon's lawyers and saying, "We need to investigate one of your customers, and since we don't know how to take one customer's data off your servers, we're coming over with a couple of sixteen wheelers and taking it *all* away until we finish our investigations." Or, as the Godfather might have said, "Nice cloud; it'd be a shame if something were to happen to it."

Amazon had a lot, so they had a lot to lose, and while

they'd been a good choice for our nice, boring campaign site, they sucked at providing infrastructure for ground zero in the new infowar. I'd heard a seminar about this from some of the Tor hackers at Noisebridge, and they'd mentioned a bunch of ballsy, free-speech-oriented cloud providers that could take us on. They were the projects of eccentric weirdos, free-speech nuts; bashed-together hackerspace side projects; sketchy-sketchy services with one foot in the porn industry and the other in organized crime. Most of them couldn't take a credit card payment because they'd been cut off by everyone from American Express to Visa to Mastercard to PayPal. Instead, they received payment through wire transfers, Western Union money orders, and other weird and cumbersome measures. I groaned and facepalmed and went and talked to Flor about this.

I'd been afraid to face Flor. I remembered her warning about dragging the campaign into anything "leet" and had a feeling that she was probably already furious with me. But I hadn't bargained on what it meant for the idea to come from Joe. Joe and Flor may have argued about this, but once Joe won the argument, Flor was behind him a hundred percent. Like most of us, she was ready to march into the sun for him, and as soon as I made it clear why I needed her to take the campaign credit card down the street to a liquor store and buy a Western Union order for a random dude—I didn't even know where he lived—she agreed.

"Just let me talk to him first," she said. I had a moment's impatience, because I felt like my parent wanted to look over my homework—finding bulletproof web hosting was my department. But then she got on the phone with the guy I'd chosen and exchanged some quick IMs with, and quickly negotiated better terms than I'd been able to get, including thirty-day billing for our future bandwidth bills and a 24/7 cellular number for support calls.

"Sounds like a good guy," she said, as she pulled on her jacket and picked up her purse and marched out into the Mission to find a Western Union office.

Joe got back in the late afternoon, just as I was finishing the switchover to our new host. I had set up two more backup clouds for us to move onto if we needed to, one in a country I'd never heard of in Central Asia. Flor had gone out for two more money orders and I'd written the scripts to keep us all in sync. I also made sure to register a bunch of variants on our domain, joenossforsenate.com, in other countries, snagging the .se (Sweden) and the .nz (New Zealand), figuring that it would be a lot harder to convince two countries on the other side of the planet with totally different legal systems to nuke our DNS than it would be to just get Verisign, who runs all the .com domains, to take down the U.S. version.

Joe listened to me report on all this and nodded his head soberly. "Marcus," he said, "I knew you'd be the right guy for this. Thanks for all the good thought and hard work you put into this. Now, Flor tells me you've been in jail. Were you at the chicken farm?"

I found that my voice had disappeared and tears had welled up behind my eyes. I nodded silently.

Normally, Joe looked, well, *statesmanlike* is probably the best word for it. Like someone who might be photographed at any instant and, if he was, would look as though he were carefully considering how to pilot the nation and its interests. But for an instant, something flashed to the surface that I'd never seen on his face before, a momentary glimpse of something like an Old Testament prophet who's about to lay down some smiting on a foolish tribe that had strayed from the path. The fact that he felt that way on *my* behalf made it all the more powerful—made me like him even more.

"Marcus," he said. "I have been around the block a few times. I've seen all manner of brutalities inflicted in the name of public order and keeping the peace. But the *premeditation* of what happened to you and the others, the sheer *militarization* of it—" He shook his head. "All I can say is, it's not to be tolerated. The fact that the SFPD had prepared for the future of protest by buying fleets of gas-spraying drones and turning a titanic building into an internment center—it can't stand. It won't. I'm sure you've heard about the class action suits pending against the city." I hadn't, but then I hadn't been doing *anything* except trying to get our infrastructure secured. "As someone who served in this city's government for many years, I wouldn't blame you if you joined them."

"Thank you," I said. The lump in my throat had gone down, and Joe had regained his normal "statesman" look. We were back to baseline.

"Now, about these documents. I'm sorry if I stepped on your toes by having Liam work on this while you were away. He told me that he couldn't do as good a job as you could, but perfection wasn't as important as timeliness. There was a lot of interest in those documents after the demonstrations, and I felt that we could seize on that interest if we moved quickly."

"Uh," I said. He was apologizing to me? "Well, it's your campaign, right? I'm not going to chew you out for running it the way you want to."

He smiled. "Yes, of course. But I hired you to do a job, and the last thing I want to do is make it harder for you to do that job."

I waved him off. "I don't mind, really. But is it working?"

There was another flash, and I got a glimpse of Joe Noss, the imp. The glee in his eyes was unmistakable. "Oh, it's working. I've gotten more airtime in the past twenty-four hours than I have for the whole campaign. Everyone seems to get the connection between the weekend's events and the documents we're publishing. We can barely keep up with the requests to act as official campaign volunteers, going through all that data and making sense of it. I only check in a few times a day, but from what I hear, there's plenty there for Sacramento—and the rest of the country—to chew on. My advisory committee squawked and one of them quit. They're worried, sensibly enough, that there's stuff in that archive that could expose us to liability, and they're right to worry. I tried to explain to Liam what you'd suggested about this but—" He spread his hands and shrugged.

"I know," I said. "He told me." I'd been giving that some thought. "I bet I can get it up now, though. I was going to try and do the moderation system tonight, see if I couldn't bang something together that would only show the public the checked documents. Sounds like we could use the volunteers to go through what's left pretty quickly, assuming you trust them. And then we're going to get to work on this vote-getting machine, somewhere for all that positive energy to go."

"I trust them to do a better job than is being done now," he said. "They're substantially better than nothing. But Marcus, you have been in jail, you've been gassed, you've been beaten. I don't expect you to work through the night, too."

I shrugged. "It's not that hard," I said. "I mean, no big deal. I've pulled plenty of all-nighters, and—"

He held his hands up and I fell silent. "Let me put this another way: as your employer, I don't want you to work on this until you've gotten a good night's sleep and had a chance to see your loved ones and start to recover from your trauma. It's not a request, Marcus, it's an order."

Part of me wanted to argue, but I told that part to shut up. "Yes, sir," I said.

"Good man," he said. "But if you should want to stay a

little late tonight and possibly turn up a little early tomorrow, I wouldn't take it amiss."

"Yes, sir!" I said.

"Good man," he repeated.

Mom and Dad were surprisingly cool about everything. I tried about six Skype calls to my old phone, but Dalia wasn't answering. Finally, I gave up and dialed into it and picked up my voicemail (about a million messages from Mom, Dad, Ange, Liam, Flor, and Joe, preceded by a series of panicked calls from a woman speaking Arabic whom I took to be Dalia's mother, who must have had kittens when her conversation with her daughter was so rudely cut short and redialed my number). Then I found an old phone and brought its firmware up to date and stuck in a pay-as-you-go SIM I bought at the Walgreens down the hill and changed the outgoing voicemail on the old phone to a message telling people to use this number until I could get a new SIM from my phone carrier.

I *did* work a little on Joe's darknet moderation site before bed, despite what he'd said, because while Joe was a nice guy to insist, the darknet was *my* project, and just because I was working on it, it didn't mean I was working on it for *him*. I worked until the muscles that allowed my eyes to focus on my screen went on strike, and I blinked hard, brushed my teeth, stripped off, and fell facefirst into bed, amid all the junk I'd dropped there, not even feeling the sharp corners that dug into me.

I was 99.9999 percent of the way to sleepyland when my eyes opened so fast I heard the *click* of my eyelids ungumming.

Lemmy's quadcopter.

We'd put it in the sky just before the gas attacks on the crowd, *after* the police thought that every camera had been killed. The tweet telling people where to look for its feed hadn't gone out, but that didn't mean it didn't create and store that feed. I pounced on my laptop and after a few minutes' dicking around, found the file I was looking for.

It was all in ghostly night-vision monochrome, with false-color splotches of orange and red where the people gathered. The SFPD stood out hotter than the rest, with bright red splotches on their hands and feet—I wondered if they were using boot- and glove-warmers? We didn't get the firing of the HERF gun on the camera, but we did get some *amazing* footage of the gas blimps setting sail, moving into position like sinister circus balloons, unleashing their chemical rain, a kind of gray static that fell on the screaming, terrified crowd below. The gassing went on and on and on, different blimps releasing at different times, filling the air with wave after wave of choking chemical droplets.

I'd lived through this on the ground, but I hadn't *seen* it, not the way I could see it now. Watching thousands and thousands and *thousands* of Americans of all stripes, choking and falling down—kids, moms, dads, old, young, writhing, crawling over one another, vomiting, screaming. I know that worse things have happened. I know that bombs have fallen on cities, mustard gas sent over trenches, people machine-gunned wholesale.

But this was *here*. This was San Francisco. America. The twenty-first century. I had been in that crowd. It had just happened.

And yet life was continuing the way it had. The world didn't stop. No one declared that "everything was different now." No one was going to remember September 24th as "the day everything changed."

If some foreign power, some religious terrorist, had gassed hundreds of thousands of Americans in the streets of San Francisco, they'd be rearranging all the furniture in government to make way for the new agencies that would swoop in to make sure that "never again" would such a thing happen "on U.S. soil." Why did the fact that we'd all bought the gas with our tax dollars make the gas acceptable?

I wanted to put this online, but I didn't have the energy to do it all over again, make *another* darknet site, try to get people interested in it. I was about to go back to bed when it hit me: I didn't *need* to do anything with the darknet this time. This video was *ours,* mine and Lemmy's. It wasn't a secret who recorded it or where it was recorded. I laughed. I could stick this on YouTube. I could tweet it from my own account! I'd gotten so used to operating in secret that I'd forgotten that I didn't have to.

I posted the video to the Internet Archive, YouTube, and popped a torrent on The Pirate Bay for good measure, wrote a paragraph explaining that I'd shot this at the demonstration after the HERF event, pasted it in, tweeted it, and crawled beneath the covers.

Ange woke me up at 6 a.m. by ringing my phone. When I'd set it up the night before, I'd forgotten to configure it to stay silent before 7 A.M., so the ringing drilled into my ears at oh-dark-hundred and dragged me back from the land of nod. "Morning, beautiful," I said.

"You could have told me you had video of the gassing," she said.

"I forgot," I said. I was still half asleep.

There was a long pause at the other end of the line. "You forgot?"

"I forgot I'd made the video."

Another silence. "Okay, under any other circumstances, that would be really lame, but I guess you've been pretty distracted lately. Fine. You get a walk. This time. Still—holy shit, dude, what the hell?"

"Are people talking about it?"

"It got a million YouTube views before it got taken down. The Archive version's still up and the torrent's being seeded by about a thousand people."

"Taken down, huh?" I tried to find some reservoir of naiveté in me that could be surprised to discover that the SFPD had ways of taking down files that embarrassed it.

"Temporary injunction," she said. "That's what the YouTube page says. I bet you're going to get a visit from a process-server today."

"You think *they're* going to sue *me*?"

"Sure," she said. "No recording in a frozen zone, remember?" There'd been a bunch of news stories for years about police departments declaring certain areas to be "frozen zones" because a "major operation" was taking place, and no press had been allowed.

"Frozen zone my butt. The courts've said that the press can go into a frozen zone."

"Are you the press?"

"Well, a million people looked at my video. I'd say the answer is yes."

I could hear her smiling on the other end of the phone. "Well, *I* agree with you. But you'll have to explain it to a judge if you want to make it stick."

"Great," I said. "I'll get right on that. After I get Joe Noss elected, sue the SFPD for police brutality and unlawful detention, and rescue two people I don't like very much from the clutches of a band of ruthless international mercenaries."

"You make it sound so hard," she said. "Come on, dude, you're *M1k3y!*"

"And I've got to get my phone number transferred to this new SIM."

"Yeah, that sounds like a total bitch. Phone companies suck. Good thing you've got me."

"I do," I said. "Indeed I do."

So that was that day: getting the rest of the stuff built for Joe, getting a whole raft of emails from reporters—some of whom I knew from my M1k3y days—asking if they could license "my" video for their networks. I laughed and said, "License, schmicense, it's all over the net, duh." That was good enough for Al Jazeera and Russia Today and *The Guardian,* but all the big American networks wanted me to sign these release forms saying that if anyone sued them for posting the video, they could sue *me* for letting them post it. Invariably, these "contracts" came as noneditable PDFs so that I couldn't delete the offending clauses before signing them. The first three times this happened, I just opened the PDFs in a graphics-editing program and drew big black boxes over everything in the contract apart from the bit where I said they could use the video, pasted my signature into the bottom, and filled in the date and sent it back. After that, I stopped bothering. I noticed that most of the networks I gave this treatment to later ended up running the video, sometimes with "Courtesy of Marcus Yallow" underneath, but more often with their big fat logos superimposed over the picture and "All rights reserved" messages that made me hoot with indignant laughter.

My new phone rang at 2 A.M. Like an idiot, I'd forgotten *again* to apply the setting that turned off the ringer after bedtime. I swiped at the ANSWER button.

"Ange," I said. "It's the middle of the goddamned night. I love you and all—"

"We love you, too, M1k3y." It was another one of those text-to-speech voices. This one was female and had a crappy Australian accent.

"Good-bye," I said.

"You haven't done anything about Carrie Johnstone," a

different voice said. This one was male and sounded like Yoda.

"You called me to tell me that? I already knew that."

"Masha and Zeb are depending on you." The female voice this time. I wondered if there were really two people on the call. It could have been one guy. Or one woman. Or a hundred people typing into a group-edited page and firing off the results to a text-to-speech engine.

"I've done everything I told Masha I would do and then some. If you want to save her, you should do it yourself."

"We sent you Johnstone's d0x," the male voice said.

"You did."

"Did you look at them?" This was a new voice, impossibly deep, like a cartoon bullfrog. It had a Texas accent.

"No," I lied.

"You should look at them. Johnstone's a very naughty girl. You could tell the world about it. You've got the platform. Especially now."

I sat up in bed. "Listen," I said. "I don't take advice from anonymous strangers. If you've got something to say to me, you can say it to my face. It's easy to sit there in your parents' basements telling me how I should be risking my life, but as far as I'm concerned, you're just another gang of creeps who get their kicks from spying on people."

"So much drama," the Australian voice said again. "We've handed you Johnstone on a platter. You've got the home addresses of everyone she loves, her Social Security number, her ex-husbands, her criminal record, the institution where her daddy is drying out from his latest Vicodin binge. You put all that online, you watch how fast she comes around to bargain."

"Why would she bargain with me *after* I put all her secrets online?"

"Oh," the Yoda voice said, "because she doesn't know what

else you have. We told you, Ms. Johnstone's been a *very* naughty girl. You remember what we did to your computer? You'd be amazed at how many other peoples' computers we've pwned."

I groaned and pulled my knees up to my chest. "If you guys are all so leet and badass, why don't you do this? Why aren't *you* destroying Carrie Johnstone?"

"We are, Marcus. But you are our instrument in this mission. You are the perfect weapon to use to destroy one of the worst people on Earth. You should feel special."

I hung up.

Look, you try to get to sleep after a call like that. I'd spent several mesmerized hours staring at Carrie Johnstone's d0x already, but being gassed, beaten, shackled, nearly kidnapped, taken into custody, and then released to an insanely busy work situation had managed to drive the details out of my mind. And it wasn't as if I'd gotten through all of them. There were *thousands* of files in the Johnstone d0x. It was like a miniature ship-in-a-bottle version of the darknet docs, a mammoth library of sleaze and misery blended with a million irrelevant facts, cryptic files, and weird irrelevancies. I'd become a one-man version of the Department of Homeland Security, sitting on top of a haystack the size of the universe, trying to find the needles.

I dove back into the Johnstone d0x. The conversation with the freaky, computer-voiced Anons had rattled me, but it had also intrigued me. I'd had nightmares about Johnstone, and there was something evilly attractive about giving her a nightmare for a change.

The conversation had equipped me with some search terms to use on the trove, and I saw that yup, her family was pretty screwed up, and that there were a bunch of phone numbers and addresses for relatives. Some of them were important people—there was an uncle who was a judge in Texas—and some were

only noteworthy because they were in rehab or had some embarrassing criminal charge in their records. Once I started to
search on *their* names, I saw that a lot of them had received "consulting" payments from Zyz, and while I didn't know enough
about finance to know exactly what that meant, I assumed that
it was either a way for Johnstone to rip off Zyz by sending a
lot of money to her family, or some kind of slimy money-
laundering. No reason it couldn't be both, either.

There were a few folders of photos. The most disturbing of
these were clearly taken by the webcam on Johnstone's computer without her knowledge. In several, she wore pajamas or
only a bra, and in one, she had a finger rammed up one nostril
to the second knuckle. My first thought was how humiliating it
would be to her if I released these pictures. My second thought
was to feel sick at the number of pictures like this of me that
there had to be floating around, and to wonder what all my
robot-voiced "friends" might do with them if they decided I
wasn't on their side.

A file called "searchterms.txt" turned out to be exactly
what it sounded like: everything Carrie Johnstone had plugged
into a search engine, harvested from her browser's cache of
search queries. I started looking through it and quickly looked
away. I hated Carrie Johnstone, but I didn't need to know what
kind of breast cancer she was looking into, about her research
into antidepressant drugs, or the names of the stars whose
"nude photos" she was searching for.

I shook myself like a dog shaking off water, and retreated to
the emotionally safer distance of all those payments from Zyz.
Looking at several different files, I saw that everything that had
to do with a payment used the string "IBAN," which stood for
International Bank Account Number, and had to be specified for
wire transfers. From there, it only took a few seconds to produce
a list of every file that had to do with payments and start look-

ing through them. I quickly saw that Johnstone controlled and moved a *lot* of Zyz money, and that her payments went to a lot of political action committees. I wondered if maybe her family was channeling the PAC money as well.

A few seconds on the Web and I saw that Johnstone's favorite PACs were big donors to politicians who supported easy debt-collection laws, and it clicked. The darknet docs might tell the story of the pressure to wipe out the families of kids with student debt, but here was the smoking gun, the money paid from Zyz to fronts that went on to fatten up politicians who went along with the deal.

It was 3 A.M. I had work the next day. It was going to be a big day. There was a pretty good chance all our servers would be taken down by some scary lawyer-threat somewhere and I'd have to have a clear head to fix that. But who the hell could sleep under these circumstances? Who was I kidding? I was up for the count.

I took my laptop down into the kitchen and made myself cheese on toast—always my favorite midnight feast—and dithered in front of the coffee machine for ten minutes, trying to decide whether I should or shouldn't have a cup. If I drank coffee now, I really *would* be up for the rest of the night. But even if I didn't, I was pretty sure that I wasn't going back to bed, and a little of the old bean-juice would sure help sharpen my wits.

Who was I kidding? I loaded up the AeroPress and made myself a double, and then made another to keep it company. I sat down at the kitchen table with the machine and kept on reading. I even went back to the pictures.

A chat request popped up on my screen. That didn't happen often. Ever since I'd gotten the job with Joe, I'd kept my main ID logged out, and the only handle I left logged in was one that almost no one knew about.

> hey jolu

> hey mr nite owl - good to see im not the only one awake at o-dark-hunnerd

> why are you up?

> fight with kylie

> oh

I paused.

> you mean you two are . . .

> kinda. its complicated

I had no idea that Jolu had any kind of romantic life, though it stood to reason. But Kylie? She was old! Oh, chronologically she was only a couple years older than us. But she was such a grown-up. She'd run that meeting like a boss.

> listen you want to get a slice of pie?

It was the first sensible suggestion anyone had made to me all night.

> hell yeah

> ill be there in 15

San Francisco isn't a bad place to get a slice of pie at three in the morning. I'm willing to believe that New York might be better, but it's not like we lacked for choice in any event. We ended up in the Tenderloin at one of those '50s-retro places that stayed open 24 hours and catered to a weird blend of jet-lagged tourists, hookers, off-duty cops, homeless people, and night-shifters. And us.

"I think you should do something really *lateral*," Jolu said, after I had him up to speed. "I mean, you've got these two groups of weird-ass crooks hoping to make you jump one way or the other, and they're both calculating your next move to see if they can get inside it, steer it. They're smart, nuts, and totally lacking in ethics. The only way you're going to get ahead of them is by doing something totally, absolutely whacked out.

Move to Albania. Rappel off the Golden Gate Bridge. Become a Trappist monk."

"That's really helpful, thanks."

"Oh, come on, it's a major advance on 'When in trouble or in doubt . . .'"

"Again, this is less than helpful."

"It's four in the morning, cut me a break."

This wasn't the first time I'd found myself in an all-night diner with Jolu, and all the nights we'd passed in this kind of place had a certain sameness to them—I'd swear that some of the skeezy drunks and cracked-out weirdos holding down the booths around us were there the last time we'd been here. It's funny how comforting it was to inhabit the sheer weirdness of eating a slice of bad blueberry pie and good ice cream in the middle of the night sitting next to a guy with a face full of broken veins like a map of the California state highway system, a crooked nose, and a pink ballerina's tutu around his prodigious middle. Especially when that guy is trading unintelligible drunken remarks with a skinny one-armed guy with a heavily tattooed scalp, bare feet, and long fingernails painted with glitter polish.

"Marcus," Jolu said, "seriously. This is some bad stuff you've gotten involved with, and you're letting yourself be driven by what other people are doing, instead of choosing a path and making other people decide what to do about *you*. There's no reason for that. Look at it this way: all these people—the weirdos who rooted your computer, these mercenaries—have a lot of advantages over you. They're organized, they have money, they have technical expertise you lack."

"Gee, thanks, Jolu."

"Wait for it. They also all have to have meetings to decide what to do next. *You* can just decide on your own. That means that you can do something, force them to all sit down and figure out their next course of action, and while they're doing that, you can *change direction,* so that by the time they've worked out their response, it no longer applies. They have lots of advantages, but this is *your* advantage, and you've more or less surrendered it."

I thought about it. I couldn't think of anything wrong with his logic. And yet . . . "Okay, but there's only one problem: *I don't know what to do.*"

"The first step to solving the problem is framing the problem," Jolu said with a wise smile. "What if you put together a bunch of possible courses of action, all more or less independent of one another, and had them in your pocket, metaphorically, so that you could just jump and jive and zig and zag on a moment's notice."

"Again," I said, "it's a nice theory, but it requires me to think up not just one, but *several* courses of action."

"That's not so hard," Jolu said. "You could publish everything on the Joe Noss for Senate website—explain what happened, put up Johnstone's d0x, and hit 'save.'"

I winced. "Jesus, Jolu, that'd be—"

"—Unexpected," he said. "And weird. And a little destructive, though I'd bet that Joe would forgive you. You could dump it all on Barbara Stratford. You could hit your Anon pals up for Carrie Johnstone's passwords and pastebin them, make her life busy as hell for a while, put her on the back foot. You could surrender yourself at the closest Zyz office, demand that they kidnap you, freak them right the hell out. Or call the FBI and report a kidnapping. Any and all of the above, and more."

Each one of these gave me a little shiver of excitement and fear. It was just the sort of thing Jolu excelled at—coming up with scary, smart, dumb ideas. I needed to change the subject before he got me too freaked out.

"So, you and Kylie, huh?"

He banged his forehead on the table. Twice. "I'm an idiot. First of all, I was dumb enough to date someone from work, and second of all, I was dumb enough to date someone a hundred times smarter than me. She's already figured out that there's only two ways this can go if we let it get any more serious: either we break up and one of us has to leave the company, or we stay together forever. And she wants to know which one it's going to be, *right now,* because she says it's stupid to pretend that this isn't the case, and to be forced into some big emotional scene that we can see coming from here."

I boggled. This was so totally different from what Ange and I were like. I mean, she was my *girlfriend,* but we lived at our parents' houses, she didn't have a job, much less a job working with me, and we were more worried about hacking justice forcibly into American politics than we were about what The Future of the Relationship might hold. Somehow, while I was off being a debt-stricken college dropout, Jolu had turned into an adult.

"Are you going to get *married?*"

I must have sounded pretty intense, because he laughed— and so did the weirdos at the next table. "Come on, Marcus, I'm nineteen years old. That's a little young, but it's not as if I'm a kid anymore. I don't know if I want to get married to Kylie right now, but the idea of getting married isn't the worst one I've ever heard. Lots of people do it, you know."

"I know," I said. "But—" I couldn't find the words. *But getting married is for old people.*

"My parents got engaged when they were eighteen. Like I said, I don't know for sure if Kylie is the person I want to spend the rest of my life with, but there's a good chance she is. I mean, how do you feel about Ange? Are you planning on breaking up with her?"

"No! I mean, of course not! We had a big fight last week

and I was ready to stick my head in the oven. I get sick just thinking about it."

"There you go, then. You're planning on spending forever with her. You just haven't admitted it. And from what I know about her, she's in the same place. Kylie's twenty-five, she was in a long-term relationship before, and so she knows that there's a point where you've got to fish or cut bait."

"You make it sound so romantic."

"There's nothing romantic about pretending you're not heading toward a lifelong commitment. How long are you and Ange going to stay together? It's a question worth asking yourself—and Ange."

"How come no matter what, we always end up talking about my problems?"

He grinned. "Well, it's always easier to give advice than to take it, duh."

"So maybe I should give *you* advice."

"Marcus, you're one of my oldest friends. If you had advice for me, I'd listen closely."

"And once again, I've managed to put myself on the spot."

"Yeah. It's one of your most endearing traits."

"Argh. Okay, well, for whatever it's worth, I really like Kylie. I don't know her very well, but from what I've seen, she seems like really good people. And it sounds like she makes you happy. But Jolu—" I fussed with my pie and the spreading ice cream slick beside the cooling slice. "Well, buddy, I mean, I think most people today like to spend awhile making sure they know each other really well before they commit to forever. It sounds like Kylie thinks you can't afford to do that because if you decide you're not going to keep it up, you'll have to walk away from your job or she will. But what if you promised each other that no matter what, neither one of you will expect the other to quit? I mean, that may be a hard promise to keep, but is it any harder to keep than 'I promise to marry you and be with you forever until I die'?"

He chewed this over while I felt just a *little* bit smug. He was right: it was easier to give advice than to get it.

"Huh," he said. "You're not bad. Okay, that's worth a try. Now, what are *you* going to do?"

My mood fell. "I have no idea," I said. "Everything you've told me makes sense, but I don't know where to start."

"Start at the beginning," he said. "Move one step in the direction of your goal. Remember that you can change direction to maneuver around obstacles. You don't need a plan, you need a *vector*."

I finished my ice cream and left the pie. The sun was starting to come up, and Ange would be waking up soon. We'd hardly seen each other that week, and all Jolu's talk about breaking up made me really want to see her. I figured I could go by the Korean walnut-cake place she loved and bring over a box and grab a shower and have breakfast with her family before work.

As it turned out, Ange's mom had an early appointment, and her sister was staying at a friend's place, so we had a rather indulgent time in her bed, replenishing our strength with walnut cakes as required. I had this gnawing feeling that I was going to be late for work, but every time I looked at the clock, it was still ungodly early, and we returned to our business. In the end, I rolled up to work ten minutes early, grinning like a dirty fool and feeling better than I had in weeks.

Jolu was right: I just needed to take a step in the direction I wanted to head and stay flexible enough to keep moving that way no matter what happened. And of all the problems I had, the biggest one was Carrie Johnstone. For so long as she was gunning for me, I couldn't be safe enough to do anything else. I would have to do something about her, and I was going to need Joe Noss's help to do it.

"Where's Joe?" I said. Early as I was, Flor was always earlier.

She gave me a searching look, as if trying to figure out what to tell me, then she seemed to come to a decision. "He's talking to the FBI," she said.

"The FBI? Like the FBI FBI? The guys with the sunglasses and the suits, those guys?"

"Those guys," she said.

"Oh. Um, is someone trying to kill him or something?"

Flor smiled a little. "Nothing like that. At least, not yet. If he goes all the way, the way I think he can, I'm sure that'll come.

"No, the FBI wants to talk to him about the documents we're hosting on our website."

"Oh." Of course they did. And once they started talking to him about this, it was only a matter of time until they came to talk to me. And then I'd either have to lie to a bunch of hard-core fed cops, or tell them what was going on. Neither of those were my ideal position. "Does he have a lawyer with him?"

Flor smiled again. "Yes, Marcus, he has the campaign's lawyer with him. Harry has known Joe since they were in college together. I'm sure he'll do very well."

"Well, that's good." I swallowed. "The campaign has a lawyer?"

"Yes, since the beginning. He was one of the people who pushed Joe to run as an independent."

"Does that mean that if the FBI wants to talk to the rest of us that he'll come with?"

"Marcus," Flor said, "you work for this campaign, and so yes, the campaign's lawyer will represent you any time something you've done in connection with this campaign becomes an issue with law enforcement. But don't worry too much. Joe talked to Harry before he had Liam post those documents. He understood the risks. He's gone to talk to the FBI to preempt them coming around here to talk to the rest of us. It's just part of the job."

"Okay," I said, "thanks."

"On the other hand," she said, and I glimpsed the *other* Flor, the one I'd seen the day I was hired, the slightly scary, stern one. "If you've done something that *isn't* part of this campaign, something that might make the FBI or some other law-enforcement agency want to take some action against you, something that might embroil this campaign in needless controversy, then you will find yourself answering to *me,* because we've discussed this already, and I believe we have an agreement on this. Am I right?"

"Right," I said. I felt sure my guilt was scrawled across my face, but I made myself stay calm and look just slightly to one side of her steady gaze.

I sat down at my computer to discover that I was actually a pretty smart guy. Amazon had terminated our hosting in the night, and the system had seamlessly switched us over to our first fallback cloud provider with such grace and speed that none of the uptime monitors had even noticed. That reminded me that I still needed to get my phone number back—if the uptime monitor had squawked, the messages would have gone to my phone, wherever it had disappeared to—and I dialed into the carrier's customer service line and started a timer going just to see how long it took the rocket scientists at the phone company to take my request. It had ticked past the thirty-five-minute mark when a shadow loomed over my shoulder, and I turned around to see Joe, looking like he'd been through the wringer.

I hung up the phone. "Hi, Joe," I said.

"Hello, Marcus."

"How're things?"

"Things are complicated," he said. "Perhaps you and I could sit down for a few minutes?"

I knew then that I was about to be fired. "Sure," I said. I locked my computer's screen and followed him into the boardroom and closed the door behind me.

"Let me tell you a few things, Marcus, before we get to chatting. If you don't mind?"

"No," I said, feeling that tight, bloodless feeling in my face and extremities. "Not at all."

"First: I believe that my opponents are behind this FBI business. They don't like the attention this has brought to the campaign, so they've put me in the soup with the law. Monroe, in particular, has had a longstanding relationship with Zyz and its subsidiaries through his career in Sacramento. I'm not in the least bit surprised to hear that he's hurting over this and wants to hit us back.

"Second: I value the work you've done here, and I credit you with coming up with this whole plan. I think you're a bright young man, and I hope you'll stay in touch with me no matter what happens.

"Third: That said, the FBI say that they're reasonably certain that you aren't just someone who happened to suggest posting these documents to our site. They seem to believe you had something to do with their initial publication.

"Fourth: I don't know if that's true or not, but in the course of our discussion, we covered several possibilities for what could happen with you and this campaign. In the end, they reluctantly but firmly agreed that if you were no longer formally associated with this office, they would not pursue any further investigations about your role in those documents to date. This was not an easy offer to come by, and in my view, it represents an inter-

nal conflict in their upper echelons, who are simultaneously outraged over these leaks and over the intelligence they contain.
They don't want another WikiLeaks trial on their hands, especially since this one doesn't have the same national security
dimensions of that entire affair. Very little of this material is
technically classified or even secret, and Harry pointed out that
the few documents that have surfaced with those labels would
likely have been released if they were targeted by a Freedom of
Information Act request.

"But still. They don't like the *look* of the thing. Here's this
young man with a history of what they consider to be antisocial
computer use, and he's implicated in both the release *and* the
publication of these documents. They worry that if the story
gets out, they'll look incompetent or worse."

"But if I get fired—"

"Marcus, I'm not going to fire you. Be clear on that. But
we're talking about optics here, the appearance of the thing.
You're right that if you were fired at this juncture, it would
make you look more guilty and it would make me look more
foolish. But if you were to, say, go off on your own to pursue
private consulting work, then the campaign could pay you a
decent retainer for your work to date, a sum more or less equal
to what you'd have taken home in the event that you'd worked
through to election day. You'll be paid your normal salary to
the end of the pay period, in exchange for being available to
Liam if he needs help getting up to speed on the really excellent
systems you've built for us. And should I take office, well, there's
always the possibility that you would find work in my office
doing the very consulting you'd set out to do while you were
on your own."

"I thought you said I wasn't being fired?" The anger bub-
bled in me, made me want to do something *stupid*. I literally bit
the inside of my cheek to keep from saying anything more.

His expression didn't change. "You're not being fired, Marcus. You're not being thrown under the bus, either. That's what the FBI expected of me, you know. They wanted me to turn you over, denounce you as a criminal who'd used my office and its technology to commit your crimes. That was what my opponents were hoping for, too."

He dropped his voice. "The Bureau has some pure fools and vicious idiots in it, but it is not, at its core, rotten. What's more, even the most foolish, vicious Feeb at HQ has some self-respect and doesn't want to be used as a game token by scheming politicians who're hoping to score points with the electorate during the midterms. It wasn't easy to broker this deal, and Harry is still surprised we got it out of them. It's the best deal we're likely to get. It's a deal that keeps you from being investigated by the federal police, and one that lets you keep your pay. It does mean you can't keep coming here and you can't be a part of our team, and I promise you, Marcus, that however much you hate that idea, I hate it even more. I think that losing you is going to *cost us,* and if I get elected, it will be in spite of losing you."

I believed every word. When Joe Noss told you something, straight and even, looking you in the eye, you couldn't help but believe him. My anger drained away.

"I can't take the money," I said.

He shook his head once, minutely, but it was a gesture of total negation. "That's not optional. You were hired for this job, you were counting on that wage. The political machinations of unethical men and women shouldn't take money out of your pocket."

"That was money that you fund-raised for your campaign. Your donors didn't kick it in to pay me not to work for you."

"Marcus, that's very big of you, but I anticipate paying

that sum out of my own savings. Flor will paper it over. I can afford it."

"I'll just donate it back to your campaign."

He sat back, looking suddenly exhausted and beaten. "I can't stop you from doing that, but I urge you to give it some thought before you rush into this."

"I will," I said. "I think I need to go now." The lack of sleep from the night before was catching up with me. Tears were welling up behind my eyes, which was always a sign that I wasn't in my right head. I decided that Joe was right about making up my mind about the money later. I started to wonder how much of a good guy Joe Noss could be when he was ready to fire people for "optics" and then quietly rehire them later. I think I said thank you or words to that effect, and stepped, wooden-faced, into the office. There were always ten or fifteen people in the office: volunteers staffing phones or collating literature, a cluster of desks where the campaign strategist and the speechwriter and the PR guy all sat, people whose jobs I didn't even know. I'd met them all, but I only knew half of them by name. Now they were all staring at me, and pretending not to, as I crossed to my desk. There was a cardboard banker's box on my chair, and as I drew up to it, I saw that the few things I'd brought into work had been gathered into the box. I looked at Flor, and she nodded at me and gave me a sympathetic look. I supposed she had packed the box for me, and I supposed that this was a kindness, since it let me leave faster. I got into my jacket, slid Lurch into my backpack, picked up my box, and left without saying another word.

Liam met me on the sidewalk just outside the office.

"Dude," he said. "This is *weak*." I hated the way Liam talked, but I decided to forgive him. I knew that if I lost my temper, it would be ugly. I wasn't in a good place.

"You've got my number, right?" is what I said. "In case you've got any tech problems? You know where the passwords are, too. I'll email you the full server details and customer service info for all the hosts and stuff when I get home."

He looked searchingly at my face. I looked back into his eyes. He blinked. "Is it true you were behind the darknet docs all the time?"

I didn't say anything. I was tired of lying, but I still reflexively felt that going public about this was a bad idea. I was pretty sure that Carrie Johnstone had been the one to tell Joe's opponents that he had someone working for him who was behind the darknet. She must have figured that isolating me was the first step to neutralizing me. She was probably right.

"Thanks for everything, Liam" is what I said.

He studied my face a moment longer. "I don't want the job," he said. "I'm going to quit."

"Don't do that," I said.

"Why the hell not?"

"Because the world will be a better place if Joe Noss is elected to the California Senate than it will be if one of those other two schmucks makes it into office."

He barked a laugh. "You're kidding, right? You really think it makes a difference who we vote for? After you've seen the darknet docs, seen how someone uses the system to get rich, then uses their riches to change the system to keep them that way? Jesus, Marcus, what is this, high school civics? Come on, bro, you of all people should know better than that."

"If you really believe that, why were you working for Joe in the first place?" It was weird sticking up for the guy who'd just fired me, especially since I was starting to get pretty pissed off about being fired. I mean, *optics*? What the hell kind of reason was *that* to fire someone? (The nagging voice in my head told me that it was a perfectly good reason if you were running for office, especially if the person generating the bad optics had lied to you—or at least failed to mention some very important information.)

"It's a job. Who gives a damn? Might as well be flipping burgers or walking dogs."

I started to say something about how you shouldn't do a job you don't care about, but I remembered all those months I'd spent knocking on every door I could find, handing out résumés like chewing gum, and all the big, fat NOs that had got me. "Listen, Liam," I said. But there wasn't anything to say to Liam. The fact was, he was probably right. "Forget it," I said. "Call me if you need tech support, okay?"

"Yeah," he said. There was a second where we might have given each other a big, back-slapping dude-hug, but neither of us moved. Liam had looked up to me so much, and it had been nice, but it had also been *weird,* all that adulation. I had a feeling I wouldn't have to worry about it anymore.

Once upon a time, my government turned my city into a police state, kidnapped me, and tortured me. When I got free, I decided that the problem wasn't the system, but who was running it. Bad guys had gotten into places of high office. We needed good apples. I worked my butt off to get people to vote for good apples. We had elections. We installed the kind of apples everyone agreed would be the kind of apples we could be proud of. They said good things. A few real dirtbags like Carrie Johnstone lost their jobs.

And then, well, the good apples turned out to act pretty much *exactly* like the bad apples. Oh, they had *reasons.* There were emergencies. Circumstances. It was all really regrettable.

But there were always emergencies, weren't there? My whole nineteen years on this earth had been one long emergency, according to all the papers and the TV. When would

the emergencies finally end? Would there be a day when uni-
corns pranced through the Mission and pronounced an end to
hostilities around the world, a return to the promised normalcy,
with jobs and freedom for all?

Hell no. If someone like Joe Noss could turn out to be just
another politician, then so could anyone and everyone. Carrie
Johnstone had been fired, but she ended up getting more money,
more power, and more authority, with even fewer checks on
her ruthlessness. Carrie Johnstone was always going to end up
on top. I'd been an idiot to think that we could elect someone
who'd make it all better. I once thought that Liam was an idea-
listic fool who lacked the sophistication to appreciate just how
good it could all be if we just had the right people out there,
passing good laws and making good government. Now I saw
who the fool was. It was the idiot I saw in the mirror every
morning, and I was getting pretty sick of his face.

Ange didn't answer emails or IMs, and didn't pick up
her phone. Who cared? What I was about to do wasn't about her,
it was about me.

Setting up the first darknet docs site had taken a fair bit
of work. It was a lot easier the second time around, and now
I had all of the Johnstone d0x in a nice, safe, untraceable place.
I wrote a blog post explaining what these docs were, who they
belonged to, and even how I'd come by them, gritting my teeth
until they hurt and typing out the admission that I'd been
rooted by a gang of anonymous trolls who'd done the same thing
to my archnemesis.

Jolu was right. I'd spent far too long letting Johnstone drive
me ahead of her like a terrified, bleating sheep. It was time I
started leading the chase, instead of just running away in terror.

I didn't publish the post. I almost did. But I didn't.

Instead, what I did was email the post, along with the dark-

net link, to <pr@zyzglobal.com>, <carrie.johnstone@zyzglobal
.com> and <press@zyzglobal.com.> I copied in <webmaster@
zyzglobal.com> for good measure—practically no one read the
webmaster@ account for their domains these days (the address
was a spam magnet like no other), but it seemed like a good time
to be thorough.

I had just hit SEND and begun to (metaphorically) crap my
pants when Ange called.

"What's up? I had class."

"I got fired. Carrie Johnstone told Joe Noss's opponents
that I'd been the one behind the darknet docs, and they called
the FBI. Joe negotiated my freedom in exchange for shitcanning
me. So I got home and emailed Carrie Johnstone a copy of her
d0x. I've just sent a copy of the darknet address to your Tunisian
Pirate Party email address. If I go missing, spread it around, okay?"

"Marcus?"

"Yes?"

"What did you just say?"

I repeated it.

"That's what I thought you said." There was a long silence.
"Hello?"

"I'm here."

"I'm not going to apologize," I said. "It's my life. I'm tired
of running away. I'm tired of being a stupid idealist. It's time to
take charge, time to *do* something. I'm sorry I didn't talk to you
beforehand, but—"

"I wasn't going to ask you to apologize," she said. "You
don't owe me an explanation. It's pretty clear you don't owe me
anything. Don't worry, I'll get that darknet address and keep it
safe and make sure everyone knows about it if you go missing."
I had never heard the tone of voice she was using at that moment.
I couldn't tell if she was angry or scared or maybe even . . .
proud?

"Oh," I said. "Well."

"Well, I think I'd better go," she said, and the line cut off. Not proud, then.

My parents were both out for a change. Dad was doing some grocery shopping and Mom had a client meeting. The house felt more than empty—it felt hollow. Spooky. Every creak and bang was a squad of Zyz mercs about to break down my door and kidnap me.

And even though I knew that was the one thing they couldn't afford to do now that I had my finger over the button, I was sure I was about to get snatched. Or maybe they'd take my parents. Or Ange. What had been Jolu's other suggestions for actions I could take? Move to Albania. I didn't even have a valid passport—the one I'd used to go see Mom's relatives in the UK had expired two years before. I could dump it all on Barbara Stratford. Well, why not? She'd helped last time.

I got my bike out of the garage and set off for the *San Francisco Bay Guardian*'s offices. I was nearly there when my phone rang. The caller ID didn't know the return number. I answered.

"Yeah?"

"You're some kind of trouble-magnet, aren't you?"

It took me a minute to place the voice, mostly because I'd internally decided that I'd never hear it again.

"Masha?"

"You busy?"

"What?"

"From what I can see, you're somewhere by the Embarcadero. Judging from your rate of travel, you're either on a bus that's making a lot of stops, or a bicycle. And from what I can see, you're no longer listed as CTO of the Joe Noss for California Senate campaign on their website, so I'm thinking you might not be totally busy. So how about you turn off your phone altogether, remove the battery, and meet me where your idiot school-buddy tried to wrassle me. Do you know the place?"

The day Masha had disappeared—the first time—she'd tried to take me with her, and we'd been shadowed by Charles Walker, a drooling gorilla from Chavez High who would have dearly loved to nark me out to Homeland Security. Masha had kicked his ass, flashed her DHS ID, and threatened to arrest him. It had been on one of the alleys off Jackson, up on Nob Hill. I wasn't exactly sure which one, but I thought I'd recognize it again if I saw it.

"I know the place."

The line went dead. People kept hanging up on me. It wasn't a very pleasant experience. As I pedaled for downtown, I realized I didn't want pleasant experiences anymore. I was done with trying to optimize my life for what would make me happy. From now on, I was going to optimize my life for whatever worked at the moment. Happiness was overrated.

Chapter 15

I was nearly convinced I had the wrong alley. I waited ten minutes, then fifteen, then I walked off. I got to the end of the block and I turned around and walked back. I looked down the alleyway. It wasn't much of an alleyway—just a narrow space between two buildings, wide enough for the fire exits and trash cans. The fifteen minutes I'd spent standing in the alley had been enough time for me to memorize every single feature of the place, from the ancient, mossy urine streaks on the wall to the dents in the trash cans. And now I could see that something was different. Hadn't *that* trash can been over *there*? It had been. I took a cautious step into the alleyway and my palms slicked with sweat, because I could tell, somehow, that there was someone in there with me. I took another step.

"Back here," a voice said from behind the trash cans. I tried to peek over them, but couldn't quite see, so I went deeper in and came around them.

Masha was sitting with her back against the wall. She looked like she was on her way to the gym, in track pants and a loose T-shirt, her hair in a pink scrunchie, a gym bag beside her. Her hair was mousy no-color brown, and she was wearing big fake designer shades. She could have been rich or poor, teenaged or in her late twenties. I wouldn't have given her a second look if I'd sat next to her on BART. I wasn't sure it *was* her, until she lowered her shades on her nose and skewered me on her glare.

"Have a seat," she said, and gestured at the space next to her behind the trash cans. She'd put down a piece of new cardboard there, which was a nice touch and made me think this wasn't the first time she'd done this. I lowered myself into a cross-legged position.

"Nice to see you," I said. "A bit unexpected."

"Yeah," she said. "Zeb and I walked out of there a few days ago, but it's been busy."

"Walked out of there."

"Those Zyz people, they're mostly meatheads that couldn't cut it in the DHS, so they went private sector, tripled their pay, and set out on their own. They have a *lot* of faith in their systems. Like, say, if a vendor says a CCTV is secure, they believe it. Same with electronic door locks, tracking ankle cuffs, and perimeter sensors."

"Oh," I said. I'd always known that Masha was a million times more badass than I was, but in all this business about saving her, I'd somehow come to think of her as a damsel in distress. "Did you have to come far?"

"Are you asking where I was held?"

I shrugged.

"Are you sure you want to know that?"

I shrugged again. "Probably not. All this spy shit, I pretty much totally hate it, to tell you the truth. Is Zeb okay?"

"Zeb's as good as he has any right to expect. Better. He's doing some stuff on his own for a while."

I mentally translated this as *We had a big fight and split up.* "Oh."

"So I wanted to say thanks," she said. "You've done some stuff that needed doing, but you did it for me and Zeb and that was damned good of you. Even if 'spy shit' isn't your thing."

"Yeah," I said. "Well, glad to be of service, even if you didn't need me in the end."

"Oh, I needed you. Zyz's been in an absolute *panic* pretty much since the moment they grabbed us. I figured out pretty quick that you were behind it. They were awfully anxious to know what had gotten out, what else might come out, and how they could stop it. They had a lot of really *sincere* questions for me. But it was an excellent distraction, and from what I can tell, all the people who supplied me with that material are happy with how it's gotten out. There was a *lot* more material waiting for me when I got back online. Enough to keep me busy for a really long time." She was being super macha, but I was starting to see that there was something wrong with her. She rooted in her gym bag for a water bottle and took a slug of it. I saw big, ugly bruises—no, *welts*—on her wrists and at her throat. I swallowed.

"Well, glad to be of service. Wish I'd known, since I happened upon some more 'material' of my own recently." I told her about Carrie Johnstone's d0x and the source of them.

"I see," she said, in sober tones. "And where are these files now?"

"I emailed them to Zyz corporate headquarters," I said.

I have to admit, I was a little proud of the silence that followed. She might have been James Bond–meets–Spider-Man, but I'd managed to do something so heroically crazy-stupid-brave that I'd rendered her speechless. But the silence went on, and on, and on. I peered at her shades, trying to see if she'd fallen asleep behind them.

"Um?"

"Shush," she said. "I'm figuring angles."

"Oh."

She lowered her head for a moment, and I heard her muttering to herself. There was a raw ligature mark around the back of her neck, which disappeared beneath her chin.

"So if I have this straight, you've sent all this in to Zyz and to Johnstone personally. You've implied that you're ready to publish it at the drop of a hat, but as far as they know, you haven't actually done anything about getting it published, right?"

"Pretty much. I've locked down the server my blog is on six ways to midnight, because I figured they'd be after it with everything they had. I'm half convinced they're going to come after me personally again, but that was always a certainty. They've tried to snatch me twice now. There's nothing I could do that would stop them from coming a third time."

She nodded along with me and held up her hand as I came to the end. "What if I could stop them?"

"What do you mean?"

"What if I could negotiate something with them, so that they made a meaningful promise to leave you alone, and you agreed to leave the Johnstone d0x alone?"

"Just so I'm clear on this: you've just escaped from a secret prison run by these goons, and now you're proposing to negotiate with them for *my* safety? As we say on the Internets: double-you-tee-eff."

"Oh," she said. "Marcus, come on. I'm not doing this to negotiate for *your* safety. I'm negotiating for *mine.*"

Derp. "Right," I said. "Right. And Zeb's."

"Zeb, you, me, your little girlie, all of them. Zyz is stupid and evil, but it's a *business.* Money talks and bullshit walks. What you're about to dump, it will cost them plenty. If we give them a chance to cut their losses, they're going to do that."

"What about Johnstone? Won't she come after me after she's fired?"

"They won't fire her," she said. "Whatever reasons they have to fire her, you can be sure she has amassed a fat dossier of reasons why they *shouldn't* fire her. That woman's got the survival instincts of a cockroach. She only goes when she's ready to go. The U.S. Army only fired her once she was ready to be fired, once she'd set up the Zyz deal to step into. She *let them* fire her."

"You sound almost like you admire her," I said.

"The only day I wouldn't piss on Carrie Johnstone is the day she caught fire," Masha said, without the slightest hesitation or expression. "But if you're not prepared to learn from the teachers that life gives you, you'll always be ignorant. I've paid for every lesson that Carrie Johnstone has taught me, and I'm going to get my money's worth."

Sitting with Masha was like sitting on a razor's edge. On one side was my old life: safe little Marcus with his safe little life, in the system, applying for jobs, building his little electronics projects. On the other side was the life that I'd have if I followed Masha: violence, secrecy, poverty—but also power, strength, and adventure. I could disappear from the world, become a ghost and a legend, a fugitive who only gave the system what I deemed it deserved, not what it demanded.

After all, wasn't the *system* the problem? No matter who we voted for, the government always seemed to win. What was the point of living out my little fantasy of democratic change and justice when the real action was being fought out in secrecy, with anonymous envelopes of cash, encrypted whispers, secret bunkers, and secret deals?

Masha got to her feet and I was alarmed to see how slowly and painfully she moved. I was even more alarmed by how heavily she leaned against the wall. "Gimme a little help here," she said.

I hastened to stand beside her and let her put her arm around my shoulders, putting a lot of weight on me. Her hair tickled my cheek. It still smelled of her hair dye, a smell I remembered from being a kid who tried a different hair color every week. Back when I felt like I could express who I was and what I felt with my *hair*.

"Come on," she said. "Let's go use your network connection to do some negotiating before they scramble the black helicopters and nuke your ass."

"I haven't agreed to the deal," I said. I was practically holding her upright at this point, and I was amazed by how light she was, how little there was to her under her exercise clothes.

"Yeah," she said. "And what else are you going to do, dipshit?"

"Yeah," I said. "All right. Let me go get my bike."

"Screw that. If it's locked up, you can get it later. If it's not, someone else will get it and you won't have to worry about it. Get us a cab. I've got money."

Mom and Dad had left me a note saying they'd gone to a meeting with their accountant and telling me they'd be home for dinner. I raided the fridge for Masha while she used the shower and settled in in my room. I sat down on the end of my bed and watched her gnaw at a hunk of cheese and a tray of cookies while her fingers flew over her keyboard. She stopped typing after a while and spun around on my chair, her wet hair whipping around her shoulder, leaving watermarks on her T-shirt. "Okay," she said. "Now we wait. I gave them an hour, so let's assume they'll get back to us within two hours."

"I don't like the idea of Carrie Johnstone just getting away with this," I said.

She looked at me like I was a simpleton. I hated that look. "People like Carrie Johnstone always *get away* with stuff, until someone shoots them or they retire to some distant dictatorship where no one can get at them. She's not going to court. She'll never go to court. No one will ever arrest her. No one can afford to arrest her. You need to get past this romantic idea of justice and realize that some stuff just *is*."

"I hate that," I said. "It's like there's no human beings in the chain of responsibility, just things-that-happen. It's the ultimate cop-out. The system did it. The company did it. The government did it. What about the person who pulls the trigger?"

"Yeah," she said. "Well, that's a nice fairy tale. Have you got any juice or soda, something with sugar? I'm crashing here. Maybe some coffee."

I made her an *epic* cup of coffee. I may not be a ninja secret agent, but that's one thing I could most certainly do. She drank it with something approaching the proper reverence, sent me for another, drank that, and said, "Okay, this'll do." But the way she said it, I could tell that it was Masha-ese for HOLY CRAP THAT IS *AWESOME* COFFEE.

Then she typed some more. Then she typed some more. Then she made a face like she smelled something bad and her fingers bounced over the keys like a troupe of ten meth-addled acrobats on eighty-nine little trampolines. Then some more typing, her teeth bared like an animal. I tried to peek over her shoulder—I used a polarized laptop shield that made it impossible to see the screen unless you were looking at it straight on—and she batted me aside without even seeing me. More typing.

"Yeah, that'll do it," she said, and pulled out the plug and the battery in two smooth motions, thoroughly nuking the virtual machine she'd been working inside of and erasing all the passwords and keys she might have entered. I didn't even bother to object. I wasn't even particularly offended.

"That'll do it, huh?"

"You just nuke any copies you have of those files, starting with the darknet site you gave them details on, and you can forget about Zyz and Carrie Johnstone forever. I've taken the precaution of emailing myself a full set of docs, so that's that. They want to know if you want your old phone back."

"Huh?"

"They burgled some Egyptian girl's house after grabbing your old handset's location from the carrier's network."

"Jesus. Did they hurt anyone?"

"They didn't mention, so I'm assuming no. They're capable of *some* subtlety. Sounds like it bought you some time, in any event. You want it back? They've probably filled it with every bug and trojan known to the human race, of course."

"Forget it," I said.

"Smart guy," she said.

"Yeah," I said. "Well, thanks, I guess." It felt like something simultaneously monumental and *boring* had just happened. Once again, someone else had solved my problems for me. People thought M1k3y was some kind of action hero, but I was just a player in someone else's plot.

She climbed painfully to her feet, faced me. "You did pretty great, Marcus. I gave you a lot of shit, but you did great. I relied on you, and I got you into trouble. I'm glad I was able to clean up my mess. And I saved my own ass, too, I think." She wobbled a little on her legs, then put her arm out to steady herself and caught hold of my shoulder in a death grip that I barely noticed, because she was staring at me with huge, liquid brown eyes.

It was one of those moments, those girl-boy moments, where there's breath passing between you, gazes locked, a kind of falling feeling from every nerve ending, inside and out. I let the moment move me and her together, and let the kiss that had been waiting inside us come out. It went on for a long, long time and she squeezed me like I was the only thing holding her up. We came up for breath and she went on holding me, turning her face into my chest. I could feel the dampness from her hair, but I could also tell by the little shaking movements of her back and chest that she was crying. Hey, so was I.

She snuffled up her snot and wiped her cheeks on my T-shirt

and let go of me. "Well," she said, with a sad smile, "nice to see you again, Marcus. I'll look you up the next time I'm in the neighborhood."

"Yeah," I said. "Sounds good."

The door opened downstairs and my parents' voices came up through the vents, talking about money worries and what to have for dinner. We stood, eyes locked, until they moved into the kitchen, then we descended the stairs in silence. I opened the front door and Masha slipped out into the street, limping down Potrero Hill with her gym bag over her shoulder. I watched her until she turned onto 24th Street, but she never looked back at me.

Then I went inside and told my parents I'd lost my job.

Ange could tell something was up from the minute I called her, I could hear it in her voice, and she met me at a burrito joint around the corner from Noisebridge, coming straight to the table and sitting down opposite me without a hug or a kiss or any of the other normal pleasantries.

"I saw Masha," I said. "And she spoke to Johnstone's people, and they say it's over."

"Over," she said, flatly.

"As in, we don't have anything to do with them, they don't have anything to do with us. Over."

"Oh," she said. She bit her lip, the way she did when she was thinking hard. "Over. You believe her."

"Yeah," I said. "I do."

"Oh."

I'd thought about this next part a thousand times, rehearsed every way it could go, hated all of them, decided I needed to do it anyway.

"Ange," I said.

She started crying before I said anything else, so I guess my voice must have conveyed some secret message to her in the cipher known only to our bodies and subconscious minds.

"What comes after this?" I said, trying to keep my voice even. Other people in the restaurant were staring at us, even though I'd deliberately staked out a place in the back corner.

"What do you mean?" she said, taking napkins out of the dispenser on the table and wiping at her eyes.

"I mean, do we just keep dating forever? Do we get married?"

"You . . ." She blinked. "You want to get married?"

"No," I said. "Do you?"

"No," she said.

"Ever?"

"Well, I don't know. Maybe."

"But not to me."

"I didn't say that, Marcus. Jesus, you're being such a freak. Are you breaking up with me?"

I willed myself not to flinch away from her angry gaze. "I just feel like there comes a point where you have to ask yourself: is this going to go on forever, or isn't it? Are we doing this for the long haul, or is this just something we're doing for now?"

"That is the stupidest thing I've ever heard," she said. "This isn't binary. We can be boyfriend and girlfriend without being husband and wife. We're young. What the hell is this all about?"

I thought about the weird silences with Van, the kiss with Masha, the times I'd woken up next to Ange and just watched her breathe, in love with every curve and angle of her face. "I—" I thought about being a person who did things, instead of someone that the world did stuff to. I thought about the system and how broken it all was. "Look, it's been intense lately. I don't know what I'm feeling anymore. I'm just not sure about anything anymore."

"That's it? You're not *sure*? Since when was anything *sure*? Listen, you lunk, you say that you're not sure about anything. Are you sure that you're happier when you're with me than when I'm not there? Not all the time, but on balance, most of the time?"

It was such a weird, Ange way of framing the question. But I gave it thought. "Yeah," I said. "Yeah, I am sure about that. But, Ange—"

She wadded up the napkin and dropped it on the table. "That's something I'm sure of, too. But you're clearly going through some crazy mental crap, and if you need to work it out, you need to work it out. Give me a call when you've sorted it out. Maybe I'll still be around."

It took everything I had not to chase after her as she left the burrito place, but I stayed in my seat, facing away from the door, staring at the burrito cooling in front of me. I gave her a decent interval to get a ways down Mission Street, then I left the place myself, leaving the food untouched.

I hung around across the street from the Joe Noss for State Senate campaign office, wearing track pants and a hooded sweatshirt and carrying a gym bag, figuring that what worked for Masha would probably work for me. Autumn was upon us, and the sun had set early, making me just one more anonymous, slightly menacing guy with his hands in his pockets on a street in the upper Mission. But I wasn't clutching a vial of rock. I was holding onto a USB stick.

I hadn't been able to talk this over with anyone. Talking to Darryl meant talking to Van, and that meant being a theoretically single man talking to his theoretical best friend's girlfriend who had some kind of theoretical crush on him that might or might not be theoretically mutual. Jolu was busy with Kylie, because what had failed so miserably for me had worked really well for him. And of course, there was no way to talk to Ange about anything now, and maybe never again.

Liam left the building. Then the speechwriter and the researchers whose names I forgot. Then some volunteers, with Flor behind them. I was sure I'd seen Joe go in there, but Flor locked the door behind her, so maybe I'd missed Joe somehow. But I'd seen a few lights on inside the office as she shut the door, and so I hung tight. Joe came out twenty minutes later, wearing his Joe uniform, his cardigan buttoned high against the chill night.

I crossed the street and matched his stride. He looked at me, did a double take.

"Hello, Marcus," he said, his voice gentle and unconcerned. Statesmanlike.

I held out my closed fist, hand down. "Here," I said.

He held his hand out, let me transfer the USB stick to him. He felt it, put it in his pocket.

"Do I want to know what this is?"

"No," I said. "But your friend in the FBI might."

"Aha," he said, and patted his pocket. "Well, I'll take that under advisement."

We walked on for a few steps.

"Is this going to get me into trouble, Marcus?"

"No," I said.

"Is it going to get *you* into trouble?"

"Don't know," I said. "Are you going to win the election?"

"It seems likely," he said. "That vote machine idea of yours— Woah. Though nothing's certain in politics."

"I know," I said. "I'm a member of the network. I recruited sixteen people from my contact list. Maybe I'll get a pizza-and-beer party invite."

He stifled a small, sad laugh. "You're always welcome to pizza on me, Marcus."

"Well, that's good," I said. "Keep them honest, okay?"

"I'll certainly try."

"And keep yourself honest."

"Yes, that much you can be sure of," he said.

I walked away.

As I walked into the night, back toward home, I felt a huge weight lift from my shoulders. It's funny, because I assumed that after I started the chain of events that would lead to Carrie Johnstone's d0x ending up in an FBI agent's possession, I would be clobbered by worry. Would Carrie Johnstone come back for me? Would Zyz come after me? They'd have no reason to assume I turned over the d0x to the FBI, but no reason not to, either. Hell, maybe the FBI wouldn't do anything—what had Joe said? *Even the most foolish, vicious Feeb at HQ in DC has some self-respect and doesn't want to be used as a game token by scheming politicians who're hoping to score points with the electorate during the midterms.* Maybe they'd just drop it in a shredder.

But somehow, that little voice I knew to be my own, the little voice that told me all the time about the ways I'd screwed up, the way I'd let other people do the driving, the way I let life push me around—that little voice shut up the instant I did something. And not just something: the exact thing I knew to be right. Because if the system was broken, if Carrie Johnstone wasn't going to ever pay consequences for her actions, it wasn't because "the system" failed to get her. It was because people like me chose not to act when we could. The system was people, and I was part of it, part of its problems, and I was going to be part of the solution from now on.

Epilogue

I'd had eight months to debug Secret Project X-1. I even made a special midsummer trip to the Mojave, where the gypsum dust was nearly identical to the stuff you got out on the playa. I'd watched with glee and pride as X-1 sucked up the sun's rays, turned them into a laser beam, and used that to sinter fine white powder into 3D shapes. First a little skull ring. Then a toy car. Then some chain-mail, the links already formed and joined, one of the coolest tricks 3D printing had to offer. I gave a presentation on my progress one night at Noisebridge, and resulting praise had given me a glow you could have seen with a spy drone.

But *now, here,* on the *actual* playa, the goddamned machine *wouldn't work.* Lemmy sat in his lounger nearby, sipping electrolyte drink from a CamelBak and making helpful suggestions, as well as several unhelpful ones. Burners passing by stopped and asked what I was doing, and I let Lemmy explain it to them so that I could concentrate on the infernal and stubborn machine.

I only stopped when I found that even the light from my headlamp wasn't sufficient for seeing what I was doing, and then I stretched all the aches and pains out of my body, swilled a pint of cold brew, and proceeded to dance my skinny ass off for forty-five minutes straight, chasing after a giant art car blasting

ferocious dubstep as it crawled across the open playa. I stopped
as a thunderstrike of inspiration struck me, and I *ran* straight back
to camp, unlocked Lemmy's car, and used its dome light to con-
firm that yes, I had in fact inserted a critical part of the power
assembly backwards. I turned it around, slotted it in, and heard
the familiar boot sequence kick in as the stored power from the
solar panels kicked the 3D printer to life.

I wasn't a total moron after all.

It didn't matter how much dancing I'd done the night
before, I was for goddamned sure getting up at first light to
crank up X-1. I had a lot of printing to do. I puttered around it
as the blue arc of laser light shone out of its guts, making it glow
like a lantern in the pink dawn.

People stopped and asked me what it was doing. I gave them
trinkets: bone-white skull rings; renderings of perfect knots and
other mathematical solids; strange, ghostly figurines. I had a
whole library of 3D shapes I'd plundered from Thingiverse
when I realized that I was going to have a real, functional 3D
printer on the playa this year. Word got around, and by the
time Lemmy got out of bed, a huge crowd had gathered around
our camp: dancers who'd been up all night, their pupils the size
of saucers; early risers with yoga mats; college kids who'd somehow found themselves at the burn; and a familiar jawa with
crossed bandoliers over her chest, emphasizing her breasts.

"Hi, Ange," I said, leaving Lemmy to run the machine while
I grabbed us a jar of cold brew and walked off a ways with her.
She pulled down her mask. The sun had toasted a smattering of
freckles around her nose and cheeks. I gave her first slurp at the
coffee, then I had one. Then we hugged. It was awkward.

It was wonderful.

"Hey, Marcus. Congratulations on getting it working."

"Yeah," I said. All I wanted to do was hug her again.

"So," I said.

"So," she said.

"I'm an idiot," I said.

"Yeah," she said.

"I've missed you."

"Yeah," she said again. "I missed you, too. Like fire. Like part of me had been cut away."

I dropped my voice. "I gave Johnstone's d0x to the FBI."

She blinked twice. "When?"

"Back in October."

"And you're still here, huh?"

"Yeah," I said. "I guess that means they didn't do anything with it."

"Or maybe it means they *did* do something with it."

I found my mouth was hanging open. "You know," I said. "That possibility never occurred to me."

"Yeah," she said. "You have a tendency to see the bad side of things."

"I guess I do."

We didn't say anything for a while, just drank our coffee.

"Have you seen anything great yet?"

"No," I said. "I've been working on that goddamned machine since the moment we arrived."

"I haven't been to the temple yet," she said.

I took the hint. "I bet Lemmy'll be okay with the printer for a while."

"You think?"

"Yeah. Let's go."

"You spending much time at the protests?" she said.

"Every day," I said. "Trying to figure out how to do more with the kind of technology we build at Noisebridge to help make them harder to bust up. Better antikettling stuff, HERF shielding, effective treatments for gas poisoning and those dazzler lasers and sound cannons they're using now. Been arrested a few times, but I keep going back."

"I think that's great," she said. "Seriously great. I'm proud of you."

"Thank you," I said. "That means a lot." It really did. I didn't hold her hand, but oh, how I wanted to. "What about you?"

"College," she said. "College, college, college. Doing a double courseload to get out as fast as I can. My student debt, God, it's like the national debt of some drowning island nation."

"There's still time to drop out," I said.

"Yeah, yeah. We can't all be professional revolutionaries."

Not if you're drowning in student debt, is what I didn't say, because I didn't want to fight with Ange. More than anything, I didn't want to fight with Ange.

The temple came into sight. It was even more amazing than last year's, and it was surrounded by art bikes and milling crowds of people dropping off their memorials or reading them or making them. By some unspoken agreement, we walked to them in silence.

By the same unspoken agreement, we took each other's hands.

When we sat down in the central atrium and the first deep *Omm* moved through us, tears began to flow. Ange was crying, and so was I. Our fingers were interlocked, and squeezed so hard that my knuckles creaked. But the sound kept coming, and with it, a kind of peace. Peace wasn't something I'd had much of in the last year, and I barely recognized it—and then I sank into it.

My eyes closed, I sensed someone settle to the floor next to me. I opened my eyes. I knew before they opened who it would be.

Masha's hair was pink again, and she looked better than she had the last time I'd seen her, but she also looked older. There were deep worry lines around her mouth and eyes. They looked good on her somehow. Her eyes were the same, and just as I'd remembered them.

She and I looked into each other's eyes for a long time. I squeezed Ange's fingers and sensed her looking at Masha, too. The three of us stared at one another, three pairs of eyes, three brains, three sets of hands, three *people* inside the crowd, inside the temple, inside Black Rock City, on the skin of the planet.

Then Masha stood up, blew us both a kiss, and smiled in a way that made her look ten years old and made me feel like I'd been blessed by a holy woman. I gathered Ange into a hug that started off stiff and awkward and then turned into the most familiar feeling in the world.

Afterword

by Jacob Appelbaum, WikiLeaks

"Utopia is impossible; everyone who isn't a utopian is a shmuck."

Cory asked someone to write to the children of the newest generation and to say something to inspire them. To write something that would encourage them to take up the cause of bettering the world. That's you or someone you love—when you're finished, please pass this book on to the person who needs it most.

Everything good in the world comes from the efforts of people who came before us. Every minute that we are able to enjoy in a society that is not ruled by senseless violence is a minute given to us by the hard work of people who dedicated their lives for something better. Every person we meet is carrying his own burdens. Each person is the center of her own universe. There is so much left to be done, so many injustices to right, so much suffering to relieve, so many beautiful moments to be lived, an endless amount of knowledge to uncover. Many secrets of the universe wait to be uncovered.

The deck from which our hands are dealt need not be stacked against us; it is possible to create societal structures that are just and capable of reasoned compassion for everyone. It is possible to change the very nature of our lives. It is possible to redesign the entire deck, to change the very face and count of the cards, to rewrite the rules and to create different outcomes.

We live in the golden era of surveillance; every phone is designed to be tapped, the Internet passes through snooping equipment of agencies that are so vast and unaccountable that we hardly know their bounds. Corporations are forced (though some are willing enough!) to hand over our data and the data of those whom we love. Our lives are ruled by networks and yet those networks are not ruled by our consent. These networks keep us hooked up but it is not without costs that they keep us hooked together. The businesses, the governments, and the individuals that power those networks are incentivized to spy, to betray and to do it silently. The architecture of the very systems produces these outcomes.

This is tyranny.

The architecture of our systems and of our networks is not the product of nature but rather the product of imperfect humans, some with the best of intentions. There is no one naturally fit to survive in these unnatural systems, there are some who are lucky, others who have adapted.

This letter to you, from your perhaps recent past, was written with Free Software written as a labor of love by someone who wished to help the children of Uganda while flying over an expansive ocean at difficult to understand heights; it was composed while running under a kernel written by scores of people across every national line, across every racial, sexual, and gender line by a socially and politically agnostic engineer; it was sent through multiple anonymity networks built by countless volunteers acting in solidarity through mutual aid; and it was received by an author who published it for a purpose.

What is the common purpose of all of these people? It is for the whole of our efforts to be more than the sum of our parts—this creates a surplus for you—to give breathing room to others, so that they may take the torch of knowledge, of reason, of justice, of truth telling, of sunlight—to the next step, wherever it may lead us.

There was a time when there were no drone killings, societies have existed without armed policemen, where peace is not only possible but actually a steady state, where mass surveillance was technically and socially infeasible, where fair and evenhanded trials by impartial juries were available for everyone, where fear of identification and arrest was not the norm but the exception. That time was less than a generation ago and much more has been lost in the transition from one generation to the next.

It's up to you to bring those things back to our planet. You can do this with little more than cooperation, the Internet, cryptography, and willingness. You might do this alone or you might do it in a group; you might contribute as a solitary person or as one of many. Writing Free Software empowers every person, without exception, to control the machines that fill our lives. Building free and open hardware empowers every person, without exception, to construct new machines to free us from being slaves to machines that control us. Using free and open systems allows us to construct a new basis by which we may once again understand as a whole, the systems by which we govern ourselves.

We are on the edge of regaining our autonomy, of ending total state surveillance, of uncovering and holding accountable those who commit crimes in our names without our informed consent, of resuming free travel without arbitrary or unfair restriction. We're on the verge of ensuring that every person, not one human excluded, has the right to read and the right to speak. Without exception.

It's easy to feel hopeless in the face of the difficult issues that we face every day—how could one person effectively resist anything so much larger than herself? Once we stop acting alone, we have a chance for positive change. To protest is to stop and say that you object, to resist is to stop others from going along without thinking and to build alternatives is to give everyone new choices.

Omission and commission are the yin and yang of personal agency.

What if you could travel back through time and help Daniel Ellsberg leak the Pentagon Papers? Would you take the actions required, would you risk your life to end the war? For many it is easy to answer positively and then think nothing of the actual struggles, the real risk or the uncertainty provided without historical hindsight. For others, it's easy to say no and to think of nothing beyond oneself.

But what if you didn't need to travel back through time?

There are new Pentagon Papers just waiting to be leaked; there are new wars to end, new injustices to make right, fresh uncertainty that seems daunting where success seems impossible; new alternatives need to be constructed, old values and concepts of justice need to be preserved in the face of powerful people who pervert the rule of law for their own benefit.

Be the trouble you want to see in the world, above nationalism, above so-called patriotism, above and beyond fear and make it count for the betterment of the planet. Legal and illegal are not the same as right and wrong—do what is right and never give up the fight.

This is one idea out of many that may help you and your friends, may free our planet from the tyranny that surrounds us all. It's up to you now—go create something beautiful and help others to do the same.

Happy hacking,

Anonymous
000000/002012/00/00/00:00:00:00

Afterword

by Aaron Swartz, Demand Progress
(cofounder, Reddit.com)

Hi there, I'm Aaron. I've been given this little space here at the end of the book because I'm a flesh-and-blood human and, as such, I can tell you something you wouldn't believe if it came out of the mouth of any of those fictional characters:

This stuff is real.

Sure, there isn't anyone actually named Marcus or Ange, at least not that I know, but I do know real people just like them. If you want, you can go to San Francisco and meet them. And while you're there, you can play D&D with John Gilmore or build a rocket ship at Noisebridge or work with some hippies on an art project for Burning Man.

And if some of the more conspiracy-minded stuff in the book seems too wild to be true, well, just google Blackwater, Xe, or BlueCoat. (I myself have an FOIA request in to learn more about "persona management software," but the Feds say it'll take three more *years* to redact all the relevant documents.)

Now I hope you had fun staying up all night reading about these things, but this next part is important, so pay attention: what's going on now isn't some reality TV show you can just sit at home and watch. This is your life, this is your country—and if you want to keep it safe, you need to get involved.

I know it's easy to feel like you're powerless, like there's nothing you can do to slow down or stop "the system." Like all the calls are made by shadowy and powerful forces far outside your control. I feel that way, too, sometimes. But it just isn't true.

A little over a year ago, a friend called to tell me about an obscure bill he'd heard of called the Combatting Online Infringement and Counterfeit Act, or COICA. As I read the bill, I started to get more and more worried: under its provisions, the government would be allowed to censor websites it didn't like without so much as a trial. It would be the first time the U.S. government was given the power to censor its citizens' access to the net.

The bill had just been introduced a day or two ago, but it already had a couple dozen senators cosponsoring it. And, despite there never being any debate, it was already scheduled for a vote in just a couple days. Nobody had ever reported on it, and that was just the point: they wanted to rush this thing through before anyone noticed.

Luckily, my friend noticed. We stayed up all weekend and launched a website explaining what the bill did, with a petition you could sign opposing it that would look up the phone numbers for your representatives. We told a few friends about it and they told a few friends and within a couple days we had over 200,000 people on our petition. It was incredible.

Well, the people pushing this bill didn't stop. They spent literally tens of millions of dollars lobbying for it. The head of every major media company flew out to Washington, DC, and met with the president's chief of staff to politely remind him of the millions of dollars they'd donated to the president's campaign and explain how what they wanted—the only thing they wanted—was for this bill to pass.

But the public pressure kept building. To try to throw people off the trail, they kept changing the name of the bill—

calling it PIPA and SOPA and even the E-PARASITES Act—
but no matter what they called it, more and more people kept
telling their friends about it and getting more and more people
opposed. Soon, the signers on our petition stretched into the
millions.

We managed to stall them for over a year through various
tactics, but they realized if they waited much longer they might
never get their chance to pass this bill. So they scheduled it for
a vote first thing after they got back from winter break.

But while members of Congress were off on winter break,
holding town halls and public meetings back home, people
started visiting them. Across the country, members started getting asked by their constituents why they were supporting that
nasty Internet censorship bill. And members started getting
scared—some going so far as to respond by attacking *me*.

But it wasn't about me anymore—it was never about me.
From the beginning, it was about citizens taking things into
their own hands: making YouTube videos and writing songs
opposing the bill, making graphs showing how much money
the bill's cosponsors had received from the industries pushing
it, and organizing boycotts putting pressure on the companies
who'd endorsed the bill.

And it worked—it took the bill from a political nonissue
that was poised to pass unanimously to a toxic football no one
wanted to touch. Even the bill's cosponsors started rushing
to issue statements opposing it! Boy, were those media moguls
pissed. . . .

This is not how the system is supposed to work. A ragtag
bunch of kids doesn't stop one of the most powerful forces in
Washington just by typing on their laptops!

But it did happen. And you can make it happen again.

The system is changing. Thanks to the Internet, everyday
people can learn about and organize around an issue even if the

system is determined to ignore it. Now, maybe we won't win every time—this is real life, after all—but we finally have a chance.

But it only works if you take part. And now that you've read this book and learned how to do it, you're perfectly suited to make it happen again. That's right: now it's up to you to change the system.

Let me know if I can help.

Aaron Swartz
<me@aaronsw.com>

Acknowledgments

Many thanks to the people who helped with suggestions and technical details to make this book work: Jacob Appelbaum, Aaron Swartz, Quinn Norton, Tiffiniy Cheng, Nicholas Reville, Holmes Wilson, Joe Trippi, Danny O'Brien, Tim Hardy, Nat Torkington, Thomas Gideon, Roger Dingledine, Barry Warsaw, Gord Doctorow, James Gleick, Lee Maguire.

Thanks to my campmates at Liminal Labs for introducing me to Burning Man and making me so welcome there.

Thanks to John Perry Barlow, John Gilmore, Mitch Kapor, and Wil Wheaton for letting me give them a cameo (and thanks again to Gilmore for his plotting suggestions!).

Thanks to my agents, Russ Galen, Danny Baror, Heather Baror, and Justin Manask, for the awesome work in bringing *Little Brother* and *Homeland* to the world.

Thanks to all the fans and readers, the librarians and teachers, and hackers and remixers and *especially* the booksellers who put my books into peoples' hands.

Thanks to my editors, especially Patrick Nielsen Hayden, who has always improved my books.

Bibliography

When I was a kid, facts were hard to come by. If you wanted to know how to hack a pay phone, you'd have to find someone else who knew how to do it, and get them to teach you. Or you'd have to find operating manuals for pay phones and pore over them until you came up with your own method. There's nothing wrong with either of these solutions, except that they're slow and can be tedious.

Today, facts are cheap. As I type this in early 2012, a Google search for "How to hack a pay phone" gives back a full screen of detailed YouTube videos full of fascinating and often practical advice on getting pay phones to dance to your will. So if you know or suspect that a thing is possible, it's easy to discover whether someone has managed it, and how they did it. Just bear in mind Arthur C. Clarke's first law: "When a distinguished but elderly scientist states that something is possible, he is almost certainly right. When he states that something is impossible, he is very probably wrong." If you're trying to do something that everyone on the net swears is impossible, it may still be worth a go on your own in case you think of something they've never imagined.

With *Homeland*—and in *Little Brother*—I've tried to give you some scenarios and keywords that might expand your impression of what is and isn't possible, to give you the search terms you'll need to educate yourself and get yourself doing cool stuff. So, for example, if you google "hackerspaces" you'll find that places like Noisebridge are very real and have spread all over the world (Noisebridge is also real!). You can join your local hackerspace. If it doesn't exist yet, you can *start* it. Just google "how do I start a hackerspace?" And while you're searching, try "drone" and "tor project" and "lawful intercept." You'll be amazed, scared, energized, and empowered by what you find there.

Wikipedia is an *amazing* place to do research, but you have to know how to use it. Your teachers have probably told you that Wikipedia has no place in your education, and I'm sorry to say that I think that this is a lazy and dumb approach. There are two secrets to doing amazing research on Wikipedia:

1. Check the sources, not the article.

In an ideal world, all the factual assertions in a Wikipedia article will have a citation to a source at the bottom of the article. Wikipedia hasn't achieved this ideal state (yet—that's what all those [citation needed] marks in the articles are about) but a surprising number of the facts in a Wikipedia article will have a corresponding source at the bottom. *That*'s where your research should take you when you're reading an article. Wikipedia is where your research should start, not where it should end.

2. Check the "Talk" link.

Every Wikipedia article has a "Talk" link that goes to a page where everyone who cares about the article discusses its state. If someone has a weird idea about a subject and finds a source somewhere on the net to support it, they might just stick it into the Wikipedia article. But chances are that this will spark a heated debate on the Talk page about whether the source is "reputable" and whether its facts belong in an encyclopedia.

Armed with the original sources *and* the informed discussion about whether those sources are good ones, you can use Wikipedia to get an amazing education.

Beyond Wikipedia, there are some other sites you should really have a look at if you want to learn more about the material in this book. First Codecademy (www.codecademy.com), which contains step-by-step lessons to learn how to program, starting from no knowledge. You can even get them by email, one page at a time. While you're chewing on that, check out the Tor Project (www.torproject.org) and find out how to run your own darknet projects. If you're looking to use an operating system that lets you control your whole computer, down to the bare metal, then you want GNU/Linux. I like the Ubuntu flavor best (www.ubuntu.com). It runs on any and every computer, and is really easy to get started with. And if you have an Android phone, get jailbreaking! The CyanogenMod project (www.cyanogenmod.com) is a free/open version of the Android operating system, with all kinds of excellent features, including several that will help you protect your privacy.

Now, all this stuff is well and good, but only if the Internet stays free and open. If your country acquires the same awful censorship and surveillance used in China and Middle Eastern dictatorships, you won't be able to get at this stuff and learn to use it. There are lots of threats to this freedom, and every country has groups devoted to stopping them. In the United States and Canada (and worldwide!) there's the Electronic Frontier Foundation (www.eff.org), where I used to work. In the UK, there's the Open Rights Group (www.openrightsgroup.org), which I helped to found. In Australia, there's Electronic Frontiers Australia (www.efa.org.au). In New Zealand, there's Creative Freedom (www.creativefreedom.org.nz). There are also global groups like Creative Commons (www.creativecommons .org) and groups with lots of local affiliates like The Pirate Party (www.pp-international.net).

There are lots of thinkers on this stuff whom I have a lot of respect for. If you want to know about teens, privacy, and networked communications, read danah boyd's blog (www .zephoria.org/thoughts). For more on Anonymous, 4chan and /b/, read Gabriella Coleman's blog and papers (http://gabriel lacoleman.org/blog/). For the future of news and newspapers, read Dan Gillmor (www.dangillmor.com), especially his excellent recent book, *Mediactive* (www.mediactive.com). For the relationship of leaks to the news, follow Heather Brooke (www .heatherbrooke.org) and read her history of WikiLeaks, *The Revolution Will Be Digitised*. To understand how the net is changing the world, read Clay Shirky (www.shirky.com), and his latest book, the kick-ass *Here Comes Everybody*. If you want to fight for free and fair elections in America without undue influence from power and money, read Lawrence Lessig (www.twitter.com /lessig) and join Rootstrikers (www.rootstrikers.org), where activists are making it happen.

Finally, if you want to understand randomness, information theory, and the strange world at the center of mathematics, run, don't walk, and get a copy of James Gleick's 2011 book *The Information*. It's where I got all the good stuff about Gödel and Chaitin from.

There's plenty more—more than would ever fit between the covers of a book, so much that you need the whole net for it. I write on a daily website called Boing Boing (www.boing boing.net), where I keep up to date on the latest stuff. I hope to see you there.